The Pale Huntress

By B.D. Weddell

This is for my wife,

My love and best friend

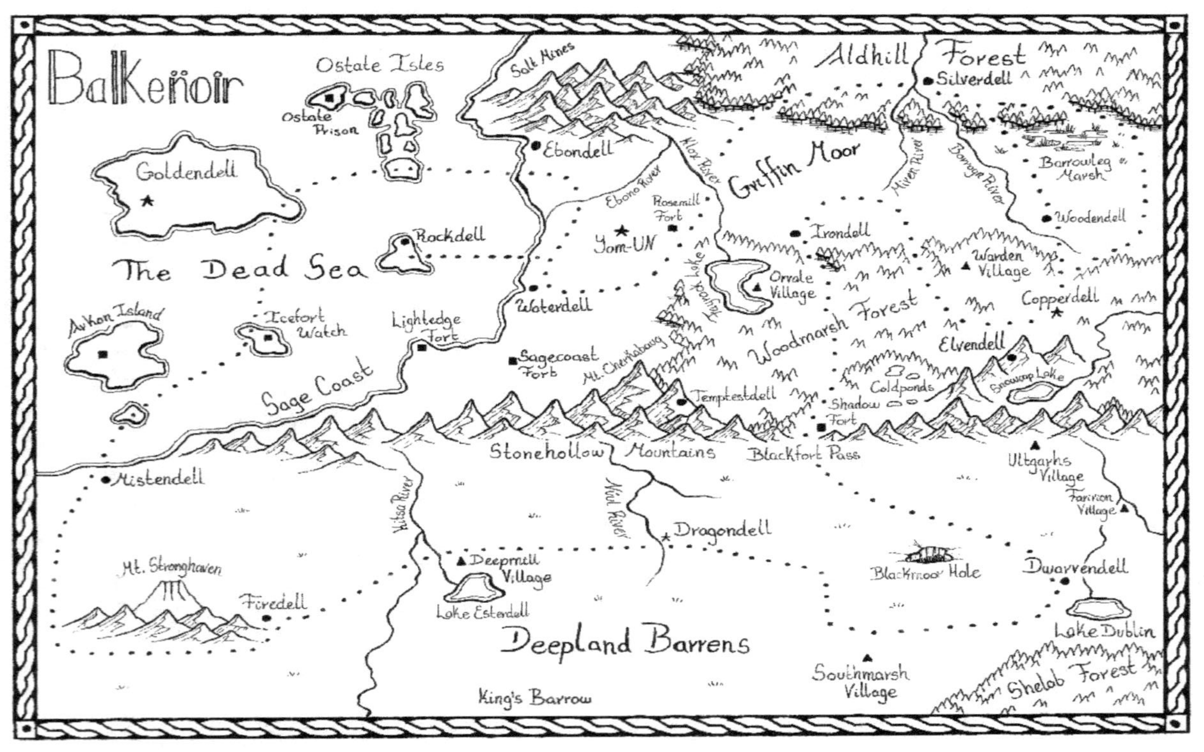

Balkeñoir
Ostate Isles
Ostate Prison
Salt Mines
Aldhill Forest
Silverdell
Goldendell
Ebondell
Griffin Moor
Barrowleg Marsh
Woodendell
The Dead Sea
Rockdell
Ebono River
Rosemill Fort
Yom-UN
Klox River
River River
Irondell
Warden Village
Copperdell
Avkon Island
Icefort Watch
Lightedge Fort
Waterdell
Fayrock Lake
Orvale Village
Woodmarsh Forest
Elvendell
Sage Coast
Sagecoast Fort
Mt. Cherkabaug
Temptestdell
Coldponds
Shadow Fort
Snowcap Lake
Stonehollow Mountains
Blackfort Pass
Ultgarhs Village
Mistendell
Niol River
Dragondell
Farrixon Village
Mt. Stronghaven
Deepmill Village
Blackmoo' Hole
Dwarvendell
Firedell
Lake Esterdell
Deepland Barrens
Lake Dublin
Southmarsh Village
Shelob Forest
King's Barrow
Kitsa River

Table of Contents

Do

Once upon a time, in a land far away, lies the country of Balkeñoir; a harsh forested land with many grand kingdoms, and a place full of shadow and deceit.

With the mountains to the south and east and the sea to the west, the entire region was enveloped into what many felt like the longest winter the people had ever seen. So long in fact, that many believed that the Stars had abandoned them, and had cursed the precious soil that had been fought for time and time again. Years of cold harsh winds brought in snow that covered the entire world it seemed, and on days when the sun seemed to never come out, it left everyone huddled together by the fire with dreams of warmth. Warmth and comfort from both the cold, and the horrors of night. Like many strange countries, Balkeñoir was home to many brave and terrifying men, and with night, came terrifying beasts. The creatures of night plagued the land; always fighting if not for survival, then dominance.

The Emperor who ruled over the empire, took many precautions to secure the realm and bring a sort of peace to the people. The Witches were hunted down and burned, with those remaining hiding out in the woods or abandoned caverns in the mountains. The Werewolves hid among their lesser cousins in the reservation south of the empire, and other bottom-feeders such Goblins and Ghouls were eventually pushed back to make way for Man; who remained at the top of the food chain regarding all of Balkeñoir. But still, with every creature of land, earth, and sky, there is always prey, as well as predators.

The most feared in Balkeñoir however, were the Immortals and their Vampire brethren. Like the Witches and Werewolves, precautions and hunts were made to fight the horrible creatures who rule the world of night. To stop another outbreak of Vampirism as well as Vampiric nobility, the people of Balkeñoir call upon the help of an expert in hunting beasts. These are the Hunters. Banded together into many guilds and even loners, they traveled across the landscape in search of fame and fortune; cleansing the world of the darkness that still lies beneath the glare of Emperor Ion's reign. Among these Hunters, one of them was out on the road one wintery night, traveling to the city of Irondell deep in the Woodmarsh Forest.

She thought to herself, *What a cold evening.*

The mooned shined big and yellow like the blotted and rotted eye of a witch. The sky was cloudy, patching the darkness beyond and threatening another snowstorm to ravage the land that was already blanketed with snow, making travel by horse uncomfortable and difficult for many. On nights like this, many would have taken the train or stayed at home where it was safe. With winter being at its longest season yet, the sun would not be up for many hours, and so the land was plunged into a world of icy fog and darkness. It was reason enough for many to not even dare to travel, let alone hunt for beasts.

But not this rider, who rode her horse at full speed down the stone road cutting through Woodmarsh Forest. The icy daggers of the wind did not bother her, nor did the dark stretch of black pine that nearly covered the entire region of Balkeñoir. The forest was teeming with wildlife, both as small as a black beetle, and as large as wild Nephelim. It would snow again, sooner or later, but the rider didn't believe it would happen for some time. Not that it really mattered. The cold never really bothered her, and she was used to riding alone to avoid the trains. It was better this way anyway; just her, and her horse.

Midnight, as she called it, was of elegant beauty and black as the darkest night. His coat, lush and beneath it ripped with muscle due to years of long travel. His heavy hooves clicked across the road as he galloped in the direction he was called to go, and his gleaming red eyes peered through the darkness while his ears swiveled in search for the slightest of sounds. His rider, remained silent, her head straight facing towards her destination.

Wearing chiseled leather armor as black as her horse's coat, the woman appeared lean and as strong as any capable warrior. Her cloak shrouded her like a pair of raven's wings, and her hood covered her entire head save for her pale chin. Her hands that gripped the reins were just as pale, with a single ring on the right hand, gleaming with a crimson ruby with an unknown insignia printed on top. At her side was a revolver, and opposite of that was a blunderbuss with a single heavy round in the chamber. Across the woman's back was a hand-and-a-half sword, the hilt sticking out from beneath the black cloak with dark leather wrapped around what looked to be a silver pommel carved into the shape of a snarling wolf. From her broad shoulders spiked with armor down to the spurs on her leather boots, the Huntress looked to be a warrior from the darkest shadows of Lunokean.

The mere sight of both horse and rider, made the air feel chillier to even the Sprites who hid within the branches of the pine even as the two passed on by without a sound other than the clopping of hooves. The two continued to ride without straying the path or even slowing down; their destination mere miles away at this point: the kingdom of Irondell.

What a cold evening, the Huntress thought to herself again as she turned her head to the sky, her eyes as violet as lavender and reflecting the moonlight like a cat's, taking in the millions of constellations visible through the line of clouds, all the Stars watching over the world, or so everyone hoped.

And another storm is coming soon...

That morning, the city came into view through the fog that enveloped the kingdom. Walls as tall as the largest Nephelim circled the city, and peeking over the top were several large towers; some with spires so tall they appeared to pierce the very sky. Amidst the many stone buildings and towers, the castle stood in the far distance with its many flags and statues watching over the city of Irondell.

The Huntress had noticed a few Watchmen patrolling along the walls close to the two towers that stood on either side of a large gate with flags with the sigil of Irondell fluttering in the breeze; a horse's head with an armor plating over its black face. Two more stood just out front, trying desperately to stay still despite the cold fog that snaked around them like ghosts. When the rider slowed down in front of them, they approached her. Both of them wore simple leather armor, as well as had a sword at their hip and a rifle in their hands. One of them removed his helmet as he approached the closest to the horse and its rider.

"You Black Hand? You look the part."

The woman said nothing but merely turned her head to peer at the man from beneath her hood. From within the shroud, the man could see two catlike eyes of purple glancing down at him coldly; studying him with such sternness that he could just feel them crawling all over him. He had obviously never seen eyes such as that, and it frightened him.

He cleared his throat and proceeded to ask, "Well, are ya or not?"

"No need to be rude, ya daft," the other Watchmen said sneering at his comrade. He turned to the warrior and bowed his head. "My apologies, Miss, me mate here, he be new. Jittery. Please forgive."

The woman said nothing still. In fact, she appeared indifferent as if she hadn't heard anything at all.

"Heh," the man said nervously. "Well then, are you a member of The Black Hand? If not-"

"Yes," the woman said coolly. Her voice was strong, but melodious like the honeyed voice of a flock of doves. She sounded as if she was in her later years, but her physique and beautifully crafted face revealed otherwise. She looked like a young girl despite her stature and the way she carried herself on the horse.

"Not a big talker," the Watchmen said proceeding to rap against the gate with a knuckle. "No worries. Head on inside, the Count will be waiting in the town square." He waved to the guard standing on the wall. "Alert Count Andrei!" The man hurried off to carry out his orders.

"The first victim," the woman then said startling the Watchman. She threw a long leg over her horse and landed softly in the snow. To the Watchmen's surprise, she hardly sank into it, as if she weighed nothing at all.

"The first victim of the attack, was here at the gates, yes?"

The man swallowed, looking to his companion for help. When no help came, he returned his eyes back to the woman's, whose own were staring violet and full of mystery. "Y-yes, that be right."

"How did he die?"

"Broken neck, it was," the man who removed his helmet said. "Snapped right to the side, didn't even utter a scream."

"And *he* proceeded to enter into the city?" she asked.

"That is right. Look, Miss, I really ain't the guy-"

The rider held up her hand and nodded. She then held out the reins of her horse. "Will you watch my horse?"

Without even waiting for an answer, the woman dropped them into the man's hands and then turned to the other.

"Lead me inside, please."

"R-right." After nodding to his companion, the Watchman proceeded to lead the warrior through the gates and into Irondell. When they disappeared, the second Watchman gently stroked the horse's nose.

"Interesstin' rider you got, doncha?" he asked the beast who gave no reply other than a snort.

"You Hunters sure are fast," the Watchmen said to the Huntress as they entered the narrow streets of Irondell. Thin cobblestone streets snaked their way around the tall and gothic buildings. Small shops, houses and inns, bars and even a giant clock tower which reached up towards the sky like a great stalagmite. The clock tower was made of complete black metal and large stone gargoyles sat squatted on four arches that stuck out on all corners, snarling silently at any passerby.

The Huntress thought she felt the eyes of the stone creatures following her as she continued to stride past the clock with the Watchman, and as its large hands struck the eleventh hour, the city itself seemed to take notice of the new visitor as they came out to see the time. Upon seeing the cloaked warrior being escorted by the Watchmen, many retreated back inside while others stayed and watched as the two passed on by. Children stopped playing, and old men smoking their pipes held their beaths at the beauty of the young woman, wishing themselves to be both younger and more heroic.

Going deeper into the city, their boots clicking on the cobblestone streets, the Watchmen continued to try and make conversation.

"Must've been a rough ride from Blackfort Pass, eh? Heard that's where you reside, though is it true no one else can find your hideout?"

The Huntress said nothing but merely followed in continual silence. She hardly wasted her breath on stupid and unimportant questions such as that. The way her footsteps crunched more quietly in the snow opposed to the Watchmen's steps infuriated him a bit and made him self-conscious about his own weight.

"Apologies, Miss, I've just heard so much about you… you're almost as famous at the Blue Rams."

"The Blue Rams are mercenaries," said the Huntress. "Despicable lot."

"Eh, perhaps, perhaps. Not like loyal Watchmen or those of the Goldendell army. No offence, of course. Say, your eyes, how did they get to be that color?"

Again, the Huntress ignored his question.

"Packing a lot a gear as well," he then attempted taking notice of the weapons under her cloak. He knew that on average a trip through the pass on horseback from Irondell alone took an average of a week. Yet this Hunter made it in almost three days. "Tell me, is it hard riding from the south?"

Still, no response. Instead, the rider simply gave her escort a look of annoyance.

"Chilly bitch, ain't ya?" he muttered under his breath so that she couldn't hear him. Unfortunately for him, she had, though she made no comment on it even as the Watchman then said loudly, "Well, the name's William. Pleasure to meet you too."

"Charmed," the woman said sarcastically.

William scowled at the reply.

"The children here," the Huntress then said, and William turned to see that from beneath her hood, the warrior was looking over at some children drawing pictures in the snow in front of a small bakery. From the shop the smell of cinnamon filled the air, and the laughter of the children making fun of each other's drawings followed. They were beautiful little creatures, unaware of the horror that had taken their city a couple of nights ago.

"What about 'em?" William asked.

The woman shook her head. "It's nothing." She still seemed disturbed, but William figured it would not be wise to pry.

"Okay," William muttered. He then turned his head and pointed up at the town clock, which had finished striking the tenth hour. Across the front of the black tower was a stain of brown which could only be dried blood. "Some poor bastard got thrown up there. Everything practically squished out like a tomato."

The woman looked down at the base of the tower where the body had to have landed after the impact. A good clean revealed no sign of such a thing.

"Where is the body now?"

"With the others," William answered. "Sent to the church to prepare for burial. They were requested however to be left alone so you can see them. Count Andrei will show you after he shows you the scene."

The warrior nodded and then asked, "Was it only Watchmen who were the additional casualties?"

"That's right. Main focus was Kuroi Te themselves." William shook his head. "Poor bastards, that's whatcha get from becoming Hunters- eh, no offence."

The woman said nothing once again, clearly annoyed at the man's arrogance.

"Jeez," William muttered beneath his breath so that she could not hear. "The sooner I get this woman to the Count the better."

"I can hear you, you know," the woman revealed which made William's blood run cold.

"Oh! Er… He-he, I was jesting," William said quickly trying to save his own hide. "Only jesting… Oh look! That be our pride and joy: Frostbite Fountain! And lookie there, Count Andrei himself!"

Count Andrei was a stout old man cloaked in the finest of Lycan furs of many shades. His black beard covered most of his face and his long black hair stretched down to his shoulders. Behind him was a massive fountain carved in the shape of a large spear sticking out of the waters and sewing crystal droplets from the top that dribbled down its length. Unlike the princes and counts that homed most of the forts and castles of Balkeñoir, the brown doublet that the Count wore made him look like a silly fat king from a children's tale.

The Count was talking to some soldier who stood beside him. The Huntress did not recognize the soldier as a typical Watchman from Irondell. Instead, the man was garbed in the golden armor of The Empire; the emblem of Goldendell on his breastplate. Keeping her thoughts in check, the Huntress allowed William to introduce her to Count Andrei, who appeared overjoyed to see her. She bowed her head in respect, but kept a keen eye on the Count's other visitor, who was watching her like a hawk.

The count looks so much like his father, she noticed.

"Ahh!" the fat Count exclaimed with arms wide open like a father greeting a long-lost decedent. "A Hunter of The Black Hand graces us with her presence. Thank you so much for coming, milady. And dare I say, you are really too beautiful to be a Hunter…" With lust in his eyes, he reached out to take the warrior's hand, but she did not relinquish it.

"Ahem," William cleared his throat and to the Huntress, he said, "When a Count offers to take your hand, it's normally polite to give it."

"Kuroi Te," the woman said ignoring both William's warning and the Count's hand altogether. "I'd like to see where they had been killed."

The Count retracted his hand and chuckled softly, hiding the displeasure of the woman's rudeness. "Right. Right this way please."

He then started to trot away, leaving the soldier of The Empire alone at the fountain with William. The Huntress took one last glance at the soldier before following the Count close behind. She noticed a strange look in the soldier's eye, even as William said something to him.

"Tell me," Andrei then to her said breaking into her thoughts. They passed under one of the gas-fed streetlamps which lit up the fog around it and making it difficult to see- at least for him anyway. "What shall we call you? As a guest of my city, I would like to know your name, so I know how to properly thank you for coming."

"My name doesn't matter," the Huntress said coolly. "What matters is why you have summoned The Black Hand." She often tried to never relinquish her name out to any client- at least not to someone of royal blood with connections to the Emperor of Balkeñoir. *Especially* those who were direct descendants.

The Count gritted his teeth behind his beard but nevertheless he managed a small smile. "Yes, of course. Right this way."

The Count then turned, leading the warrior into a bar by the name of The Bad Wolf. The sign that hung over the obviously destroyed door was of a wolf chugging down a tankard of ale. Like many of the surrounding buildings, this bar was set beneath a great stone bridge that cut right across the city high above as if a lot of traffic had to cross over all the buildings in order to reach the castle beyond. Unlike most however, this bar was boarded up with wood and had caution written across one that covered the entrance.

The Huntress allowed herself to be led through the smashed doorway to survey the carnage within.

Di

What was once a standard run-of-the-mill tavern had been completely reduced to what the Huntress would imagine what the inside of a butcher's shop would look like

Tables and chairs had been smashed and strewn about, and the bar in the back had been completely crushed with the bottles behind it shattered and empty. It was as if a Nephil had stuck its fist in and smashed the entire tavern flat. There was a heavy copper-like smell that struck the Huntress' nostrils as she delved deeper within. It was the smell of blood that completely painted the entire room. It was everywhere; on the walls, saturated in the floorboards and there were even more splattered brown stains across the ceiling. Among the blood, were the few remains the cleaning group of the church had not bothered to pick up, now all dried up and shriveled like kelp washed up on a beach.

The Huntress stepped in deeper in, ignoring the squishy sounds coming from beneath her boots where some blood was still a little tacky. Some bullet holes were visible in the splattered walls, and upon taking a knife and digging out the object in question, one of them the warrior saw that the bullet was silver-tipped; ancient metal from the moon itself.

Many other weapons of silver were scattered across the bar, one of them still having a hand holding onto it- the owner nowhere to be found. Guns, swords, even an axe. All of them splattered with blood but it was impossible to tell whose or what it belonged to. A couple of other body parts littered the floor as well, including a pile of guts resting in a tangled mess near one of the barstools. It was as if they had been torn out and simply tossed aside like garbage. Another hand and a chunk of meat was spotted near the back stage where a piano had been left untouched, and finally the Huntress noticed a leg dangling over the side of the bar, the stump rotted and coated with brown and red. It hadn't been hacked off by some weapon or blown off by a gun. It had been *ripped* off. On the wall beyond it, sticky bits of gray matter coated the back, which the Huntress knew was bits of brain that had been smashed into the woodwork.

"What of the bartender?" the warrior asked not looking back at Count Andrei who remained in the doorway of the tavern. "The owner of the place?"

"He was killed in the attack," Andrei replied. "That's part of him, dangling there." He was pointing at the leg she had noticed.

The warrior's purple eyes narrowed slightly. So much for the Watchmen being the *only* additional casualties.

"Why did you remove the bodies, but left a few of the parts scattered about?" she then asked turning back to the Count. "You left a feast for the rats."

Andrei shuffled a single foot nervously. "We didn't think the more complicated organs were necessary to understand the nature of the wounds. As for the hand and leg, well, it is obvious the damage done."

"In other words, your men were too lazy to gather everything in order to ensure I wouldn't miss anything," the Huntress said patiently. "Where are the dead now?"

The Count's jaw twitched as he said, "In the church."

She nodded. At least the Watchmen had done one thing right. "They have not been touched yet?"

"No. I told the priest to wait until you came to examine them."

The Huntress nodded. At least this man managed to do *something* right. "I was told that there was a single survivor in Kuroi Te, is that correct?"

"Yes. Only one. But we don't know why…"

"No bites?"

"None that we could see."

"Where is she now?"

"Resting. If you would like to see the bodies first, I can have someone wake her up so that you can meet her in the church guesthouse."

The Huntress looked back at the bloody room. "She is unhurt?"

"As far as we know."

"Hmm. Let us go."

Then turning on her heel, the Huntress followed the Count out and shut out the gruesome scene behind her. She followed Andrei closely as he took her through the city and towards the dome-like church that towered above some of the minor buildings.

"You should have someone condemn the building, get it cleaned up before more rats come, especially if it has been a few days."

"Y-yes, of course." Andrei said obviously feeling silly for not thinking of that before. But he should have left the bodies there as well, so she could have a greater understanding as to what had happened. A greater feasts for rats possibly, but at the very least she would be able to deduce every single detail both significant and not.

Oh well. She would still be able to find something out from the deceased, as well as the surviving member. So walking alongside Count Andrei in silence, the Huntress and he started their way down the street again towards the church peeking up over the buildings in front of it; its glass dome reflecting what sunlight escaped the clouds above.

She happened to notice that the soldier from The Empire, was no longer near Frostbite Fountain.

Upon their arrival at the beautiful temple of Yohnah, Count Andrei took a left before the main sanctuary as soon as they entered and led the warrior down into the basement where the deceased were often prepared for burial. As they entered the dark room lit with only a few torches, the Huntress looked upon the five bodies that laid peacefully on tables of stone, only one of the six tables being used to hold various tools for cleaning. The room smelled musty with both dust, mold, and decay. The priest who stood behind the empty table wearing a plague mask, looked up from what he was doing and bowed respectfully to the Count and his guest, appearing momentarily like a hunched crow.

"Is this the Huntress you have called for?" the priest asked stroking his long white beard which poked under the mask. He was garbed in long black robes and the hood he wore covered most of his head. But the Huntress could see the godly man look upon her with lust in those pale gray eyes of his peering through the mask. Around the man's neck was a bird with outstretched wings and looking upward as if flying towards the sky, the symbol of Yohnah, the Morning Star and god of Lunokean and beyond The Veil.

"Aye," Andrei replied. "She will inspect the bodies now."

"Let me know if you need any help," the priest said to the Huntress with greater hunger in his eye.

Disgusting old man.

"Thank you," the Huntress said instead as she stopped at the first table and peering down at the naked body of one of the male members of Kuroi Te.

The man was strongly built with dark ebony skin that was roped in great muscle. His belly was a gaping hole however and the Huntress deemed this member to be the one who had been gutted. Upon sticking her long fingers into the slit opening the hollow belly a little more, she took note that the wound had not been done by a weapon, but more like it had been *punched* in.

The second member was also male with multiple scratch wounds over his bearded face. He was missing one of his arms and his throat looked to have been ripped out and not by teeth. The nubs on one side followed by a sickening tear on the other suggested it to be possibly caused by a *hand* instead. The other two members were female, both missing a leg or a hand. One of them had her severed head sitting next to her body, and upon observing the wound, the warrior determined that the head had been ripped clean off her shoulders. The other had her eye sockets pushed in and her neck was snapped to the side;

and another series of scratches lined over her chest and breasts as if she had been scratched by a giant cat. Lastly, the bartender who was an old man with a bald head laid peacefully on the stone table despite the obvious puncture wound that seemed to have run him through the chest and the fact that he was missing one of his legs. In a small bowl beside him, his heart rested like a lonely apple, rotted and black.

All have been literally torn apart as if a wild beast got to them. The warrior thought that this was strange. She saw no markings on the necks of the victims, and if this was a Werewolf, there would be nothing left but bloodied bones. If this was a Witch, there would be a Raven summoned from Goldendell to handle the investigation instead. Neither was this caused by a Ghoul, Shade, or any other beast that the Huntress had knowledge of.

It could be a Vampire… but then why didn't it feed?

She supposed that she could have very well have drunken the blood that spilled from the wounds without necessarily biting them, but until she learned more there wasn't much she could do as to figuring out what exactly had caused such wounds.

This was no man to be certain. No human is strong enough to punch a man's chest through and rip their heart out.

She turned to the priest. "Where is the lone survivor?"

"Upstairs in the guesthouse," the priest said in a raspy whisper. "Are you done with them then?"

"I've seen enough. They are yours now." The Huntress then turned to head back upstairs without waiting for the Count who begged her to wait. As the two left the priest got to work preparing the bodies for their burial.

"What a woman..." she heard the priest say as they ascended the stairs. The thought of what could possibly be going through his mind made her sick to her stomach.

"Madam!" Andrei huffed and puffed as they finally made it to the top of the stairs. "Wait!" He followed her down the main corridor and into the sanctuary.

As she passed the pews the warrior looked up at the many statues that seemed to hold up the stained-glass window depicting the white dove of Yohnah. Turning immediately right before the alter, she then proceeded to climb up a second set of wooden stairs, leading up to the guest houses opposite of the dome.

"Madam!"

"What is it?" she asked the Count in annoyance as she continued her ascent. It was probably a bad idea to leave someone in such a powerful position in such a matter, but the Huntress didn't care. No law bound her to any specific city. None of them ever would.

"That's it?" Andrei asked still huffing. "What do you even make of it? Do you have some idea concerning that you are, well... done with the bodies?"

"A crude way of putting it," the Huntress responded. "I don't know what to make of it yet, to be honest. If this was a Werewolf attack, we would see nothing more of the bodies. However, if this was meant to be a feeding, there would have been very little left. Also, why only Kuroi Te? Usually if this was a Vampire attack, the victim would have been asleep and wouldn't have known until they saw the marking on their necks. If this was a Shade, then there would be no bloodshed at all. This couldn't be a Ghoul or some evil spirit; it all just doesn't add up. Therefore, I would like to speak to the survivor. I am hoping that they could shed some light for us."

"She may not be so eager to talk…"

"If she cares about her comrades, she will," the Huntress assured the Count this as they eventually came up to the door leading to inside the guest house.

Upon opening it and crossing down a short hall they came across another door guarded by another Watchman. After stamping his spear into the floor, he stepped aside to make room for the two visitors. Without another word, the Huntress turned the small knob and pushed the door in to meet the sole survivor of Kuroi Te.

She was young with pale skin with freckles on her cheeks, her hair as black as night. Her upper torso was covered by a sleeping gown offered by the church, and her expression looked like one of the dead. She looked up to see the Huntress coming in and immediately started to squirm nervously in her bed as if she was unsure whether to stay or flee. By the way her eyes looked to the nightstand by her bed where two silver daggers rested, the Huntress figured she might even just fight if necessary.

"It's all right, Akira," Count Andrei assured the bounty hunter. "This is a Hunter, one of The Black Hand. She is here to help."

The woman named Akira slowly started to relax, looking at the Huntress with curious eyes now. "Help?"

The Huntress nodded and then pulled up a small stool up to the bed. She then raised her right hand, where her guild tattoo of an outstretched black hand rested on the flesh between her thumb and index finger; the ink as dark as her black fingernails. When Akira seemed satisfied that she was indeed real, the Huntress then pulled back her hood, revealing a head of long hair that was as white as pale moonlight.

Count Andrei was taken aback by this startling and mysterious beauty, as did Akira who gaped at the warrior in amazement. The purple eyes, pointed nose, dark eyebrows in contrast to her hair, and high cheek bones made the Huntress look like a Noblewoman rather than a Huntress; perhaps even a close approximation of what an angel would look like.

"My name is Angela Dragos," the Huntress said those glistening purple eyes never wavering from Akira's bright green ones. "It's a pleasure to meet you."

Akira licked her lips nervously and nodded in a way of greeting.

She was a bounty hunter, and she had been reduced to such a state...

Angela then reached out with her right hand and gently took up the girl's chin. She then turned Akira's head from side to side like a doctor inspecting pox marks, and studied her neck.

"Tell me everything that happened that night of the attack," she said as she examined her other side. "Leave out no detail, please."

After her chin was released by the chilly fingers of Angela, Akira pursed her lips nervously. "It was horrible... unlike anything I have ever seen..."

Angela frowned. The girl was still in shock, and would need some time. She decided to try a different approach.

"Akira," she said. "Do you have any idea *why* the creature attacked, and why it allowed you particularly to live?"

Akira shuddered as if a Shade had passed through the room. "It is because... I've killed his brother."

His. Not *it*.

"Who?" Angela asked.

Akira gulped and looked Angela directly in the eye. "It was a Vampire that got us."

Angela's purple eyes narrowed slightly. *So it* was *a Vampire after all.*

Andrei chuckled. "*That's* what it was? Preposterous... I mean, there hasn't been a Vampire around here in ages!"

Ignoring the Count, Angela pressed on. "Tell me everything that happened."

Akira looked down at her hands which were gripping the edge of her blanket nervously.

Comforting people had never been her strongest suit, but Angela reached forward and took ahold of Akira's hands into one of her own.

"Take your time," she said. "I want to help you, okay?"

Akira nodded nervously and she began to tell the story. As she did so, Angela imagined every detail as the bounty hunter described it' painting a picture in her brain that moved along like a show wheel.

"We were celebrating. One of our guys, Johnny, had killed his first Ghoul. So we went to the bar, and started having out celebratory drinks. Ghoul's aren't a big deal, I've slayed seven of them, including one Riff and a Vampire, but it was still a victory for him. He had been new. We had kicked everyone else out, so that we could have the place to ourselves. Eventually, we got a knock on the door, and our leader opened it for the bartender. The man, he looked like royalty, almost younger than me it seemed. When he made eye-contact with me, I remembered feeling... cold. The man then asked to be let in, so that he could buy a drink for the road, and Cass, our leader, said yes. Why not, right? But the man then smiled and he stepped in... in one quick swipe, he had slapped her head clean off her shoulders.

"After we got over our shock, we all went in weapons free to attack, but we were all cut down one by one. This thing... it moved so fast, we didn't have time to react. There was so much blood... The bartender then took out his blunderbuss and tried to shoot him. The shot tore through his side, but immediately the hole just *filled* up with his flesh, like he was made of clay. I had never seen something do that before. Before the guy knew it, he was attacked by the Vampire as well, and I watched as the man was torn part limb from limb and had his heart *pulled* out of his chest. I was charging at the creature at this point but before I could stick my blade into him, he grabbed me, and slammed me down into the floorboards...

"He then leaned over, grinning over my face. I tried to kick him off, but he was too heavy… Or maybe I was just simply too weak. He held me, pinned to the floor, and he started to inch his head towards my neck. I saw his fangs, and that horrible purple tongue… but then he stopped. He was staring at my neck, and then he grinned at me, before letting me go and getting off me. He then turned around, and then he just started to walk away. My team, my friends, they were all strewn about me like chunks of meat in a butcher's shop, and I was left alone…"

Akira shuddered as the memory played through her mind again. "I have fought a Vampire before, but… this one was on a *completely* different level. On his way out, the Vampire turned his head and said, 'This is for you killing my little brother.' The only thing I could think of was the Vampire I had hunted a week earlier. I had stormed this old castle the locals had been afraid of, and I slew it. I never knew he had *family*. I never knew… Dear God, they're all gone… *dead*…"

Akira shuddered again as if she were cold and hugged herself as she rested her forehead on her knees. The memories seemed to be taking a heavy toll on her for telling such a tale. She was finished.

Angela pursed her lips in thought. This was indeed a strange tale, and it made little sense. But she knew why the Vampire didn't kill her or even bitten her. It was a rare case, but not impossible; she had only seen something like this once in her long, long life.

"You've already been bitten," she eventually said when it seemed appropriate to tell Akira. "That is why you have not been attacked by this Vampire yourself."

Akira stared at the Huntress in fear. She reached for her neck and started feeling around for evidence as if the marks would finally reveal themselves. "But…"

"Some Vampires don't leave puncture marks on their prey's neck. It's how they hide themselves, having needle-points in their fangs it makes it almost impossible to see the bite marks. Not all Vampires have them, it's like a second set that can extend past the regular canines. It's a mutation some are able to achieve and manipulate. I could see the markings the moment I stepped into the room. I wanted to hear your story first."

Then taking Akira by the chin, Angela gently turned the bounty hunter's head slightly to the left to expose her throat a little more. "And your story tells me exactly as you have said: this was not an attack for a source of food. The Vampire had come out of revenge upon your group and turn you into the very thing you hunted. He's let you live because he saw that his brother had already gotten you."

"But how… how am I still… still…" Akira didn't seem capable of finishing her sentence.

"Human? From Immortals, depending on what their motive is, it could take weeks to turn into a Vampire. If he wanted you to turn into a Dearg or some lesser Vampire, you would have turned that very night. But it seems that he wanted you to become sentient; *aware* of what was happening to you."

"This is horrible," Andrei said speaking for the first time. He looked upon Akira with an expression of fear, as if she had already become a monster. It was a look that Angela had seen many times before. "And you said you were bitten a *week* ago?" he then asked.

"I guess…" Akira said nervously.

"There may still be time," said Angela. "We need to get you into urgent care." She then stood up, and looked down upon the bounty hunter, those gleaming purple eyes never wavering as she said, "You are coming with me. If we hurry, I can have someone make a vaccine for you."

She then turned to the Count. "There have been no other attacks the last few days?"

"None that we know of…"

"Then hopefully the Vampire moved on…" said Angela but she didn't seem convinced.

Andrei then said, "Shouldn't we do something about the girl now? I mean, if she was bitten, she will turn. We need to take care of her here and now."

"There is still time," Angela said. "My group are experts concerning the supernatural, and we will be able to make a vaccine that will slow the process or even stop it. I would rather try to do that rather than killing her here and now. The fact that she is still with us means the Vampire wants her for something else."

"And what of the Vampire?"

"We will see about that. If he turns up again, then we might be able to destroy him. In the meantime, we must try to help this girl."

She turned back to Akira who still appeared shaken up. "We have little time. I need you to be ready to go soon. Unless you want to end it now. The way I see it, there are only two options. Come with me, and risk being healed if we are not too late, or be staked through the heart to completely eliminate the threat entirely. Either way if you begin to turn, then there is only one way out, and that is death. With my people, you have a small chance at being saved. It's your choice, Huntress."

Akira asked, "What about the Vampire?"

"Again, we don't know that it is here still, nor can anyone help me in this regard. But that is none of your concern now. The Vampire should it rear it's head again will be dealt with when it does. For now my priority is you. It is best for you to head for Blackfort Pass and meet with my people, or to be staked. What do you decide?"

"Miss," Akira said looking back at her. "What will I do, once I am healed? I don't have a guild anymore, and I got nowhere to go…"

"That is not for me to decide," Angela answered. "You still have two legs, and you will have to walk on your own."

Akira looked down, nodding solemnly. "My comrades are gone…"

"I know," Angela said really feeling sorry for the bounty hunter; she knew what it was like to lose people you cared about. "But we will deal with the Vampire later. Right now, we need to get you some help. If you come with me, I can ensure your safety as well as promise to make sure you never turn- one way or another. If the Vampire is no longer here and you are capable, then I will personally hunt it alongside you. Do we have a deal?"

Akira was silent for the longest time. For a moment, Angela wondered if the bounty hunter would even *want* to go at all, or just simply give up before her fate was sealed. Humans rarely faced such opposition when it already felt completely hopeless.

Eventually, she *did* speak and there was a fire in those green eyes that had not been there before.

"I have stuff back in my room," Akira said. "Notes, some weapons, I need to go get them."

Angela couldn't help but smile. "Then hurry. Where do you live?"

"Just the local inn. It won't take more than a few minutes, I promise."

"Then go," Angela said standing and with a whoosh of her cloak, she started back down the stairs with Andrei in tow. "I need to make a call," she announced.

There was still hope for the Huntress it seemed.

"Madam?" called the Count once they were outside and back in the cold. Angela had pulled up her hood to stay the chilly air and when she answered the Count, her breath came out in puffs of thick vapor.

"What is it?"

"Are you sure this is wise?" Andrei asked her not shivering in the slightest thanks to his pelt robes; as well as probably all the fat in his cheeks. "Allowing an infected girl to just *leave*?"

"Do you want her to *stay*?"

"What? No, I…"

"I think we can agree that she is safer out there than she is here," Angela replied. "She won't be alone for long, however. If she remains, she will be either killed or turn on your own subjects. We need to see if we can help her before that happens."

"And the Vampire? Are you truly capable of finding it and killing it if it's still here?"

"I will worry about that later."

"No, I mean, will you be all right, I mean. I mean… not to be rude or anything, but you are just a young woman. Young enough to be my daughter almost I'm willing to bet."

Angela gave him a sharp look which made the fat count wilt under. "I am an expert on this, you don't need to concern yourself with my safety."

"Well, a beautiful thing like you, I would hate to think what could happen…"

Sure you would. "Flattering, but unnecessary."

Andrei made a face as if he had been slapped right across it. He then puffed out his chest as if trying to regain his wilted pride. "Whatever the case, I do hope you know what you are doing."

"I appreciate that. You have taken a considerable risk in calling for The Black Hand in these dark times."

"Who else could I ask? Kuroi Te was the best of the best in these parts, and now they are gone. I couldn't think of anyone else to call, and I prayed and prayed for one of you to arrive. Besides... I didn't want a *Raven* coming here."

Angela nodded. "I understand. Though it might have been unwise considering your relationship with Goldendell."

Andrei shuddered, his family matters affecting him even now. "Even so, you have the better reputation- aside from the rumors. The Empire has been demanding more and more laws to be put in place, and I don't want any part of Ion's security especially upon my subjects."

Then what was a soldier of The Empire doing here?

Angela decided it was best not to ask. It was none of her business.

"Well, now your problem will be taken care of- immediately." She then stopped before a telephone booth sitting beneath a gas-fed lamp beside the nearby bakery. She then gave Andrei a look that clearly said, 'go away,' and the Count stepped aside to give her privacy. After stepping into the glass case, she sat cross-legged in the case and closed her eyes, sending her mind out towards Velinar of the Black Hand.

"Hunter of Darkness I call upon thee as a sister of blood," she spoke in a low voice. "Answer me, a Hunter of the Black Hand."

Who calls to me? came the voice inside her head, cold but kind.

"It is I," Angela responded. "Angela."

A feeling of warmth and satisfaction. A welcoming sensation that was also just a little hesitant. *Angela Dragos. Have you arrived in Irondell? What seems to be the problem?*

"I have. I need a vaccination made for Vampirism. I have an infected girl, and it is about a week old."

How unfortunate. I can make it up, but what of the beast itself?

"I will stay and Hunt. Someone will have to find her in the Pass."

Unsatisfaction, but understanding. *Can she get here on time?*

"She has to," Angela told the deity on the other side.

Very well. I will inform Oskar and we will have someone waiting at the bottom of The Steps. Make sure she is not late.

"I will. Thank you, and Amen." Thus the prayer was complete, and Angela opened her eyes and stood to step out of the phone booth. She ignored Count Andrei's eyes of wonder, for he no doubt witnessed what she had done inside the phone booth.

"We are good to go," Angela said to him. "Where is the local inn?"

"This way," the Count said showing the Huntress the way as they passed through the chilly streets. As Andrei continued to give a useless tour and history about Irondell, Angela was keeping a watchful eye on the rooftops beyond the gas-fed lamps. She felt as if someone was watching them.

She could smell them, hear them, light feet running along the roof tiles, watching from the shadows.

"What will you do," Andrei then suddenly asked. "Once Akira is cured?"

Angela replied, "As I have told her: I plan to hunt the Vampire who slaughtered Kuroi Te, and eliminate the threat to Irondell entirely."

"Threat?" Andrei asked nervously. "I thought you said the Vampire might have moved on?"

"It's a *possibility*. However, I am hoping that if Akira is gone, the Vampire will look for her. I can only think that he let her live for a greater purpose, and hope that it will drive him out. Once the threat is eliminated, then it should be safe in Irondell for the time being."

"The sooner the better," Andrei muttered. "Although you have a strange idea of 'greater purposes'.' You have my thanks for coming here. Will you be expecting payment?"

"We will handle that once the contract is complete." Angela said. "Until then, no pay will be given."

"Fair enough," Andrei said sounding relieved as he held up a hand towards the large rectangular building that served at the city inn. "Here we are, 'The Ol' Inn'. Not as classy as most places, but still the best place for a long night's rest."

As if the count ever stayed in such a place.

"Thank you," Angela said uninterested.

The front door then opened, and Akira emerged from the mouth of the building. Angela had to take a second to take in the beautiful armor the bounty hunter wore, seeing that it was not of traditional Balkeñoir fashion.

Having looked like it was forged of bronze and steel, the armor that covered Akira's torso shined brightly in the rays of the dimmed sunlight hiding deep within the clouds far above. Beautiful designs were etched in the armor itself as well as the thick shoulder pads that covered her thin arms. Angela could see designs of wolves, crows, bats and other creatures of night etched into the armor, and beneath the heavy set was simple leather armor of brown that covered Akira's entire body. Noyiian by the looks of it. At her belt was the pair of silver knives about as long as her forearm, and in her loved hands was a small notebook of black with a scarlet ribbon marking a place within the pages.

With her hair tied back, Angela could see Akira trying to keep a good posture while at the same time looking a little flustered at the attention she was getting from the Huntress herself.

"Little bright... isn't it?" she asked.

Angela shrugged. "I think it's beautiful. That is not Balkeñoir attire, is it?"

Akira shook her head. "My father came from across the sea, met my mother here. It's... the last thing I have to remember my parents."

"Well, it is beautiful," Angela said again.

"Very much so." Andrei agreed.

Akira smiled sheepishly. "Thank you. You are too kind."

Angela eyed the notebook in the bounty hunter's hand and gestured towards it with her chin. "What is in the notebook?"

"Notes, drawings, logs concerning my training and my journeys. I like to keep it close by, so that I can look back on what I have learned for the future."

Angela nodded with pursed lips. "Very nice. Well then, shall we go?"

Akira smiled. "Yes, let's."

Angela turned to Andrei. "I don't suppose you can spare a horse?"

The Count puffed out his chest with a bright smile. "But of course! You can take your pick by the stables at the gates."

"Thank you," Angela said. "She will need to ride fast and-"

She heard it just when it was too late. A sharp whistling sound in the air as it was cut; the sound of the misty air being cut by a sharp object. It was then followed by a wet tearing sound, the sound of flesh getting sliced open. Angela turned around fast to see Akira falling against the wall, clutching her eye which had a black bolt sticking in it.

The bounty hunter slid down the wall before collapsing to her side as blood and jelly seeped into the snow by her head. Angela started forward but she heard the sound again and she spun about and caught the second bolt between two fingers before it even had the chance to strike *her* in the head. She saw the tip and recognized the tint as silver. Following the trail that the bolt had come from, she saw a man garbed in black standing on the rooftop of a clock shop, a crossbow in his arms which he reloaded with another shaft.

The man had armor of leather with a cloak that looked to be made of crow feathers. His face was covered by a mask of silver which was carved into the shape of a beak with thin eye slits for the wearer to see. At his belt, Angela saw the gleam of two silver swords about as long as an arm and curved with a barbed end. The man hoisted the crossbow on his shoulder as he peered down at Angela, who snapped the bolt intended for her in two with her fingers.

Andrei ducked into the snow and started to crawl over to a pair of barrels that sat by the inn, mere feet away from where Akira laid dead. "What is going on?!" he demanded. "Guards!"

Angela peered over to the fountain area again. The soldier from the Empire was long gone still, nowhere to be seen. Fixing her purple eyes back on the man on the rooftop, she answered the Count's hectic question.

"It is a Raven," she said. "Sent by your all-knowing Empire."

"What!?" Andrei demanded. "Why would a Raven be *here*, in my city!? I didn't call for him!" As he said this a bunch of Watchmen started to rush into the streets, wielding rifles and blunderbusses.

Lowering the crossbow, the Raven laughed as he leapt from the building and tucked the crossbow behind his back beneath his feathered cloak before landing nimbly in the soft snow. He then slowly approached the Huntress with boots that crunched softly as he reached for his two blades and twirled them in his hands.

"Just performing my duties, Count Andrei," the Raven said behind his mask. "Simply because, you have brought a *monster* to your town to join the one you have been harboring."

"What are you talking about!?" Andrei demanded. "I demand an explanation! You killed that poor woman!"

"'A man bitten, is a man cursed.'" The Raven stopped about twenty feet away from Angela, who remained standing silent while glaring at the man with those piercing eyes of hers. "You know the necessities for the good of the realm. There was no hope for the bounty hunter; you are wasting your breath calling for The Black Hand and their quote-unquote 'ancient' ways. There is no cure for Vampirism except death."

Angela was still glaring at the man, who seemed to finally catch on that she was looking. Both stared the other down while Andrei still blubbered with confusion and strain.

"But the Huntress-"

"The Black Hand is useless now that the Empire is strong enough to care for it's own people better than ever before. They are a relic lot, and there is no need for them or any other guild that risk more than just themselves. The future is now standing before you." He held his hands up dramatically, an actor in his own play. "The Ravens will now be taking responsibility of all Hunting expeditions foreign and domestic. Hunting by any guild or persons is now illegal, for their own safety as well as those associated with them.”

“Since when?” demanded Andrei. “The Black Hand-”

“Are an unreliable lot now,” said the Raven. “Especially, considering they have a *monster* in their ranks.” He then removed one of his swords and with the tip of his blade, pointed it at Angela as some Watchmen started to come near them, surrounding the two.

“Count Andrei,” the Raven then said. “Are you aware, that you have been conversing with a *Dhampir*?”

Angela at last stopped glaring at the Raven; her eyes now closed as the inevitable began to unfold.

“What!?” Andrei exclaimed at last, speaking everyone’s stunned thoughts. Immediately, all eyes turned to Angela, who remained standing silently. Not only their eyes, but some even turned their weapons on her as well. Some stepped back and started to tell some townspeople who came out to see what the commotion was to get back inside- where it was safe.

“That’s a Dhampir!?” Angela heard one Watchmen whisper.

“But she’s too beautiful...”

“Idiot, it makes sense! She is a half-demon!”

“Monster...”

Angela ignored the Watchmen and opened her eyes and focus them on the Raven before her. “You killed an innocent woman. She had a chance to be cured.”

“Oh, I cured her,” the Raven said lowering his blade to his side. “A lot more than you would have done. Who’s to say that you wouldn’t just suck her dry once you left town? Demons like you are always full of deceit, especially since The Black Hand took you in. Criminals, the lot of you! The woman was doomed anyway- just like you are. By my honor as a Raven and for the glory of the Empire, you will be slayed as a creature of the night."

"Don't," Angela warned but to no avail.

"Time to die, *Vampire*!"

"Men!" Andrei said still shaking in his boots behind the barrel. "Don't just stand there- shoot that *thing*! Shoot it!"

That thing... Angela thought somberly as the orders were carried out.

The Raven looked to all the Watchmen with hopeless eyes. "No! Don't!"

But it was too late, for the eruption of guns and the resonated throughout the city. Just as the bullets hurled towards Angela like angry hornets, the Huntress leapt aside faster than any human could move out of harm's way as the projectiles crashed into the snow in a series of ricochets.

"Don't shoot!" the Raven shouted again lunging towards the Huntress with his feathered cloak flapping in the wind and both of his silver blades gleaming in the dim sunlight. "This demon is mine!"

He brought both blades together and stabbed forward with all his might towards Angela's heart with a smile of victory hidden beneath his beaked mask.

However, both of his blades were caught by Angela's own which she had unsheathed in a flash of movement almost no one had been able to follow. It caught and held the Raven's swords which trembled against the unique blade as the Raven stared at Angela in awe at her strength.

It was about as long as one of her arms and was curved on one side like your usual hand-and-a-half weapon. However, the back of the sword was riddled with curves like the teeth of a cog, and it was these numbs that caught the Raven's swords and held him steady without the fear of his blades sliding across her own sword.

"Wha-!" the Raven gasped as Angela suddenly spun about, disengaging and shifting the balance of the swords before kicking him in the stomach. The power of the kick was enough force to send him flying across the street and crash right into two other Watchmen who were still mesmerized by the strength behind the kick. The Raven curled up there momentarily with the wind knocked right out of him.

Spinning her blade in hand, Angela looked upon the Watchmen with gleaming eyes. "Anyone who wants to live will stay far back. Anyone who attempts to attack me, will be injured. Those who persist, will *die*."

Then sprinting with the speed of a whirlwind, the Dhampir came to a stop before Akira's body. To the Watchmen, it looked like she was trying to get a bite out of the fallen bounty hunter. However, she was merely searching Akira's body so that she could take the notebook she had in her possession. Even if she might not be able to save the woman anymore, there was still a possible chance to hunt the Vampire who attacked her. *If* Velinar allowed her to, anyway.

"Shoot that thing! Shoot it!" Andrei shouted ducking behind the barrel and Angela heard the click of the gun before the hammer struck down and the blast of igniting gunpowder.

Before the bullet could tear into her side however, Angela sidestepped out of harm's way just as the bullet crashed into the wall beside her just above Akira's body. Then taking a throwing knife from her belt, she hurled it at the man and it stuck right into his hand. Crying out the Watchman dropped his revolver into the snow staring wildly at the knife that was stuck right through his palm.

Then propelling herself forward, she took off into a sprint. Many of the Watchmen dove aside as the Huntress barreled towards them but a few unsheathed their short swords and brought them up ready to intercept her.

However, one by one Angela knocked the swords aside as easily as if she was fighting children with wooden swords. Their weapons flew through the air and grabbing ahold of one of the Watchmen she spun about and hurled the screaming man towards those who have clustered together and knocked them all flat into the snow. She then proceeded to bolt for the main gates which was only a few hundred feet away from where she once was. All the while, bolts and bullets whizzed past her like angry hornets shot by the Watchmen who stood on the rooftops.

She was just about to reach the gate when she heard a rush of wind to her left. Looking over she saw the Raven coming at her again blades spinning around him. "Gotcha!" he cried out as he came in close for the kill.

Angela planted a foot into the snow and then swung her blade with all her might, her movement a mere blur of speed to any who witnessed. She knocked away the first blade coming down towards her while the second fell into the snow- the right hand of the Raven still holding it tight.

"Grrh!" the Raven grunted tumbling past the Huntress and falling to his knees clutching his bleeding stump to his side. Blood continued to drip as he stood back up glaring at the Huntress through the slits of his mask. His breathing was heavy, hissing beneath his iron mask. "You goddamned wench!" He reached for his revolver and pointed it at her with venomous hatred.

Blam! Blam! Blam! Three consecutive shots, none of them hitting their mark. Angela had twisted and sidestepped, avoiding two and using her sword to deflect the third. If it had been silver, the metal would have damaged her sword but as it was of standard lead, the slug bounced harmlessly off the strongest metal in all of Lunokean.

"I warned you," Angela said with a sigh and as soon as the Raven started to go for another weapon, she closed in the man and with a whoosh of her cloak he was blinded by darkness and could not see her coming around to his side where she punched him in the kidneys causing him to falter and grabbing him by the scruff of his cloak, she turned and hurled him away, sending him flying into the nearest street lamp. Her opponent now immobile, Angela took off towards the gates once more, her weapon still drawn as the Watchman named William came out in front of her as the gates started to close.

"Stop!" William shouted. "In the name of Count Andrei, stop!" He had his sword in one hand and his blunderbuss in the other, ready to fire should he have to.

Still, the half-breed in front of him didn't change her pace nor her direction and kept coming straight for him.

"Move," Angela warned him holding her blade up so that the Watchman could see his own reflection in the silver edging.

"HALT!" William insisted but Angela could tell he was afraid. The man reeked of it, and the sweat that glistened on his brow despite the sun still being hidden by the dense clouds above made it all the more obvious.

But Angela didn't want to hurt the man too badly and wanted more than anything to just escape. So, when William raised his weapon and fired it, Angela leapt aside and lunged forward swinging her blade and slicing the weapon in half. With a cry of terror, William swung his own sword, but it was a clumsy strike and Angela got her blade up with the teeth facing the incoming sword and with a clang she caught it and held him there. Now they were mere inches from one another with William staring into those pale purple eyes that just weren't human. They were dilated into thin slits, cat-like, and predatory.

"Forgive me," Angela said before ducking and punching William hard in the gut and causing him to double over and collapse at her feet. She then left the man in the snow without breath as she sprinted forward and slipped right through the gates as they slammed shut; closing off the city from the escaping Dhampir who then deflected an arrow hurling from a nearby tower with her sword.

Then, leaping nimbly upon the man who held her horse Midnight, she knocked the man clean out by hitting him square in the forehead with the butt of her sword.

Then leaping from him and onto the black horse, she dug her heels into Midnight's sides, causing her spurs to click and command the horse to run. Rearing back, Midnight neighed loudly before galloping forward at break-neck speeds. They thundered down the snowy path and away from Irondell where the alarm bell was still tolling by the gates. In a matter of minutes, the city walls were out of sight, hidden behind the miles of trees that made up the forest Angela had escaped not too long ago.

When the only remaining sound was the clopping of Midnight's hooves and the soft moan of the winds through the trees, Angela willed the horse to slow down to a steady strut and she finally sheathed her unique sword over her shoulder and took hold of the reins with pale white hands that gripped them in frustration. At this point, she was well used to how she was treated because of the cursed blood in her veins.

But that didn't mean it got any easier.

Being a Dhampir, Angela Dragos was cursed the day of her birth, being hated by both humans and Vampires alike. With the attributes of both races coursing through her body, she was cursed to be scorned and treated with fear and hatred. With nowhere to go, nowhere to belong, she had dedicated her life to the Black Hand; ever since her own family casted her out like a leper from a city. But even then, the castle hidden deep within the mountains offered no place she could call home. Doomed to hunt the creatures of the night for the rest of her eternal life, she has accepted the life of a Huntress, and understood that even if she did save someone, they would still hate her for what she was. Not even the

Vampires would accept her, for her blood was tainted by the very beings who feared her still.

Hated and feared by both the races that sired her, all she really knew was what she was not. She had accepted this, but that did not make it any easier.

Even if she had been able to help Akira, and eliminate the Vampire threat, the city of Irondell would have found out and chased her away- or worse send a Raven after her. With her contact dead, and the Ravens at large, there was no point in staying in Irondell.

So instead, the Huntress started for home; the only sanctuary for a creature like her. A home, that wasn't home.

The only place a creature such as herself, could find a small sense of peace.

Velinar will want to know what the Empire has decided…

The Raven ground his teeth as he stuck his stump into a fire basin on top of the walls overlooking the forest beyond Irondell. The pain was excruciating and sent shockwaves up his arm all the way to his head. Still, he kept it there. He had to stop the bleeding and cauterize the wound. He had used his belt to staunch the bleeding and he had come up here to watch the Dhampir flee with Count Andrei.

The Count stood close by, with one of his Watchmen by his side. After the Dhampir had been chased away, the people came out demanding what had happened. The useless Count managed to keep them busy while the Raven watched the men give chase to the demon in the woods. Unfortunately, they came back just as he was burning the stump to cauterize it. The monster had taken his hand, a crying shame next to actually losing the creature.

Everything hurt. His back, his head, the fire that burned his flesh in order to stop the bleeding as well as the ghostly fingers that he tried desperately to move again; everything. Especially his pride. What would his guild say about such a failure? To have such a creature still loose in the country, was an abomination all on its own. Especially with the new order coming to the country.

There was still time too. There was still a mission to be completed.

"Um… sir?" Count Andrei stuttered with a nervous expression, chewing on his thumbnail.

"What is it?" the Raven said now wrapping the burned stump with some fresh bandages brought to him by a pretty maiden with black hair. The smell of cooked flesh filled his nostrils, making him sick but he kept his calm demeanor up for the sake of The Ravens. He studied the young girl closely as well for the sake of a distraction, and he was surprised to find himself not disappointed in what he saw.

Andrei licked his lips nervously. "Not to be rude, you *do* have my thanks concerning that beast. But why are you here? I don't remember calling for a Raven to come."

"It is a good thing I was here, otherwise you might just have another massacre on your hands," the Raven replied coolly. He reached into his satchel and removed a scroll of parchment. He held it out to Andrei who took it and broke the wax seal of the Goldendell sigil; the eagle of The Empire. He began to read, and the Raven watched as the Count's eyes widened.

"It is by the order of His Majesty the Emperor that we check up on every city within his realm. As I had mentioned earlier The Ravens will now be handling any and all investigations supernatural or otherwise if His Majesty so chooses. It was a very poor decision, calling for the Black Hand instead of The Ravens in the first place. You really have made a terrible mistake, Count Andrei."

Andrei scowled, brought his eyes up from the parchment which trembled in his hands. "I was not informed of any new order of Hunting expeditions. As far as I was concerned-"

"My informant didn't alert you to the new order?" asked the Raven.

Andrei's brow furrowed. "Are you calling me a liar?"

The Raven shrugged, not caring in the slightest. "In any case, I will be handling the Vampire infestation of your hold, Count Andrei. As for The Black Hand, they are soon to be disbanded along with every other Hunting Guild in the country. The Ravens will be in complete control of the situation, to ensure nothing like what happened today ever happens again."

"That wasn't my fault," implored the Count. "Besides, I didn't know that they would have a… a…"

"A bastard of a Vampire and human?"

Andrei fell silent, no more excuses to give.

"It hardly matters now," the Raven said retrieving his sword from a Watchman who had come up to give it to him. He sheathed it as he continued. "I am upset that the Dhampir had escaped. But, she is gone now, and the city is safe- for now. With the victim gone, the Vampire shouldn't have any reason to come back. Although, I would heighten your security around the city walls, just in case. I plan to do a thorough search throughout the city. The Immortal who had given her the kiss may very well come back. It may very well still be here."

"What about your arm?"

"Don't worry about it."

Andrei gulped loudly, his expression stretched in newfound fear. "I do apologize…"

"No need to be. The city is now under my investigation, and I shall perform my duties regardless. In the meantime, I will also be following up on your orders that you have there."

Andrei frowned at this, but the Raven continued.

"The Emperor will be happy that I have thwarted the monster's intentions. However, there *must* be punishment for calling in the criminals of the mountains instead of us first."

"Eh?" Andrei said confused.

The Raven nodded. From his satchel, he removed another small piece of parchment which he handed to the Count. After a quick read, Andrei's expression grew pale, his eyes widened to the size of dinner plates. It was more amusing than the look he had from the last message.

The Raven relished in his following statement. "I am in charge here from here on out. You are now under my command, Count Andrei. Place the city under a quarantine. No one is allowed in or out of the city until I find the Vampire. Also, there is some work to do regarding your... faith."

"Preposterous!" Andrei practically yelped, the parchment crumpling in his fingers. "I am the Count here, not y-"

"I didn't give you a suggestion," the Raven warned the Count. "But a command. For the safety of your people and those outside the walls, one is allowed in or out until I find the Vampire responsible."

"But-"

The Raven turned a sharp eye towards the Count which rendered him speechless. "Would you like to argue this with the Head of The Ravens? Or perhaps, the Emperor?"

Andrei gulped audibly. "The Emperor would ensure the safety-"

"Of the *realm*," the Raven cut the man off. "It is my duty to ensure that the Vampire does not escape this place, and no one will be allowed in. This will be taken into effect- immediately. I am in charge here, and if you have a problem with that, then let us call Emperor Ion and you can try to explain to him how you made a foolish decision and nearly ended up with an epidemic on your hands."

All the color flushed right out of the Count's face at the thought of what the leader of the country would have to say. To call upon The Black Hand when he blatantly declared them outlaws of the motherland because of their insolence against his new order, was a grave mistake for anyone in Balkeñoir, whether they be Count, General, or even a city sweeper.

"What will I tell everyone?" Andrei asked. "I don't understand how you expect this situation to be handled- especially considering the fiasco that you and that Dhampir caused!"

"Are you *really* trying to shift the blame onto me?"

"N...no... but also the church-"

"Then you better figure it out. Tell them what they need to hear and then report back to me immediately." He Raven looked to the Watchman present. "Make sure that he does, sir."

The Watchman cleared his throat.

The lack of response sent Andrei aback. "You cannot do this to us! I am the Count of Irondell! I still have a city to keep! We are one of the biggest trading posts this far from the Capitol. If you cut us off-"

"You'll what?" the Raven demanded in a bored tone. "Cut off supplies from the Emperor and Goldendell?

Yeah, *that* will go well. Especially, if turns out I am right. You really want me to go? Then good luck finding the Immortal without any support." There was no guarantee that the Vampire was still around, but Andrei was not stupid enough to try and dismiss the possibility. Especially not with what was to take place here in the meantime.

"Be reasonable! You're cutting us off completely! And if that Immortal is still on the loose-"

At this point, The Raven was getting short on patience and so cut the man short with a sharp wave of his hand. "Don't fret, I will ensure that the situation will be taken care of. You just have to make it out, and pray that nothing else like this should happen again. Also, concerning your phone call, I'd make sure you are truthful with the Emperor."

"My… phone call?"

"I am sure the Emperor would like a personal response to what he has commanded you. As well as an account as to what happened here. On that… I think we can stretch the truth out a bit. I am sure he will be greatly upset if he found out a Dhampir had not only been here in Irondell, but *invited* in. He might even consider pulling me out, and leaving you all at the mercy of the Immortal if he is still here."

Andrei's eyes widened at the mention of this. "Surely he wouldn't-"

"I *could* put in a good word for you," said the Raven with cruel delight. "Say the Black Hand happened to just wander by. Just think of this as… an act of mercy. Do we understand each other, Count Andrei?" He looked at the

Count with a piercing glare through the eye slits in his mask, daring him to say the wrong thing.

Instead, as usual, the Count of Irondell gulped again and nodded. He really was a spineless worm, just like the Emperor wanted. As long as leaders such as this man existed, the power will always belong to Goldendell and the Emperor.

The Raven, smiled beneath his mask. "Good. Very good."

He then turned to go with a flap of his feathered cloak. Irondell was his responsibility now, both in terms of finding the rebellious demon that stalks the streets, but also in terms of setting the new standards in the minds of the influential. The Emperor had big plans for the future, and for it to work, all the major cities would have to be on the same page; and on the same *god*.

And Raven Vicar Virgil was more than happy to help in the spread of the new religion for Balkeñoir and make mankind the strongest beings in the world; more powerful than any beast or angelic being. It was his destiny, and his mission.

Kawfka guide me, he thought as he left Count Andrei and went to prepare for the hunt. After a quick but thorough search, then he will meet with the Count again.

The Anguis Express was making its daily rounds down the track that cut through the landscape of Balkeñoir at incredible speeds, carrying with it both goods and passengers to different cities where it would make its stops.

Faster than any demon-horse, the black engine that pulled the many cars thundered through the Woodmarsh, disturbing the many creatures sleeping within the trees that it thundered past. It was a magnificent machine of transportation, the most well-known of Professor Clockwork's inventions that kept the kingdoms and holds of the Empire together; as well as provide safe transportation of goods and people through the harsh and yet to be tamed wilderness. While much of Balkeñoir was inhabited, there were still areas none dared to tread.

Within the civilian cars on this blustery night, were a few families and travelers heading for Copperdell, a small hold at the base of the Stonehollow Mountains to the far east of Balkeñoir. From there the train would loop back up northwest and then curve back south through Irondell, and from there, through Blackfort Pass. Unbeknownst to the passengers however, the Anguis Company had received orders not to stop at Irondell until further notice. The goods meant for Irondell however, would be taken to the Copperdell warehouses; much to the dismay of the tradesmen.

Men and women, old and young all huddled close together in the cars of beautifully crafted seats of leather and wood. The ceiling was dotted with beautiful lamps of bronze and glass that illuminated all of their faces both asleep and awake. It was a warm and luxurious ride for little Adina, who sat with her mother and older brother, Adam.

Bored of watching out the window only to see the flurries of the night blaze by that obscured any 'good' sightseeing, Adina had taken up people-watching to try and pass the time. Her mother was reading a book and her brother was fast asleep and fogging up the window he rested against. As the train rumbled on, making the seat beneath her bounce occasionally, Adina watched the other people on the train who all seemed to be in their own little worlds. At times, her mother noticed this watching behavior and was concerned about it, but has yet to speak to Adina about it.

A young couple sat together, buried beneath a blanket of patched fabrics. The man was handsome with a little stubble on his upper lip, and his girlfriend was particularly beautiful with pale skin and hair as brown as chestnuts. The girl was sleeping against the man's shoulder, who would occasionally look down at her with a worrisome look. Were they two young lovers trying to escape their families? A tragic romance between two lovers torn apart by family or politics? It wouldn't surprise Adina. Her mother and father were in the same situation, particularly because he took it upon himself to become a Werewolf Hunter. She hoped that the same situation was not set on this young couple. They looked so young, full of love and care, Adina hoped that they would be happy one day, and even wondered if she would ever be looked down upon with that same caring look. Being only ten years now, she still had a few years to go. It wouldn't be long for even her brother to one day find a lover and run away with her as well. This thought depressed Adina, and so she looked somewhere else.

In the seat across the aisle from the couple, sat an old man with a cane of black wood resting in his lap. He wore a simple tan suit with a hat that covered his eyes as he slept. His hands were dotted with liver spots, and he had hair that appeared silver in the dim lamplight. How old was he now? Sixty? Seventy? It was anyone's guess. Was he ever married? Did he have kids, or family that he was visiting? Was he heading home? Traveling? So many questions seemed to radiate from the sleeping old man, but none would be answered, for Adina was to stay where she was seated until they reached the train station in Copperdell. Mystery shrouded the man, which only made him all the more interesting. But alas, some mysteries could not ever be solved until the answer finally reveals itself.

Another woman sat in the seat right across from Adina and her family. She was garbed in all black, including her large wide-brimmed hat that shaded her from the lamplight. In her gloved hands was a paperback novella, the cover having a rose and what looked like a naked woman dancing around the thorny stem. Her neck and shoulders were covered by hair as red as the rose on her book, and her crimson lips turned into a smile as she no doubt got to the good part of her novella. Adila liked to read as well, and wondered if the woman would like any of the books that she herself has read. Stories like Cinderella and Rapunzel.

Lastly, there was a man sitting alone just behind Adina and her family, and peering over the back of the seat she looked to see that he was now eating from a tin of cookies. They looked like muffins at first, they were so big. Many different shades of color depicted different flavors, and the aroma was still coming from the open tin as the man took one with nimble fingers and popped it into his mouth. His black beard was crisp, clean of both any crumbs and graying hairs. His head was bald, reflecting the light from above like a polished orb on a sunny day. His glasses were large half-moon styled with lenses that made his blue eyes large, especially when he looked up at the feeling of being watched.

He smiled warmly and offered the tin towards Adina. She declined politely however, for her mother had taught her to never take sweets from strangers. She sat back down onto her seat and adjusted her pink skirt as the train continued to rumble on. It has been a long ride, and it would be longer still until they reached the station of Copperdell by sunset.

Copperdell... their new home.

Train rides really were extremely boring after a while, even with all the books in the bag at her feet, which she had already read- all of them, twice.

At some point the door at the far end of the car opened up, revealing one of the workers on the train. The man wore a tailored blue uniform and a hat to match it. He was terribly pale, making the rosiness in his cheeks even more visible than usual. His perfectly white hair revealed him to be Noyiian, because he was too young to have such white hair. He blew into his cupped hands, trying to warm them up as he approached the center of the car and stopped dead center between all of the passengers. He was about to make an announcement, his whistle now in his hands and ready to unleash the chirp which would bring everyone to attention.

But she never got to hear the whistle's shrill cry, nor whatever the man was about to say, for his words were cut short by the black projectile that had speared him through his back and shot out his chest before getting stuck halfway. The man gasped and coughed out violently as blood spilled from his lips, his eyes staring at the spike protruding from his chest. He collapsed to the ground convulsing and slowly dying as Adina screamed; waking her brother and bringing everyone's attention to the dying man who continued to twitch on the carpeted floor of white which was now being stained by crimson. Upon seeing the curved hilt of the cane in the man's back, Adina turned to see that the old man further up had gotten out of his seat and was standing just fine without its support. His teeth were bared in a terrible grin, and now that he faced her. Adina noticed that the man's eyes glowed yellow with no pupils, as if they had been replaced with buttered ball bearings.

"Guess that means they're finishing their rounds, eh?" the old codger said as he started forward caneless and with a deadly purpose. The couple who sat across from him shifted as the boy got up and blocked the man's path. He was about to say something but suddenly the old man lashed out and his hand shot out from the man's back through the stomach, spraying crimson back and speckling his girlfriend in the dew.

"Ander!" the girl screamed as the old man dropped the unfortunate to the floor. She rushed to his side screaming his name until the old man backhanded her face- and sent her *head* flying over the heads of the rest. It bounced off the back and was lost somewhere beneath the seats, leaving a gory stain wherever it went.

"Bloody nuisance," the old man said raising his soaked hand and started to lick his fingers with a tongue that wriggled out like a long and purple snake past teeth that appeared sharp like a shark's.

"Mommy!" Adina cried out as both she and her brother were taken by their mother towards the back of the train. Leaving their belongings, the mother violently pulled Adina back when she tried to go back. She shielded them, keeping them both behind her as the remaining passengers agreed with what they were doing and ran after them, desperate to get away from the old man who was now coming at them, his skin changing from white and smooth to black and almost moist, his hair falling out and his bodyweight increasing.

"Adam!" their mother shrieked pushing them back against the door to the point where she might crush them. "Get that door opened!"

"I'm trying!" Adam struggled against the door, but it was no use. All the locks beyond that door were set on the other side so that the rear could get out after this car was supposed to empty. The clamors of the rest of the passengers certainly didn't help either; in fact, the man who sat behind them eating sweets had squeezed his way past their mother and was trying desperately to help Adam wrench the door open. Meanwhile the woman in black screamed her head off and Adina peeked around her mother's skirts to see the old man who was no longer there.

In his place standing with a pile of torn fabrics scattered around its feet, was a creature of terrifying proportions. It wasn't any bigger than it was before, but it was bulging with muscle; humanoid, but entirely inhuman. Black shiny skin webbed with ropy muscle beneath, its long black hair appeared thicker than usual as if actually tentacles or feelers. If Adina didn't know any better, she would have thought they were ears at first. Its hands were big enough to hold the headless body of the woman in its fist, its long fingers crushing it as it raised the body up to its mouth where it squeezed the blood from the stump and guzzled it like wine. Long curved teeth that appeared sharper than any dagger were stained red and with claws curved and sharp it shredded the woman's clothes to clear the way for its teeth to sink into the fleshy meat in her naked abdomen.

Adina moaned and cried at the sight, a horrible sound of pure terror. Her mother absentmindedly tried to shield her daughter's eyes from the gruesome scene, but she too appeared frozen in place as the creature turned its baleful yellow eyes upon the huddled crowd and tossed the half-eaten body aside and it lumbered over the body of the two men and started its way forward to the group.

The bearded man shoved his way past the group again and stood in front of them, holding the woman in black back next to Adina's mother while her brother continued to try and break the door down behind them. Compared to the beast, the man was no bigger, nor more intimidating even with a switchblade out.

"Get back!" the man cried out at the snarling creature as he grabbed ahold of his tin and chucked it at the monster. It bounced harmlessly off the creature's head and without even blinking, it hissed in laughter.

"That ain't gonna work," the monster said bringing up its bloody claws to scare the man even worse as it got closer and closer. It relished with the terror of it's victims. "Poor little morsels, stuck in a corner. You gonna cower as I feast on you alive, or are you gonna fight like rats?"

Adina clenched her eyes, not wanting to see what would happen next. She would keep her eyes shut throughout the screams, the rendering of flesh. She would keep them shut even if the monster came upon her and tried to get her to open her eyes. She tried to make herself as small as possible, burying her face into her mother's clothes and sobbing miserably.

The monster suddenly let out this harrowing scream that resonated against the glass windows, causing them to vibrate and Adina clamped her hands over her ears to protect them from the horrible sound the monster made. She opened her eyes to see what had happened.

It whirled around fast and she saw that a silver arrow protruded from the creature's muscled back, and leaning to the side to peer around it best she could, she saw that someone had come in from the other side, allowing the cold winds to billow through the car as he stood there before the angry Ghoul.

"Should have checked the rear cars after all," the man said reaching back to pull another arrow out of its quiver before he nocked it on a bow of black bark and pulled back on the taunt string.

He was a handsome man, appearing no older than Adam with long black hair that was tied back in a ponytail under a black bowler hat. He had an eyepatch over his right eye, and he wore simple black leather armor with a cloak to match; which flapped around him like wings in the wind. At his sides were two dagger sheathed next to one another and a revolver, as well as another circlet of throwing knives around his black boots. He peered down the arrow shaft with his one blue eye, aiming right for the Ghoul who roared at him in indignation.

"You little bastard!" the Ghoul snarled and then forgetting its previous prey, it charged forward with outstretched hands, ready to grab the Hunter who stood where he was. "I'll rip your arms off!"

"Oh, thanks for coming closer" the man said with a calm expression and lowing his bow fast and just as quick, he grabbed a second arrow from the quiver across his back and nocked both of them at the same time on the string. When the monster was almost upon him, he suddenly crouched and tilted his bow to the side and released both projectiles which flew straight and true before sinking right into both of the Ghoul's glowing eyes.

"Reaargh!" the Ghoul screamed out clutching at it's face as it continued to barrel forward. "My eyes!"

As it came upon the Hunter, the man leapt up and ran across the seats past the Ghoul who slammed right into the doorway which was too small for it to slip through. Whirling around it wrenched the arrows out of its eyes and screamed out once again as black blood sprayed from the sockets. It tossed the arrows aside angrily, one of them still skewered through one of the creature's eyes like a gory kabab.

"That was close," the man said landing on the floor and turning around. His cape blew behind him because of the wind, giving everyone a better look at the broad shoulders he had. The Hunter then hooked his bow behind his back by a strap beneath the cloak and then reaching down he pulled out the two daggers from their sheathes, their blades sparkling of curved silver. He spun them in each hand and got into a defensive stance as the Ghoul started to feel its way back to the rear of the car.

"You bastard!" the monster snarled as the black slime continued to dribble down its face. "You took away my eyes!" It then began to sniff around like a bloodhound, trying to locate its prey.

"Good. They were creepy," the man said rushing forward. The Ghoul turned its head as its ears caught the sound of approaching boots and it raised its arm, ready to claw at the approaching Hunter.

"There you are!" It slashed at the man with all it's might, tearing through the cloak as easily as it did the woman.

"No, I'm not," the Hunter said now directly beneath the beast and fast as lightning, he drove the daggers in one after the other again and again randomly into the monster's groin and lower belly. Black blood spilled onto his boots and the white carpet, and the force of the attack started to slowly drive the beast back as it gasped and coughed. Every time it tried to reach and grab at the Hunter he would nimbly dance away before coming back in and creating a large gash in the arms or severing a finger. Then driving both blades in at once on the leftmost side of the Ghoul's gut, the Hunter then jerked to the right and slide them right across; ripping the belly open as easily as he would gut a fish. The intestines spilled from the belly like wet eels and the Ghoul fell to its knees as it tried to scoop it's guts back in unsuccessfully. It looked up blindly with a terrified face and held up a shaking hand to its adversary who stood panting before him, dripping with black gore.

"Have mercy…" the Ghoul begged in a weak voice. It froze however as it felt the two daggers press against its throat. Then in one quick, fluid motion, the Hunter slid both the blades apart, slitting the creatures throat and letting loose one last spray of black before the Ghoul collapsed to the carpet.

Wiping the black dew off his sleeves, the Hunter looked back to the group. "You all alright?" he asked.

Everyone stared, amazed and horrified by what had occurred. Some got over their initial shock and allowed the man to come closer and check in on them personally, individually. All the while, Adina was staring at the Hunter in wonder. He really was handsome, a beautiful strong face free from marks and a thin shade of stubble across his chin. Her eyes soon followed him still as he returned to the corpse of the couple and train worker who had been killed. Taking the drenched blanket they were previously using, the Hunter then covered the woman's naked and chewed body. He then stood up and sighed, peering at the two men who perished before her.

"I should have checked the rear cars..."

Once the train had stopped at the station just under an hour later, the remaining passengers on the other cars were told to remain seated to allow time to remove the bodies and calm the traumatized victims of the attack.

The Copperdell Station was an old, small building of wood and stone just right off the main street leading into the city. Everyone had left aside from the passengers from the attacked car while doctors took a look at them. They were all huddled under blankets during the checkups, and Adina was glad to be in her mother's arms next to her brother. The Hunter who had saved them was speaking to the Head of Control who owned the railroad tracks as well as the trains who rode them. Adina watched from a distance as the Hunter accepted a bag of gold from the pudgy little man who had apparently hired him to kill the Feral Ghoul. If he hadn't been there, Adina wouldn't be here now, being hugged by her loving mother.

This was exciting! An actual member of The Black Hand had saved them! Adina had heard stories of the group of Hunters who were not tied to any city or ruler, who hunted the creatures of the night in the shadows as opposed to the Goldendell Ravens. Terrible rumors were told about The Black Hand; in fact, many were afraid to even discuss about them because of their reputation of dealing with dark magic as well as working with dangerous creatures as well as humans. There were even rumors that they were in league with a few of the most powerful monsters of Balkeñoir. Whether this was true or not still remained a mystery for no one had ever captured a member or killed one and lived to tell the tale. So, the fear of the unknown remained, and only the bravest or those with no one else to turn to dared to summon them.

"Thank you so much," the Master of the Railway said behind his gray mustache to the Hunter who accepted the bag of coins gracefully. "That beast has been giving us trouble for days now. Every night a whole car would be emptied 'cause of him, and we could never tell just who he was. He must have been taking a new form of the victim every time. I knew if we called The Black Hand, they would take care of it! You guys always do, and now thanks to you, the Anguis Express can continue its business as smoothly as-"

He was cut short as the Hunter suddenly stomped hard on the man's foot, seizing him by the throat when he started to buckle in pain. The passengers of the attacked car as well as any other onlookers gasped at the sight, but none seemed eager to get out from under the blankets provided for them. Adina couldn't blame them, the Hunter looked angry as he stared down at the man who choked and gagged as his windpipe was being crushed.

"You had this problem for a *while* now," the Hunter said through clenched teeth. "And *still* you kept the train running at night." This was not a question, but a very cold statement. He released the man's throat but kept his foot down, pinning the man down as he fell over on his butt and began rubbing frantically at his swollen throat.

"We-well you see sir," the Master croaked, grimacing at the weight on his foot. "We have a schedule to keep, you understand, right? Profits to be made, goals to keep- ahh! C-could you kindly, please, remove your foot? Ow! Ow!"

"You goddamned idiot," the Hunter sneered grabbing the man's mustache and turning his head so that he could see the two bodies being loaded into the cart a couple yards away. "Look! Take a good look! You put these people in danger, and those two are dead! They're death is on *your* hands." He shoved the old man to the ground again, only now removing his foot. It would have been funny had it not been under the current circumstances.

The man glared at the Hunter as his face turned beet red. "Y-you incompetent- do you know who I am!?"

"No, and I don't give a shit," the Hunter said. He pointed a finger at the man's face, who immediately froze. "Their blood is on *your* hands. Remember that when you close your eyes at night. May the Flutemaster bring you their faces every time you dream."

Then with a whoosh of his cloak he started for the exit of the station, ignoring the looks from all the spectators as he passed through the arch and started down the steps to the main street of Copperdell where a horse was waiting for him. Time was of the essence, especially if the right authorities were notified about his involvement with the word spreading about what happened on the train.

The Master got up and glowered at the man's back. "What do you care anyway?" he demanded loudly. "It's not like you and your guild cares anyway! You're only in it for the money, just like us! You're no different than us! Thank Yohnah the Emperor has named you criminals; I hope the Ravens bring you all to heel!"

The Hunter stopped abruptly, and the man held his breath, as did everyone else. Was the Hunter going to do something? For a long while, he said nothing, but then the man turned his head to peer at the Master with his one good eye and said, "I'm not the one who called for help." And with that, he continued on, ready to mount his horse waiting for him at the entrance.

Adina pulled the blanket off her little body and she hurried forward, ignoring her mother's calling for her to return. She stopped at the top of the stairs just as the Hunter was just about to mount his horse. Telling him to wait she doubled her speed taking two steps at a time if she could, and stopped near the bottom a few feet away from him. Her mother and brother were up on the staircase, concerned for Adina's safety but also too afraid to approach the Hunter who waited patiently for the curious little girl.

"Sir…" Adina said nervously descending down the rest of the stairs and meeting at the base. "Thank you, for saving us."

Now that she was closer to him, now that the horrible shock was over now, Adina was able to see his features better. He really was handsome, like a prince out of a storybook she once read. A wide nose, chiseled cheeks, and his one visible eye as blue as the clearest sky.

What caught her eye the most however was the fact that the man wore only one glove on his right hand. She wondered what happened to the other, and if his left hand would be cold on his way home.

The man turned to look at her, his one eye studying her as he kept a hand on his horse. He offered a small smile, and Adina could have sworn her heart had skipped a beat.

"It was nothing," he said. "I only wish I could do more, for the other three."

The graphic image returned to Adina's head with a vengeance. She quickly shook it away and she looked back up at the Hunter. "Still, you saved us. Thank you... Sir, are you really a member of The Black Hand?"

"That I am."

"Do you like doing what you do?"

"I don't *hate* it."

"A lot of people... they don't like you, do they?"

The man shrugged his broad shoulders. "No, not really. Not a lot of people like politicians either."

"I like you," Adina said meaning it. "I like that you did what you did, saving my family and I. My daddy... he was a Hunter too. A Werewolf Hunter. What kind are you?"

"I hunt all beasts." The Hunter said. "But, my specialty is Witches."

"Oh..." Adina said. Witches were terrible folk who have taken up contacting evil spirits to cast horrible spells upon those they deem prey. There was even a legend of one who lived in the woods and fed on children with teeth of sharpened bone taken from those she had slain.

"Well... thank you. One day, maybe I can be a Hunter too."

The man chuckled and nodded to Adina's mother who Adina saw was at the top of the stairs still, staring *daggers* at the Hunter. "I don't think your mother would appreciate that."

"What about *your* mother?" Adina asked.

The man frowned and Adina immediately got the message to not ask any further.

"Um… sorry." Adina said.

"Don't be," the man said flashing one more handsome smile at her. By the Stars, he was handsome… "I must go." He then mounted his horse and then gently spurring its sides, the beast started forward.

"Wait!" Adina said but the Hunter kept on going, his back remaining to her as he rode slowly through the streets to the city exit. "What's your name?"

"Adina!" Her mother was now by her side, hugging her close. "Are you mad? Don't ever *approach* a Hunter like that again!"

"Yeah," Adam agreed hurrying down the stairs after them. "They can't be trusted, just like Dad."

But Adina wasn't listening. Her attention was focused solely on the rider and just before he was out of earshot, he threw a name over his shoulder as he disappeared through the main gates.

"It's Jacob."

Adina would never forget that name. She promised herself. And she never did forget that name. She wouldn't for the rest of her life.

Facing upwards at the 'Thousand Steps', Angela dreaded what awaited at the top of the stone staircase which were hand-carved long ago by the Nisthgúlian's long ago; the castle at the top of the mountain being one of the very last strongholds used by the Vampiric Nobility back when Immortal's were more prominent and attempted their own hand at conquering a developing nation. The mountain's true height was obscured by the thick clouds and blustery snow. Further below in the pass behind her, the village of Blackfort was enduring the cold.

The wind blew terribly down at the base of Blackfort Pass. Somewhere behind her, the Anguis Express whistled in the distance, echoing through the many trees and against the icy face of the mountain where her place of refuge hid. It would be a long climb, especially for Midnight, but Angela had promised the horse that he would get to rest for a long while without disturbance. As one of the guidelines of the Black Hand, if a town or contractor was either dead, unable to pay or even didn't want the Hunter's help any longer, they were to leave immediately and instead of continuing to travel, return to Shadowfort to report. Because of the new law concerning the Ravens, Angela figured she would not hear from Irondell for quite some time- if ever again.

Besides, once the other Hunters realize that she had come home emptyhanded, they would probably try to keep her locked up inside the castle for quite some time. Contracts were hard enough to come by nowadays, with many monsters now residing far from human residences and very few daring enough to come by, as well as the Ravens practically taking over the Hunting business- while also overlooking the Emperor's realm with an iron fist. The Guild's reputation was bad enough as it was, having making deals with the Demon Hunter, Velinar and other supernatural phenomenon's over the last century. Angela was the last straw for the Empire once the rumors got out that a half-breed was a monster hunter.

All of this, Angela thought of as she climbed off Midnight, and taking her horse by the reins, guided the beautiful beast up the icy stone steps where Shadowfort Castle sat hidden in the snow and clouds high above the world of Lunokean. As they climbed, they passed by many clearings where hikers and travelers seeking the top of the world would stop and rest; where some stones for worship and meditation were also left behind by the Nisthgúlians of old. Sources of power left dormant and hidden in the snow, where only the bravest and faithful would dare make the climb to find them. Many came to the Thousand Steps to pray and meditate, others seeking the Black Hand themselves, but the mountain was enchanted with Velinar's wards, which caused those who sought out the ancient castle to return to The Steps or get hopelessly lost in the woods in order to protect the guild. Only those bearing the black handprint of Velinar were able to find the castle hidden in the mountains.

After the long climb through the bitter cold, the stairs soon leveled out to a smooth pathway cutting through the crest of the mountain, the wards that would otherwise send Angela off course recognizing her brand

and allowing her passage through the mist. The two continued to travel deep within the foggy winds cutting through what little black pine sat on the great mountain's back. Angela pushed on in the direction she had to go, and eventually the fog cleared to reveal a clearing where little trees stood surrounding Shadowfort Castle in the distance; the jagged peak that marked the highest point of the mountain casting its shadow upon the monument.

It was a vast and wicked thing of black stone that for all anyone knew, it could have been carved out of one of the very mountains peaks by the Nisthgúlian's who once inhabited the entire continent before the arrival of Noyii and other empires seeking to gain more land and power. Tall black towers stood tall above the bulk of the monument, and statues of snarling demons and gargoyles sat perched on the tower walls and shingles. The tallest tower in the center of all stabbed at the sky with a wide-brimmed arrow of darkness, pointing out to a shredded flag that fluttered black in the moonlight.

In the many towers, Angela could see the light of candles and lanterns growing brighter and brighter as she and Midnight rode together the rest of the way up the slick pathway to the stables that sat before the castle to the right. Hours of climbing had exhausted the horse, and Midnight deserved a good long rest.

After sticking her horse into his own stall with a bed of straw with plenty of food and water, Angela left the stables while the other horses within snorted at her and didn't dare move until she left their home and went to her own. They didn't trust her any more than their owners did;

only Midnight was brave enough to bear the inhuman weight of a Dhampir.

She finished walking the path up to the large double-doors of oak wood and steel, and after placing her hand on the white handprint seal above the curved doorknob to the right, she pushed the door open with a thundering squeak. Her Mark was recognized, and she was allowed passage. The castle door closed shut behind her like a mouth of a great monster.

The main hall was simple but elegant in its own way. Years of proper occupation as well as some reconstruction and refurbishment would have made this place a spectacle for the wealthy and powerful. A crimson rug covered the black marble floor which reflected the light coming from the golden chandeliers that hung on the high ceilings. Pillars of stone held up the ceiling, each one carrying a sconce which was lit with a brilliant flame. The walls on either side were filled with woven tapestries depicting brave warriors and monsters of the night, and between each one was a small painting of the Hunters of old, brought to life with oils and pencil. At the end of the hall across from the front door was another set of double-doors, with a spiraled stone staircase on either side leading up to the second floor on both sides of the entrance to the Grand Hall. Statues of Hellhounds sat next to each entrance to the staircases, keeping guard and watching all who entered. Beside them, next to the great doors themselves were two pairs of Noyiian steel armor who also stood guard with battle axes gripped in both of their hands.

The Hellhounds remained still for they were only statues, but the pieces of armor suddenly stood at attention as the Huntress neared the door, their axes now at their sides.

"We were not sleeping, Ma'am!" the one on the left chirped, the soul inside sounding somewhat high like a young adult.

"Yes," said the other his own voice deep like a true and experienced warrior. "We were simply-"

"I don't care," said Angela. She wanted to get everything over and done with. The sooner she was in her quarters with her books the better. "Who all is inside?"

"Hmph," said the armor on the right. "Always in a hurry with you it seems."

"*Who is inside*?" Angela asked again her purple eyes flashing dangerously.

"Everyone should be home for the night," said the one on the left. "I believe Vladimir came in from a job about an hour ago."

"Two," corrected the armor's brother. "Also, there is that new guy who should be in soon."

"Oh, right. That's right. So almost everyone."

Vladimir... damn.

"Thank you," Angela said starting for the door. Her hand barely touched the handle before the armor to her right asked her a question she dreaded to answer.

"You got run out again," he asked. "Didn't you?"

"Mind your own business," Angela said throwing the door open and damning the consequences to come.

"This will be good," was the last comment she heard as she closed the door behind her and delved deeper into the Grand Hall of Shadowfort Castle.

The hall was beautifully elegant and warm. Beautiful chandeliers hung from the ceiling, illuminating the stone ceiling that was domed and arched with pillars that looked like giant angels holding it up. The ballroom floor was full of wooden tables that lined up evenly like a mess hall, and to the left was a long bar table with many barrels of beer and mead stacked behind it. A fermentation barrel was nearby, sacks of potato peels close by to make vodka. A Ghoul in his human form stood behind the bar, wearing the figure of a tall lean man with a mustache while cleaning a glass while wearing a butler's outfit. At the far end of the hall, was another set of doors, which led to the lower chambers where Velinar dwelled. Upon entering the Grand Hall, all the Hunters present and occupying two tables ceased their chatter and stared at Angela with tired and weary eyes that immediately changed to expressions of aversion and disapproval.

Everyone mostly sat together, taking up two tables in total. There wasn't many, hence so many empty tables, so it made sense for everyone to try and sit together; everyone who was *human* anyway.

One of the veteran Hunters, Matei Coventon and the newest Hunter, Jacob, were both missing, leaving only eight more Hunters who remained in Shadowfort for the evening- at least presently.

"Look who made it for the night," Vladimir Kane called out from his seat which was on top of the table itself. His hunting attire was gone, and he wore a simple tunic and a belt to hold two revolvers beneath his armpits. Even though he was in for the night, he still had his gear on.

"How much did you bring home?" Kane was always the first to pounce on Angela whenever she returned to Shadowfort, eager to demean her in any possible way it seemed. Being one of the most respected Hunters aside from maybe the old and 'retired' Hunter, Damion, the other Hunters who sat in their seats around him like worshippers looked upon Angela expecting a silly or nasty reply.

Giving nothing to the Hunters, Angela stalked past them without a word.

"You got run out again, didn't you?" Kane demanded bitterly, his question an echo of the suit of armor outside.

"Give it a rest, Vlad," Nicolae Stoker muttered after taking a sip from his tankard. "If she don't wanna talk, she don't have to."

Angela appreciated that. Nicolae seemed to be the only Hunter who pitied Angela, and she appreciated him more than the rest of the lot. His short hair revealed a thick scar on his forehead from some monster; probably a Werewolf or perhaps a Leshy.

"That ain't the point," Kane's partner, Luca Harker said glaring at the Dhampir distastefully. "If she ain't bringing in no profit, then what business does she have being here?"

"Maybe she is just after something more valuable to her than gold," Adriana Whitby suggested next to her partner, Sabina Irving. "Who is to say she ain't paying any of us a visit in our sleep?" She said this loudly to anger Angela. It was untrue, of course, but the group chuckled along anyway.

"Do they do it the same way as Vampires?" Sabina asked flicking some golden hair out of her face. "Do they seduce the males to their whim before killing them?"

"Better keep Matei away," Adriana warned her friend eyeing Angela as she continued to walk to Velinar's chambers. "You don't want her to take him away."

"She wouldn't dare. I would kill her."

"Silence," The Demon Hunter, Livia Auerbach hissed at the girls from across the table. Having no hair on her head and skin the color of dark chocolate, she was a from the southern nations of Deepland Barrens, a desert realm full of Sand Demons and even more monstrous creatures. A descendent from a warrior of Ved'máled, she had come to the Empire to escape the jungles and fight more than just Leviathans and Trolls. She was the oldest of the group, and all were silenced by her words. She had no heart for Angela either, but she did have a problem when there were tensions between the Hunters of Shadowfort.

"We shouldn't be saying such things. She can hear us from that far away, can't she? What if she says something to Velinar? We're supposed to be a team, yes?"

"Heh!" the last Hunter at the table snorted. Bram Helsing, having used to be a Witcher before joining the Black Hand, was missing an arm that was replaced with a crudely-made prosthetic made of bronze. He had lost it with a fight with a Kraken in the Dead Sea.

"Really, Livia? Tattle on us?" he demanded. "We can't go nowhere- and she knows it. If she knows what's good fer her, she ain't gonna say nothin'- or better yet just *leave*. The Black Hand has enough trouble keeping a demon like her around."

"What was Velinar thinking?" Kane grumbled again, loudly, on purpose so that the Dhampir could still hear even as she reached the back of the hall. "Doesn't he and she know she ain't wanted here?"

"She belongs with her *own* kind," said someone else. But Angela didn't bother to register who the owner was, for she pushed the door to the inner sanctums open and ventured down into the ancient crypts; making sure to close the door behind her and shut out the voices of those who dwelled in the castle.

Besides, there was no one of *her* kind. Not as far as she was concerned.

The staircase descended deep within the core of the mountain beneath the castle. The ancient halls were carved with the artwork and proverbs in the Nisthgúlian language that was rapidly dying in the nation now known as Balkeñoir. Very few people could read the ancient language, save for the few who had been around for as long as the occupation of the continent. Even the people subjugated in the reservations to the south of the empire rarely spoke the entire language.

After flying down the stairs lit by dimmed torches that burned a pale green color of eternal fire, Angela eventually came into the inner sanctum; a circular room almost hexagonal with many candles lit on tables of stone along the walls. A thin stream of light shined down into the middle of the floor form an unknown source, where the Fallen Star and founder of The Black Hand sat perched on the top of a large and vicious-looking scythe.

Velinar, also known as Velinar the Hunter, had the appearance of a young child, garbed in simple black pants and a hooded undershirt. His feet were bare, and his thin hands and face were paler than the moon itself on a clear evening. He was small, and nimble as he sat on the head of his scythe which was carved to look like the skull accessory was spitting out the blade. His nails were as black as his eyes, which sat in his little skull like obsidian marbles. When he sensed the Dhampir's presence, he lifted himself off the head of the scythe and slid slowly down the length.

When he landed onto the ground, he took up his scythe and with a swing, rested it on his shoulder.

"Angela Delilah Dragos," Velinar said in a voice that did not match his body. Though he had the figure of a youth, his voice was deep, and cold like a dark icicle from the highest peaks of the mountains; the voice of the god Angela and all who served The Black Hand prayed to. "You have returned."

"Master," Angela said dropping to one knee and bowing her head.

"You've had some trouble in Irondell," said the Fallen Star.

Angela bit her lip, not wanting Velinar to see the frustration on her face. "Aye."

"'Aye'," Velinar repeated and nodded. He padded softly across the room and touched her chin. "Come on, stand up. I'm not the Pope." When Angela brought herself back up to her feet, Velinar studied her, his expression a mixture of disappointment and yet of fatherly concern.

"You are unhurt?"

"I'm fine."

"Good. At least you came back."

"Penniless," Angela reminded him.

"Yes, yes, I know." Velinar sighed. "It can't be helped. You were run out- again."

"It was worse this time," Angela informed him. "A Raven was there."

The dark eyes sharpened, intrigued. "Really? A Raven? Irondell has been independent from such policies for decades now- I wonder why the Emperor felt it necessary to send one of his lapdogs to the biggest trading post?"

"They say they knew because of the Vampire attack," Angela explained. "Thing is, Count Andrei didn't summon them."

"Hmm, this is interesting. Maybe the Emperor is really starting to try and track down how we work. Or maybe, he's just trying to cover more land; more control and whatnot with his damnable policies."

"He won't," Angela said. "Your Hunters are brave, fearless, and resilient. They will never allow themselves to be captured."

"Especially you," Velinar said turning a black eye to the Huntress.

Angela bobbed her head. "Yes."

"Well, what is done is done. There will be other contracts. *Hopefully*." With that, Velinar turned and started to go back to his normal spot.

"What difference will it make?" Angela called to the Fallen's back. Velinar was no longer a god, lesser or otherwise, but he was old, ancient, and held power that even witches never held. Beneath Yohnah Himself, Velinar would be considered closest of the Fallen among the human race.

Velinar paused in step, waiting for her to explain her question.

"Master Velinar, what good will it do, keeping me here?"

"Do you want to leave?" Velinar asked.

Angela pursed her lips. "Of course not. Where would I go?"

"Then stay," Velinar shrugged. "It is that simple."

"I'm not doing any real good here," said Angela. "I am not even welcome. If I do not bring any coin soon, the others might convince you to send me away."

Velinar chuckled, amused. "They can certainly try. As long as you do not partake in your predatory nature, and you wish to remain here, you may stay. You pay off your debts in your own ways," Velinar added. "Your knowledge with the Vampires have been and will continue to be useful as long as they exist. And of course, I *do* appreciate the help you put into keeping the castle looking pretty. I know that Jecklyn appreciates the help in your knowledge as well. Not to mention, you've kept your promise. A lot of Dhampir's would have lost it if they have lasted as long as you have."

Angela remembered their deal very well. She hadn't hesitated to agree to it, for that was what she wanted as well. Still, it is difficult for a Dhampir of all creatures to keep such a promise.

"Still," Angela said. "I don't belong among the living."

"Neither do I," Velinar said setting his scythe into the floor and then ever so carefully, climbed up the staff and took his usual place sitting on top. Perfectly balanced like a master acrobat. "All things considered, you are very much more alive than I."

"Still, the other Hunters, I don't belong with them."

"'Still, still, still.'" Velinar sighed, exasperated by the word. "Do you know that, or do you *believe* that? Both are two completely different things."

"When I came to Shadowfort Castle," Angela said leaning against the doorway with her arms crossed. "I came to seek refuge. You gave me a home. You gave me safety and allowed me to work among your followers. But... This home, it doesn't feel like home. I feel like a failure when I do not bring in as much coin. Also, concerning *what* I am-"

"What you are hardly matters, Angela, and you know that," said Velinar. "*Who* you are is what matters most."

"People do not care for the 'who.' They do not see that at first. They see what you are first and foremost, and sometimes only that."

"Is it really that bad here? You really feel that much alone?"

Angela shrugged. It wasn't any new feeling for her. She had felt this way her entire life. Ever since she was born, she knew she didn't belong among the living- *or* the dead.

"No one walks alone in the world, Angela," said Velinar at last. "Until you learn to trust others, and give them reason to trust you, then it will take longer. But eventually, everyone finds the place where they belong."

Angela sighed. "I'll try to remember that, Master."

Velinar nodded. "And besides, you may not bring in as much coin, as necessary as it is, but how many Vampires have you slain?"

Angela didn't even bother. "I don't know."

"More than Livia, or Sabina, or anyone I had the pleasure of having in my counsel. How many demons from Oblivion have the others slain compared to you?"

"I've only met a few…"

"A few is more than what many could stand," replied Velinar. "Your knowledge is necessary for us to move forward not as a guild, but as society. Never since the Vampire Wars have we been so advanced as a society to ensure our rightful place in the world."

By 'our,' Velinar meant the human race, the most blessed creations of Yohnah and the most favored among the rest of the Stars, except of course Kawfka, who despised the humans and to spite Yohnah, created the Vampire, who in the end, defied him as well as the Morning Star. Velinar used the word 'our,' because as one of the Fallen, he was closer to a human than any other deity in the entire universe.

"Have more faith in yourself," Velinar told Angela. "Your place is here, as long as you wish it to be."

Angela sighed and said, "I will… try, Master."

"Good. I will let you know when another contract becomes available."

"Thank you. Goodnight." And with that Angela left Velinar's presence within the dark of Shadowfort Castle, feeling more ashamed than ever that she had once again failed The Black Hand.

When she stepped outside, she should have seen it coming. She should have paid more attention to her surroundings, and she damned herself for a fool.

When Angela stepped out of the doorway the entire room fell silent again. The group of Hunters were talking about her, no doubt. But she ignored them as she brushed right past and started for the exit. The sooner she was in her room, the better. She only nodded a hello to Cithro, the Ghoul butler, and didn't say a word to anyone else. Not that it would matter seconds later.

"Hey, Angela, hold up."

She stopped and turned her head. Nicolae Stoker was coming her way, and stopped within a few feet from where she stood. "I just wanted to say, I'm glad you're home."

"And not out there terrifying all of Balkeñoir," Kane called out which earned a few chuckles among the group, but Nicolae waved at the man, telling him to be silent.

"Why don't you join us?" Nicolae said. He was trying to be nice, Angela knew this.

"No, thank you." She appreciated Nicolae for offering, but she didn't trust him. Though he was nice to everyone, he had his own thoughts about her and all Dhampir's and half-breeds. After all, he was a Vampire Hunter just like her. He has killed two Vampires in his time, and one Dhampir; the only other half-breed of a Vampire that Angela was aware of. Though he was trying to be nice, his words were empty with his thoughts on her and her kind. There was no telling what his true intentions were. For all Angela knew, it could result in the bad end of a joke.

With a nod of respect, Angela started to go.

But then, Nicolae reached out and grabbed her wrist. "Come on, don't be like-"

Angela whirled around on instinct, striking Nicolae right in the chest and sending the man flying across the room and right smack on top of the table in the middle of the group who gawked down at him. Nicolae sat up, his kind demeanor gone now and his face twisted with rage as he rubbed at his sternum. Kane and the others went for their weapons but didn't advance on her.

"What the hell!?" Nicolae snapped angrily. Maybe he was in the right to be upset, but that didn't matter to Angela who was glaring at him with a venomous stare.

"Do not touch me again," Angela said in a low voice. With a swish of her cloak, she continued towards the exit, doing her best to ignore Nicolae's words of outrage behind her.

"Stupid leech," Nicolae muttered.

"You okay?" Adriana asked.

"Goddamned cunt," Kane said. "Let's go after her."

"Forget it," Nicolae grumbled. "It ain't worth it."

"I can't believe you tried to talk to her," Sabina scolded.

"I had to."

"Doesn't matter," Luca argued. "She's a monster. Just let her go back to her chambers. Velinar should really just put her in a kennel."

"Shh!" Livia hissed. "You can't-"

Angela cut off the rest of the conversation with a slam of the door. She stood on the other side, trying to control her anger between the two Hellhound Guardians. It was pointless; stupid to get all upset. It wasn't like any of this was new or anything like that. It wasn't like they could understand even if they tried.

"So," one of the suits of armor mumbled. "How'd it go?"

Angela growled at the spirit within the armor and stalked away without a single word to them. As she made her way to the staircase on her right, two more Hunters were heading for the Grand Hall. Matei Coventon, Sabina's lover and the oldest male Hunter of the current group. He was a wiry man with a dark goatee that matched his hair. His suit of gray armor was strapped with two swords and a large rifle that was slung across his back. Beside him, was the newest Hunter of the Black Hand, Jacob Tepes.

Angela had only met the man once, and thought him no more than a passionate child. He was young, reckless, and worst of all, annoying. He had this snobby attitude most boys his age had, and Angela had decided she didn't like him. He looked worn from his travels, and so Angela didn't bother the two men as she hurried by.

As the two passed by her, Jacob stopped and asked what was wrong. Angela ignored him, and stalked up the stairs like a wraith retiring before the dawn.

"Don't bother," she heard Matei say at the bottom of the stairs. "She don't talk to anyone."

"Who is she?" Jacob had seen her once as well, but immediately after his acceptance into the Black Hand, he was off on a Hunt with Luca. After a few trips, he was sent out on the Ghoul assignment; his first one by himself.

"Angela Dragos," Matei said, and Angela heard him whisper upon making it to the upper level. Even though he whispered, her ears caught every single word. "Stay away from her, she's a Dhampir. A spawn of a Vampire and some entranced human. Keep right clear if you don't want to wind up shriveled up bloodless as a dried fruit."

That was all she was to these people: a monster; a freak of nature. Angela didn't disagree, but it still didn't make her feel any better. It mattered little though, for as soon as Angela found her room, she closed off the rest of the world and locked the door.

Now, she was truly home, alone, where she belonged. Let the Hunters drink themselves silly, laughing at how she failed. Let them prepare and train for future contracts; let them mingle and be the family that the world never let them have. None of it was hers to begin with. Ever since she came into this world, Angela never belonged. The only place of refuge she has was right here, in this room of hers. Her work was done for now, and now was the time to rest.

Her bedroom was elegant, simple, and very homey. Upon entering her chambers Angela passed by her bed on the right wall which was a large thing with thick comforters and an overhead with a curtain should she wish for complete and total darkness. On either side of the bed was a nightstand with a small, elegant oil lamp and a drawer containing spare keys as well as a pistol should an intruder come in. On the back wall was the window overlooking the vast valley beyond the mountain, the wind blowing furiously against it and coating the glass with frost. Next to it, taking up most of the stone wall was a large bookshelf that was untidy and littered with books stacked on top of one another.

Angela loved to read, and always had plenty of time to do so. Though there were other beasts within Balkeñoir for The Black Hand to hunt, Angela hardly got a direct request and if there was no such thing, she and the rest of the company would draw sticks to decide who and how many would take on a job. So, on days when she did not have to venture out into the cold world of beasts,

Angela would reside here, reading in the comfort of isolation. It just was never the same reading on the road, although she tried to buy a new book every time she ventured out.

In the back corner opposite of the window was a grand piano, its teeth covered by a glossy black cover. It was a magnificent; beautiful instrument that Angela would play very little of, but would play it with the grace of a true pianist playing within the capital of Goldendell. She had learned at a young age, before she had discovered her heritage and what she really was.

To her left was a large brick fireplace empty of any flame, the mouth howling with the wind passing over the chimney far up its throat. On either side of the mantle were more pairs of ancient armor similar to the pair downstairs; should she have to be summoned in a timely matter.

After tossing a log into the fireplace and lighting a match to get a flame burning, Angela passed the fireplace down a small threshold to the right, entering the second room of her chambers. In there was a desk with a typewriter on it, and piles upon piles of paper and notebooks littering the surface. Above the desk was a map of the whole country; what territories that belonged solely to Balkeñoir and what groups laid hidden in the new country. Aside from the Nishthgúlian Reservation in the south beyond the Stonehollow Mountains, there were still many wild groups in the north that refused to bend to Emperor Ion and his vast Empire. Some newspaper clippings hung on the walls around the map itself as well as wanted posters nailed into the mortar between the stones. On the desk itself, Angela tossed the notebook she had retrieved from Akira's body before taking her weapons over to the workbench on the opposite wall and began to remove her gear.

First, she placed her sword, crafted by a blacksmith from Mistendell onto the table next to her Blunderbuss and pistol. Her crossbow she hung on the wall, her quiver of bolts she sat near a grindstone for later use. All of her ammunition and daggers were also placed in their proper place on the table for Angela to sharpen and tinker with for the next job- if one came any time soon.

She then crossed over to the side where her mannequin was, and upon removing her hood and her cloak, Angela removed the leather armor from her body, relieved to feel the weight leave her. Though it wasn't at all heavy by her standards, it still relieved her to have the filthy thing removed. When her armor was now worn by the mannequin her boots at its feet, Angela went to the back room beyond her little workshop now in her underclothes as she entered the bathroom.

The bathroom itself was beautifully set with another small window over a large porcelain tub with a faucet that would release gallons of hot water. Next to the washing basin in the corner was a shelf with salts, soaps and towels, and a small table for books and snacks sat beside the toilet that led to a shoot that would dispose of any waste into it into the unknown chambers deep below the catacombs within the mountains. That chamber along with the hot water system had been by far one of the most difficult projects to bring the old and crumbling castle to the modern age.

Angela started up the water and threw some salts into the tub. As the tub began to fill with the aroma of lavender and lemon, she left the bathroom and returned to her workshop to retrieve the notebook left behind by Akira. Curious to know just what she had possibly left back in Irondell, Angela decided to read whatever notes Akira had written before her untimely execution at the hands of The Ravens.

The goddamned bastards... Angela felt her grip tighten around the leather-bound pages, nearly crumpling them until she caught herself in the midst of the memory of Akira being shot in through the eye. It had not nearly been a precaution to prevent vampirism as it was an execution; an unjustly one at that.

She returned to the bathroom with the notebook in hand and then upon placing it on the little table and scooting it closer to the tub, she began to undress; happy to be rid of the stench of sweat and dirt that had covered her body since she had left for Irondell. With her clothes and socks in a ball on the floor, Angela slipped a pale foot into the tub and slowly sunk her body into the salty waters with a sigh of imminent relief. It felt good to be so warm after weeks of traveling through the cold. Stretching her lean body, Angela soaked in the water from head to foot as she slipped her head beneath the surface and allowed herself the feeling of sinking just beneath the surface to elude her from whatever strain was on her mind. She saw her white hair float like weeds around her face, and when she could hold her breath no longer, she came back up like a corpse rising from a coffin, feeling refreshed as the humid air opened up her pores and cleansed her of the frigid world beyond.

Comfortable now, Angela reached over to the notebook on the table and after studying the worn cover for a moment and respecting the hands that owned it, she opened up the booklet and began to read what Akira had written during her time with Kuroi Te and her experience with hunting the beasts of Balkeñoir.

As it turns out, Akira had been somewhat knowledgeable about the Vampire; the most feared creature in the world. Though Lycans and Werewolves are also greatly feared, and the Witches that lived in the woods made the country wary of pagan black magic, Vampires continued to be considered the most dangerous of beasts; being walkers of the night and the primary predators of humans, Vampires were the bane of the existence of man. Akira was aware that different Vampires meant different threats that came with them; their eyes, their infection, their age, all of this had to be kept in mind should you decide to hunt such unholy creatures; especially in the midst of a mutation since vampires were now so rare that their very bodies would change to adapt to the world that was slowly driving them to extinction.

What caught Angela's eye however, was how much Akira had kept note on the Immortals; the pureblood Vampires.

She skimmed through the notes concerning the nights and the whereabouts of certain Immortal Counts within the area of Irondell, and among them, Angela found exactly what she was looking for; Count Takeshi Horla.

According to Akira, the Immortal had been hanging around the woods near Irondell, and had been terrorizing some of the local villages that lived within. She had a lot of notes on Horla himself; what kind of eyes he had, how old he was, and if he had any what they called Disciples. Right to the letter, Akira determined that Takeshi was a loner; and refused to work in a covenant. This must have been what made it easy for Akira to track the Immortal down and hunt him in an abandoned castle beyond a wheat field.

Angela then read about Akira's encounter with the Count, and what she had experienced in their fight after breaking through the line of gargoyles that had been instructed to protect their master.

With the gargoyles dead, I continued up to the main chambers where Count Takeshi Horla appeared to be waiting. Though he looked to be a youth, I knew he was much, much older. Within his presence I felt like a mere child; an inferior compared to him. His eyes flashed yellow like the sun, just as I had predicted. Immediately, I was trapped in his illusions; my past revealed to me like a picture show with my young self looking down upon the graves. Though I felt compelled to hug the girl-sobbing beside it and I <u>had</u> for a moment, I pushed through and stabbed her in the heart with my silver blade. Immediately, the illusion shattered like glass, and Count Horla laid dead at my feet.

From what I can gather, I have taken some interesting lessons in my fight with the Count- aside from the bounty money offered by the village leaders. One, it is true: Immortals are capable of certain psychological influence on the weak-minded. Though I am not an expert on all the different kinds of Immortal Eyes, it is true that yellow, if you look into them will trap you in an illusion; whether it be something the Immortal wants you to see, or if he plucks a memory straight from your brain. I have no explanation why he showed me my broken home, my dead, and myself. Maybe he simply remembers, but it felt so real just like it had many years ago. The only logical explanation that he saw what I saw through my own eyes. 'The eyes are windows to the soul', it all makes sense now. I shall return to Irondell in a matter of days, and I will report my knowledge to the rest of the guild. Hopefully this information will prove invaluable as we make our way to the top.

2nd of Elul, 2229

Oh, the poor naïve girl.
Angela truly felt sorry for Akira, though she was truly impressed. Akira really did know quite a bit about Immortals; and her knowledge was probably what saved her life. When it came to Vampires, Immortal or otherwise, knowledge was your greatest weapon. Even for a crossbreed of the creatures and the humans, Angela herself had to do her own research from time to time which helped her in the past- when she actually was able to complete her contract without getting chased out by the Ravens or the citizens of whatever village or city she ventured to.

What held Angela's attention however, was the fact that Akira's notes held no information regarding Horla's bloodline, including the supposed brother who had attacked her and her guild in Irondell itself. It made her curious, and after draining the water, Angela merely wrapped herself in a towel and marched back out into her workshop and pulled out her own notes. Among the many stacks of papers, she eventually found what she was looking for and laid it out in front of her. An ancient scroll, containing the bloodlines between different Immortals that she was aware of, divided into a sort of 'family tree' revealed the many purebloods out there or rumored to be a part of the Immortal Nobility. Tracing her fingers along the many lines, she eventually found Takeshi Horla, and connected to him, was another name; both having been converted by the Immortal, Loana Alnwick.

Josef Horla.

Angela wondered where she had heard the name Horla before. She knew it had to have been a Count back when the Vampire Nobility attempted to overthrow the previous Emperor and rule the continent, only to fail in the end. But Josef Horla, had been a very influential Count near the land of Griffin Moor. He had a couple of small villages under his 'protection,' but there had been rumors whispering through the forests that the Count himself had a dark secret hidden in his castle. But now, looking at the bloodline of Immortals, it was clear to Angela just who the Vampire who attacked Akira and her group was. Josef Horla, one of the overthrown Immortals who managed to flee, along with his little brother, who was now dead.

How powerful he was, Angela hadn't a clue. She and the rest of the Black Hand had never received a contract concerning him, but she now wondered just what was happening in Irondell as of now. For the sake of Andrei and all within his city, Angela hoped that the Raven she had encountered was strong enough to handle the situation. In fact, she hoped that the Count simply left, knowing already of Akira's fate placed upon her by his brother. But deep in her heart, Angela knew that the possibility of that not being the case was very high.

Immortals never gave in to fear of anyone- and the Ravens were of no exception. They were disbanded, the Nobility crushed, but those who remained in hiding having evaded those who still Hunt them today, they were still incredibly dangerous and powerful. Horla was no exception.

But it wasn't Angela's problem anymore. Her contact was voided, destroyed the moment the Raven entered the city. She had been chased out by the Watchmen under Andrei's orders, so as far as the Black Hand was concerned, the Empire had this under control. To interfere without another contract, was not their way. Unless they were called to Irondell again, the Black Hand would allow the Raven stationed in the city to proceed with their duty to the loyal subjects of the Empire and assist in the Vampire infestation. Hopefully, it would not last long or it had already been taken care of in the weeks Angela had spent traveling back to Shadowfort Castle. Whatever happened in Irondell now, was not Angela's concern any longer. All she had to do, was sit, and wait until her next contract came about.

Angela turned her head to her feet, where she felt a coat of fur brush against her pale leg. It was Sebastian, her black cat who had at last come out of hiding and was nuzzling against her, purring pleasantly at his master's return. Smiling softly, Angela stooped down and stroked the cat's lean back, the creature curling and stretching like water beneath her hand.

"Hello, little one," she said. "Did I wake you?"

The cat meowed in response, its bright blue eyes looking back at her like whirlpools taking in everything in its wake.

"I'm glad they kept feeding you. Come on," Angela said reaching out and scooping up Sebastian in her arms. "Let us go to bed."

Allowing the towel to slip off her now dried body, Angela slipped beneath the covers of her bed- the bed she had missed during these weeks of travel. Sebastian curled up in the small pocket where her legs were, and as soon as her head rested upon the feather-filled pillow, Angela closed her eyes and slipped away into the world of dreams.

It was good to be home, at last.

That same evening, Emilia Crawford was fleeing for her very life.

It had begun to follow her after she left her friend's home, after a late night of celebrating. The Quarantine of the city had prevented her from having to go and visit relatives in Dwarvendell, and her friend Jessica was having a little cocktail party and was gracious enough to invite her at the last minute. A night for their book club and to drink and gossip had been exactly what the doctor ordered. With a belly full of fattening cakes and blood running with four or five Cosmopolitans, Emilia ventured out into the cold streets to home as a light snowfall began to drift onto Irondell.

It was as she was passing through the town square when she realized that something was wrong. The city was all too quiet. She had not heard the mew of a cat, or the bark of a dog; nothing. Not only that, but the Watchmen who would usually be out and about this time of night-especially with the Vampire attack on the nearby bar, were nowhere to be seen. It was like the entire world was plucked in the darkness of night, and she was left all alone. The silent snowfall only made the foggy atmosphere all the more eerie and caused her to sober up. Nervously, Emilia began to hum a carol sung by her ancestors in order to calm her nerves, one of the ancient psalms of the Flute Master herself.

That was when she first heard it, the faint, scraping sound of nails against stone, and the occasional patter of bare feet. Emilia would look around but in the darkness beyond the lamp posts around the street, she saw nothing. When she would start walking again, she would hear it closer every time. At some point, she began to believe that over the sound of her beating heart and the blood roaring in her ears, she could hear faint breathing somewhere above her. That was when she just started running.

She felt the pain of panic suddenly seep into her heart, as if the Stars themselves were telling her to run. She did not know why she was afraid, but she willed her body to hurry as she fled with her brain seeming to blare like an alarm bell. She would run all the way home and as soon as she reached her flat, she would lock the door behind her and probably laugh at herself for being so silly when she finally calmed down.

That was when she heard the giggling. Amused, terribly gleeful giggling like a manic child playing a silly game and she was now running and screaming out for help for whatever Watchmen were out in the foggy streets. But no help came to her aid, and she was left to run, crying, lungs burning from lack of breath as she fled the creature now closing in fast behind her. It was closer now, and the damned giggling threw her into a fit of hysteria.

"Get away!" she screamed at the darkness while hiking up her skit just a little more and willing her burning legs to run faster. Her shoes clopped against the cobblestone street as she ran from door to door, banging on it with all her strength and begging for whoever was inside to let her in. In most cases, she would only receive silence or be told to go away.

"Shoulda thought of that before you went out at night!" one even shouted behind the door of the local bakery. "Piss off, will ya? *Now!*"

Emilia stood aghast at the door, wondering just what happened. It was like the city had suddenly gone under a spell; her fellow man had never behaved like this before.

"Please!" she cried as she turned and continued to flee. She could hear it, laughing, giggling like a child as it followed her from the walls of the buildings towering around her.

"Get away!" she shouted again as she took off running again. "Help me! Somebody!"

But her cries continued still to fall on deaf ears. No one came to her aid. No citizen, no Watchman, and not even the newly-arrived Raven. She was left alone; abandoned in the cold of night as the wind howled around her. Her skirt clung to her skin as her sweat froze around her, and her very coat choked the life out of her, but also saved her life as she heard the distinct sound of fabric tearing as something clawed across her back, leaving her skin exposed to the elements.

"Missed ya!" the voice cackled and Emilia's terror reached a new height. Screaming even louder now, she then turned the corner and then started fleeing towards the Church of Yohnah; her only hope in her time of need. She ran through the small closure before the large domed temple and upon reaching the doors she tried to pry them open only to find them locked. The hinges and rotted wood groaned defiantly against her strength, and she winced and cried as the frozen door handles bit into her palms.

"Father Gaston! Father Gaston!" she cried banging on the door with both of her fists. "Sanctuary! Please! I beg of you, let me in!"

A voice, muffled, quiet with regret sounded on the other side of the door. "I am sorry, my child, but I cannot let you in."

Emilia stared slack-jawed at the door. Behind her, she heard something strike the ground, but she didn't dare to turn around.

"Father, please!" she begged. "You have to let me in! Let me in! Protect me!"

"Nothing can protect you, child," Gaston said still unwilling to let her into the sanctuary of the church. "Not me, or this church."

"You let me in *now*, dammit!" Emilia screamed. "I am a member of your choir, you let me in *right* now!" The desperate screams turned her voice hoarse, and the sounds of someone trudging through the snow-covered steps to the church sent a chill down her spine- colder than the winds that licked her exposed flesh.

"God have mercy on you, Emilia." Gaston said as his voice quietly departed within the sanctuary of his church. "God have mercy on me..."

That was when Emilia was suddenly grabbed by the shoulders and thrown into the snow-covered lawn. Screaming, she tried to crawl away, but she felt claws dig into her skirt and coat, and with the tearing sound of fabric, she was stripped naked right there in the snow that bit her bare flesh. Still screaming, she felt a hand cover her mouth followed by a slight pain in the side of her neck. She moaned as she felt something slither beneath her chin, and she realized that it was a tongue.

"This is *my* religion," the horrible childish voice said as the figure pulled Emilia's thighs up and began to force himself inside of her, the loathsome sensation of cold, dead flesh invading her like a parasite.

The monster then proceeded to suck at Emilia's neck while at the same time driving her into the snow with the force he thrusted into her. She moaned, she cried, begging for help and for whoever it was to stop. Cold and in pain, she begged the creature to stop. But the creature didn't stop, only laughed every time it pried it's mouth away for a moment.

Eventually, she did not know when and was beyond caring, Emilia Crawford knew nothing. Nothing but coldness, deep pain inside her, and horrible, horrible pleasure.

All the while, a figure from within the church watched from behind one of the windows, his silhouette casted by a single candle in his hand. All he did was watch in horror as the woman was raped of her very life, and pray like the gargoyles and statues that watched over Emilia on the rooftops of Irondell; their frozen expressions displaying nothing but stern disappointment, and yet also pity.

"Yohnah," said Father Gaston from within the safety of the church. "Have mercy on me…"

Jacob was out in the castle courtyards practicing with his bow the next chilly morning.

The sun was out over the sea of clouds obscuring the view Balkeñoir and what rays *did* manage to slip through was caught in his raven hair; making it blaze like fire. The winds howled around the peaks of Blackfort Pass, and occasionally he would hear the shrill cries of the Wendigo that haunted the mountains but also protected the castle from any unwanted intruders; something about having befriended Velinar the Hunter when he had first founded the place.

The other Hunters were either still asleep, eating, or training in their own ways. In the solitude of the courtyard feeling the harsh winds that whipped about him, Jacob kept his body strong and still as he notched and released each arrow into the various straw-stuffed dummies he had set up with targets painted on their chests and heads. Every single time, every single stance or position, he got a perfect bullseye on all but one; even under the influence of the high winds. There was a reason why he preferred a bow over a gun; he was naturally good at it and loosing arrows was faster than reloading a blunderbuss or a bolt rifle like a JR-Scout or a Jackal. Still, that never prevented him from carrying a .44 Hornet revolver just in case.

He heard the door to the castle open, but Jacob kept his focus on his next target; his leather glove on his right hand groaning against the pressure as the bowstring pulled back against him. It took a strong man to pull the bowstring all the way back to one's ear, and Jacob didn't even tremble or waver against the strength of the bow. When he was sure of his target, he released the arrow and watched it sail straight and true, right into the bullseye of the last dummy; the head jerking back with the impact of the projectile.

"Aren't you cold out here?" the voice of Vladimir sounded behind him.

"Helps me stay focused," Jacob said turning to smile at the Hunter. "What's going on?"

Vladimir stood in his tunic and pants, a cigarette pinched between his fingers and trailing a thin tail of smoke. He took a puff of this and answered, "The rest are inside eating for now. Biscuits and gravy."

"Yum-yum," said Jacob sarcastically.

"Hey, the ghoul's make 'em good. You just got back, why don't you come join us?" Vladimir was looking at the dummies with an impressed expression.

"Sounds great," Jacob said adjusting the strap on his eyepatch. Damn thing was always itchy it seemed. "Is Matei up as well?"

"He is still tired from his hunt near the sea," Vladimir said taking another puff of his cigarette and blowing the smoke into the wind. He offered it to Jacob who accepted the stub gratefully, letting the smoke fill his lungs and calm the tensions in his body.

Meanwhile Vladimir was still talking. "I'm sure we will see him too; after he is finished with Sabina and whatever unfinished business of theirs."

Jacob didn't bother to ask what sort of business that was. "And that one girl?" he asked instead between puffs. "The one with the white hair. Will she be joining us?"

Vladimir smiled and shook his head. "You don't want to deal with her, rookie."

"I think my work on the Express proves that I am *hardly* a rookie," Jacob tried for a laugh.

"No doubt, but you still don't know much about the Black Hand nor the secrets it keeps. You still got some learning to do."

"No doubt. But who is *she*, exactly? Matei mentioned something about her last night. Come to think of it, you two seem to have the same opinion of her and I don't understand why."

Vladimir sighed and the looked off into the distance beyond the nearest peak, watching the snow swirl around it like a flock of white birds in the fog. "She is just another member, but she is not one of us- humans I mean."

"Matei said she was a Dhampir," Jacob said giving the rest of the cigarette to Vladimir who told him to have the rest. He smoked the last of it, and then stomped it out into the snow.

"That all he told you?" Vladimir asked still not looking at the new member.

"He wouldn't say anything else. Other than she is supposedly the spawn of a Vampire. I've never heard of a Dhampir before."

"They aren't very common in the world today, especially with the overthrowing of the old Nobility. Heard of them? Well anyways, she ain't 'supposedly', she *is* one of their spawn. A bastard of a human and a Vampire."

"How does that work?" Jacob said. "I thought that all Vampires were supposed to be dead. How can they fornicate?"

"They are dead, or at least the closest thing to dead anyway," said Vladimir. "But there are some that *chose* the fate of Night. The Immortals are the ones that can have children. Some Vampire fell in love with a human, and Angela Dragos was the end result." He then turned to Jacob, a serious expression beaming to the man. "Stay away from her, Jacob. She might be a member of the Black Hand, for whatever reasons that Velinar has, but she is *still* a monster. She still has Vampire in her blood, and she would suck you dry with zero warning."

"Has that ever happened before?"

"With her? No. But that doesn't matter. Dhampir's have a bad reputation, and the fact that they are the closest thing to humans other than the Vampires themselves, make them even more dangerous. She is dangerous. You cannot trust her, even if she bears the same mark as us."

"That so?" Jacob asked marching over to the small bench at the edge of the courtyard where his shirt and morning coffee sat; now cold and unable to be drank. He dumped the remaining contents into the snow, watched it become soaked in while Vladimir followed close behind as he gave his answer.

"You better believe it." He eyed the Hunter as he sat his black bow down and began to put on his shirt. "You are not attracted to her, are you?"

Jacob chuckled. "When I see a beautiful lady, I can't help it."

"She ain't no lady." Vladimir said this with a smirk but was serious. "That's the problem: she's *too* beautiful to be human. I guarantee that if you saw a male Dhampir you'd fall in love with him as well."

"That so?"

"It's happened before. They are indeed beautiful creatures; that's what makes them dangerous. That's how they trap you. They are spawn of the greatest creation of both Yohnah, as well as Kafcaw. They are dangerous, and any Dhampir, especially Angela Dragos, cannot be trusted."

"She can't be *that* bad," Jacob said taking a seat on the bench and taking a sip from his wineskin. The brandy inside warmed him up almost instantly. "When she saw me she looked more like she wanted nothing to do with me or Matei, not suck our blood." He offered the wineskin to Vladimir and the Hunter accepted the offer.

"Believe what you want, it's your neck." Vladimir said after taking a quaff. He shook his head and sighed. "Don't say I didn't warn you when she goes for that neck. It *still* bewilders me why Velinar let her in the castle in the first place. I get that she has nowhere to go- and she is good at hunting Vampires, but still..."

"She doesn't have anywhere else to go?" Jacob asked. "No family, or anything?"

"Does *anyone* in this organization have any family? She has that much in common with us, and that's it. Think about it: we humans don't want her around because she's a bloodsucker. The Vampires don't want her around because she's a bastard child of a human. It's sort of a… purity thing that the Immortals used to vow. They only want purebloods to be sired, and they hate Dhampirs just as much as everyone else. She doesn't have anywhere else to go, so she and Velinar made a deal and lo and behold: she's a Vampire Hunter working for the Black Hand."

Jacob frowned. "That's kinda harsh…"

"That's just the cold hard truth. It ain't nothing personal, that's just the way it is. She doesn't belong with either humans or Vampires. To be frank: it would be best if she was never born. Dhampirs are not meant to be in this world."

Vladimir then turned his attention back to the castle, as if he was looking through the walls with incredible vision, trying to see beyond it, and even further. "What must it be like, I sometimes wonder, to be born without a people to go to? To have no one in the very end."

"Why don't you offer a place to go then?" Jacob asked. "Just… let her in."

Vladimir snorted. "Yeah, right. That would only mean our deaths. I stand by what I said. Do not mistake me: I do not pity such a creature as her." He then started for the castle, and then said over his shoulder, "I'll say it one more time: for your own sake, stay away from her. You're better off far away from that she-devil."

Jacob watched the Hunter disappear into the castle. Vladimir's caution was justified: Vampires were terrible creatures of the night. Cunning, intelligent, unpredictable, dangerous… no man in his right mind would risk being near a Vampire, Immortal or otherwise. But the thought of having no place to go, made Jacob pity the beautiful Dhampir he met last night. He had his share of experience with Vampires, but a Dhampir was new knowledge to him. But to know what the organization had such a dangerous creature in their midst- one that was on her own with no place to go; no people to turn to, it made him pity Angela Dragos. If she was a mindless monster, that would be one thing. But the fact that she was sentient, and almost human, made him place himself in her shoes.

He hoped that he would eventually see her again before either of them had to go out on a mission. He was curious, and wanted to learn more about Dhampirs and Vampire-lore.

That, and he wanted to see if the Dhampir was really the monster everyone said she was. After all, the two of them might have a lot more than common than anyone else within the Black Hand.

Sol

Jacob ventured up the spiraled staircase leading to the east wing of the castle where the female Huntresses slept.

He had gone to the meeting hall to eat a quick breakfast as well as ask some questions to the other members including the ghoul servants he could run into.

Unfortunately, every single person he asked gave him a similar if not the exact same answer to his questions. He already knew about many of the members the moment he swore his life to Velinar, as well as last night when he returned from his first job. He knew their expertise, names, part of their backgrounds, quite a whole lot. But this was the first time he had actually *heard* of Angela Dragos, and being the newest member, all he wanted was to meet everyone in the castle; and that meant *everyone*.

Unfortunately, any information the others gave him was almost exactly what Vladimir had told him and more.

"Angela?" Adriana asked along with Sabina who practically glared at the mention of the Dhampir's name. "Why would you be interested in that dreaded creature? You should pay more attention on your training and future jobs."

"If women are on your mind," Sabina said with a tantalizing smile. "You can always talk to Adriana." This earned her a jab in the ribs by her friend and while Jacob had played along with this he immediately went to the other Hunters for more information; turning next to Bram Helsing who was readjusting his mechanical arm.

"Not much to tell," the Hunter had said. "I hardly ever speak to her- hardly anyone does."

"Can't tell you for certain," Livia had said at the bar, even the Ghoul merely shrugged.

"Angela?" Nicolae said next. "Probably what everyone else says: she's a Dhampir and that is reason enough to not get involved with her. Thankfully she keeps to herself, spends more time in her room than she does with us and only goes out if she has a job. Other than that, no one really knows a whole lot about her."

He had been rubbing at his chest a lot from where she had struck him, and he didn't seem eager to forget it either.

Matei was next, sitting not too far from where Jacob and Nicolae had been conversing.

"Yeah," he said looking at some charts of the southern regions. He looked up at his new friend with a concerned expression. "Look, Jacob, I know you want to get along with all the Hunters here, but Angela is not like any of us. We wouldn't be telling you this if it wasn't so."

"Neither is Velinar," Jacob tried to reason.

"Velinar isn't a part of a race who tries to kill our kind," Matei pointed a glass pen at his friend, almost like a sword. "Stay away from her, Jacob. I don't want to have to deal with another dead rookie."

"Another?"

"Aye," Nicolae said leaning closer. "Rumor has it that when Angela first joined, she killed a member. This was way before any of us came in, but it matters not. She is not meant to be spoken to- *stay away from her*. She's a monster."

"She killed someone?" asked Jacob. "That ain't what Luca said."

Matei shrugged. "That's what I heard." Nicolae confirmed it as well.

Jacob left the two feeling confused given as he had gotten two different stories about the Dhampir. Every single member he came across after all told him to stay away: that Angela Dragos was nothing more than a tamed monster. There was nothing but that fear that everyone could agree on while she was left in the dark.

Despite their warnings, Jacob, now wearing a simple pair of slacks and unbuttoned dress shirt with the sleeves rolled up, ventured down the hallway where the women slept. Many doors lined the hallway and the torches kept it lit as he made his way to the very end of the hall on the last door where the Ghoul butler had mentioned she lived. When he stopped by the door, his ear caught something; a melody of sound, beautiful and sad, emitting from behind the door.

It was the music of a grand piano. Heavy, booming low notes conversed with the twinkling of high notes; all working together to create incredible music. A mixture of black and white keys that sang out every emotion known to mankind, rang through the room and passed through the door that Jacob stood before. It was so lovely, so sad almost, that Jacob found himself mesmerized by the musical notes. He stood there for almost thirty seconds, losing himself to the music.

He just about hardly noticed that the keys had stopped playing, meaning that the player inside was done. Raising a hand, Jacob was just about to knock on the large door of wood, when it suddenly opened a crack to reveal something so beautiful, and yet terrifyingly inscrutable.

Angela Dragos, the Dhampir, stood within the crack of the door, glaring at Jacob almost as if he actually *had* knocked and interrupted her. Those bright purple eyes, like pools of liquid lavender, took him in like a predator eyeing prey almost. There was an intelligence in those eyes that Jacob had not seen in any eyes in the years he had lived on this planet. Her hair, white as freshly-fallen snow, hung loose around her lean shoulders. She wore a simple black house gown, and looking at her bare hands and feet, Jacob saw that her nails were as black as coal. Was that nail polish or was it something to do with her bloodline?

Jacob's second thought besides how terrifyingly beautiful this woman was, was how she knew he was there and answered the door before he could even knock. He had not been making a lot of noise coming to the door he had thought. He wasn't heavy-footed; no one in the castle was.

"Can I help you?" Angela said in a low voice; not unkindly, but definitely not welcoming and it snapped Jacob's attention back to her.

"Uh..." Jacob muttered gathering his wits about him. "I don't know if you knew me or not... I'm kinda new here, and I figured I'd pay my respects and introduce myself to everyone in the organization." He held out his hand, smiling. "Jacob Tepes."

"You are the one who took the infestation job on the Anguis Express." Angela said with those cold eyes unwavering before his own gaze. "Killed a feral Ghoul."

"You know about that?"

"Nothing goes unsaid here in this castle."

Jacob couldn't completely argue about that. Angela herself was one of the things definitely talked about around here.

He flashed her a smile. "Well, I heard there was one more Huntress up here, so I'd thought I'd stop by." He reached out with his gloved hand once more. "Jacob, Jacob Tepes. You, uh, saw me yesterday."

Angela's eyes lowered to the hand, and immediately they rose back up to his face, her face as still and expressionless as a statue. "Angela Dragos," she said coldly.

Jacob lowered his hand, smiling still despite the obvious message the woman was giving him. She definitely was... cold. Yes, that would be a good word to use for her.

"I hear you are very, eh, informative about hunting. Vampires for the most part, right?"

"Is there something you need?" Angela asked impatiently, that same low voice cutting deeper than any knife; telling Jacob to get to the point as to why he was here. "If you have any questions concerning contracts, Vladimir or Velinar are the best sources to ask from. Livia is the oldest member here."

Jacob flashed a confident smile. Though he was clearly being told to piss off, he wasn't one to give up so easily. "That's not what I heard. Besides, maybe I wanted to learn from the company of a beautiful woman?"

"Then ask Sabina or any of the other Huntresses," Angela said uninterested.

"I *could*," Jacob said deciding to play his last trump card. "But, see, I wanted to meet and speak with *you*. I've never met… you know, a Dham-"

"You are annoying." The blunt message felt like a shot through the heart, and Jacob felt all his confidence shatter life glass as he stared at Angela still smiling but in incredible shock. "Do yourself a favor, and stay with your own kind. You will only get in trouble if you associate yourself with me."

"So everyone says," Jacob said defiantly. "But I don't believe it. I mean… you seem…"

He couldn't even lie. He was wanting to say 'nice person', but Angela… she was cold. Colder than ice and was just as mean as any winter storm he had ever ridden into.

"You are annoying," Angela said again sticking a foot out and Jacob looked down to notice that she was trying to keep a black cat inside the room. The little beast stared up at Jacob with bright eyes, as if asking him to rescue him or her.

"Cute cat," said Jacob. "What's his name?"

Angela's eyes narrowed as she pushed the black cat back into the bedroom. "Do us both a favor: Go downstairs, stay with your own kind, and leave me alone." And with that, Angela closed the door on Jacob, shutting out the conversation completely, and leaving him alone in the hallway.

Jacob frowned at the door, not because he was upset with the Dhampir, but because he pitied her. What sort of things had she heard or seen while working under the Black Hand- or even her entire life, to make her behave so coldly towards a new face?

With a sigh, he said to the door, hoping that she could hear him. "Nice to meet you too. I just want to thank you all, for accepting me. I hope that we can become good friends on our hunting trips together." And with that, he turned and left the hallway, without another word.

Though he had tried and failed, Jacob still walked down the staircase with a thin smile on his face. Angela, while such a stiff, was very interesting. There really were an exquisite group of Hunters within the Black Hand, and Jacob was eager to learn as many secrets as he could in order to fulfill his destiny- and his own contract. Getting inside the organization was no easy feat, and the deals he had struck were soul-binding, and dangerous. He would have to fulfill his end of the bargain, little by little, but in the meantime, he could hunt a few beasts and learn a thing or two. He would be killing two birds with one stone; and looking down at his gloved hand, he clenched his fist tight in excitement.

He was so close; there was just a little more work to do.

Angela Dragos... What to make of her, I wonder.

Angela sat on the edge of the bed with Sebastian curled in her lap. As she pet the graceful creature, he purred lovingly while she sat looking at the door leading outside, troubled. It was rare to receive a visitor in the castle unless it was one of the Ghoul butlers or even one of the girls who had been asked by Velinar to join them on a meeting or something.

It was rarer still to have a *rookie* come up to *her*.

Normally, as soon as one was sworn in by the Blood-Oath of Velinar, the other Hunters would immediately frighten the new Hunter with stories about her. The knowledge of the Black Hand having a Dhampir in their midst was a rumor sometimes whispered in Balkeñoir; the monster that hunt the most dangerous in the land, and so sometimes newcomers already suspected, but in the end it always resulted in the same treatment: she was outcasted.

But this time, the arrogant confidence of the young Hunter, it *irritated* Angela. The fact that he even tried to stall for time chewed through her nerves and almost made her hate the man. But at the same time, maybe he was just a curious child, unknowing about the true horrors and secrets in Balkeñoir, especially the Black Hand. That eyepatch obscured a lot of his handsome features, but that damnable smile of confidence made Angela want to punch every single tooth out.

"Such an annoyance…" she muttered as she stroked Sebastian's back. "He'll understand, soon enough. They all eventually do."

"Ahem."

Angela turned her attention to one of the suits of armor in her bedroom who stood up and saluted her.

"Pardon the intrusion, Ma'am," the armor echoed within the steel plates. "But Master Velinar is calling an emergency meeting down to the hall. Please, head downstairs- immediately."

"A contract?" Angela asked slowly standing up so that Sebastian had time to climb off. He meowed in indignation as he scurried across the room and out of sight.

"Not sure," the spirit admitted. "He didn't say, just told us all to inform all the Hunters in the castle."

Must be important. Angela dismissed the armor and then crossed back to her workshop. After changing into some regular pants and an undershirt, it occurred to her that the new rookie, Jacob Tepes, would be there as well. If what he had witnessed for himself here wasn't enough, maybe he would understand when everyone was in the same room together.

Strapped up and ready, Angela made sure Sebastian had some food in his bowl under her bed before venturing down the dark hallway and she made her way down into the Grand Hall where everyone would soon be waiting.

As soon as she entered the majestic and warm hall, all voices suddenly fell silent. The majority of the Hunters took up two tables and their eyes followed Angela as she crossed the room to the opposite end. They all sat up close to the entrance to Velinar's chambers, and patiently waited for the ancient being to arrive. Angela leaned back on her own bench with her back resting against the table. She crossed her arms and her legs and patiently waited while whatever conversation the others were having hesitantly resumed.

At some point, Matei and Jacob entered the hall as well and sat behind the larger group. Sabina sat with them and started talking to Matei, while Jacob turned his one eye towards Angela and flashed that handsome smile of his in greeting. Angela ignored him coldly.

"Would you like a drink?"

Angela turned her head to see the Ghoul butler, Cithus, standing there with a platter full of tankards. Angela accepted one graciously and reached into her pocket for a few pieces of gold.

"Don't bother," the Ghoul said in a bored and rehearsed tone. "It's okay."

"Don't argue," Angela said seizing the shape-shifter's hand and dropping two sovereigns into the palm. "It's a thanks."

The Ghoul nodded appreciatively and pocketed the gold. "In that case, come into the kitchens sometime, and I'll make you a tart." He started to go, when Angela asked him to wait.

"What is this meeting about?" she asked him. "Velinar never asked everyone so suddenly before." Normally he would just call the Hunter he had in mind for a job.

"Dunno for certain," Cithus said with a shrug. "The Master hasn't said."

Figures. "Thank you." Angela said allowing the Ghoul to return to his duties.

She sipped at her cup of warm honeyed ale patiently until the doors to Velinar's chambers eventually opened wide like a moaning mouth, and the little deity stepped out. His bare feet slapped against the stone floor and his scythe screeched as he dragged it behind him. When he came up close to the now silenced Hunters, he stood the scythe up and climbed up the shaft like a salamander on a branch to sit perched like a bird on top; those black marble eyes acknowledging each and every single one of the men and women before him.

"Thank you all for coming on short notice," he eventually said, his voice chillier than usual. There was no hint of him being a youth now, but a frail old man and Angela wondered what exactly was going on for him to appear as such. "I suppose you are all wondering why I've called you all here? Well, I've received a message from Professor Daniel Clockwork."

Immediately the Hunters began to talk amongst themselves. Angela couldn't blame them. Dr. Clockwork was a mechanical genius; and was the creator of the locomotive in Balkeñoir after the division between the northern and southern regions were taken down with the creation of Blackfort Pass. He was also the one who created a natural gas made from the burning of coal and whale oil to power up various electrical appliances throughout the country; lights, water boilers, and even the ignitors for some of the Zeppelins used during the Great

War against the last of the Noyiian Empire. The man was an incredible legend throughout the country, and was respected by many of the top-state scientists and alchemists; and even philosophers at the Yom University.

"It would appear," Velinar spoke up rubbing his hands together as if they were cold. "That my old friend is in Irondell right now, and all is not well."

That caught Angela's attention. If the professor was there asking for the Black Hand, that could not mean good news. With Irondell now part of the call, that was even worse.

Velinar continued. "In his prayer, he says that there is a Vampire infestation within the walls of the large city. Unfortunately, a quarantine has been set up around the city, and no one is allowed in, or out by order of his majesty, Emperor Ion."

"Master," Vladimir said standing up to speak. "What is the Empire doing to stop the infestation?"

"Please, Vladimir," Velinar said. "I will explain if you will be patient." When Vladimir sat down with his partner, the deity resumed. "The quarantine was put up by a Raven who wanted to cut off the city from major supply-lines in order to make sure no one left the area as he hunted for the very Vampire that Angela was originally supposed to find."

Angela felt the eyes of all the Hunters glaring right at her- like daggers driving into her. She felt their obvious hatefulness towards her as if she was being stabbed already.

"Unfortunately," Velinar continued. "The situation has apparently gotten out of hand, and now even the

Irondell Watchmen are having trouble containing the infestation. However, no one is allowed outside the walls and anyone who ventures too close are shot on sight. The Raven in charge is clearly taking no chances of this infestation spreading throughout the region. Unfortunately, there has been no way for anyone to call for help outside the city. The phone lines had been cut, and anyone who tries to send a letter by raven has their bird shot down."

Velinar looked at his Hunters with a grim expression. "I don't know much about your modern traditions regarding an infestation, but this sounds too suspicious to me."

Velinar was right. This sounded too strange for a normal quarantine. Though quarantines in general were naturally used nowadays to prevent an outbreak in major cities, this one was just way too extreme if the Raven Angela fought was simply trying to prevent a spread of the vampiric disease. Not only that, but what about the Watchmen? Wouldn't they or even Count Andrei find this way too strange as well and contact The Emperor? Something really wasn't right, and it made Angela's skin crawl at the thought of it.

"This doesn't sit right with me..." Nicolae spoke up. "That's... *ridiculous*. They are trapping a lot of people in there with an outbreak that *clearly*, they cannot contain. Why wouldn't they at least ask for help?"

"Because we believe there is a sick game afoot."

Everyone turned around to see a large man from the southern lands walk down the middle of the room. He wore a dirtied lab coat with many stitches and his ebony skin seemed to glow in the torchlight. He wore large microscopic glasses and he had a large mess of white hair that was fluffy like the wool of a sheep.

"Dr. Jecklyn," Velinar then said. "Thank you for joining us."

The man smiled. "Please, Velinar, for the hundredth time, call me Oskar." He then noticed Angela and winked at her as he passed by. When he stood next to the deity of Velinar, he continued to explain to the Hunters.

"No one can get out of the city, that's understandable. But no one can get inside, not even the Empire? Now that is strange- stranger still that Count Andrei is allowing such a thing to happen. According to Clockwork as Velinar had said, he also mentioned that the Watchmen are usually out during the day taking care of whatever Vampires they find in homes and nestling in the sewers, but during the night, just like everyone else they are staying near the castle. Apparently, no one is allowed to be out at night while the Raven is hunting the beasts. Clockwork is very much annoyed that nothing seems to be getting done during his time there, and would like us to assist in eliminating the Vampire horde."

Luca chuckled. "Kinda ironic. We get labeled as criminals for Hunting, and they are the ones who need help."

"Then what are we waiting for?" Adriana demanded. "Let's all go."

"And leave everyone else without a Hunter to call?" Velinar asked with a soft and amused tone. "Now *there's* an idea." His words cut like a knife, and rendered the Huntress silent.

He shook his head. "No. After what happened with Angela, we cannot risk a whole horde of us to go there. They had made it clear that the Black Hand was not welcome in this fight. However, we cannot ignore the calling of a good friend in need. Besides, Daniel Clockwork, has requested specifically, that Angela Dragos herself is to return."

This caught everyone including Angela even by surprise. "Me, Master?" She sat as still as a statue with her tankard forgotten in her hand.

"Sir," Vladimir said standing up again. "I really must protest."

"Your reasons?" Oskar asked with a gruff voice as he tucked his hands behind his back.

"She failed when you sent her, Master," Vladimir said not speaking to Oskar but to Velinar himself. "She couldn't finish the job before, so why should she get a second chance now?"

"So she can redeem herself," Velinar said. "This was originally *her* contract, and unfortunately for the lot of you, none of you have as much experience hunting Vampires as she does. Therefore, the only logical choice is to send her back out there and hope she does not fail again."

"But, Master-"

"I have spoken," Velinar said his eyes suddenly flashing bright with sternness. A shadow filled the room, and with it snuffed out any warmth the hall once had.

It was rumored that if Velinar looked at you hard enough, he could reveal your death. He must have done that to Vladimir because the Hunter fell back into his seat and didn't dare speak again.

Velinar said, "Angela Dragos will be the one we send back to Irondell, and she will be the one to put an end to this infestation. If she is able to do this, then she will get paid whatever Clockwork offers her and she will be able to return to this castle. But if she fails, then she may never be allowed to set foot within the halls of the Black Hand ever again. Is that reasonable?"

When no one answered, he turned his eyes over to the Dhampir. "Do I make myself clear, Angela?"

"Perfectly, Master," Angela said with a bow of her head. She sat her half-finished tankard onto the table and stood. "I shall leave immediately."

She could not afford to fail now, and besides, there was some unfinished business and unanswered questions that she herself wanted to investigate. She wasn't concerned with what Velinar had said. She knew that he hadn't said she wouldn't be allowed to return because she would be banished. He had said that because if she did fail, then it was most likely she was dead. And if she was right about this Immortal...

"Before you do," Oskar then spoke up. "Velinar has made a decision."

"You will be taking a partner with you this time." Velinar explained. "You will not be allowed to go alone on this one, and with two Hunters in the vicinity, it will be easier for you to be rid of the outbreak in Irondell."

Now, it was Angela's turn to protest. "Master, will all due respect, I prefer to work alone."

"Not this time you don't," Oskar said.

"I'm not-"

"This is not open to discussion, Angela," Velinar said in a stern but not unkind voice. Though he wore a firm expression, his eyes were soft, as if asking Angela to simply trust him. "You cannot and *will not* do this alone. Besides, Clockwork has requested someone to go with you. He already knows your predicament concerning your last visit to the city. With two of you, you can cover more ground- and to top it all, whoever goes with you might learn a thing or two about Vampire-hunting. This is not a suggestion, but a command. You will have a companion go with you."

Angela bit her tongue to keep it from lashing out. This arrangement, it was madness! No one wanted to work with her, and she didn't want to have to drag anyone around. Vampire-hunting was a delicate business, unlike many other beast hunts. If she had a companion with her, she'd merely be babysitting and the two of them might end up getting killed if not by the Vampires than by the hands of the citizens or Watchmen. On top of that, she had the Raven to worry about, she didn't want to have to concern herself with anyone who hated her.

Still, she held her tongue back and bowed her head. "As you wish."

Velinar nodded a thank you, and then returned his attention to the others. "Do we have any volunteers?"

Unsurprisingly, no one stood up. For a long while, everyone just looked at one another, unwilling to look Velinar or even Oskar in the eye.

"Sir," Luca eventually said standing up. "With all due respect, I for one would protest even if you asked me specifically to volunteer. No one wishes to work with a half-breed like her. She is dangerous, and I personally will find myself hanged before I work with someone with vampiric blood in them."

"She is your companion," Velinar said calmly, unoffended by Luca's words. "She is a member of the Black Hand; your ally."

Luca chuckled humorlessly. "A Dhampir, a half-breed of a monster, will *never* be my ally."

Everyone else nodded in agreement, and Angela was not surprised. She would never be accepted by her so-called 'brothers-in-arms' and she would never be considered one of the Black Hand's own. It was clear to her, that no one was going to be willing to take on the job with her. She would have to go alone, and if she failed, that would mean she was either dead or no longer able to return to the castle. Either way, she loses.

But then, someone stood up tall and proud, acknowledging the looks of everyone with a proud smile.

"Master Velinar," Jacob Tepes said. "I know I am not an experienced member of the Black Hand, nor am I a Vampire Hunter. But I volunteer to join Angela on her Hunt in Irondell."

"What are you doing?" Matei hissed at Jacob as everyone just stared at him in shock and bewilderment.

Angela thought the same thing. She *glared* at the young Hunter with a venomous rage. The sheer nerve the man had! What was he thinking, deciding to jump head-first into a hunt he knew absolutely *nothing* about?

He had already sealed his fate and his reputation by the looks of the other Hunters. Unsurprisingly, they disapproved of this movement greatly, and evidently desired nothing more than for Angela to go alone in order to die or fail to never return again.

And Jacob... he was willing to do such a stupid and reckless thing without any prior knowledge or even a second thought!

"I am doing my duties as a member of the Black Hand," Jacob finally answered Matei. "It is our duty to protect people from the beasts of Balkeñoir, and the people in that city is trapped with a Raven who clearly doesn't know what he is doing. Meanwhile, you are all arguing about who will go with Angela or not and wasting precious time in the process. If none of you are willing to fight with Angela to aid those who need us just because of her bloodline, then I say you are all cowards."

Immediately, Vladimir and Nicolae were on their feet with their hands on their weapons. The girls and even Matei stayed seated however, as they watched the two confront Jacob who remained as calm as ever.

"You want to say that again, rookie?" Vladimir challenged.

"I said," Jacob said without a hint of hesitation in his voice. He paused between each word, letting each strike home like the toll of a great bell. "You, are, *cowards*."

"Why you-" Nicolae started forward, but a monstrous growl suddenly sounded from Velinar, who glared at the three Hunters with a murderous expression.

They all stared, no one had ever heard Velinar make such a sound, except for maybe two people in the entire world. Around the deity, the shadows seemed to have darkened within the hall, making the air feel colder and this was evident by the plumes of vapor escaping past dumbfounded lips.

"That is *enough*," Velinar hissed in a snake-like voice. "Sit down!" When the three men sat back down, he took a deep breath before continuing in his normal voice. Likewise the shadows around him seemed to fade back to their original shade and the temperature climbed just a little.

"Jacob Tepes, are you sure?"

"It is like you said, Master," Jacob where he sat. "We can't allow Angela to go alone. She needs all the help she can get without raising suspicion of the Irondell Watchmen, or that Raven. I am more than willing to help her if it means saving the lives of all those people trapped in the city. I want to do my part as not only a member of the Black Hand, but also Angela's guildmate; especially if no one else will."

Angela felt like vomiting with such a speech. Everyone else looked angry or ashamed that Jacob would call them out like that. All eyes were on Velinar however, as he took in Jacob's words.

Velinar stared at Jacob for the longest time before he eventually nodded in understanding. "Very well. You both shall leave immediately. Everyone else will remain here at Shadowfort for the time being. Those who remain will keep an ear out with me in case the situation in Irondell goes peril. I am hoping we can get to the bottom of this without starting a war with the Empire. In the meantime, no one is to say a word about this. Do you all understand?"

"Yes, Master," everyone including Angela said in almost-perfect unison.

What he said made perfect sense. The less Hunters that were in Irondell, the less likely that the Raven will try to go after them and get distracted from his current task at hand. Not only that, but if the Raven were to call for assistance from the Empire, they would be more interested in capturing a member of the Black Hand than an Immortal considering Emperor Ion's priorities. It was too risky to send everyone out, and the fewer people to break into the city, the easier it would be to have more control over the situation.

Angela stood immediately, ignoring the venomous glares of hatred turned towards her as she did so. "We shall prepare now, Master."

"How do you plan to get there?" Oskar asked with a chuckle. "By train or horse? The Express has been instructed to pass by the city, and the walls are under constant watch by the Watchmen. If you all get spotted, you'd be shot dead with zero warning."

Angela thought that without Jacob, she would have a better chance slipping in, but decided it was best to not say anything. Once Velinar made his decision, it was foolish to argue.

"Then how are we supposed to get in?" Jacob asked.

Only then, did Velinar smile. He told the rest of the Hunters, "You are all dismissed."

He then instructed Jacob and Angela to prepare for the trip and then to come and see him. With that, lowering himself to the floor and picking up his scythe, Velinar turned and started for his chambers with Oskar by his side. Angela and Jacob, then taking their leave, left the meeting hall to get their gear.

"Hey, Dhampir," Angela heard Vladimir say behind her. "Do us all a favor: and make sure you never come back! Just you wait, Jacob, you'll see what I meant soon enough! You fool!"

Even as the doors closed behind the two, Angela could still hear the voice of Vladimir shouting what everyone else was thinking.

It made her feel pitiful and not for the first time that she even bothered to join the Black Hand in the first place.

All these years, and humans are still all the same…

Angela returned to her quarters and began to gather up her gear. She slipped on her black armor, hooked her cloak around her neck before pulling up her hood and concealing her snow-white hair. When she was strapped up, she slipped the revolver she carried into the holster on her thigh as well as a second at her belt to her left. When her sword was strapped across her back, she finally slipped on her boots. For good measure, she slipped on her ruby ring on her right finger. She doubted that it would be of any use in Irondell, but perhaps an ancient Immortal like Horla might find it interesting to talk to her should the time ever come.

After saying goodbye to Sebastian and leaving a note for the servants to care for him, Angela stepped out of her quarters and locked the heavy door behind her. She then turned and ran right into Sabina and Adriana who were just about to enter Sabina's room. Ignoring their glances, Angela crossed down the hall with the intention of making it straight to Velinar without delay.

"Dhampir."

Angela stopped at the sound of Sabina's voice, waiting for her to continue without looking back.

"Good Hunting."

There was no sincerity on her voice, or any indication that she even cared for Angela's hunt. There was mockery, a poisonous tone that made Adriana chortle. Without acknowledgement, Angela kept on moving and started down the spiraled staircase to the main hall where Jacob was waiting at the foot of the male stairway.

His leather armor was taut over his body, and his cloak made him appear larger than he really was. Other than his throwing knives and dagger set, the only weapon Angela could see was his bow that stuck out from under his cloak, but she could smell gunpowder and various poisons on his person. She hoped that he packed accordingly, and didn't get in her way.

When her boots touched the floor, the young Hunter pushed himself off the newel post shaped like a robed woman praying, the candle in her hand flickering dark shadows across her still face. "I have brought silver-tipped arrows," Jacob said as Angela turned and pushed the door to the Grand Hall open with a loud groan. "Will that work on this hunt?"

"It will suffice," Angela said moving forward still and almost leaving him behind. "Do you have any stakes?"

"No. Just knives."

"That'll be fine. If need-be we'll make some when we get to Irondell." Angela wondered what Oskar and Velinar had in mind if they weren't to go by train or horse.

To be honest, Angela was glad she wouldn't have to take Midnight back out there. The horse was dead-tired, and the chill in the air considering how exhausted he was could kill him. It was better to take a train, but since that option was clearly out, she was curious to find out what the immortal man had in store for the two.

The *two*. What a damn joke. If Angela had her way, she would have told Jacob to return to his quarters and never come out until she left. She could feel his one blue eye watching at her, as if sizing her up as they walked. She didn't know what he was playing at, but she intended to get this job done as soon as possible and get him out of her hair.

"Are you really that angry with me?" Jacob then asked breaking into Angela's thoughts. At this point, they were just at the door leading down into Velinar's catacombs.

Angela stopped her hand before reaching for the handle, and turned her bright purple eyes upon the Hunter who flinched at the sight of the liquid pools of lavender that threatened to swallow him up should he push his luck. He quickly composed himself however, and flashed that irritating smile of his.

"Well… are you?" he dared to ask again.

"I will make this as clear as I possibly can," Angela said ignoring the arrogant child's question. "You will not interfere with anything on this Hunt. You will do everything I tell you to do, whenever I tell you to do it, and you will follow it to the letter. You will not speak unless spoken to, and you will *not* get in my way should we run into trouble. These are not Ghouls or Goblins we are hunting here. These are not Nephelim or even Werewolves. These are Vampires, and they *will* kill you if you mess up even in the slightest. Just heed every word I say, and you will be fine. But if it seems that you will become more trouble than you are worth, I will make sure you *never* return to Shadowfort Castle again. Do I make myself clear, Jacob Tepes?"

She of course had no such power, but it was good to intimidate, good to make threats even when empty especially to someone so young. Yes, Angela was annoyed that Jacob Tepes was joining her on this Hunt, but at the same time his safety was also her responsibility, and she wouldn't be able to return to Shadowfort anyway if she were to get this rookie killed.

Jacob blinked his single blue eye, and then smiled. Was it a nervous smile, or a smile of spite? A challenge?

"Crystal, Madam. I'll do my best to remember that."

Angela narrowed her eyes but then shook her head, dismissing the conversation. "Come." She then pushed the door open, and then the two of them ventured down into the darkness beneath the castle where Velinar and Oskar were waiting.

As they continued down for what felt like an eternity, she stole a quick glance at Jacob, who kept his eye straight and said nothing until they reached the bottom and into the main chambers where Velinar usually dwelled.

"I'm not wanting to cause trouble," Jacob then said as they neared the final door to Velinar's resting place. "I just want to get some hands-on experience. And besides, I stand by what I said, back in the hall. I do not care about whatever you are. We have a job to do, and I hope that you will look at me like a companion, and not a burden on this Hunt."

Angela said nothing, but she decided to at the very least keep that in mind. She still didn't understand Jacob's reasons or his motives, but she decided the worst that could possibly happen was she humor him, and he prove her right.

That, or they *both* wound up dead.

When they entered the darkened chambers, Velinar was speaking to Oskar, his leg scratching the other as if the deity was nervous about something. Upon sensing the two Hunters enter the room, Velinar turned his attention to them.

"What I am about to show you," he then said without a hello. "Has hardly ever been revealed to mortals since the beginning to time. Only a few people know of such a thing, and I am trusting you both that you will never speak of this- ever."

"Of course not, Master," Jacob said.

"He is serious," Oskar said taking out a cigar and lighting it with a match. "If anyone else found out about this, it could mean bad news for the Black Hand- and anyone else who knows of its existence."

"What is it?" Angela asked, curious to find out what exactly it is.

Velinar leaned his scythe against his right shoulder and reached into his black sleeve. Upon removing it, his little pale hand was revealed holding a silver key with a two-faced skull to make the bow, and the cuts and shoulder shaped into what looked like a jagged saw. Upon seeing the metallic key, Angela felt as if the room had suddenly gone cold, and by the looks of it, Jacob noticed the change in the atmosphere as well.

"This," Velinar then said turning the key in his nimble fingers. "Is one of eight identical Skeleton Keys crafted by the Star Pandei. They were made as portal keys in which to pass through the different dimensions of Lunokean. With it, one can pass through the dimension through one door, and end up in a completely different area by another. You two are not able to take the train into Irondell, and there won't be enough time by horse. Therefore, you will infiltrate the city by meeting Professor

Clockwork where he is staying. He is a Keymaster, and he will allow you both to pass through the gate and get into the city without alerting any of the Watchmen."

"That's..." Angela started.

"Incredible." Jacob finished. It was such a ancient and powerful artifact, that Angela couldn't blame the Fallen Star for being so cautious. The ability to teleport anywhere in the world with two of those keys... if such a power would fall into the wrong hands, then Balkeñoir would have more than its fair share of problems.

Velinar nodded. "Indeed, it is." He then turned to Oskar, who now held a golden pocket watch in his hand. "What is the time, Dr. Jecklyn?"

Oskar checked his pocket watch and with a puff of his cigar, answered, "Thirty seconds until noon."

"Perfect."

Velinar then motioned the two Hunters to follow him to the very back of his chambers, where from within the darkness appeared a door of mist and silver. Angela had been down here many times, but such a door never existed. In fact, nothing but the torches and the unfamiliar light source coming in from somewhere high above was the only thing in this room aside from Velinar. The door... it just appeared out of nowhere.

"Come." He motioned to the door, and he placed the key into the keyhole just beneath the skull doorknob.

"When Oskar says so, you both will walk through the door when I open it. You will then keep walking straight, and you *will not* steer off course. There are many vast dimensions of darkness and nightmares unseen by mortal eyes, and if you do not walk straight towards the light, you will slip off into the far shore and possibly end up in Oblivion, or some other realm that you will both will never be able to return from. Keep this in mind, as you head for Clockwork's door, and pass through the gate."

Angela was nervous, but she refused to let it show. She was the one who lived among the living, *and* the dead. Death was not something she feared, not after the hell that the real world had put her through. She would pass through the gate, and she would return to show that Velinar had not wasted his time or his resources in allowing her to join the Black Hand. She would return victoriously, or she would die trying and allow her own namesake to bite the dust.

And Jacob? Well, as far as Angela was concerned, he just needed to stay out of her way, and let her work.

"Ten seconds," Oskar warned the three.

"Do you both understand your mission?" Velinar asked.

"Yes, Master," both Hunters responded in unison.

"Then go. May your swords stay sharp, and good Hunting!"

"Now!" Oskar Jecklyn barked and with that, Velinar turned the Skeleton Key and opened the door to Darkness itself.

It looked like the door opened to a great long hall shrouded in total shadow. Ghostly mist lingered at the floor that wasn't there, and the moans and cries of the damned echoed down the abyss. At the very end of the hall, was a bright light that was rectangular and shaped like a doorway. Even as Angela and Jacob passed through the door, she felt as if the end of the hall was lingering further away; and she would fall at any moment in the darkness that surrounded them both.

She felt invisible hands, cold and clawed scratch at her, calling her to turn to the left or right. She heard the tongues of ancient languages piercing her brain, calling her name and sink into the mist that clung to her boots like mud. She felt as if a great many bugs crawled along her body, and she felt terribly ill. But still, she kept her focus on the doorway at the very end of the 'hall,' and thankfully, the young Hunter beside her didn't linger away from their path and kept his own sight straight and true. The two continued on and on, ignoring the cries of Oblivion calling them to stay, and soon they passed through the threshold and a bright light blinded them as they suddenly collapsed onto the hardwood floor of a completely different building.

The sun shone through a dirtied window, and the room they were now in appeared to be that of a sickroom with walls lined with bookshelves and benches of strange chemistry labs and beakers. Cots and crates littered the room, and even the candles that were lit on some of the chairs stacked against the wall seemed to be melting to the last of their wick. It seemed that this was a room that someone was recently moving into, and before Angela could even process any more than what she already have seen, she heard a door close behind her and she whirled around fast with her hand reaching for her sword over her shoulder.

"So," the man in the wheelchair said upon removing a silver key with a two-faced skull from what looked like a closet door. He wore a dirtied suit with no tie and a tweed flat cap. He also wore a monocle over his left eye, and Angela noticed that the man was missing his legs at the knees. "This is the Dhampir I have heard so much about. And she has brought a friend."

Jacob turned and regarded the man with a sharp blue eye. "Professor… Clockwork?"

The man nodded with a smile. "In the flesh, and at your service."

La

Angela allowed her body to relax as she stood up from her position. She bowed her head respectfully to the man and said, "Professor Clockwork. An honor, and a privilege, my lord."

Clockwork smiled warmly and bobbed his head. "And an honor to meet you as well, Angela Dragos. And you must be...?" He stretched out a hand to Jacob who shook the professor's hand.

"Jacob, sir. Jacob Tepes."

When the two released their hands, Clockwork wheeled back slightly and looked the two Hunters over. "I am sure this is all a bit... overwhelming. You hardly had any time to prepare, though I see you both are eager. I see that Velinar's ways have not changed in the years I've known him."

"You two are good friends, sir?" Angela asked.

"More like pen-pals, but yes, we are," Clockwork answered while rubbing his smooth chin. "He is always willing to share some secrets of the worlds beyond the one we stand in now, and I in turn, more than willing to assist in the advancement of whatever weapons and gear you Hunters need before the Empire requires them. The perks of knowing one of the most brilliant minds in the world, not to sound arrogant of course."

"Helpful in the world of Hunting on top of being a brilliant author and scientist," Jacob spoke up with that confident smile of his. "We have heard so much about you, sir."

Clockwork smiled. "You flatter me. But I am afraid we have much more important matters to discuss. I assume Velinar has given you the brief insight on the situation here in Irondell?"

"We are in the city now, sir?" Angela asked.

Clockwork pointed to the window behind them with a long and bony finger. "See for yourself."

Upon looking out the pane of glass, the two Hunters saw that they were indeed in the city of Irondell, though in a different area than when Angela had entered before. Not only that, but the city itself was not in the same condition as she had left it.

In fact, it looked like something out of a nightmare.

The short walls surrounding the city were not even visible due to the smoke and smog. Many of the sharp towers piercing the skies above appeared hollowed out and on the verge of collapsing. Far down in the streets below, Angela saw bodies being burnt on crosses, as well as heads placed on spikes. She caught the distinct smell of garlic in the air and the occasional sound of a gunshot sounding somewhere in the vast city. Now that they were deeper within Irondell, Angela realized just how large the city really was, and with many different bridges and towers crisscrossing over one another, it dawned on her just how difficult this contract might be.

The people that she saw marching the streets and dragging others out of their homes were not Watchmen, but normal citizens armed with torches and farming tools. Though the sun was slightly obscured by the smog that hung over the city like a cloud, Angela was able to watch as a citizen dragged a small child out into the street and stepped back as it screeched and snarled an inhuman cry. It's body began to smoke and flake out into burning ash and soon the creature went still, still burning by the glare of the sun that shone past the tall towers of the large stone citadel that towered in the center of Irondell like a jagged piece of bone. All that was left indeed was a set of charred bone blackened and ashy.

All the atrocities, burning, beating, killing, it all happened under the watchful eye of the sun, and the many statues that decorated the towers of the city; as if Kawn and Oblivion were both watching the terror of Irondell tearing itself apart.

"Dear Yohnah above…" Jacob whispered his eye wide with horrified shock.

"Where are the Watchmen?" Angela asked turning back to Clockwork. "I do not see any down there."

"They hardly ever come out anymore," Clockwork said sadly. "It has gotten so bad, that the citizens are taking matters into their own hands. Therefore, the Watchmen that are still around stay on the walls or near 'important' buildings such as the castle or the local churches."

"How many are dead?" Jacob asked leaning an arm against the glass as if looking for some sort of support.

Clockwork grimaced as if the number stunned him. "This morning, the citizens counted almost two-hundred, not even including those who are just missing. After today, and even tonight when the sun sets, who knows?"

"What about the Raven in charge of the Hunt?" Angela asked. "What about Count Andrei?"

"Ha!" Clockwork suddenly croaked. "That bloody idiot has been nowhere in sight. Well… not entirely. He would sometimes be in the presence of a major attack, investigating the aftermath, but other than that, hardly anyone ever sees him either. As for Andrei, no one has seen or heard from him since the day that Raven made his arrival. None of the Watchmen are eager to talk about it either. It's as if, they are scared of something."

"So, the citizens are on their own?" Jacob asked. "No help from the Watchmen, the Raven, or even the Empire who promised to protect them?"

"Unfortunately so," Clockwork confirmed.

Jacob slapped the pane of glass angrily and stalked away, seeking a moment. Angela couldn't blame the young Hunter, but this was what happened when an infestation got out of hand. The people got scared, and the men and women who were to protect them leave them at the mercy of the beasts. Justice, and protection was a thing of the past, once fear took over like a plague. If this had been a century or two ago however, it could be a lot worse. A whole city of the living dead.

"It has been like this for the last week or so," Clockwork continued rubbing his hands together as if washing them. "In the day, men, women and children are dragged out and burned for being discovered to be Vampires, and at night, the people lock themselves in their homes in hopes that the undead don't reach them. The Watchmen stay on the walls and only come out every so often, and the so-called men in charge are nowhere to be seen."

"Do you think the Raven has left?" Angela asked.

"We don't know. No one knows anything here it seems or is willing to talk about it. But the fact that Andrei himself has gone missing as well, concerns me most of all. I have come to Irondell to conduct some experiments with the owner of this house. The fact that I cannot return back to Mistendell disturbs me, and considering what you have already seen out there, it is getting much worse. I need you both to eliminate the Vampire threat in the area, and if possible, find out just what exactly is going on with the leader of this city."

"We'll do our best," Angela ensured the professor. "We just need all the information you got."

"We should go out there right now." Jacob suggested.

"No," Angela told him. "There is way too much excitement happening out there. We cannot risk being caught and risk our identities being found out. We wait until nightfall."

"Wouldn't that just be trading one danger for another?"

Angela glared at him and he fell silent. She returned her attention to the professor. "Until then, Dr. Clockwork? Shall we sit and talk?"

"Yes," Clockwork said wheeling his way towards the door exiting the sickroom. "Let us talk downstairs. Ava is making a delicious beef barley soup."

Angela started to follow, but she stopped as she felt a hand grab her wrist.

"Angela, wait," Jacob's voice said. "This all sounds too strange. We shouldn't waste any time. We should-"

Whatever he was about to say was cut off as Angela spun beneath his arm, twisting it across his chest and with a strong hand grabbed ahold of the front of his armor and slammed him right against the wall, making the shelves shake and even a bottle of some clear liquid shatter onto the floor. Clockwork whirled around fast in his chair, but Angela ignored him, her eyes burning with a fiery hatred towards the Hunter in her grasp.

"Maybe I wasn't clear when I told you this," she growled to the now shocked Jacob in a low and dangerous tone. "You *will not* speak unless spoken to, and you *will not* get in my way."

"I was just oomph..." Jacob groaned as Angela increased her pressure enough to make him stop talking.

"You will follow my guidance to the letter," she continued. "Whether you agree with it or not. I know you want to help the people out there, but there is nothing we can do right now. For now, you will *sit*, and *listen* until I say we go out."

She then tightened her grip and forced more pressure onto his chest, making it difficult for Jacob to breathe. "And one more thing: you *ever* put your hands on me again- or even *touch* me again, and I will break your arms and legs and force you to stay here like a leper. Are we clear, *rookie*?"

Jacob tried to resist but Angela held him firm. "You're crushing me..." he groaned trying to stare her down defiantly. "Goddamn, let me go..."

"Do you understand me?" Angela asked, pausing with each word while placing more pressure on his chest. She heard the wood in the wall groan against the strength pushing against it. Still, Jacob glared at her defiantly, unwilling to back down. Unfortunately for him, Angela was very patient, and she had the upper hand on this.

"Oh, for Pete's sake…" Jacob groaned. "Alright, I understand. I get it."

"You get what?" Angela demanded.

"Seriously?"

Angela only stared back.

Jacob grunted and muttered another curse. "Fine. I get that you're in charge and I should never touch you again. Now for the love of Yohnah and all things holy, put me down!"

Angela obliged, releasing the man and allowing him to drop onto the floor with a *thud*. He coughed and rubbed his now sore chest as she turned her attention back to Clockwork.

"I apologize for that."

"No, no," Clockwork shook his head although he was clearly startled and uneasy still. "In fact, in all honesty, I find it quite interesting. I've never seen a humanoid move as fast as you did."

Humanoid. What a word.

"Still, I apologize."

Jacob grumbled as he pulled himself back up. "I'm fine too, thanks for asking."

"Well then," Clockwork said clearing his throat before turning around where he was. "Let us go eat and talk. *Are* you good, Jacob?" He asked this as if he were talking to a specimen undergoing experimentation and not a human being that had been crushed against a wall.

Jacob gave the right answer: "Never better."

“Good. Come.”

And so, Angela followed him out, leaving Jacob to follow her behind. Though they were only in Irondell together for a few short minutes, the man had already crossed a line. She dreaded this Hunt, and the days she would have to spend here.

Jacob ate his food silently at the table while Clockwork and Angela did most of the talking. The small dining room consisted of just a smaller room next to the kitchen and lit with many candles for the power was out in the district where Dr. Ava Manchester lived. Some crates and boxes were stacked against the wall, their contents unknown to the trio. As they ate, they spoke of Watchmen patrols and where the city appeared to be most watched during the night. They then went on to where most attacks took place, and what the major religion in Irondell was; if there was worship of only Yohnah or any other Stars. He didn't see the point of that, but Angela was firm and so he decided it was best to just sit quietly still and listen.

The stew that Ava had made was brilliant. Being a sweet old shut-in, she practically dotted over the three like a grandmother- unaware of course that Angela was a Dhampir. According to Clockwork upon introducing them, Ava owned the sickroom upstairs and occasionally worked as a local nurse for those in the district. Apparently, she used to work in the capital city of Goldendell before she retired and moved across the country. She was and still is a good friend of Clockwork and was working with him on an antidote for certain flu symptoms. Jacob thanked her gratefully and enjoyed the stew in silence as Angela and Clockwork continued their conversation.

It amazed him how well-mannered Angela was. Though she hardly ate as much or as fast as he or Clockwork, her table manners were that of a noblewoman. The way she handled her silverware and positioned her back and her elbows, she could really pull off being in one of the major rulers' courts if she wasn't a Dhampir. He wondered where she learned such manners from. His chest still hurt from the impact on the wall.

He still couldn't conceive how fast and strong Angela was. It all happened so fast that he had no time to react, and the strength holding him there, it was incredible; definitely inhuman.

Also, for a moment, brief but noticeable, he noticed her eyes having a strong look about them, like the intent to kill. When she spoke to him, her teeth were more noticeable up close, and he could see her irregular-sized canines. What he had pissed off was not a normal Huntress. He could now understand the fear the other Hunters felt around Angela. She was clearly... just, *incredibly* dangerous.

But still... she was so well-mannered, and spoke politely to Ava despite the obvious fear in the old woman's eyes. She even offered to help with the dishes afterwards, as if she was not speaking to clients but to friends. Even when she spoke to Jacob at the table she was gentle, despite her dislike of the young Hunter. How could something so beautiful, so kind to others, be so dangerous? What made Angela the way she is, and what was it about Dhampirs specifically that made so many fear them? When she was like this, she looked like any other woman Jacob would have met back out in the streets before he joined the Black Hand. Were all Vampires like this? Or was there something more?

"So, the best chances to avoid too much detection," he then heard Clockwork tell Angela. "Would be the lower cisterns. You can navigate through the city with ease using them, but I can guarantee you that some Vampires might be nesting out down there."

"Good," Angela said taking a sip of her wine before speaking again. Jacob wondered if Dhampir's were just as intoxicated to alcohol as humans. "Because the first thing we need to do, if find a Dearg to find the Immortal responsible."

Jacob cleared his throat and thankfully, Angela looked at him and didn't tell him not to speak. "If I may ask, you keep using the term 'Dearg' and 'Immortal' when it comes to Vampires. Forgive my ignorance, but, what is the difference?"

Angela nodded as if the question was reasonable. "The difference is what the word represents when it comes to the severity of Vampirism.

"An Immortal is what is known as a pure-blooded Vampire. One that *chose* the darkness rather than forced into it. Very few choose this path since the original Prince of Darkness; the Riders of Dragul back before the Empire was founded. They are neither alive or dead, but instead something of an entirely different reality than the one you and I know of. Deargs, or lesser-Vampires or just known as the infected and common Vampires, are bodies drained of blood, and brought back from the dead due to some strange toxin that Immortals have in their saliva, although many suspect it to be a way of cursing the living which they would be correct on."

"So when someone says 'vampire' it's just a broad term?"

"Correct. Unlike Immortals, they are easy to track and easier to kill, for they are like mindless zombies, fixated on sin and feeding. Though, to the Immortals themselves they call their undead their 'Disciples.' But Immortals, they are not like normal Vampires. They have mystical powers of conjuration and all other things supernatural. They can shapeshift, often into animals but also demonic creatures that are not so common anymore. They are usually the cause of outbreaks throughout Balkeñoir. However, they are not usually the real ones responsible for the outbreak as a whole. A bite from an Immortal can take about a week or two depending on how old the Vampire is and how thick their fangs are. If you are bitten by a common Vampire, it is usually to suck all the blood in your body, and by then the toxin will bring you back immediately the day after."

"Why does it take the next day for a regular Vampire and a week or two for Immortals?" asked Jacob. "Shouldn't it be the other way around?"

"More time for the Immortal to feed on the same victim," said Clockwork. "There has been cases in the past where young men and women would be given to Immortals who would slowly drink their blood for as long as almost three weeks before they finally perish. They purposefully hold back their toxins in order to prevent sudden death."

"Very good, Professor," said Angela sounding impressed.

"Oh," said Jacob. "So if we get bitten by a Dearg or Disciple, whatever, we're screwed. Done deal. But if the Immortal bites us, we got a fighting chance?"

"Unless," Angela said with a raised finger. "The Immortal chooses you to join them in the darkness, or you gain their power yourself. What this means is that if a human gets bitten by an Immortal who doesn't want them to turn into a bloodthirsty demon, then the amount of toxin it can release will slowly curse the human into a more sentient Vampire. This is what a common Vampire is like, and there is a possibility for them to become an Immortal over time. It is a slow rebirth, so to speak. But the fastest way to become an Immortal, is by relinquishing your humanity and accepting the darkness completely."

"What does that mean though?" asked Clockwork clearly interested.

"Think about it," said Angela. "A Vampire is essentially the opposite of a human. They are the embodiment of sin itself, whereas humans were made in the image of Yohnah, all things pure and virtuous. This of course does not mean that humans are not capable of evil just like Vampires are not capable of doing good."

"Doing good?" Jacob chuckled. "Like what?"

But Angela ignored him, continuing with her explanation. "What separates the two beings entirely, is their soul. If a human gives up their humanity, turn their face from their god whomever that may be, and accept the blood of an Immortal, they will become powerful; a being beyond rebirth and beyond salvation. The key difference is that if a common or sentient Vampire is able, there is a chance they can end their curse. Die as a human in the form of suicide. A true Immortal houses the demon of the Nosferatu; the true form of the Vampire. If an Immortal can end their lives or undergo treatment through potions and antidotes before that demon settles in entirely, then their souls can be saved and they will die as the humans they were born."

"You make it sound like Vampires are merely possessed humans," said Jacob.

Angela nodded. "In a way, yes. But it is more of a symbiotic relationship. The spirit of the Nosferatu is the curse of which the Vampire is created. Depending on how much toxin is transferred will depend on how the Vampire will become. Either a gluttonous and bloodthirsty zombie or a Dearg; soulless and sinful. *Or* as a man slowly transforming into an Immortal as the Nosferatu demon slowly takes hold, combining with the soul of the human in question until they are one and the same."

Jacob nodded, understanding the differences now. "So, based on the timeframes you have described, we have to assume that the outbreak started a week or two ago, spread by the first victim who has become a Dearg, and from them, the hordes of Vampires that are now out there. Just when you said the attacks began, Professor."

Clockwork nodded. "That is correct. It would only take one Immortal to infect one person, and that person could affect as many as it could drink."

"Killing the Immortal however, will stop the spread of the Disciples who live to serve their Master," said Angela.

"So, we have to find the Immortal," Jacob gathered.

"And to do that," Angela continued. "We need to first find a *sensible* Dearg."

Jacob raised an eyebrow. "Sensible?"

"Coherent, able to speak. Just because they are no longer human does not mean that they are incapable of thought or planning."

"Oh. That makes sense."

"And there are sure to be plenty out there tonight," said Clockwork. "Everyone will be inside, so only the Watchmen will be out there. If they see anyone, they will expect they are Vampires and shoot to kill. It has been the... unfortunate cause of some of the deaths in this city."

"That's... despicable," Jacob eventually was able to spit the last word out.

"That is how the Raven sees fit to deal with this situation." Clockwork said.

"Which is why we are also here to find out why." Angela said. "All these precautions, all these measures, are all too strange, even for an outbreak. A quarantine, I understand; you can never be too careful. But driving everyone into hysteria with no answers?" She shook her head, her white hair flowing like silver strands around her shoulders. "The sooner we capture a coherent Dearg, the easier it will be to find out what is going on here."

Clockwork then looked at the Dhampir. "Do you have an idea who this Immortal might be? You had come here first to help that one affected girl from Kurou Te."

"I have a hunch," Angela admitted. "But until we get out hands on a Dearg, I won't be able to find out if I am right or not just yet."

"Who do you *think* it is?"

Angela shook her head. "Let us pray I'm wrong."

Her tone was thickly blatant; clearly telling him that she wasn't going to discuss it any further than necessary; not until whatever suspicions she currently had were confirmed. Jacob wanted to press the matter more; telling Angela that she should trust him with the information she was keeping to herself, but the last thing he wanted was to make her angry again. He didn't want to start a fight in front of Clockwork again- or the wonderful Ava.

So instead, he asked a question that had come to mind while Angela was discussing the Nosferatu demon. "If Deargs or Disciples are just undead, therefore not possessed by the Nosferatu demon, does that mean that the souls of those people are untainted?"

"Think of them as dead," said Angela. "Say for example, you were bitten and died as a result. You would die, your spirit would go to Kawn and join the Stars or wherever your soul belongs after death. Your body however, would belong to a minor curse by the Nosferatu demon. Simply undead, but not the Jacob Tepes who is sitting in front of us right now."

That made Jacob feel a little better. Maybe that would make it easier to slay some Vampires tonight if that was going to happen.

Suddenly, Ava peeked her head into the candle-lit dining hall with a smile on her face. "Apologies, Daniel, but would you dearies like some cookies?"

"Cookies!" Clockwork chirped. "Sounds splendid! Come!" He beckoned to the two Hunters as he wheeled back and started for the kitchen. "Ava's cookies are to simply die for!"

"Thank you, but I must decline," Angela said politely. "I am not a huge fan of sweets."

"Oh," Ava said sounding almost disappointed. "Well, that is a shame. Jacob, would you like some?"

"Yes'm," Jacob said standing up. As he followed Clockwork towards the kitchen, he took one last look at Angela who started clearing away the table for Ava.

She had hardly touched her stew.

After the dishes were washed and dried, Clockwork assisted Ava to her bedroom to retire for the evening. Although she protested at first due to his handicap, the professor would not take no for an answer, leaving Angela and Jacob alone for the time being as he led her to the stairs.

The sun had disappeared behind the clouds long ago, but now it was starting to dip behind the walls of Irondell, and with it the activity seemed to go down as well. People were quickly returning to their homes, locking up their doors and barring up their windows. Cloves of garlic were hung by the windows, and crucifixes and many other religious artifacts were set around nearly every home. The Watchmen were already out with torches and lanterns in hand, ready for the long night ahead of them.

All of this, Jacob watched from afar next to the window. The glare of the setting sun pierced through the dirty glass, forcing him to squint his one good eye. With the dawn of nightfall upon him, Jacob could feel his bad eye beneath his patch throbbing slightly. It was worse tonight than any other night. Maybe it was because he was nervous, or maybe it was… something else.

"Relax," a voice said beside him and he nearly jumped at the sight of Angela. After Ava and Clockwork had left, she had laid across the couch to rest for a bit. She didn't look so well, and to now see her appear out of nowhere like this, and without a sound to boot, it startled him. "We'll take care of this."

"You feeling any better?" he asked returning his attention back to the window.

"There was nothing wrong."

"You looked sick."

A pause, consideration perhaps, and then, "There was garlic in the stew."

Jacob looked back at Angela with a confused expression. "So that thing, the way garlic affects Vampires, it's real?"

"It's minor, but yes. It stunk."

"That's all garlic is?"

"It is one of the most pungent natural herbs in the world. Vampires have stronger sense of sight, hearing, and smell. The smell of garlic to a Vampire, is like..." She paused, thinking of a good comparison.

"You don't need to explain." Jacob said. "I think I get it. Your senses are stronger, so you smell it stronger than I do."

"That's right." Angela sighed. "It's a horrible smell, but since I am partly human, I am able to endure it. Some Vampires are able to endure it as well, but it is very rare."

Jacob looked back at her. "It's kind of funny, the way you say that."

Those pools of lavender turned to Jacob, not hostilely, but curiously. "What do you mean?"

"That you are partly human. I don't know, it seems sort of... funny. Because you don't seem 'partly' human to me."

"Then you are blind," Angela said coldly.

"No! No, I don't mean to offend you, and if I had, I'm sorry. Just fascinates me how you say it like that."

"Why?"

"Because like I said, you don't seem partly human to me. You're just as human as I am."

"That doesn't mean anything, Jacob."

He frowned. "Why not?"

"It is because I'm not human. Not entirely. You don't have to be modest. I'm aware of what I am. I don't need you to remind me."

"I wasn't trying to-"

"Doesn't matter." Angela crossed her arms. An awkward silence followed for a few seconds, and then, "But you didn't offend me. So don't worry. Should I not feel natural stating the truth?"

Jacob was stumped. "I don't know. I just didn't think you'd be so casual about it."

"If a person with black skin tells you he or she is black, would you be so shocked then?" Angela asked this question almost like a parent the way the tone of her voice was so stern; telling Jacob to really think before he answered. "Or a person with white hair saying they're Noyiian? Or one with warts saying 'I have warts'?"

"Well... no," he answered. "But..."

"Then why are you shocked about the fact that I acknowledge about what I am?" She looked at him again. "I *am* aware of what I am, Jacob Tepes. There is no point in denying that I am not human, no matter how I 'seem,' as you put it."

She got him there. The fact that she used his last name as well, made Jacob feel even more foolish. "Wrong thing to say, I guess. I'm sorry. Open mouth, insert foot."

"Excuse me?" asked Angela.

"It's an expression. Mean's I said something stupid."

"Why don't you just say that?"

Jacob looked at her, debated whether not to explain what a figure of speech was. The confusion in her eyes were all too real though.

"Forget it," he said turning his attention back to the window. "Just... making conversation."

"Right," Angela said. She then suddenly snapped her head towards the entrance of the living room. When Jacob looked in the same direction, he was just in time to see Clockwork turn the corner.

"Ava is asleep," he announced. "Thank you, for your assistance with dinner tonight."

"It was our pleasure, sir," said Angela.

Clockwork looked over to the grandfather clock. "It's nearly five o'clock. Sunset will be official in about five 'til."

"Not all Vampires come immediately at sunset," Angela corrected the professor. "They are not animals set on a schedule, they will come out when they feel safe from the sun."

"I am sorry," Clockwork appearing uncomfortable. "I did not know you-"

"You know what," Jacob said stepping in. "I think we should take her word for it. In all honesty, it would make it easier for us to hunt for one, right?"

Though he was curious with what Angela meant by defending how the Vampires think and behaved, he didn't want to dwell on the matter any longer.

Thankfully, the professor had the same opinion. "Of course," Clockwork said with a bashful smile. "Forgive me, I didn't mean any disrespect."

"Do not worry, I take no offence." Though Angela said this with a polite tone, she looked at Jacob with a murderous rage. What had he done now?

"Very well," Clockwork said. He clapped his hands together. "Now, business. You both must take the back door, and pass through the gardens to get to the cisterns. Use them to transverse through the city without being seen by the Watchmen. Get what you need, and then come straight back here. I will prepare a room for you to hold the Vampire."

"Make sure we have *two* beds ready," Angela told him. "We may need a second."

"A second?" Clockwork asked just as confused as Jacob was. "May I ask why?"

"It may not be necessary. But I want to be sure." It was clear that Angela was not going to be saying more, and thankfully, Clockwork respected that.

"Very well then," the professor said. "Get what you need, and bring it back here. And one more thing: beware of the Raven. Though he hasn't been around, there have been whispers among the Watchmen. He's out there still. We don't know what he is up to, or how he is working for the good of the people, but he is out there. If you find him, I trust you will be careful when you investigate him as well."

"One thing at a time," Angela said. "But rest assured, we'll find out for certain." She then turned to Jacob, and said, "It's time to go."

Jacob readjusted the bow on his back and nodded. "Lead the way."

"Good luck," Clockwork said. "May Yohnah watch over you, and Good Hunting."

Within the depths of Irondell near the eastern and western walls, were the cisterns where the fresh snow and rainwater was set apart from all waste and sewage that would rush like a river down into the sewers beneath the streets and towers of stone. These cisterns were large gaping holes near the walls with many tanks and containers lining the stone walls in the shapes of women in robes holding up mighty bowls where this water would then flush into the water system and offer clean water to the people.

Beneath them, laid the sewer drains that would soak into the soft earth under hundreds of feet of stone. Many poor souls had fallen into these gaping mouths along the pavements beyond the iron-picketed fences despite both the fences and the warnings. Still, whether by accident or by heinous acts, many have still fallen into the depths only to remain among the wastes of the people of Irondell. The further down the drain your traveled, the deeper beneath the city you would go, and the further away from the sun you would become.

Outside, snow and ash from fires still burning fluttered into the sludge like leaves and watching the falling snow in the safety of the tunnel entrance while he fed, was a Vampire.

Markus... yes, that *was* his name. Sometimes he would forget. Since yesterday morning, he had nearly forgotten such a name. He had forgotten many things, and it would strain his brain to remember who he was. His clothes were blood-soaked and torn, now discarded so he now roamed naked without fear of either eyes or the elements.

That's right, he used to be a banker. They were probably wondering where he had been all day, but the sun... the cursed light, it burned his skin. It made him sick just seeing the rays outside the tunnel where he lied in wait. That was when the Watchman came, carrying a torch and a gun.

What was his name again? Think...

Markus!

That's right, Markus was afraid. He hid in the shadows, as the man trudged through the sludge, smelling of sweat and shit. The Watchman was looking for something, but what?

That was when the smell struck him. A flowing river, the roar of blood passing through the veins... Dear God Yohnah, the rushing... like a river. Markus could hear it. It was enough to make the man sick, it was.

He couldn't help himself. He had rushed the man, and bit him on the neck. The Watchman had started to scream, and Markus had panicked. In his fear, he snapped the man's neck to the side, killing him instantly. He had started to apologize, for a moment or two. But that was when the coppery, sweet taste like sugared honey trickled down his throat. He licked his lips, tasting the blood further and smelling it. The sweet stench, it was so enticing that apologies were no longer necessary. He was hungry, and as his instincts took over, Markus lowered himself to the man, and he drank.

He drank, and drank more despite having his fill. His gluttonous belly was gorged, and yet he wanted more. He was aroused by the blood, revitalized by the blood, better because of the blood. He had felt sick, the sun glaring at him like an angry eye; it was the blood that was curing his disease. Like alcohol used to be for him, the blood made all his problems and worry vanish like vapor, made everything better.

The view of the sun slowly fading away, would have made... Markus' heart thunder if he was still alive. He longed to go out into the city. He longed to go back home to his wife and daughter. What were their names again? They were... They...

Markus groaned in his blood-soaked throat. He could not remember. Try as he might, he could not remember, and instead continued to hunch over the body of the Watchman, naked and smothered with gore, drinking his fill and... and...

He froze. He had heard a splash; two of them. The splashes were then met with footsteps, trudging through the sludge. Afraid for his life that he might be found, Markus leapt back deeper into the tunnel, and hid behind one of the gargoyle statues holding up the ceiling of the sewer drain, sewage spilling from it's spout-like mouth.

He peeked around it like a prowler, keeping his eyes on the entrance as two figures emerged from the fading light. They had stopped at the body of the Watchman, and one had stooped low to inspect it. He could smell that one of them was a woman. The scent of her skin, the taste in the air as she moved, the moisture of her cunt. The other was male, no doubt. The difference in the stench of his sweat and his pheromones warned Markus that he was strong. Among the smell of sweat, he also smelled metal, gunpowder. What he did not smell however which the Watchman certainly had, was fear.

Deep within his instincts, Markus now felt fear. These were predators, not like the Watchman. The one with the woman however, he was a man, just as dangerous by his own scent. A bow was in his hand, and he watched his partner inspect the blood-drained body Markus had left behind, his head constantly swiveling in search of the perpetrator. The tracker, and the one to watch her back.

They were here for him! Yes, that was why they were here. They were friends with the Watchman, and have come to kill him.

No, Markus had done nothing wrong. He had done *nothing* wrong! "Away! Away!" he hissed not loud enough for them to hear. He did not want to be dragged out into the sun. He didn't want the stick the girl was plunging into the Watchman's heart to be in his own. He didn't want to be found out. He was a good man, a good husband and father! Did he have children? He couldn't remember. Who was his wife? Did he even have a wife?

My name...

He hissed to himself while feeling around on the shit-covered walkway lining the tunnel walls. Workers had been here before, rebuilding some of the collapsed tunnels. There were tools here. Tools... why did he need tools? His hand soon came across a hammer, and he took it in his hand with such a grip as he hid further back into the shadows. The two were coming in! They've come to take him away! He would not let them! He would return home! He had done nothing wrong! He lived in... he worked at...

His name... He no longer knew his name. All he knew was that he had to live. He had to survive, and pressing back against the walls of the sewer, the Vampire watched the two tread closer and closer.

He could hear the rush of blood again, and in his cold dead heart, he felt the need, the desire to drink again. He clenched the hammer tighter, and waited. He waited, and watched.

Angela had said nothing when she stabbed the dead Watchman in the heart before standing and venturing towards the sewers. The horrible stench nearly crippled her, but she kept her composure as she led Jacob and herself into the depths of Irondell.

The young Hunter however, had asked why she had staked the man.

"It prevents him from coming back," she explained. "Without a heart to reanimate the corpse, it cannot be brought back. He can rest in peace now, until someone finds him."

Somewhere outside the tunnel, inside the city, Angela heard a horrified cry followed by a gunshot. The sun was now down, and the Vampires would come out to meet the Watchmen marching along the streets. Taking the back alley and down the stone stairs to the wedge of the wall to make it to the sewer dump was nerve-wracking on its own, and it had caused even Jacob to be more alert. The man hardly let go of the arrow he had notched. Even inside the sewer where such a weapon might be useless, he still kept a firm grip on it, never letting up or letting go. He had to have been strong, to keep the bowstring taut like that for so long.

"I see…" Jacob finally said taking a peek behind them. "It's too quiet in here. I don't like it. Do you think-"

"Shh," Angela said trying to pick up the scent. Among the dirtied water and shit in the tunnel, her sharp nose caught the distinct smell of copper.

Blood.

The dead Watchman was proof enough that a Vampire was still lingering inside the tunnels. But how infected it was and how many were in here, she didn't have a clue. If there was ever a good place for them to be attacked, it was here. Though the tunnels themselves were lit with dim lanterns left on by someone earlier in the day, the sewers were dark. But even in darkness, Angela could see as if the sun was shining inside the tunnels. She continued to lead the way, as the two ventured deeper into the sewers of Irondell.

The tunnel was crafted elegantly, at least at some point in its life. Statues of gargoyles and other hellish beasts held up the tunnel walls, their mouths open to unleash water and sludge like spouts. The walkways on either side were covered in sludge and the lanterns set on the sides of the circular walls were flickering dimly, threatening to go out as the last of their oil were licked away by the flame inside. As the two ventured deeper and deeper, Angela could see them. Pairs of eyes, three of them, icy blue spheres with no pupils, all down the length of the sewer vain. The closest one, was hiding behind one of the statues, and he had something in his hand. If there was an ambush to come upon them, it would be now.

"Jacob," Angela said ready to give her orders to the young Hunter. Though she was still angry with him for his behavior in front of Clockwork, they were out here now, and such squabbles had to be set aside if they were to make it to the end of the vain. She reached over her shoulder, and grabbed ahold of her sword. "There are three of them in here."

"Where?" Jacob said his one eyes blinking blindly in the darkness. "Tell me."

"Stay behind me," she instructed. She ventured closer to the closet pair of eyes, steadily, oh so steadily. She could smell its breath, rancid and thick with the stench of blood. As she got closer, she saw it's body tense, as if it was contemplating whether to fight or flee. Whatever it decided, Angela would be ready.

And she was, as the creature suddenly unleashed a hellish scream and lunged for her swinging the makeshift weapon in his hand.

It happened so fast, that Jacob's own eye could not comprehend the ferocity in which Angela ducked beneath the lunging Vampire and upon spinning her cloak and shrouding her into deeper darkness, her sword was revealed and in one swift movement, the undead creature fell into the sludge screaming with his torso separated from the right shoulder to the left hip. There was only a small flash of blood and no resistance as it's sliced entrails erupted from the two halves. Angela had cut through the creature as easily as if she had cut a slab of butter with a dull knife.

She's fast! was his only thought as his eye adjusted to the darkness and he saw two more pairs of glowing blue eyes reflecting whatever light the lanterns could give. They were closing in fast on Angela, and he could hear their claws scraping the walls as they climbed like salamanders right towards her.

"Above you!" he shouted, and he took aim with his bow. He released it while aiming right between one of the pairs and he heard a scream that sounded like many souls screaming in agony. It resonated and echoed in the tunnels and just as quick, Angela plunged into the darkness and Jacob heard the wet crunching sound of bones shattering and the rendering of flesh as her sword cut through the creatures. He could not see what had happened, but as fast as the attack took place, it was suddenly over.

Jacob didn't move for a long time, breathing heavily and not allowing himself to relax until Angela stepped out into the light. There was a little blood on her strange sword, and with a swift flick of her wrist, it was made clean again; the strange teeth on one of the edges gleaming wickedly. All around her, some still and sometimes floating in the muck, were the bits and pieces of the slaughtered Vampires

"These all have different marks," Angela informed him, sheathing her weapon almost casually. "They were all infected by those already bitten."

"So, they are not the Dearg we are looking for?" Jacob asked, his heart still racing his body ready for action.

"Not yet. Though if we do not find one that we are looking for, then we will take the next one we have alive. We need to keep going, until we reach the center of the city. Until then, keep quiet and stick close."

She then started back towards the darkness without another word.

Still amazed by how fast and swift she dispatched the Vampires, Jacob eventually followed close behind, keeping a hand over his mouth as the smell of shit and decay and death grew stronger and stronger.

Te

Upon taking the ladder that Angela deemed appropriate, the two eventually ended up near the main entrance of the city, close to where the fountain Count Andrei had shown her during her time in Irondell before.

The two immediately closed the hatch leading down and then ducked behind an alleyway as some Watchmen came running past the fountain, their guns erupting in bullets and fire as another unholy scream pierced the otherwise silence. The falling snow continued to float softly among the embers of the burning crosses and bodies still hanging in the dirtied and trashed streets. After a long period, the screaming and gunfire had ceased, only to resume this time with the Watchmen themselves screaming in agony as their adversary attacked them once more.

The situation was indeed far worse than how it looked in the safety of the sickroom which has now near a mile from where the two were now. Angela saw bodies of men and women burnt and scorched black sitting against the walls and lying in the snow. The tall hollowed towers and buildings whistled in the cold winds, and the thundering toll of the bell tower in the far distance echoed like a bad omen. Every shop that Angela remembered seeing before was now barred up with wood, garlic cloves hanging by the also boarded windows. Light shone through every house, no doubt holding in some terrified citizens who dreaded the night. More cries, and screams echoed in the vast city, sending shivers down the spines of those unlucky enough to be left out on the night of the Watchmen's hunt.

"Come," she eventually said to Jacob. "We need to get up high."

The two transferred through the crooked and dirty alleyways, avoiding the main streets at all costs. But no matter where they went, what turns they took or what abandoned chariots and carriages they hid behind, they could never escape the watchful eyes of the guardians carved into the very buildings. Heroes and villains of the past, monsters and creatures of night, all watched with stony expressions at the duo who hid from the Watchmen and continued their hunt for the Vampires that Angela had in mind.

The narrow alleyways eventually led to an iron ladder leading up to the rooftop of a building that stood next to what looked like a bridge leading across a large gap of slums to the main road. There would no doubt be heavy foot traffic on the bridge itself, but Angela saw that within the sides of the carved bridge behind the many stone nuns praying for safe travels across the landmark, there was room for the two to slip beneath the watchful eyes unnoticed. She told Jacob to keep close, and the two began to climb up the cold ladder that bit into their palms to the bridge.

Johnathon Lawrence chuckled upon the spires of one of the towers close to the bell tower.

The tower itself, taller than the one close to the fountain, overlooked the entire city of Irondell and beyond the walls. The Vampire could see everything from the smoke that rose from one of the smaller churches, to the destroyed carriage upon the great bridge crossing over the slums. In his hand, he held the arm of a dead woman who was covered in blood.

The foolish thing had gone out in search for her husband, William. The Vampire knew the man's name, for the woman wouldn't stop screaming his name as he shredded her clothing and drained her of her precious blood. Having drank the last drop in her naked and frail body, having had his fun with the corpse all the way up here, he dropped it; allowing it to flail and fall, crashing down into the streets below. He had his fill, and yet was hungry for more.

This was a lot of fun; he did not understand why he was so worried before. Two days of evading the damned Watchmen, watching them scurry about like frightened rats looking for a cat, it was enough to drive him into a fit of ecstasy. Though he sat perched on the spire naked and covered in blood, the cold didn't bother his bare skin. He was simply having too much fun, and he didn't want to stop. The massive face of the clock behind him with the black beasts of stone glaring down at him, he prayed that his Master found what he was looking for in this dying city.

Johnathon turned his eyes to the main gates at the entrance to the city, and thought about maybe searching around there- maybe grabbing another bite to drink. Though he preferred the blood of young beautiful women, it never hurt to have the tart bite of soldier blood on his tongue. Still, it was always so grand to see a face he remembered having rejected him in life, to take what he had always wanted from them and then some was the greatest blessing he could have ever hoped for.

Still, as much as he enjoyed being a terror for the women he once knew, there were still too many Watchmen in Irondell. But there was more of *them* being made every single night. Before they knew it, the foolish Count would find his city overrun, and nothing could protect them from his Master's wrath. So, Johnathon tensed his legs upon the top of the roof, ready to leap down and head for the gates. Afterward, maybe he would pay Kirstein Anderson a visit, show her what he had become, and do everything he had ever wanted to do to her while they were growing up in school.

This, the soul of Johnathon thought, corrupted by the Nosferatu that made him what he was; one of the first Disciples chosen by The Master.

He caught something in the corner of his eye, and he turned to face the Great Bridge that crossed the cluster of buildings and slums. The bulky and practically useless thing was of course guarded by a mass of Watchmen with horses and guns that fired silver rounds. So many of Johnathon's brethren would normally keep their distance from the monstrosity of stone. But along the sides of the bridge, hidden among the many statues built into it, he saw movement.

Two figures, scaling along the side and crossing without being seen by the soldiers. At first, he thought they were members of the brethren, trying to find better hunting grounds without running into the Watchmen. But as he peered his glowing blue eyes towards the two, he saw that they were not dead, but alive, and judging by their attire, he made them out to be Hunters. He knew that the Count didn't call for any Hunters other than that Raven, and yet here they were. Were they hired by some poor soul within the city, or was it something else?

That was when Johnathon noticed something very peculiar about one of the Hunters. Beneath the hood she wore on her head, he saw a gleam of white on her head; hair white as snow. And beneath her bangs, he saw two orbs of purple that glowed bright and dangerous. With the realization of what the Huntress was, Johnathon hissed with the burning knowledge that came with the instinct that was given to him upon his baptism.

"Daystalker…" he whispered hatefully.

His eyes then lingered to one of the nearby towers close to the bridge itself. Some Watchmen were setting up a Gatling in order to provide cover-fire for the men hunting for the others. A smile stretched across Johnathon's blood-smeared face and sinking his claws into the brick of his tower, he began to scurry over to the three men; a dastardly idea swimming impatiently in his brain as he hurried.

Jacob refused to look down as he and Angela shimmied beneath the main railing of the Great Bridge.

Thankfully, the space behind the statues that held up the railing with lanterns in their hands provided the support he needed to take rests in between the gaps. He absolutely *hated* heights, and it amazed him how Angela acted so calm even from way up here. With her hood up, it was impossible to see her facial expressions. Above them, he heard the clopping of hooves and the clicking of boots striking stone. She was not kidding when she mentioned that the bridge might be heavily guarded. Now that they were higher up, the smoke rising from far below now choked Jacob of breath, making crossing the bridge all that more daunting.

"Just relax," Angela told him as she kept on going without even waiting for him. "It's not that high up."

"Maybe not for you," Jacob muttered under his breath. "The sooner we are off this thing the better."

"While we're moving," Angela said. "Please, next time shoot them in the heart. Shooting the head won't do anything but make them angrier- or in the very least leave them stunned. Silver can hurt a Vampire, but you need to make it a heart-shot if you want to kill them- or at least leave them in crippling pain. The only other way to kill a Vampire is to cut off its head if you cannot drive a stake or silver into it's heart. It will keep them from reanimating. If not, we can leave it to the Watchmen or the sun to finish the job."

"I'll keep that in mind," It was just too dark in the sewer; and everything happened so fast that Jacob didn't have time to consider such a thing. But he saved his breath, he didn't want to sound like he was complaining.

"By the way," he said instead. "What is it about silver that hurts the undead?"

"Not just undead, but any supernatural monsters or entities. No one understand for certain, whether it is a biological defect or something more... spiritual. Silver is also the most common metal used in the making of holy artifacts. Since silver is from the moon, it's an interesting contrast, considering it is the moon which bring out the undead and unholy creatures of the night. Though the moon is their friend, it is also their enemy."

"Interesting..." Jacob groaned taking another peek down. They were now at the mid-point of the bridge, and at its highest point. The talking made it easier for him, despite everything going on. "So if a Vampire's hand for example was cut by a steel sword, what would happen?"

"It would regenerate. Silver would prevent the wound from healing over for a course of time, which is why silver is used when hunting Vampires in the first place. Because if you cannot make the kill, you can seriously wound them and make it easier once you track it down again."

"I see," he said slipping behind yet another statue. "Since garlic obviously isn't your favorite scent, does silver have an effect on you as well?"

"Yes," Angela answered bluntly. "Despite being partly human, the compound metal can burn me, but it isn't as potent as it would be towards one of the undead. Physically, if you were to shoot me with one of your arrows, it would hurt only a little worse than iron-tipped arrow would. It would just take longer for me to heal."

She halted and turned an eye to Jacob. "Are you asking because you are curious or because you are trying to get under my skin?"

"In all honesty?" Jacob asked using her pause to catch up with her. "It makes it easier to get across this bloody thing."

Angela stared at him for a moment longer, and then turned her head in understanding. "I see."

"Very cautious, aren't you?" Jacob then asked. "About your business of your... you know."

"I just don't have a lot of people asking me such things," Angela said. "I'm not used to having a companion to worry about making it across bridges. It would have been so much easier if I had just come here alone."

Jacob frowned at that comment. "I that much of a burden to you?" he asked.

She didn't answer.

He prodded again. "You seriously think you could have done all of this on your own?"

"Yes," she said. "I've done it many times before, probably since before you were even born."

That struck another question into Jacob's brain. "How old are you anyway?"

"That is none of your business."

"I'm nineteen, so how old are you? You can tell me."

"I said that's none of your business. Ask me again, and I'll throw you off this bridge myself." Was it just Jacob, or did he see her pout at the mention of his own age?

Jacob smiled cockily at her evasions of his question. "Touchy," he muttered.

"I heard that," Angela said.

"What did I say then?" he challenged, eager for at least a little banter.

"Just remember that my sense of hearing is stronger than yours. I can hear you breathing right now, trying to calm yourself." A pause, and then, "I can even smell your breath as you smile through those rotted teeth of yours."

Jacob immediately clamped his mouth shut. "Rude."

She ignored him again.

"Can I ask at least one more thing?"

"If it has anything to do with me, then no."

Jacob thought of something else really quick. "Do you have any questions for *me*?"

"No."

At this point they were just a quarter of the way across when Angela suddenly stopped. She turned her head forward and Jacob nearly bumped right into her, causing him to forget his planned retort.

"What is it?" he asked. That was when he heard it. Gunshots, the sounds of metal clashing, and the screams of men in agony. He looked across the smoking buildings, but he couldn't see anything through the hazy blackness.

"What was that?" he whispered when he suddenly heard an ear-piercing screech that echoed across the city. The sound made his spine tingle, like a thousand fingernails scraping against a chalkboard. It reminded him of a bat that had flown close to his head and screeched at him, not as loud, but of a similar pitch. He winced at the sound when suddenly, Angela spun on her heel and grabbed ahold of him-

And the two plummeted off the bridge as the place they were originally standing on was struck with a rainfall of bullets. Chunks of splintering stone fell away and he heard the explosive cranking sound of a Gatling as he fell screaming in Angela's arms as the two suddenly turned in mid-air. They came to a crashing halt as Angela used her own body to take most of the impact of the fall onto a stray carriage left behind in one of the abandoned alleyways. The weight of them both crushed the cart, sending straw and pieces of fragmented wood sailing everywhere. Jacob turned his body so that he was hunched over Angela as the fragmented stone of the bridge came crashing down around them. A small chunk got him on the shoulder but otherwise they were okay.

He got up then, aware of how close he and Angela were, making sure he himself was alright before scrambling back up and checking on Angela who was groaning in pain.

"Are you alright?" he asked out of breath and wanting to feel her for any broken bones but too afraid to even dare. It had been risky keeping his body on top of hers to shield her from the debris but she didn't seem to care or notice.

Thankfully, the Huntress sat up rubbing the back of her hooded head. "I'm fine," she groaned. "It just hurt..."

The sound of the Gatling suddenly stopped, and the sharp scream pierced their ears again. Angela snapped her head up towards the buildings now towering above them, and Jacob even heard the shouting of men up above.

He was then suddenly aware of a great many screams, lower in pitch than the last one but there were many of them- and they sounded close.

"We got company," Angela said rolling off the crushed carriage and dropping to the ground. She grunted upon landing on her feet and Jacob knew instantly that she was injured.

"You're hurt!" he exclaimed slipping off the splintered wagon and landing next to her.

"Don't touch me," she warned him while reaching for her sword. "Get your bow out- if we get overrun, we're dead."

"Overrun?!" he demanded whipping out his bow and nocking an arrow between his fingers.

"That was a call for help…" Angela said her purple eyes darting back and forth between the many entrances to their location. "A Vampire shot as us, and knows we survived. He is calling for help."

Jacob didn't dare ask how she knew all of that but instead stood ready for the fight about to happen. He heard chuckling and scraping of nails, and it got louder and louder from all directions until it overcame the shouting of men up top.

"Here they come," Angela said gripping her sword tightly just as some of the creatures came crawling out of the woodwork and down the length of the surrounding buildings and pillars like invading spiders.

They looked human but Jacob could see their black nails in their hands and feet digging into the stone, their large fangs baring as they hissed at the two Hunters beneath them. Men, women, and even children all glared at them with cold blue eyes and snarling like wild beasts. Some had mere rags left of their clothing, while others had none at all. Some even had pointed ears and some were now missing their noses, their transformations further along than the rest. All bearing their teeth, their ugly faces wrinkling back with animalistic malice.

The Hunters were completely surrounded; and there was no way out.

"Don't get bit," Angela then told him. "If you are bitten by any of these Deargs, you are dead."

"No shit," Jacob said taking aim at the closest Vampire and releasing his arrow.

It flew straight and true before it pierced the creature's heart. An unholy scream escaped its lips as if fell the rest of the way down and crashed onto the pavement with a sickening *crunch*!

That was when the horde suddenly lunged with fangs bared and rolling tongues wriggling for the taste of blood.

Jacob released arrow after arrow as fast as he could. He watched as many of the undead horde dropped like flies and those that were on the ground were caught in mid-lunge before they could reach either him or Angela who charged right into the thickest of the ambush.

Jacob proceeded to leap aside as a Vampire landed right where he was standing. The creature snarled at him and came at him swinging what looked like a Watchman's sword. Jacob, using his bow to deflect the blow, hooked the string around the creature's neck and upon vaulting over it, he pulled back with all his might upon landing, severing the head at the shoulders in a sharp motion. He then crouched as he notched another arrow and proceeded to shoot at another Vampire coming at him, the blood that had coated the string flinging off as it snapped the arrow. Then reaching into his belt, he threw a silver throwing knife into the eye of another. The woman screamed and writhed as it clawed the silver out of its head. Angela was not exaggerating when she said that it would only make the creature's angrier.

Speaking of which, every time Jacob was able to even catch a glimpse of the Dhampir, all he could see was a blur of black and silver before a Vampire was immediately cut down, followed by another. With such speed and agility, Angela would close the distance between her and her target; her unique sword slicing through enemy after enemy with hardly any resistance at all. Every stab, every dagger thrown, and bullet or bolt fired from a gun or crossbow, it all happened with fluent movement that nearly represented dark water. The way the Dhampir fought was ferociously fast, and yet was as coordinated like a ballet dancer; never ceasing no matter how many foes were cut down, how many skulls were smashed in, how many hearts pierced.

Even spinning about and using her cape to startle a larger group Angela looked like a dark angel who would proceed to kick the undead away with the strength of a mighty Nephelim, and her sword sliced through flesh and bone with hardly any bloodshed as many of the horde fell dead at her feet. Jacob had noticed that when the Vampires were hacked apart, they were always cut across the chest or stabbed dead center where the heart is; if not that then their heads would go flying with their faces frozen in a silent scream.

One particularly brutal killing was when a large black man came at her snarling with a mouth that had split into four parts, it's tongue lashing wildly out like a snake. It's face was wrinkled back to appear more bat-like and it donned large inhuman ears that were pulled back like a cat's. It came for Angela, reaching for the Dhampir who ducked out of grasp and kicking out and forcing the left knee of the Vampire to bend in a way it was never meant to go. When it dropped to the floor, she stabbed it in the heart. It snarled and tried to grab at her again, and while it managed to grab both her arms, she held it down and pushed it to the ground before suddenly wrenching her sword upward and slicing the Vampire open from the chest all the way to it's weird mouth before standing back up and slicing another Vampire's head clean off. The first laid dead on the ground, it's head split in half and spilling brains that forced their way out to spill into the opened cavity of it's chest.

Before he knew it, there was only two Vampires left and with his arrow and her sword, both were brought down almost immediately; their screams echoing through the alley as they fell dying in agony.

But it wasn't yet over, for Angela was soon dropped on with a sword plunging right into her back. Jacob found himself merely staring in shock as the Dhampir's rampage suddenly halted as she dropped onto the ground as the attacker Vampire crushed her underfoot, his sword piercing her back and sending up a light squirt of blood which stained the steel. Chuckling like a little kid, it wrenched the sword out, now slick with gore. It then proceeded to lick the blood off the blade with a long purple tongue, shuddering at the taste.

"Oh… Daystalker… that's good, so good… Gah!" Where it's tongue had licked the blade, a long burn mark had appeared.

The sword it was made of silver.

Jacob turned and reached for an arrow, only to find that his quiver was empty. He had used them all to take down the many dead that were now littering the alley. The Vampire then turned it's bright eyes towards Jacob, and rose on it's haunches, still perched on Angela like a crow protecting a claimed corpse.

"Hunter…" it hissed stepping off and setting its bare feet into the blood-soaked street. It remained hunched, it's legs bent and ready to spring when ready. It hissed at him again, it's fangs stained pink from whatever or whoever it had just killed. As it began to circle around Jacob who tossed his bow aside and went for his two daggers, the creature's eyes lingered around the dead sprawled about in hacked pieces.

"Dead all over the shop…" it hissed disappointedly. "You'll be one of 'em, sooner or later." It then turned on him, and with another hiss, it's eyes glowed bright as it charged towards him at incredible speeds.

Jacob just barely managed to get both his daggers up to catch the attack as the Vampire swung his sword. The sound of silver clashing rang together loudly and the force behind the creature's attack nearly knocked Jacob back should he have not caught himself in time.

The Vampire swung at him again in a haphazard arc, this time going for the head. Jacob ducked and rolled out of harm's way, slicing behind the creature's legs and cutting open I'ts calves. It hissed angrily as a little blood pissed out and muscles were severed like taut ropes. Still, the creature spun on it's heels and swung it's sword again, the blade just barely slicing through Jacob's cloak. It then lunged for the wall it was facing and kicking off the stones, it sprang back towards Jacob and swung its sword in order to knock the Hunter down before tackling him to the ground.

Before the creature could bite him however, Jacob had managed to free one dagger from the sword and drive it right under the beast's chin. It growled and hissed as blood seeped from between its ruby-red lips. It then clawed at his face, cutting his cheek and Jacob rolled away, putting him on top of the beast as he held the arm holding the sword down and then with his other dagger began to stab repeatedly at the monster's face.

But the Vampire managed to get it's feet underneath the Hunter and with inhuman strength he was kicked off and sent sailing through the air before crashing into the wall behind him. His head smacked the stone and Jacob dropped like dead weight onto his side, the Vampire now trying to get up and pull the dagger stuck in it's now malformed face.

"You fuckin' *tosser*!" the Vampire snarled, his face cut up and sliced open from the dagger. His cheeks had thick slits spilling blood and he even one of his eyes had been driven out and now hanging by a tendon. It moved in on the hurt Jacob, its sword still in hand and a look of rage on his face. "I'll wring your scrawny little neck- Oh…. Argh…"

It had paused in step, clutching at it's face as if in terrible pain. Jacob was able to see the lower jaw splitting where his dagger had cut into, and the two lower halves seemed to try to stretch apart from each other, making the Vampire look like some humanoid bug that bled profusely from the malformed mouth.

Jacob was watching the creature with bleary concentration, but saw something past it. On her knees, her tongue licking up the blood that was on the ground, was Angela, and upon raising her head, he saw that her eyes were glowing brighter than before. He smiled and began chuckling. The Vampire noticed and stopped just a few feet away with a look of irritated confusion.

"What the fuck is so funny?" it demanded with a snarl, it's changing mouth momentarily closing together in order to form such a sentence.

"I'm gonna enjoy watching this…" Jacob groaned pushing himself up and getting comfortable just as Angela closed the distance between herself and the Vampire in less than a second. The creature realized too late as Angela grabbed the arm that held the sword and with a sharp turn of the hip, she had broken the humerus as easily as if she were breaking a branch off a mighty tree.

"Reaargh!" the Vampire squealed like a pig and spun about to claw at her with the other. Angela caught the fist with her other hand and then turning her wrist slightly, Jacob heard another bone snapping and the Vampire cried out just before Angela kicked out and snapped one of the legs backwards at the knee. The Vampire dropped and proceeded to try and kick at her but once again Angela was too quick; grabbing ahold of the foot and with the sword that the Vampire had used on her, she severed the leg right at the knee. Blood sprayed and the Vampire howled in agony as it writhed on the ground, it's limbs now entirely useless as Angela dropped him to the ground.

She then walked right past the wriggling thing and made her way over to Jacob. She then extended a hand out and helped Jacob to his feet. He nodded a thanks, noticing the blood that was now dripping from her torso.

"How are you…?" he asked still amazed that she was even up after taking a direct hit like that.

"I'm fine now," Angela said. "But we need to get back to the clinic so I can rest before I pass out from the blood loss."

"Argh… me arms… me arms…" the Vampire continued to groan as Angela turned and went to retrieve her sword. As she did so Jacob began to gather whatever arrows he could from the dead, the tips slathered with gore. All the while, the Vampire cursed them with venomous and vulgar threats.

"Fuckers! You damned Hunters! Daystalker! Daystalker! I hope you burn in hell!"

Angela sheathed her weapon, the wound in her back still spilling profusely and making Jacob worry even more. Even if she wasn't entirely human, that was a lot of blood to lose. She then turned and returned to the Vampire, who squirmed and tried to crawl away but only succeeded in squirming back and forth like a fetus forcibly removed before birth.

"No!" it snarled. "Stay away from me!"

But Angela stepped on its one remaining leg, making it cry out in pain as she continued to walk across its back and step on the back of it's head. Her prey now pinned down, she glared down with eyes full of dark rage.

"*This* is definitely the Dearg we want." she informed Jacob.

"Let's get him back then," Jacob said now picking up his now bloodied bow and hooking it across his back.

"Of course," Angela said and then planting a sharp heel into the back of the head, she knocked the Vampire out cold. She then grabbed ahold of his tattered clothing and hoisted it over her shoulder.

"Let's go," he said and started towards the exit.

"Hold on." Jacob said marching for her. "You're bleeding! We have to stop it."

"I'm fine."

"You're going to pass out!" he said reaching out to her but catching himself before his fingers made contact with her cloak. "At least let me wrap it up to slow it down. Who knows how horrible the wound is?"

Even as it came out of his mouth he knew it was a dumb question; Angela had been run through with a sword and smashed down into the ground. No one, not even someone like her should even be standing after receiving a terrible blow like that.

"I don't need it," Angela said still moving towards the exit of the alleyway. "We don't have time, we need to-"

Her words were cut off as she suddenly froze. That was when Jacob heard it as well; many footsteps rushing towards them as well as the barking of dogs. He was still buzzing with adrenaline from the sudden attack that he hadn't heard it before, and before he knew it the alleyway was completely blocked off by men in armor. They took aim at the two Hunters with their Blunderbusss and rifles while their dogs stayed at their feet, barking and snarling at the two and daring them to try and run.

They were now trapped, this time by the Watchmen who had heard the commotion.

"Holy shit!" one soldier exclaimed. "Look at all of 'em... they are all dead!"

"Are they?"

"Keep your guns on 'em! Don't move!"

"Wait, wait!" Jacob said raising his hands and flashing a charming smile. "I get it, we went past curfew, we understand gentlemen. We shouldn't have gone outside, we will return home immediately. We're sorry, truly we are!"

"What's that then?" demanded who might have been the leader of this particular group. He was indicating towards the body Angela was about to drag away.

"They might be Vampires, sir..." one man whispered.

"No, you bloody idiot! They are Hunters! The Black Hand! Look at that one's tattoo!"

"The Black Hand? I thought the Raven was in charge!"

"He was, *and* is. This has to be reported to the Count."

"Think we should bring them in?"

"No, they are too dangerous. We shouldn't..."

Jacob tuned the men out as he turned his head towards Angela, who stared at the men without saying a word. He could see that she was already working a plan, but nothing would work here. Not with her injury and with that many guns trained on them. Not without anyone else getting killed or hurt.

He smiled, and told her to relax. Then ignoring her glare that clearly told him to not do anything, he reached up to his eyepatch and lifted it up from his eye.

"My turn to save *you* this time," he said enjoying the look of shock and surprise on the Dhampir's face as she saw what he was hiding under his patch. Though he wished it would have never come to this, he had no choice; he turned his attention to the men before him and took a single step forward.

He felt his eye throbbing and his head hurt from the effect of his eye, but still he kept it still on all who looked at him as he acknowledged them all. The eye he had kept hidden beneath his eyepatch glowed bright red, capturing the attention of all before him as they were suddenly transfixed on him alone.

"Friends!" he said in a loud and proud voice. "You have all worked hard tonight, Irondell owes you plenty! However, there are more pressing matters to attend to as of now! All of you will let me and my friend go. You will turn around, and return to your original posts. You will not come after us until the sun is up and whatever Vampire you find is slain before you. Now all of you; you are dismissed!"

His red eye had flashed bright and red like a crimson camera-flash, and then suddenly the men went rigid; even the dogs stopped barking and became tranquil. The men then began to mutter as if they were in a dream, and they began to disperse. When their path was cleared, Jacob covered back his eye and turned back to Angela who was now staring at him with awe. The look on her face, needless to say, was priceless.

"Well," he said gesturing towards the mouth of the alleyway. "Lead the way, Madam."

Angela clamped her mouth shut and proceeded forward. She said nothing as she brushed past Jacob still dripping blood as she carried the Vampire over her shoulders. Deciding it best not to question her any further, Jacob followed close behind, his bow now out in order to protect her from anything else that came after her.

Thankfully, the Watchmen who walked among them in the streets paid them no heed, as if they weren't even there. Angela never once looked back, as if she had simply accepted what had happened; and she remained silent all the way back through town as they slipped out of sight of all Watchmen and took the backstreets back to Ava's Clinic.

They didn't run into another Vampire for the rest of the cold night.

Ti

William Blackwood had seen some horrible and strange things in his lifetime.

When he was a young boy, living in a small village before his family had moved to Irondell, he had seen a lot of crazy things that still offered no explanation even in his thirty years of life. Horrible and strange events that he longed to forget. Struggles and dangers to the farm that made a rabbit infestation or a starved bear look like nothing in comparison.

This last week alone, he had seen the most horrendous things happening to the very people he swore to protect, both by the Vampire Infestation and his own fellow Watchmen. The Count's orders made no sense, but he had carried them out all week in their constant search for more of the undead to assist the Raven who was hardly ever around anymore it seemed.

But tonight, he never would have believed he would run into that white-haired woman ever again. The Dhampir had returned, and she had backup.

After seeing what happened to the men down in the alley, William had debated whether to follow along the rooftops or even to just shoot them here and now, but every time he tried to raise his rifle, he found that he couldn't; as if it had become a heavy weight in his hands. So instead, he watched them as they walked through the streets among the Watchmen and simply slipped away again; his comrades not once seeming to register who they were at all. All the while carrying with them the naked and crippled form of a Vampire.

William didn't know what her partner did; what sort of witchcraft he had performed, but it frightened him just as much as the Dhampir *terrified* him. Just looking at her alone made his belly clench tightly due to their last encounter when had she fled the city.

This wasn't good... The Raven gave specific instructions that no one was allowed inside the city- or even out for the good of the realm. One of the Watchmen tried to let his own family back into the city after they had left to see their relatives and both him and his family were ordered to be burned at a stake. At first, the rest of the Watchmen including the citizens were outraged by this, especially William. But then Count Andrei backed up the Raven, telling them to fulfill their orders. The Count was on the Raven's side, and if he found out the Dhampir was back...

He had to tell him. He had to seek an audience with the Count who had been silent since the infestation truly began to spread, and tell him what he had seen. The right thing to do was to alert the higher powers of who was now in the city, whether they were truly on Irondell's side or not. He didn't know how the Raven in particular would react, but he had a good idea. What made William struggle and question what he was supposed to do now was the fact that the Dhampir really had slain a great many Vampires as easily as an army of men could. Her partner, whoever he was, only added to the numbers. They were clearly not Irondell's enemies, but would Andrei or the Raven think the same?

William did not know. He didn't know anything.

In the end, when he saw the two Hunters disappear from sight, he decided he would tell them. It was his duty as a soldier and a Watchman of Irondell; he *had* to tell them. He would go when the sun was up, and he retired from the morning shift instead of going to his wife first thing. He would return to her afterwards; he *had* to see the Count first.

It was the right thing to do; for the good of the realm.

By morning, Angela was now sitting in the sickroom with the Vampire they had captured. The creature was strapped down onto a cot with leather strappings and shackles, it's head strapped back across the forehead. With the sun up, it had placed itself into a deep hibernation-like trance to conserve energy and heal. Already it's limbs had regrown, much to Jacob's obvious displeasure of seeing it grow almost instantaneously, as if the Vampire had infant arms and legs that recreated bone and marrow and grew to it's original length. As it slept soundly, she studied it; studied the bite marks on its neck and taking blood samples of what was still inside the creature.

According to Ava, she knew the man as Johnathon Lawrence; a local warehouse worker and a kind man. It was hard for the old shut-in to see a familiar face turned to darkness, and Angela had consoled her. After all, it was Ava who assisted in bandaging Angela's side upon returning to the clinic.

As she was healed up, Jacob had been watching while cleaning his bow. He had even asked how she was still alive and she simply told him, "The blood on the ground helped heal me."

She could tell he wanted to talk more about the matter, but instead he had gone to sleep; tired from the night's prior events. Angela had watched him on the couch until he fell asleep, not once congratulating him on the work he'd done last night. The man *had* done good, but he still had a long way to go.

Having slept only a little bit, it was now early afternoon with the sun hidden behind a mask of clouds as more snow began to fall upon the city. The Watchmen were already beginning to clear out any Vampires hiding inside homes and buildings, and the citizens had come out as well; armed to the teeth wherever they went. From where she sat, Angela even saw riots break out in the streets; the people demanding Count Andrei's attention. They wanted the Raven, and they wanted him to fix the problem. In the light of day, the damage was inexcusable and unable to be covered up or hidden, and the people demanded answers that Angela doubted anyone would give.

The bite marks on Mr. Lawrence's neck were old, and even Professor Clockwork noticed that when he had come to assist Angela in her investigation.

"Incredible..." he had muttered while taking notes on the blood he had helped place in vials as he turned it in his hand. "Amazing, really, how long it takes for an Immortal to infect a human as opposed to a Common Vampire or Dearg as you mentioned..."

"Indeed."

But the time it took for the toxin in the bite wasn't the first and only clue that the man held; but what kind of bite it was. For Angela's hunch was unfortunately true, and she dreaded what the future may hold. Though she could see it, Clockwork had needed help with finding the bitemark because to the naked eye, it looked like the man hadn't been bitten at all.

But he was; he was bitten by an Immortal with needle-teeth.

"The same bite-marks as Akira of Kuroi Te?" Clockwork asked Angela, mesmerized at the sight of the bites under a scope given to him by Ava.

"That's right," the Huntress answered standing from her seat and pacing around the room. With her armor off and her torso covered with only a shirt with her bandage around her waist, the chilly air felt good on her body. The warmth of the fire downstairs would feel even better when they head down for dinner.

But food was the last thing on Angela's mind; if she was right about *who* the Immortal was...

"Though the bite is clearly different at least in size, they *are* needle-teeth."

"I'm still amazed that you can tell the difference." Clockwork said looking back at the Vampires neck. "They are so *small*! How does an Immortal feed so patiently?"

"It's how some choose to hide. It's a mutation brought upon themselves influenced by the Nosferatu spirit. Though the disadvantage of needle-teeth is that they are more fragile and easier to break, they *can* help the Immortal hide in public." Angela rubbed her eyes tiredly. "It would explain why he has been able to evade the Watchmen and the Raven. They are all probably just looking for normal visible fangs like the rest of the infected spread by the Dearg."

"Or simply shooting anyone out at night," Clockwork pointed out. "Like what nearly happened to you and Jacob."

Angela's cheek twitched at the reminder. "Yes, we uh… had a sort of falling."

"He mentioned how you and saved him," Clockwork pointed out taking ahold of the Vampires hand and feeling the cold veins beneath the skin. "I assume he did well after all that?"

"He was… sufficient."

In all honesty, Angela was glad he was there. If Jacob hadn't been there, she would have probably been in greater danger. It was of course nothing she couldn't handle on her own, but at the same time, she had allowed it to go out of hand. Never before had she been so careless, and she was determined not to let it happen again.

But what happened back at that alley… it still haunted Angela even now; nearly as much as the fact that they were dealing with a needle-toothed Immortal.

"Anyways, there is a connection to the Huntress Akira's condition, and Johnathon's here."

"About time you explain."

Angela looked up to see Jacob standing in the doorway. His own cloak and armor were off, and he was wearing a shirt and trousers. He leaned against the frame of the door with his arms crossed. He looked tired but determined. Alert.

"You know who we are dealing with," he stated. "Do you? Your hunch, you think you're right?"

Angela nodded, and she felt the eyes of both Jacob and Clockwork upon her, expecting her to answer. "I believe we are dealing with Count Josef Horla, half-brother of Takeshi Horla who had bitten Akira. The Immortal had come to Irondell in order to get to Akira, but saw that his brother had gotten to her already. I believe that Horla was still around, waiting for Akira to turn so that he could take her away, make her his eternal servant or perhaps a concubine."

"But now she is dead," Jacob said placing the pieces together to the best of his abilities. "And so now you think he's taking it out on the town?"

"That is what I'm hoping our friend here can clarify for us," Angela said looking back at the sleeping Johnathon. "I still hope I am wrong. Come sunset, we will know for sure and will be able to plan our next move."

"May I ask something?" Clockwork said peeling back the lip of Johnathon with a pen to observe the thin and sharp canines curving over the normal lower teeth.

"You may," Angela said taking her seat again but this time keeping clear of the table so that Clockwork can do his research.

"Josef Horla, the known Count in the East, he has been quiet for almost two-hundred years since the fall of the Pudidrac Nobility." Clockwork jotted down some notes and then continued. "For him to suddenly return like this and cause an *entire* city to fall into chaos… it is almost like it's said in the history books."

"What's this Pudidrac Nobility?" asked Jacob looking at Angela.

"A large coven of Immortals once tried to overthrow the Empire as it was winning the war against Noyii," said Angela. "They were trying to start their own country, and many Immortals actually owned lands and holds and even ruled over many people in Balkeñoir. Thanks to many great Hunts against the courts of Pudidrac, their leader, it has been disbanded. Many of the Immortals have either died or gone into hiding. Horla was one of them."

"Oh," said Jacob. "I've never heard about it."

"It's a rare discussion," said Clockwork. "A lot of folk wish to forget it. Can't say I blame 'em. Now, back to Horla pretty much taking over the city. All for the sake of a girl who is now dead. It seems a little… overboard, even for an Immortal. Why go through so much trouble? Doesn't he have better things to do? And even if he doesn't, what does he have to gain coming here now?"

"The Count is over a thousand years old, Angela said. "I can only assume that he was bored, and decided that the best way to start a show would be here. But… you are right, something *does* seem off about that. There has to be a greater purpose to this. No Immortal ever does something without a purpose, and revenge is a silly thing for them to carry out…"

"You say that like Immortals are noble or something," Jacob said stepping inside the sickroom.

"Forgive me if I am being ignorant again, but isn't an Immortal just a more powerful Vampire?"

"No. They believe in a high-standard set of rules and respect," Angela answered him. "If an Immortal owned an estate with many followers, they are usually respected and respectful like high-class aristocrats; as traditionally portrayed as. They believe that courtesy is a major virtue that must never leave them even after many years of longevity. Those who do not respect a fellow Immortal is considered what one might call 'savages' to an uncivilized member of society."

"That is kinda funny," Jacob said now resting against one of the shelves behind Clockwork so that he could face Angela. "A Vampire calling another a savage."

Angela shrugged. "That is just how they are. Since they live a long life, they simply believe in politeness and respect for their fellow man. There was once even a Hunter in the Black Hand who once took contracts for Immortals."

"Really?" Clockwork asked raising his eyes from his clipboard. He seemed just about as surprised as Jacob- as expected. "That's news to me. Velinar never mentioned it."

"What would the contracts be for?" Jacob asked, also deeply intrigued.

"Other Immortals who did them wrong, or even creatures that the Vampires find to be nuisances. As far as my knowledge goes, there was never a contract from an Immortal placed on a human. The most common bounties were placed on Witches and members of the Wildesding Cult."

"Wilda-what?" Jacob asked with a raised eyebrow.

"Wildesding," Clockwork explained. "It's a cult that practices black magic through the Demon Lord, Kawfka. It was made when the Empire was first formed and spread across Balkeñoir. They are a savage bunch determined to overthrow the government through anarchy and Witchcraft. They have been responsible for major attacks on small villages and war camps, and even Immortal estates. They are criminals known to the contribution to the Witches Covenant, studying Witchcraft in general, and committing atrocities of rape, theft, and murder. There are also some Ringleaders who are rumored to be Lycans."

"That's frightening..." Jacob said uneasily. This must have been the first time he had heard of the group. Angela wasn't at all surprised, the cult was very secretive and hardly ever showed themselves in major cities. They preferred to work in the shadows, and it had been beneficial to Angela in the past. They always appeared in the worst of times as well...

"Incredible," Clockwork eventually said, his attention now returned to the Dearg. "I never would have guessed any of that concerning Immortals. They really are incredible creatures. Please, tell me Angela, what else separates an Immortal from the Dearg we have before us? Or even the Common Vampires running amok? Their eyes, how they are blue like crystal, does it give them any advantage? Is it similar to actual Immortal Eyes?"

"Excuse me, sir?" Jacob then said pushing himself away from the wall. "Can you actually give me a minute with Angela? I'd like to talk to her really quick- alone."

"Oh! O-of course!" Clockwork placed his clipboard onto a table and then proceeded to show himself out; his rickety wheelchair wheels squeaking as he made his way out the door and pulled the door shut behind him.

With the professor gone, Jacob pulled a chair away from the wall and sat across the cot from Angela backwards, his arms draped across the backboard. He looked down at the sleeping creature, his mind lost in his own thoughts. Though he was annoying and cocky at times, Angela liked how serious he looked when he really put his mind to something and studied something with that intense blue eye of his- the other one hidden behind his eyepatch.

Di

"How are you feeling?" Jacob eventually asked after a minute or two of silence. It was a question that Angela had expected.

"I'm fine," she replied somewhat relieved that Jacob finally spoke instead of just sitting there, still as a statue. "You don't need to concern yourself with me. With the little blood from the alleyway, I will be fully healed by nightfall. This is nothing." She patted the bandage on her side as if she needed to show proof that she was unhurt.

Jacob nodded, understanding. "So, you *do* drink blood?" A blunt question, one that Angela was sure he had been wanting to confirm since he first met her. Everyone always did.

"I try not to," was her response.

"Why?"

Angela shook her head. "I don't want to be seen like that. I don't…"

How could she explain it? How can she explain what her instincts longed for, while at the same time what her contradicting desires were? How could she explain that while she still had that wanting of blood as any Vampiric being did, she did not want to indulge herself by increasing her strength from the blood of a human being. Because deep down, Angela wanted more than anything to simply *be* human, and yet understood that she would never be.

Seeming to understand where she was coming from, Jacob nodded, saying she didn't have to answer. He fell silent once again, leaving the two of them alone for a moment with their thoughts and the sleeping Dearg.

"Guess it was a good thing that guy wasn't human anymore," Jacob said in an attempt to lighten the mood.

"Can I ask you something?" Angela then asked, deciding to take control of the conversation this time. Though something was clearly on the young Hunter's mind, there was something on hers as well; and it had been bugging her all night.

Jacob looked at her with that confident smile of his. "Interested in *me* now, are we?"

Ignoring the comment, Angela continued. "That eye," she said pointing at the eyepatch. "Where did you get that?"

Jacob's smile remained on his face, though it now looked sad, like a child who knew he was caught concealing a secret and knew there was no point in denying it. The strained marks around his eyes told Angela just how touchy a subject this was.

"So, you know what it is, huh?" he asked.

Angela nodded. She very well *did* know what it was. The eye wasn't anything from a human. She remembered seeing it when he flipped off his eyepatch, revealing it to both her and the Watchmen last night. The iris was crimson-red like blood, and the sclera was as black as his pupil; and it glowed slightly just like Angela's own.

The eye was one that once belonged to an Immortal.

Jacob sighed, resting his head against his arm which still laid across the top of the chair. "Where do I even begin?"

"You don't have to answer if you do not want to," said Angela. She didn't expect him to do what she herself couldn't.

Jacob shook his head. "No, I'll tell you. I trust you."

A pain in Angela's chest. All the while Jacob thought about his story for a moment, while she sat patiently, allowing him to take his time. If he chose not to speak, she would respect that just as he did the same with her when she saw fit to cease his many questions last night.

"Well…" he eventually said. "I got it when I was a little kid. My mother was… not the most pleasant woman in the world. She was a member of the Witches Covenant, and my father was a warrior from a nearby village close to Elvendell. He was sacrificed in order to appease whatever pagan god she worshiped in order to gain her power. A little after her ritual, I was born. By then it was too late for her to join, because you cannot be pregnant and become a witch. They don't like children, except to eat them I suppose."

Angela nodded. She knew of the Witches rituals and traditions, what they sometimes had to do in order to release their spirits and gain supreme power. What they considered godly powers as ancient as Lunokean itself.

Jacob continued. "Growing up with just her and I, she used me as a test subject for all her spells and experiments. She got a big kick out of creating abominations out of the animals that lived in the woods with us."

Angela felt a fist close around her stomach where the sword had pierced her body. She had seen the aftermath of Witch workshops; all the dead animals and humans mutilated and practiced on for their spells; and even more locked in cages for sacrifices and the Stars know what else. To think of such a fate placed on a child… She wondered just how much Jacob had endured, and how it had affected him even today behind that smile of his.

"One such experiment, happened to be this one." Jacob pointed to his covered eye. "Mother-dearest plucked my eye out like a fruit off a tree, and while casting a spell, fused this one into me. I didn't know what kind of eye it was at first, but I eventually found that it was capable of hypnosis as long as I looked into the eyes of another. After it was put in, she forced me to practice on rabbits, forcing them to rip each other's throats out. It got worse, when she captured travelers in the woods…"

Angela noticed that Jacob was now clenching his fist- the very one that he always kept a glove on.

"Is that another thing she's done?" Angela asked her eyes lingering away from the glove back to Jacob.

Jacob slipped his hand out of sight with a small smile. "Yes," he admitted stiffly. "Though, it is only the second out of the few experiments that were actually considered 'successful'. The rest only left traumatizing pain. But I'm okay now."

"I can't imagine it being at all easy for you," Angela said softly.

"It wasn't. The Empire eventually came through, after the old hag had already… passed away. Though, when they saw me, and what she had done to me, they thought I was a lost cause. They were ordered to kill me.

But not having it in their hearts, they left me in the woods to die. It wasn't until much later when some Bell-Ringers came through to meditate, and they took me to their church back in Elvendell. While I was there, the people feared me, called me the Son of a Witch, the Demon Child; oh how especially cruel the kids were."

Jacob chuckled humorlessly. "But the Bell-Ringers, they were kind to me. Taught me about the faith in Yohnah, how to read, write, and even how to shoot a bow. They were more my parents than my own ever were..."

"I'm so sorry," Angela said which surprised even her. What was this she felt for the man? Pity? Sympathy? Did she *really* feel sorry for him? Such a terrible fate placed upon a child... She understood that sort of pain very well. What kind of horrible acts did his mother perform on him, and how has that not changed him for the worst? Even now, Jacob still put on that smile; like a mask hiding the terror his body really was.

Jacob nodded, grateful for her words. "Thank you." He chuckled then. "You know, I never told anyone about that before. What happened to me, I mean. That is just the icing on the cake. Feels good to talk about it though."

"I'm glad," said Angela, unsure of what to say now.

"I guess... this means you and I have more in common than you thought, right?"

Right on the spot, as if he had read her mind.

"... Maybe." Angela admitted.

She wasn't experimented on, but she knew what it was like to be called a monster; to be left behind and forgotten; forsaken by man and tortured by the ones who called themselves your guardians. But Jacob... he has had his own struggles as well. He was… not close, but something like her.

"Kinda creepy, isn't it?" Jacob said. "Having the eye of an Immortal, huh?"

"Not at all," Angela said. "It just… caught me off guard." Why did she feel the need to defend such a ridiculous notion?

"Heh, sure," Jacob said, that smile still bright and confident. Just what happened to him, that made him the way he is now? He was annoying. Childish. Why hasn't his past destroyed him like it should have?

"I guess this means the cat is out of the bag," he continued raising both hands up as if in surrender. "You're working with a cursed man. I know that you're probably going to do whatever you want, but, if possible, I'd like to keep this a secret between us. I don't want to…"

"I understand," Angela assured him. "Don't worry, I'll keep your secret." *Not like I could tell anyone anyway. I wonder if Velinar knows…*

"Thank you," Jacob said with that smile still on his face, like he knew she would have said 'yes.' "I really appreciate that."

"You shouldn't be so concerned though. What happened, what your mother did, it has nothing on you as a person."

"Others don't look at it that way," Jacob said with a chuckle. "They just see what they wanna see and make of it what they please. Besides, if that was *really* the case, then why does it bother you so much when the others don't even know *you* as a person?"

Angela looked away. Though she has accepted what she was and knew that her blood didn't define her, that didn't matter to the others. In their eyes, she was simply just a monster; nothing more, nothing less. Jacob had good reason to be cautious. That didn't make it right, but it was the way the world was.

"Anyways. You *sure* you're going to be okay?" he then asked again. "With your injury and all?"

"I'll be fine. Really, you don't have to worry about me."

"I can't help it," Jacob said. "When you grabbed me and took the impact of the fall, I was worried about you. When you got stabbed, I…"

"I'm fine," she told him again. "Don't worry, time is all I need."

"And…" Jacob caught himself before he said it, but Angela knew what he was thinking: Blood.

"Right," she said stiffly. She looked out the window, as smoke continued to rise in the sky.

It would be worse tonight. Much worse. She couldn't afford to make a mistake this time. It was foolish to let her guard down after crashing into the horse carriage. She only made it worse by letting Jacob nearly get killed.

One thing that wouldn't shake away from her mind no matter what she did was the thought that if Jacob hadn't been there, there was that slim chance that she would have been killed right there on the spot. More than likely she would be able to muscle her way out, but Jacob made it a lot easier to do so. But at the same time, he was still in danger. He was in a city he didn't know that well, on a hunt he wasn't fully trained for.

Tonight, there would be no mistakes. She couldn't get hurt even for him. No one could afford to get hurt now.

"Look, uh," Jacob asked scratching the back of his head and making his ponytail sway slightly. "There's another reason why I wanted to pull you aside."

Angela looked at him, waiting for him to continue.

"When you drank the blood of that Vampire... won't that affect you?"

"No. Since I was born from an Immortal, I cannot be affected by the cursed blood. If anything, the blood only has a foul taste to it and nothing more. Bites don't make me turn into the undead either, although it does drain me of strength like silver. I don't understand why though."

Jacob nodded. "Then... if I may ask... have you ever bitten anyone... *human*?"

Angela knew that was coming. It was a question everyone who saw her feared; and rightfully so. She had rumors told about her about it, and the unknown fear that everyone tied her with her relations to the Immortals and Vampires everywhere. Though she never was asked the question herself before now, for no one dared to ask and would rather assume, she was still cautious about telling Jacob of all people.

But he *did* help her, and trusted her with his own dark secret, so she figured she owed him.

"Yes."

Jacob nodded, as if he knew the answer already. "Do you have to?"

Do you have to. Not *did* you have to. Not did you have to feed on the Vampire's blood, it was a more personal question: *Do* you have to drink blood at all?

"No," Angela replied. "A Vampire needs to feed on blood at *least* once a night in order to survive. An Immortal can go for a month without blood. But for Dhampirs... we don't *need* blood to survive. It's sort of... It's not a *necessity*. Blood is like wine to the spawn of the undead. Some are drunks who need it often, like Deargs and common Vampires, and then there are some who can live without it, like me. Unfortunately, the desire for blood is just like wine to humans; addicting. There have been many times when the temptation creeps up on me like a hungry wolf."

"I see..." Jacob said. "How many times?"

"Three. Once when I was just a child, and twice more before I joined the Black Hand."

"Anyone *in* the organization?"

"No. Never."

Jacob nodded. Angela couldn't tell if he believed her or not. "So blood is like a healing serum to Dhampir's, and a necessary life-force for Vampires."

"That's correct."

Jacob nodded once again, putting every piece of the puzzle together. "I see." He looked back at Angela, a serious look in that blue eye of his. "Have you ever drank someone's blood since?"

"Not from a human."

"Then how… never mind." He decided against whatever question he had before. "And the people you've bitten… what happened to them?"

"As far as I know, two of them are still alive and well. The other, I killed intentionally."

"Intentionally…" he repeated. "They didn't turn?"

"No. A human cannot be turned into a Vampire by a Dhampir. There is no toxin in the saliva of Dhampirs. I've made sure of that." Even as she said that, Angela realized that sounded very defensive when she answered that last question.

"I've upset you with asking you these questions." Jacob pointed out, noticing her tone as well.

"And I've upset you." Angela said. "It is just what everyone fears; I *do* drink blood, though I prefer not to. I've been clean of human blood for nearly ten years."

"That's good… Is it hard?"

"As hard as it is for an alcoholic to let go of wine."

"Alright," Jacob said clearly having his troubles cleared. He didn't trust her; as he shouldn't. She was just what everyone calls her: a monster.

"Well then," he then said suddenly, that smile reappearing on his face like a magic trick, as if nothing had ever happened. "You promise to keep my secret, and I'll keep yours."

Angela blinked at him. "Aren't you afraid?"

"Afraid of what?"

Angela stared at him. When he gestured for her to elaborate, she simply said, "You know what I'm talking about."

"What's there to be afraid of?" Jacob asked. "I trust you."

"Why?"

Jacob shrugged. "I just do. I mean, if I can't trust you after saving my life, then what would be the point of you saving me?"

"You shouldn't."

"Shouldn't what?"

"Trust me."

"Why?"

Angela squirmed in her seat, suddenly uncomfortable with what was being asked now. For so long she had kept a cold demeanor about herself; indifferent and uncaring. The walls she had built around her kingdom in order to protect it. But now, it was as if a sheet was removed from her body, revealing everything and leaving her naked and vulnerable.

She hated this feeling. Hated feeling like an opened book, with no privacy or that she was being scrutinized or watched. But at the same time, she felt... strange.

"No one should trust me. I am what everyone fears me to be: the spawn of an Immortal, one who consumes the blood of Man and dwell in the twilight between night and day. I do not belong anywhere, and I am not wanted by anyone, human, of Vampiric."

"I do," Jacob said sternly, rendering Angela speechless in her seat. He cleared his throat and elaborated. "*I* want you. You say you don't have anyone, or any*where* to go to. You barely know me, I know. But you have me. You and I aren't that different. You and I might be partners on this Hunt, but I'd like to think of you as a friend as well."

A friend… "Why would you want that from a creature like me?"

"Because A: you're not a creature. I don't see any extra eyes or fur or anything threatening. And B: I trust you," Jacob said with that damned smile of his. "Just like you *should* trust me. All jokes aside, my behavior at the castle included when I sort of barged in on you… You saved my life, Angela. Because of that, I trust you. And I don't just trust for free. I only hope that… I only hope that I can earn your trust as well."

Earn. Not give me your trust, but let me earn it. Don't just trust me now, because like me, you shouldn't trust for free. But give me that chance to earn your trust. That's what Jacob was telling Angela, and for the seconds that passed since his hope or declaration, she felt a slight twinge of that very same hope deep in her gut. She had not felt like this for a long time. Not since she was a child. Not since…

It happened so suddenly that Angela nearly gasped. She had a vision; a flash of an unknown future coming before her. This happened irregularly; often she had control of whether or not she wanted to see the immediate future, often in combat or to gain insight on decisions she had to make. It was how she was able to figure out what the sounds had been before the Gatling had gone off.

But sometimes her eyes showed her more than the immediate future. Sometimes whether by the hand of Yohnah or something or someone else, she was able to look into the future and see what often at times can never be changed. A future set in stone, written by a precursor neither good nor evil.

Her lavender eyes flashed, and in that millisecond, she saw Jacob but not the Jacob *now*.

She saw Jacob's face, but it was in anguish; blood splattered as he laid in a pool of it. *His* blood. He was wounded in what looked like a church with the glass depiction of Yohnah glaring down at him with brilliant color. What she saw, was his death. Why she was seeing it now, she did not know. Maybe it was by some coincidence based on what he said, but she still didn't know and when she opened her eyes again, she looked at Jacob who was now closer; a look of concern on his face.

"You okay?" he asked.

The image flashed through her mind again and Angela suppressed it, snuffing it out as she would the flame of a candle. "It's nothing."

Visions like this had come before, but not like this. It felt so real, like she was really there. That was the curse of her bloodline; her fathers' eyes, the power of clairvoyance. What she saw this time had unnerved her, and Jacob hadn't failed to see it.

"It didn't *look* like nothing," he said. "Your eyes flashed bright like a camera and then you suddenly gasped as if you were having a heart attack." He reached out with a cautious hand. "You sure you're-"

"I'm fine!" she said standing suddenly and taking a step back from him. "Just... don't come near me, okay? Don't touch me."

Jacob looked hurt at this, but he respected her space. "I'm sorry, I couldn't help it. I was worried. I thought you were-"

"I'm *fine*," she said again more sternly this time, almost defensively. She wanted more than anything to erase the vision that still played over and over again in her head like trick candles for a birthday cake. Jacob was overstepping his boundaries, and she had to make sure it was clear for him to understand. They might have a few things in common, but they were *nothing* alike. He had no idea the torment she had dealt with, nor did she understand his own. It was best to keep it like that, and keep this relationship as *partners* only.

After this Hunt, they would return to the castle and go their separate ways. Never again would she work with this man. Whether the vision would come true or not, she didn't care. She would finish this job, and get them both home before never agreeing to do a job with him again.

She had made up her mind. Jacob opened his mouth to say something but then the door opened again, and a worried Clockwork emerged.

"Pardon the intrusion," he said looking greatly disturbed. "But you both need to come downstairs- now." The urgency in his voice was clear as day, and the two Hunters wasted no time following and helping Clockwork down the stairs. The two let the conversation slip away; but they were far from being done with this.

But work came first; and their client needed them, now.

Do

After helping Clockwork back in his chair at the bottom of the staircase, Jacob followed him and Angela into the living room where Ava was tinkering with an old radio set. The cryptic thing looked to be nearly a hundred years old as she tried to bring back whatever signal she'd obviously found.

As the three waited patiently, Jacob stole another glance at Angela.

So, she *did* drink blood, but not from a human in a long time. Not only that, but her bite was not toxic and couldn't turn a human into a Vampire. As far as Jacob was concerned, she was just as safe if not safer than any other Hunter he had worked with before he met the Black Hand.

But she was still cautious of him, and he supposed he couldn't blame her. This was probably the first time she actually talked about herself like this and not get treated poorly. The two of them had similar ideals in terms of secrets, as well as their own reasons, so they had at least that much in common. They both understood what it was like to be left behind and treated like an outcast among their supposed fellow man. What he had confided in her and what she was obviously unwilling to speak of as well, was the fact that they had both been abused in some way shape or form, which undoubtedly led to the way they both were today.

However, Angela's walls had been built up high in order to protect herself. Jacob didn't know everything that she had gone through that made her as careful as she was now, but it was not his place to pry. His job was to Hunt with her, and keep her safe. After what happened last night, watching her get stabbed, he couldn't bear to see such a thing happen again. Tonight, when they found out where they had to go Hunting, he would make sure he didn't mess around. He would protect *her* this time; and prove to her that he *can* be trusted.

Because he trusted her with his very life.

"Come on…" Ava muttered and cursed while shorting some wires together to make a spark. The crystal in the radio suddenly was alit with life and a garbled voice came in on the speakers. "This is it!" she hissed victoriously. "Quiet!"

"… this message will repeat in a moment," the Radio buzzed. A burst of static ensued, and then, "People of Irondell…" Jacob noticed that Angela stiffened at the voice. "This is Count Andrei, here to give you an update on the purge of the Vampire Menace in our great city. First off, the Empire is stationed outside and making sure that the horrible plague does not spread out to the rest of the country."

That infuriated Jacob to no end. "What a crock of-"

"Shut up," Angela said sternly though she didn't look at him as the broadcast continued.

"The threat is still very high, and all citizens are asked to continue to cooperate and do all the tests that the Watchmen give you. Failure to do so will result in you being detained, and regardless of if you turn out not to be one of the undead, you will be punished *severely*.

"What kind of tests?" Jacob asked quickly as the Count paused.

"A candle test," Angela answered just as fast. "Looking into mouths or eyes is too dangerous to check for Vampirism. The easiest way is to shine a light or candle at the person. If they have no shadow, they are a Vampire. If they do, then they are human."

Jacob looked at the ground at Angela's feet. Though the candle and lamplight were dim, she *did* have a shadow, but it was faint; dimmer than the others.

"... of all," the Count's voice continued. "I have some grave news. It appears that there is a Dhampir on the loose in our great city; aiding the Vampires in their taking over of the city. As she is able to walk among the daylight immune and unstoppable to pursue her bloodlust, all citizens are asked to keep a clear distance from her. The she-demon has pale white hair, and eyes bright and purple. She has a slender figure and will most likely be garbed in black attire. It is told that she has an accomplice with her, and both are armed and *very* dangerous. All Watchmen are directed to shoot on sight, and any citizens with any information regarding the creature must report to the Watchmen immediately. Until both the Dhampir and the rest of the Vampire scourge is eliminated, everyone please remain indoors at night and no matter how many times you are begged to open the door or window, *keep it locked*. The fate of your lives as well as the future of Irondell rests in your cooperation. Thank you, and may Yohnah have mercy on us... This message will repeat in a-"

"That's a crock of bullshit." Jacob said speaking over the radio as Ava went to turn it down. "How did they even know we are here? We made sure we weren't spotted. I..."

He didn't need to explain further. The agreed plan was to not tell Clockwork or Ava about Jacob's trick of hypnotism. As far as Jacob himself was concerned, he was sure he took extra precautions to make sure that the Watchmen didn't remember them. So, who spotted them?

"It doesn't matter," Angela said turning about and started pacing across the floor in thought. Her footsteps were so silent it was as if she was walking on air like a mystical wraith. "It just means we need to be more careful when we go out tonight."

"Where do you plan to go now?" Ava asked turning in her chair.

"We just need to hope our 'friend' upstairs knows," Angela said stopping at the bookshelf and turning to face the others before her. "How often do the Watchmen perform checks on this clinic usually?"

"Around fourteen or fifteen o'clock," Ava replied. "They don't check it every day though, not enough people."

"We had it all planned out with Velinar to avoid the Watch and get you out after curfew," Clockwork added.

"I see..." Angela said. "And that's a guarantee that they won't come upstairs?"

"They haven't before," Ava replied.

"Yes, but that might change," Jacob pointed out. "If they know there is a Dhampir hiding among them, they might be extra cautious."

"There are a lot of homes in Irondell," Clockwork pointed out.

"Nevertheless, we should take extra precautions. Which means we need to find a way to hide the Vampire and hide *you* most of all." Jacob said this looking at Angela. "Your white hair just gives it away."

Angela gave him a look, that was neither kind nor angry. It was not even a look of annoyance, but a warning. She was telling him to keep his mouth shut, and not speak anymore; that *she* was in charge, not him.

"You're right," she relented at last. She then turned to Ava. "Do you have any... extra space by chance? Closets, cupboards, maybe even an alcove?"

"Actually, I just might," Ava said standing up. "Follow me, Dearie." She led Angela out of the living room, leaving Jacob alone with Clockwork. Jacob rubbed his one good eye, the urge to smoke strong now as this day seemed to drag on. It felt like one thing after the other; he never felt so tired in his life. Not on any hunt for local change or even an actual Hunt for a beast left him feeling so fatigued. Maybe it was when he smacked his head, or maybe it was the way Angela looked at him with those eyes.

It was funny, actually. So many things happening all at once, and his thoughts always seemed to return to her.

"Forgive me for prying," Jacob's thoughts were broken into by Professor Clockwork's words. "But is everything alright with you and Angela? When I came in, I could tell something was very wrong between you two."

"What gave it away?" Jacob asked him sarcastically. "Just a feeling, or catching her strangling me against the wall?"

Clockwork chuckled humorlessly. "Just by how you are acting now, actually."

"You a psychic now?" Jacob immediately regretted asking such a question. "I'm sorry, I was rude. Forgive me, Professor. I just... I got a lot on my mind is all. We are fine though, to answer your question. We cleared it all up, I'm sure."

He reached into his pocket and removed a packet of cigarettes. He placed one into his mouth and considered lighting it, but just having it in his mouth for now was enough.

Clockwork nodded understandably, and then with the front of his shirt he began to clean his monocle. "I understand. Being a Hunter is dangerous business, it leaves you wary. I should know."

"You used to be a Hunter?"

"Once upon a time. I was a freelancer; I didn't join any guild or organization. I was asked to, by both Velinar and even the Ravens, but I refused. Still, Velinar and I became good friends, even after I lost the use of my legs."

"What happened?" Jacob asked, intrigued to know the backstory of the magnificent Professor Daniel Clockwork who helped invent the locomotive as well as many other incredible inventions.

"Werewolf attack," the Professor said, pausing for a moment as if he was reliving the distant memory. "I shot the beast just as it tackled me. We fell off the train but that didn't stop him from ripping my legs off as we tumbled apart from each other. My old partner, if she hadn't been there, I would have drowned in the river. Even today, many years later, I still feel so tired like I have been up all night, tracking beasts and then killing them. The Hunting business is not a pretty workload. You have to have a lot of trust in your partners, and keep your wits about you; even if you know that that one Hunt just might be your last."

He looked back up and smiled at Jacob. "We used to fight a lot too. Just like you and Angela."

"Yeah?"

"Well, she never once did slam me against a wall, but, yeah. But that just means that your partnership is growing."

Jacob couldn't help but laugh. "I don't know about that."

"Well, whatever it is that's going on, just keep an eye on her," Clockwork told him placing his monocle over his eye again. "I may not be a Dhampir, but having to work alone before I met my partner, I know that it takes time to adjust: watching someone else's back and trusting that someone watch yours. It's something that is learned, not taught."

Jacob smiled. "I'll keep that in mind, thank you."

The front door suddenly rattled as a heavy fist slammed against it, making a hollowed booming sound. "Watchmen. Open up!"

"Shit," Jacob swore, removing his cigarette and standing up to take a peek out the window through the curtains. There were three men in total with one holding a burning lamp. The rest had their guns ready, waiting impatiently by the door. Thankfully, there was no dogs. But the girls were still upstairs...

"We got trouble."

"Brilliant deduction," Clockwork muttered. "Coming!" he called out and then turned to Jacob. "Distract them. Keep 'em down here for as long as we can, see?"

"What about-"

"A Dhampir's hearing is superior to ours. Let us hope that she can hear what goes on down here. But just in case, speak loud and clear, but not suspiciously."

The door was banged on again and Clockwork wheeled over angrily. "Comin'!" he shouted, and he turned the knob before wheeling back to open in. At this point, Jacob had returned to his seat just as Ava came slowly down the stairs.

The three Watchmen came in, all with wearied looks on their faces. Their eyes remained sharp however, as they looked at the three before them.

"Home-check," one man said with a mustache. He leaned against the far wall when suddenly the other turned on the light and shined it over Clockwork, who shielded his eyes in pain.

"Blimey, turn that down a bit willya?"

"Shadow," the man with the lamp announced then turning to Ava. He shined it at her as well, making her also shield her eyes. "Clear." He then looked to Jacob and gave him a funny look. "I don't recognize you..."

Jacob was suddenly glad that he didn't have his armor or cloak on. To be safe, he kept his gloved hand over the other in order to hide his Black Hand tattoo. "New in town," he said. "Moved in about... three weeks or so ago to help me sweet mum." He gestured to Ava who thankfully nodded in agreement.

"Where you from?" the man at the wall asked as his partner shined the light in Jacob's face. He didn't even flinch as the light glared into his one good eye.

"Elvendell," he made sure to say it loud enough, just in case.

"You a long way from home," said the other who had been quiet since their arrival.

"Back home now," Jacob answered.

"Hmph," Mustache said without caring. "Why weren't you here yesterday or the day before?"

"You missed me, I guess."

"Hmm. You all seem clean."

"Would you dears like some tea?" Ava offered. "Before you go?"

"We aren't done, Madam," the one with the light said starting for the stairs. "We have to do a full-house search.,

"Wait just a moment," Ava said holding up her arms and blocking the man. "What's this all about?"

"New protocol, Madam," Mustache said simply. "We are to check the entire premise to make sure there are no Vampires here."

"Only Professor Clockwork and I are here, as well as my son," Ava said with a huff. "If there was anyone else in my clinic, I think I would know. I might be old, but I ain't blind."

Jacob had to hand it to the old shut-in. She was actually very convincing.

"Regardless," the one Ava had stopped said in a gruff voice. "Will you allow us to search, or will we have to force you?" There was a bored tone in his voice, like he had to say it multiple times already today.

Ava let out a huff, making sure it was clear how much she displeased this. "Fine. But I go with you."

"Not alone," the other man said coming up. "I will be with him."

"I'll stay down here," Mustache said, and his two companions followed Ava up the stairs.

Jacob could hear their footsteps above his head as well as the scraping of what had to have been the doors dragging across the floor. Meanwhile, Mustache marched through the ground floor, checking every nook and cranny that was visible. He didn't bother to check the cabinets, which Jacob thought was funny. If he was a Vampire, he certainty would have tucked himself into any tight space he could find in order to keep out of the sunlight and out of sight from the Watchmen.

These guys... this whole operation really was just a huge joke.

"How goes the Hunt out there?" he asked the man from where he sat. "Killed more of the bastards today?"

Mustache grunted in reply. "More heads on pikes than I'd like to count. People I once shared drinks with, women I've shared beds with, friends I once played in the streets with. All now with their heads on poles with garlic stuffed behind their damned teeth."

Jacob nodded. At least the Watchmen were doing at least *something* right.

"And the Raven?" he then asked. "How goes his own hunt for the one responsible?"

"Ha," Mustache laughed out loud as he emerged from the kitchen. "That stupid wanker ain't been around all week except for maybe a situation at the church. But tonight, he might actually get his arse out there. 'Bout damn time if you ask me."

That definitely caught Jacob's attention. "He finally doing something, eh? Good to know. What makes him decide to finally come out and help us now?"

"Didn't you hear the broadcast?"

"Didn't you hear Ava?" Jacob turned the question around. "We didn't know you guys had to perform full searches now." There was still movement upstairs, and Jacob started to get anxious though he remained calm in front of Mustache who crossed the room and took his original position by the door.

"Right," he said. "Apparently, there is a Dhampir out here now. That is about as much trouble as an Immortal."

"A Dhampir?" Jacob asked trying to sound convincing. "What's that? Another monster?"

"Jeez, are ya *daft*, man?" the man sighed. "No, I suppose you're not. A Dhampir is a filthy spawn of a human and Vampire. What sane person would ever fuck one of the undead? The world's gone mad I say. Now we have to deal with those Daystalkers as well as the undead at night. They are almost as bad as Immortals, mate, if not worse. Imagine, a leech who ain't afraid of the sunlight."

If not worse…

Jacob felt anger when he heard those words, yet he still smiled and nodded. "I suppose they are. That truly is frightening to think about."

"Aye," the man agreed, and he turned towards the stairs as the footsteps drew near. Soon, both the two men and Ava emerged and came downstairs to meet the rest.

"All clear, sir," both men said almost in unison.

"Good," Mustache said opening the door to let them out. "Let's go." With his men now out the door, the leader nodded to Ava. "Goodnight Miss, goodnight Professor." He then turned his eyes to Jacob, and nodded as well. "Stay indoors, folks."

With that he stepped out and closed the door behind him, leaving the three now alone in the living room and sighing with relief.

"That was close..." Ava gasped.

"Where is Angela?" Jacob immediately asked. His heart was slamming in his chest the entire time the Watchmen were here, and it still didn't slow down even in the slightest.

"I dunno," Ava admitted with raised hands. "I was shocked myself when we found the room empty. I don't-"

"I'm right here."

They all whirled towards the stairs to see Angela coming down them as quiet as a mouse. The Dhampir had that stern look on her face and Jacob wondered if she had heard what the leader had said. "I was hiding in the rafters with the body tucked behind the shelving. They didn't even bother to look up."

"Incredible!" Ava exclaimed. "I thought you squeezed in there with him!"

"No. He is back on the table now."

And in almost no time at all nor a sound to be heard... it truly was incredible, to say the least. Jacob sighed in deep relief, his heart finally starting to slow down a few beats.

"Well, all is well then," Clockwork said finally relaxing in his wheelchair. "So, what now?"

"Hopefully, all we have to do is wait now." Angela turned to Jacob again, those bright eyes piercing him through like daggers. "Rest while you can. Come upstairs as soon as the sun sets." Without even waiting for another word, Angela turned and started back up the stairs as silent as ever.

"Would you both be eating dinner?" Ava asked.

"Please," Angela said. "We'll help out afterwards as well, before we go. We'll be leaving a little later tonight." And when she reached the top of the stairs, Angela turned the corner and disappeared from view.

"She doesn't expect to rest up there, does she?" Clockwork asked.

"Well, we *do* have a Vampire up there," Jacob reasoned. "I'm sure she is just keeping watch."

"As for you," Ava said as stern as a mother. "You rest up best you can. You didn't sleep all night, and you've been up all morning. Sleep, and I'll wake you at sundown."

"I appreciate that, thank you." Jacob's eye lingered towards the stairs again, but he turned his body so that it fit into the length of the couch. He then draped one arm over his face to cover his eyes, and the other he tucked behind his head as he tried to fall asleep.

It did not come to him soon enough, but the sounds of Ava rummaging in the kitchen and Clockwork wheeling about and occasionally typing in a typewriter were more soothing than the sounds he heard coming from outside. When he actually *did* fall asleep, Jacob was already hating the night, and fearing what the moon would bring on their next Hunt.

More importantly, he wondered just how Angela herself was doing, and it was the last thought in his head before he disappeared into the realm of the Flutemaster, and her land of dreams.

Di

Angela sat in one of the chairs in the sickroom, not sleeping but watching the Vampire.

When he awoke, he will be fully capable of fighting, and might resist against the many straps and restraints holding him on the cot. Angela had also taken the extra precaution to stuff gauze into the Vampire's mouth and taped over to prevent it from screaming and calling for help again.

There were still hours to go, and so, Angela waited with her arms crossed and legs curled over one another. Downstairs, she heard the boiling of water and smelled the vegetables that Ava was chopping up for whatever supper she had in store for the group. She heard Clockwork typing something downstairs on a typewriter, and she heard the slow breaths of Jacob as he slept. The entire home was kept busy, while Angela waited in solitude until the Vampire before he woke up.

As she waited, she allowed her mind to wander and collect all the data she and Jacob had gathered while here in Irondell. They still had no legitimate proof that Count Josef Horla was the cause of this outbreak; and to be honest, Angela *hoped* that wasn't the case. Not only that, but what the Watchmen told Jacob downstairs, about the Raven finally coming out tonight, *that* might pose a larger threat. Why would he come out only for Angela, when an Immortal was obviously hiding among them? If the Dearg can tell them at least *who* was the cause, then she and Jacob could probably try and infiltrate the castle, and from there find out if there was any area inside the city itself that the Immortal could be hiding.

It would be dangerous, and if the Raven was out there, both Angela and Jacob's life could be in danger.

She wouldn't slip up tonight. It might actually even be better if Jacob didn't come at all with her to the castle. But maybe if they split up…

Angela didn't know how long she had been sitting, thinking, and waiting, but eventually she heard thick, labored breathing, and her eyes turned to the Vampire lying on the cot. It's bony chest rose and fell unevenly, it's pale torso filling with air for the first time in the last few hours. Behind her, the sun had set behind the walls and the horizon beyond, and night had finally fallen over Irondell.

At that same moment, Angela heard heavy boots climbing the stairs and was not surprised when Jacob slipped inside the sickroom, closing the door behind him. Though he had slept for a good three hours, his eye was dark and baggy. Still, despite how tired he appeared, he still flashed that irritatingly confident smile. Angela caught herself glaring at the young Hunter who either didn't care or didn't notice. What had happened earlier still troubled her greatly, and only reenforced her plans for the evening.

"Is he waking up?" Jacob asked watching the Dearg who was now breathing slightly quicker- rapidly actually, as if his body was trying its damnedest to get air into its blood and getting its undead heart to beat once again.

"Slowly," Angela said standing up and walking over to the cot. "You may take a seat, or you can stick close by." Her hand lingered over to a small table, where she and

Clockwork had formulated a collection of concoctions just for the Vampire as soon as he woke up. Among these vials of different liquids and tools that lined up alongside what they had made using Ava's herbs and medicinal drugs, there was a small bowl of blood.

Her blood. A reward for the Vampire, should he choose to cooperate; though she didn't tell Jacob this but she could tell that the Hunter had noticed the crimson liquid in the glass bowl.

"Just let me know if you need help, Jacob said crossing the room and leaning against the shelving so that he could have a clear view of the Dearg and give Angela space as waited patiently as the Vampire finally woke up.

His eyes fluttered slightly, and then opened up slowly to reveal black and blue orbs. He blinked once, and sniffed, taking in the new environment around him. When his eyes lingered towards Angela, he immediately started to thrash on the cot. It shook with his might, and he tried shrieking through the gauze, but it held his voice firm. Running her hand along the tools of silver, Angela chose the scalpel and held it up to the candlelight, and immediately, the Vampire ceased struggling, his eyes widened as it looked at the Dhampir standing beside it with absolute hatred.

"Hello, Johnathon Lawrence," she said speaking to him in a soft tone. "You've finally awakened."

Johnathon said nothing, either because he thought there was no point in talking, or because he physically couldn't. Angela ran the scalpel softly across the Dearg's chest. Though the blade didn't penetrate his skin, it left a thin rash like she was running a rose thorn over his body.

The Vampire's eyes narrowed at the discomfort but otherwise made no sound. It's pointed ears turned back like a cat showing displeasure or annoyance.

"I have some questions for you," Angela continued. "And you are going to answer. If you make a sound *other* than answering the questions, I will make sure you scream for your lord to save you."

She paused for a moment, letting her words sink into the creature. She then reached out with nimble fingers, and upon taking the tape off the Vampire's lips, pulled the gauze out of his mouth. Johnathon licked his lips with a tongue that was much longer, taking care not to prick himself with his fangs while he moistened his ruby mouth. His lower jaw which had split like a pair of mandibles last night had closed up again, making his mouth appear otherwise normal.

"Who do you serve?" Angela demanded, her face looming over his like the moon; her hair tumbling over her shoulders gently. "Who took your lifeforce, and made you a Disciple?"

"Go to hell, Daystalker," Johnathon said with a hiss, baring his fangs defiantly. "I've got *nothing* to say to you."

Angela shoved the gauze back into the Vampire's mouth, covering it with her palm for good measure. Johnathon had managed to nick her fingers with his fangs but she ignored the pain. Then with the scalpel in her free hand, she sliced open a thin cut in the creature's shoulder. Johnathon grunted in pain but then he screamed in pure agony as Angela took a bottle of Holy Water and poured it into the wound. Smoke hissed from the cut and the water burned the flesh around the wound itself. Johnathon's scream was loud, but the gauze prevented it from escaping the sickroom. No one could hear him; no one *would* hear him. The smell of the burning wound was nothing like burning flesh which Jacob distinctly remember comparing it to a whole pig being roasted on a spit. Burning humans gave off the sickly sweet odor of cooked pork.

This smell, it was revolting, the smell of sickness and decay burning after a horrible plague. It was death, it was the smell of fire and brimstone and everything beyond the depths of the foulest of Oblivion.

When he finally calmed down, Angela dug the gauze out and allowed the Vampire to breathe. She then placed a hand on his face, hovering her thumb mere millimeters over his left eye.

"Do not waste my time," Angela told him. "You know how this will end for you. However, I have the power to put an end to your curse quickly and painlessly, or I can do it slowly and inflict terrible agony. Either you tell my partner and I what we want to know, or we will stay here all night."

She leaned closer, her bright eyes burning into Johnathon's own, letting him know that she wasn't bluffing. "Who, cursed, you?" she asked again, enunciating each and every word slowly.

"You goddamn *shitblood*..." Johnathon hissed. "You're a traitor to your own kind!"

"I'm not of your kind," Angela said. "Now answer my question."

"I'll never give up my master!" Johnathon snarled, his face momentarily morphed into a face that was both human and bat-like, the nose squashed and wrinkled and the pointed ears appeared more prominent.

He then took a deep breath to scream but Angela was much too fast for him. She covered his mouth with one hand and with the other, the one with the thumb hovering over his eye, plunged it in. The Vampire screamed as Angela flicked her thumb upward after digging deep under the eye and the eyeball popped out, dangling by a strand of tendon which started to pull it back like a snake seizing prey into it's lair. Again, Angela was fast, seizing the scalpel and severing the eye from it's host, causing Johnathon to scream out once again. When he had begun to calm down, hissing and groaning at the pain that was burning in his empty eye socket, which cried tears of blood, Angela took the momentary calm to swap the scalpel with a pair of pliers off the table she clamped them onto one of his fangs.

With wide eyes, Johnathon could only watch as she ripped it right out of his mouth, spilling out blood and making him scream loudly before she clamped her other hand over his mouth to prevent someone else from hearing it. No doubt someone or something already had, but no one human was going to go poking around, and unless they were invited in, no Vampire was going to be coming into Ava's clinic.

"The fangs are always the most difficult to pull out…" Angela said observing the bloody fang in her tool. "But that won't be a problem for me. We can take our sweet time, and if you happen to grow them back somehow, we'll take those too."

She kept her hand plastered over Johnathon's mouth until the Dearg calmed down again. When he did, she removed her hand now speckled with blood and she sat the pliers onto the table. She then took a syringe full of a pale, yellow liquid that represented light-colored piss.

"Who cursed you?"

"Cunting bitch..." Johnathon muttered hatefully.

"Who?" she demanded again. She was growing impatient; the night was young still, but they were wasting too much time. She held the syringe up to the light, her unvocal threat hanging in the air.

Johnathon growled in his throat, wanting desperately to keep his master a secret, but dreading the thought of Angela taking something else of his again. He knew that if this went on, she would make sure he stayed alive long enough to tell her what happened. Then, and only then, would he have her permission to die. He knew it, she could see it in his undead eyes.

With a surrendered sigh, he relented, his face shifting back to something almost human, despite the pointed ears and fangs and those horrible blue eyes. "Master Horla... Josef, Horla. Master, forgive me..."

Angela frowned, her fears confirmed at last. She could feel the weight of Jacob's eye on her, probably thinking the same thing she was.

With a sigh, Angela sat back and rubbed her eyes. "Alright. Why is he here?"

Johnathon hesitated, and Angela showed him the syringe again to get him to talk. "He came for *her*... that Huntress."

"Akira?"

"That's her… We all know of her. Some of us saw her, on our way back to the land of the living. I saw her myself. Such a shame, such a pretty whore for the Master."

"Akira is dead. So why is Horla still around?"

Johnathon hissed, as if even he himself hated the answer. "That Raven… Horla wants him."

"Then why doesn't he just negotiate with the Count?" Angela asked.

"He tried. But… the bastard declined the Master's deal, and now this city will suffer until the Raven emerges from his hiding place."

Angela frowned, disturbed. So, Count Andrei *knew* that Horla was back, and yet he defied the Immortal in order to protect the Raven, who was *supposed* to be hunting for the Immortal but instead was not noticed as often as he should have been. Angela could not think of anything more stupid that a man of power could have done in a situation such as this.

Granted, the man probably meant well, but to defy an Immortal without the aid of the Empire, was simply foolish. Also, there was the Raven as well, not doing his job properly. If the Raven was behind Andrei deciding to defy Horla, then *he* was the cause of all of this. The moment he killed Akira, he had sealed his fate as far as the Immortal was concerned. Is *that* why the Raven had gone into hiding until tonight?

If all the Count wanted was the Raven, then maybe there was a chance to stop this bloodshed. At least, Angela hoped.

"Where is he?" she demanded of the Dearg. "Where is Count Horla?"

Johnathon shook his head desperately. "I cannot tell you."

"Wrong answer." Angela stuck the syringe into Johnathon's arm and placed her thumb right over the plunger top.

"Wait!" Johnathon shrieked almost too loudly. "I cannot tell you, because I don't know! He doesn't share this with us. Many have asked to see him, and he doesn't tell us. I was just told to go make more Disciples in his name, and find the Raven!"

"And you haven't found him yet?" Jacob asked, speaking out for the first time since the interrogation started.

"Does it *look* like I've found him, you stupid prick?"

Johnathon snapped his teeth together in frustration. Angela noticed a hair-thin line appearing in the center of the Vampire's chin. It grew up his jawline and covered the chin, reaching up to the lower lip which seemed to split momentarily like a small but perfectly symmetrical harelip. It was going to happen again, she could tell.

"No, not yet," Johnathon confided, seeming not to notice the minor change in his lower jaw. "*No* one has seen him, and there is too much security at the castle to search there. So, we've just been increasing in numbers. By this time tomorrow if not by morning, we'll have enough brothers and sisters to storm the castle and tear the place apart until we find him."

He giggled then, seeming to tremble with sudden excitement. "Then Horla will reward us all greatly after we take over Irondell! A city for the undead! What a thought!"

"Indeed," Angela said. "But you know that will never work. Once the Empire realizes that the situation has gone out of control, they would simply bomb the city and you all would burn."

"Never! The Night shall always conquer the Day!"

"We don't have time to argue," Angela said seizing the Dearg's throat and making him choke. The tendons in the Vampire's neck bulged as she squeezed, her fingers clenching tighter and tighter. She kept her other hand ready on the syringe, her eyes glowing bright and dangerous. "Where is Horla?"

"I don't know!" Johnathon choked. "I swear on my life!"

"Your life isn't worth shit," Jacob said coming up and ready to say something else. Angela merely silenced him with a stern glare.

"I *really* don't know!" Johnathon insisted. "As soon as I was sent out, he disappeared!"

Angela thought about it for a second. "You've been *everywhere* in this city?"

"Yes!"

"And the others?"

"We've searched everywhere. Everywhere but the castle like I said."

Angela sighed. "One more question: Did you *choose* this fate? To become one of Horla's pawns?"

Johnathon frowned as if confused by the question. In fact, his cat-like eyes seemed to dilate further for a brief moment before returning to their deathly glare.

"No. No… not at first. But then… I felt no pain. Just… nothing. And then hunger. Bloody, terrible hunger. But then, I found the blood. The glorious blood. That was when he found me."

"Horla?"

"Yes. He found me, and told me to find the Raven."

"Very well." Angela removed her hand from the Vampire's throat, and the syringe from his arm. She then scooped up the bowl of blood and tilted it over to his mouth. Johnathon sniffed, and his eyes widened with disbelief.

Angela gestured with the bowl. "Drink. You have fulfilled your purpose. Gratitude is in order."

Johnathon's mouth suddenly split open, and Jacob gasped in horror. It was as if the chin and jawline were really too half's, extending out to either side like a pair of bony mandibles. His tongue wriggled out and reached for the bowl, but Angela pulled her hand back.

"Compose yourself," she commanded.

The jaws closed back as if they had not changed at all. The jaw looked human again. Johnathon sneered impatiently, his features turning that of a bat's again before he forced himself to relax. He gulped and then moving his lips closer to the blood in a more calmly fashion, he whispered to the Dhampir.

"You would… offer this to me?" His tongue slithered out again, and almost touched the surface of the blood.

"No." Too fast to be seen, in one quick motion, Angela plunged a wooden stake right into the Vampire's chest, piercing his heart and sending out a spray of blood all over her hand.

At that moment, just barely able to have one last taste of blood, Johnathon let loose a harrowing screech that shattered every glass bottle inside the sick room, and could have easily shattered the windows if Angela had not grabbed ahold of the man's mouth, the bowl meeting the same fate as the glass bottles and vials.

Johnathon stared at the Dhampir holding him down, his eyes begging her the question: *Why?*

Angela gave no reply, but merely stared back into those eyes glared sharply and the jaws split once more, pulling away from the hand that tried to contain it and Johnathon made one last effort to bite the Dhampir. Angela only drove the stake deeper into the chest, avoiding the Vampire's lunge as the life slowly slipped away from the undead body. When Johnathon finally fell silent, she stepped back as the skin of the Vampire turned ashen-gray. It then began to fall away like soot, and then the bones, until there was nothing left but a pile of ash on the cot; the Dearg dead for good.

"Holy shit..." Jacob groaned while digging his fingers into his ears to alleviate the pain. "That was loud..."

A knock on the door sounded, and Ava asked behind it if everything was okay. "We're fine." Angela called out. "Don't come in yet. We'll be out soon." She did not speak again, until Ava's footsteps walked away and disappeared from the door.

She looked at Jacob. "After we eat, we go. Grab your gear, and get downstairs, now." With a turn, she started for the chest where she had stored her armor and weapons. "And we do not talk about this; to anyone."

"Angela," Jacob said, trying to shake the gruesome image from his head. "What happened to him? His mouth…"

"Sometimes Vampires go through a sort sudden mutation. A reaction sometimes completed under great stress or a desire. Not all Vampires can do that, only Deargs and other abominations. It's… it's an old remnant of the true form of the Vampire."

"Oh…" Deciding to leave the matter alone at least for the time being, Jacob instead asked next, "Do you know where we are going?"

Angela knew, but she told Jacob to wait until it was time to go. They had no time to lose. They had to eat quickly, and slip out into the night before it was too late. If the Raven was all Horla wanted, then it was time to find him and give the Immortal what he wanted. There was no guarantee that it would save the city, but Angela was willing to at least try, for now.

Because the Raven would be out tonight, looking for her.

After scarfing down some bread and barley soup, Jacob and Angela slipped out the back once again and started to make their way through the sewers just as they had before.

There were a few Vampires in there, particularly some women who were nuzzling some naked corpses of men who happened to be Watchmen. Seeing the women naked and bloody as if they had escaped the womb disturbed Jacob, but that didn't stop neither him nor Angela from cutting them all down like the vermin they were.

Watching them all fall apart in chunks sickened him, and the smell of the sewers only made it worse. It was even worse when a child only five or six years old came out of the muck and snarled at them, baring fangs and claws. Angela severed the child in two where the heart should be, and that was the end of that. She scolded Jacob for not taking the shot when he had the chance.

"It was a kid," he argued. "A little kid!"

"Age makes no difference," she told him. "A Vampire is a Vampire. There's nothing human in them anymore."

Angela said nothing else throughout the rest of the tunnels, and so Jacob took it as a sign that he was doing something right. Though the ordeal left him splattered with gore, he wasn't as frightened as he had been yesterday. Last night, he didn't know a thing about hunting Vampires, and tonight he was more confident. He didn't lose his head when he had been tackled by another Vampiric child and had to resort to knifing the little boy until he was sure the creature was dead.

Children... *children* were also involved in all of this, and even though he was still breathing, Jacob felt only dread after all of this.

Still, he pushed on and didn't allow his own thoughts get in the way of doing what was necessary. Angela remained silent, even as Jacob rammed a wooden stake into the child's heart, a sign that he was doing decent tonight and didn't need correcting. With his knives back in his belt and his bow in hand, he continued to follow the Dhampir and upon reaching the ladder Angela wanted, they climbed back up to the main street, this time closer to the fountain area in the town square. They were by the smaller clock tower that stood tall and black, ringing the seventh hour.

Near the fountain, there were more bodies hanging on burning crosses, and scattered around the scorched corpses were many heads placed on spikes. Blood had soaked all the snow and stones, and it looked like a body was laying belly-up in the fountain itself, the blood churning and turning the water pink. Some Watchmen on horses were torturing a Vampire to death, poking it with pikes of steel and shooting her in the knees with silver bullets. It wasn't until she was spilling her guts onto the street when one of the men came up and beheaded the creature, stabbing her in the heart for good measure. He then proceeded to hold the severed head up high like a trophy, and continued to mutilate its once beautiful face while his men laughed.

"That's despicable..." Jacob muttered. He could only imagine what Angela was feeling.

"That is how a Hunt is," she said simply. "Bloody, and monstrous. The lust for blood is strong, even in humans. The smell, the sight, it is sometimes never enough to satisfy humans just like the creatures they hunt, so they spill more. Humankind really are violent creatures when they have to be- and worse when it comes to Vampires both old and young."

Jacob looked at the Dhampir, wondering if she had forgotten he was there.

"Come," she finally said turning back towards the alley behind the clock. "We need to keep moving."

Following her close, the two then climbed up to the rooftops and out of sight. They were soon on top of a nearby bakery, overlooking the mist-filled street below which occasionally lit up with gunshots. Anguish screams echoed through one of the houses, and in the far distance, smoke belched from a burning home. It seemed like it was a lot worse tonight than the last, and Jacob felt sick to his stomach. Gripping his bow tight, he followed Angela to the edge where she was overlooking another clearing near the church, and beyond the house of worship, Irondell Castle.

The castle stood up like a massive cathedral of stone as black as night. Standing tall over the city, its shadow shrouded half of the buildings from where the two Hunters stood. Tall towers stood up like spikes from the large building, and monstrous creatures appeared to have been carved in the sides. Thin bridges passed between the towers, all leading up to a single monolith that stood high above the rest like a beacon. The flag of Irondell wavered in the winter winds, the horse sigil practically torn by the harsh weather.

A great many soldiers marched along the bridges between the towers, and even more stood by the main gates that broke off into the large streets of the inner cities. A moat had to have been around the castle, for no building was too close to the towers of terrifying beauty.

"There's a lot of guards around the castle grounds..." Jacob looked around the buildings to see that they didn't go any further than the gates themselves, leaving everywhere else vacant like a ghost town from an old story. "You plan to go in there?"

"I do," Angela answered. "And you will stay right here."

"What?" Jacob demanded looking at the Dhampir incredulously. "You can't go in there alone."

"I can, and I will. You, will, stay, here." She pronounced each syllable clearly and sternly, as if she was scolding a child instead of a fellow Hunter. Her eyes illuminated the inside of her hood, though she didn't look mad or upset. She was simply giving instructions, nothing more and nothing less.

"No way," Jacob said not taking that for an answer. "I'm sorry, but we go in together or not at all. If that Raven is lingering near the castle, then we need both of us to take him down."

"Leave the hunting of Hunters to me," Angela said turning to face the castle again. "You don't have what it takes for that kind of blood to be on your hands."

"Like hell I don't," Jacob said angrily. "You think I haven't killed a fellow man before?" He winced even as he said it, and unfortunately, Angela took notice. "Look, I ain't some saint. I can handle anything. We're Hunters, our job is to work together to stop this whole thing. If to do that we need to Hunt that Raven, then I'm going with you. There are too many guards in there; what if you get killed?"

"I don't get killed easily."

"What if this is an exception then? What then?"

"Then I die," Angela said indifferently. "It's as simple as that. At the very least, you will be out here where it is safer. It's better if I proceed on alone. You may hunt a few Vampires, but don't go overboard. I still need you close by to keep watch in case something happens and someone tries to leave in a hurry."

"Friends don't do that," said Jacob with a scowl. "Friends stick together."

"I'm *not* your friend, Jacob. I never will be."

She started forward but Jacob just wasn't having it. He reached out and grabbed ahold of her wrist, stopping her. She glared at him, but he stood his ground, prepared to receive whatever repercussion this action would bring.

"What did *I* do?" he demanded. "What did I do to make you think that? Do you really think your life is worth less than mine?"

"That isn't the issue here. Let-"

"You're my partner, it is my job to help you as it is as much of yours to help me. You are not going in that castle alone."

"Let go of me."

"You can't expect me to just *sit* here and wait," Jacob argued further. "I don't understand why you are so determined to send me away."

"Let go of me," Angela said, her voice venomous with controlled rage, a low growl underlying her words.

"No." Jacob said defiantly. "You're not going in alone. If you really want me to just let you go, then you're going to have to-"

Whatever he said was cut off and Angela rolled into his arm and hooked her own just underneath his armpit. In one quick and fluid motion, Jacob was flipped over the Dhampir's shoulders and slammed down hard on the cold rooftop. He felt the wind get knocked completely out of him as Angela held on to his wrist, making his arm stick at an angle to pin him down. As he groaned, she glared down at him with those terrifyingly beautiful purple eyes of hers.

"You didn't have to do *that*," he moaned.

"Get this through your thick head, Jacob." She practically *spat* his name out as if her mouth was full of bile. "I don't *want* your help. I want you to stay out here, not only for your safety, but for my own. You are to stay right here, in this spot, and keep watch. You *will not* pursue me, and you *will not* leave this spot unless you plan to go hunt some Vampires or go back to the clinic if nothing happens near the castle. If I do not return by midnight at the very latest, then you are to return to the clinic and contact Velinar for help. My decision has *nothing* to do with you, it has *everything* to do with this mission. You calling me 'friend' is not going to make me change my mind."

She then released him and shook her head with an expression that looked like disgust. Jacob stretched his arm out wincing, eyeing her sharply in defiance as he did so.

"You think you've got the experience to make important decisions, when you've yet to realize just how difficult this job can really be. You are not mature enough to make the calls; nor mature enough to understand that when you're a Hunter, your life doesn't mean a damn thing. My decision is final. You will stay safe out here and away from that castle, while I go in and find the Raven, or better yet, Andrei. If you follow me," She looked back at him with a stone-cold expression. "I will kill you."

Jacob chuckled at the threat, and stood up. "Empty words, Angela."

"I mean it."

"Yeah, sure." Then reaching up he removed his eyepatch from his eye. Angela's expression softened as his Vampiric right eye glowed bright red.

"You will not go in there alone," he said in an authoritarian tone of voice. "You will take me with you, and we will hunt together, like partners are supposed to. I will protect you, and you will protect me. Together, we both will make it out of there alive. Your life isn't something to just throw away; you need to be safe as well."

Angela turned suddenly and started away, leaving Jacob sitting there flabbergasted at the Dhampir. "Hey! Hey!" he called out starting to follow.

"That trick won't work on me," was all Angela said over her shoulder. "Do *not*, follow me, Tepes."

And before Jacob could say anything else, the Dhampir leapt off the edge of the building and soared across the gap towards another. Leaping like a flea, she bounded across the stretch of buildings and stone towers towards the castle until she suddenly disappeared from sight.

With a scowl, Jacob flipped his eyepatch back over his demonic eye. "Crazy bitch…"

She really was too fast for him, and even if he *did* give chase, he wouldn't catch up with her. Those eyes… he didn't know why she acted so hostile all of a sudden; he thought that they were doing okay. He thought that maybe, just maybe, she was finally getting used to him. She said she wanted him to be safe, but that didn't stop the truth from spilling out in the end.

I don't want *your help.*

Was he really that useless to her? Did Angela really think he wouldn't have been a help in the castle? Why would she behave like that, just to send him away?

"Throw me a bone or something," he muttered. Sitting up cross-legged, Jacob glared at the direction the Dhampir had disappeared to. "Who's acting like a child now?" he asked himself.

I am not your friend.

Even if they weren't friends, they were *partners,* right?

He was angry with how Angela had spoken to him, and how she had this violent behavior all of a sudden right when he had grabbed her. He didn't know what he did to get her so angry, but grabbing ahold of her certainly didn't help the situation either. That at the very least she had every right to respond the way she had.

What was she thinking now, planning to infiltrate the castle alone and leaving him out here to just hunt a few Vampires? Sure, it would get him to become better when dealing with the undead, but what about her? Despite being angry with Angela, Jacob couldn't help but feel worried. What if she got hurt? What if something like last night happened and she was captured, or worse?

Then I die. Her cold words echoed in Jacob's head like a bad dream.

It made him sick to his stomach that someone could say such a thing. Did Angela really think that way, or was it just some way to get him off her back? Either way, it didn't make Jacob feel any less worried than he was now.

"All right," he decided, and scooping up his bow he stood up and walked towards the edge of the building. There was no way he could make the jump from this one to the next, especially across that gap. How wonderful it must be, to be more agile than a normal human being. Jacob was just now starting to look around and see if there was an easier way to follow the Dhampir, when he heard another blood-curdling scream that sounded close by.

He turned towards the church, its dome-like structure looking like a black hill in the dark of night where the screams were coming from. There were three of them, both female while one sounded like a young child's, and the other, sounding like the monsters Jacob had been hunting the last few nights.

Considering his options, Jacob turned away from the castle and started rushing towards the church- the gap between the building and the one closer to the place of worship being easier to bound across while using the many statues for cover as he made his way towards the screams.

Ti

Little Connie would have been screaming more if her lungs weren't choked for breath.

As her mother dragged her out of the alleyway and into the streets, she huffed and puffed for air that was cold and felt like daggers piercing her chest. The church of Yohnah was just ahead, and the cackling of the monster chasing them was now closer than ever.

The two of them had been locked out of their own home by Connie's alcoholic father. As soon as the curfew had begun, he had forbidden them entry and even laughed as her Mother was slamming on the door, screaming at him to let them in.

But Father simply cackled on the other side of the heavy door. "Tryin' to fool me into open this door? Poor sods, you'll bring them here! Away!"

After trying for what felt like forever, that was when the clicking began; the chattering of fangs. Connie felt complete and utter terror as her mother suddenly grabbed her hand and they started running away. She didn't explain why, and Connie didn't ask. She just ran and cried. Every door they knocked on refused to open, and despite their mother's screams, no Watchmen was around to help. It was like running around the fog of a nightmare, not knowing where they were going, but just running from the unseen terror close behind them.

They crossed the bloodied streets, and Connie practically screamed at the horrible sights around them. People hanging on pieces of wood, their skin black like burnt paper with a sickening smell coming off of them. Heads of monstrous faces stuck on iron-spiked fences and stakes, their faces frozen in terrifying snarls. Some of them looked familiar, which only made the sight even more terrifying for little Connie.

Still, Mother held her daughter close as they ran past all of it, the worst being right next to an overturned carriage with the horse gutted and it's driver headless while still in his seat. Blood was everywhere, and the intestines of the poor horse were spread out like giant worms. Connie nearly slipped in the bloody slush, but Mother quickly picked her back up and they kept going. They were just moving away from the carriage when a loud shattering *thud* sounded behind them. Both Connie and her mother whirled around fast to see a Vampire perched up on the overturn carriage like a demon overlooking the two of them, ready to pounce.

The creature was terribly thin and pale; its naked body glistening in the pale moonlight that just barely shone through the hazy skies above. It's eyes glowed sapphire blue and it's fangs gleamed sharp and long like a viper's. His shoulders being hunched made the man appear so much smaller, the stringy red hair hanging in ragged strands around its small shoulders. It stood up on its legs, its black claws extending from the fingertips.

"What a pretty lass," the Vampires hissed hungrily as it looked upon Connie. "I like me some young blood. Though, I don't mind meself a little age…"

That was when Mother suddenly turned Connie away and stepped in front of her and the Vampire. With her back to the creature and facing her daughter, Mother hugged Connie tight and then pushed her away at arms-length, all in the span of a few short seconds. Connie was just about to ask what she was doing when she saw it. Mother's tears, dripping from her eyelids and sliding down her cheeks. She was smiling, and yet... she cried.

"Run to the church," Mother told Connie before she shoved her daughter back and whirled back around, holding her arms out as if trying to block her daughter from the monster's view.

"Go!" she bellowed and now finally having the breath to cry, Connie ran. She ran across the street and towards the church just as she heard the Vampire snarl and lunge at her mother. Her screams would haunt Connie for the remainder of her life.

She didn't look pack as she passed through the front lawn before the massive church, and upon reaching the large door that appeared blood-splattered and covered in scratch marks; as if someone was clawing at it with desperate fingernails. Connie screamed for Father Gaston to come out- for anyone to come and help.

But no one answered, and all that Connie was acknowledged with, was cruel laughter.

"Look what I just caught..." the voice snarled. She turned around, and what she saw made her gasp and fall to her dirtied knees.

Her poor mother, hung dead by the neck in the jaws of the Vampire like she was a bone for a wild dog. Blood was spilling in waterfalls down the creature's front and was all over Mother. It was like it was a wolf or some terrible beast that had just caught its weak and meek prey. The Vampire then opened its maw, releasing Mother and dropping her dead at his feet. The naked and blood-covered creature then took a step forward onto the steps leading to the church and it's next meal, which cowered just at the doorway.

"C'mere, little lady…" it hissed as it licked its bloodied lips with a long and slithering tongue. He had one hand on his prick, and the other dragging its claws up the railing of the stone steps as it made its way towards the cowering little girl. "I wanna show you somethin'…"

"Mummy…" Connie started to cry sorrowfully. "Mummy…"

"Mummy ain't here no more, little lady," the Vampire said now standing right above the her. He smiled cruelly down at her, those horrible hellish eyes burning right into her soul and scorching whatever hope she had left. His "No one is here to-"

Shruck!

Whatever he was about to say was cut off as his airway was cut off by the arrow that shot through the back of the creature's neck and pierced right through the jugular, showering Connie in a spray of maroon dew.

The Vampire stepped back, choking in surprise as it wrenched the arrow from its throat. It then whirled around fast as another arrow suddenly struck it right in the chest, making it fall back and shattering bones upon impact of the stone steps. With a snarl, it turned around and started reaching out for Connie with a look of desperation.

"C'mere, you little bitch!"

Connie screamed out just as she saw something coming up right towards them, the cloak flapping behind him like a pair of wings as he took aim with his bow and shot another arrow. This one stuck into the Vampire's back, making it howl horribly. Immediately it stopped pulling as it suddenly dropping onto the staircase, bleeding out as it lied dead. It's body would not be reduced to ash until a stake was through it's heart or the sun shone on it's sinful body; whichever comes first.

At that moment, the man who had come to her rescue kicked aside the revolting body and stooped down in front of Connie, blocking her view of her dead mother who laid in the snow of red.

"Are you okay?" the man with the eyepatch said crouching down to eye-level. He looked at Connie's ankle, as if to make sure it was still there.

"You okay?" he asked again.

Connie sniffed and then reached out to the stranger, hanging her head and burying it into his shoulder. For a moment, the man did nothing, and then slowly, raised an arm and hooked it around Connie's little body. Out of the cold and into the man's warm embrace, Connie felt safe, but she was already too broken to be fixed.

"Mummy... Mummy..." she cried.

The man sighed, as if he understood her pain. She turned her head, and continued to be held by the man who was now looking up at the church. He didn't let her go, even as he mumbled to himself.

"No broken windows..."

He then stood up, still keeping an arm around Connie and pulling her close still as he sheathed his bow and with his freed fist, he banged on the door.

"Open up, we got a little girl out here!" When no one answered, the man banged his fist against the church doors again. "Hey! You alive in there?"

"Go away…" a frail voice answered and Connie recognized it almost immediately. "Go away, son. I am sorry, but I cannot open this door. It is too dangerous with the beasts lurking about."

"Did you not hear me?" the man shouted. "I have a little girl out here, open up the damn door!"

"I cannot," Father Gaston said again. "I'm sorry."

"Father!" Connie cried out. "Father Gaston!" She was so afraid, she didn't want to be left alone. Though the stranger had saved her, she didn't want to be out in the streets of Irondell any longer.

"I'm sorry, my daughter," Gaston said almost reluctantly. "But there is nowhere safe here. Please, just go. For all I know, you are one of *them*."

"Excuse me." The man suddenly moved Connie back and away from his grasp as he suddenly raised a foot and with a solid kick, he broke the lock and the doors swung open, striking Father Gaston who was right on the other side with a loud smack.

Connie saw the priest on the ground in his black robes, his bald head exposed thanks to his hood being thrown. He had a hand over his forehead where a cut was bleeding. He glared at the Hunter who was now in the process of pulling the doors shut.

"What in Kawn's name?" Gaston growled getting up to his feet in outrage. "How dare you damage church prop-"

The man whirled around fast grabbing the priest by the throat and slamming him against the nearby wall. Connie gasped though her surprise was nothing compared to Gaston's who practically wilted under the Hunter's piercing blue eye.

"Why didn't you open your doors?" he demanded.

Gaston gulped audibly. "For the safety of the church."

The man looked down the hall and Connie followed his gaze. The doors leading to the sanctuary was open, revealing the large cathedral worship room with the pews stacked up on either side of the walls to make room for what looked like thousands of lit candles. Wax covered the floor, and the eerie glow illuminated the entire room including the statues of praying monks and worshipers cloaked in stone. Above the alter etched in the painted glass that illuminated the moonlight on the other side, there was the depictions of Yohnah, in the form of a white dove that glowed beautifully silver throughout the church.

The Hunter turned his attention back to Gaston and released the man. "Safety of the church, eh? I see no one in here, save for the coward in my clutches."

Gaston panted heavily and wiped the blood off his forehead. "If those beasts got in here, they would destroy this last sanctuary. I couldn't take any chances."

The Hunter scoffed. "You ain't concerned with the church, you're using it to save your own ass."

Gaston looked away, ashamed.

The Hunter then grabbed Gaston by the scruff of his robes and forced him to look in Connie's direction.

"Look at her!" the Hunter snarled. "This little girl just saw her mother get slaughtered right in front of her!"

At the mention of this, Connie felt anguish rise to her throat and threatened to make her cry.

"You ignored her cry for help- how many times have you done that since the outbreak?" When Gaston didn't answer- or wouldn't -the Hunter released the priest and took a step back. "I need to go. You, take care of this child. If anyone else asks for help, it is your duty to help them."

"If you give them permission to come in," Gaston said still on the floor. "They will storm this place like an infestation."

"Not if they wish to burn on Holy Ground," the man countered. He pointed a finger at Gaston, making him flinch. "I'll be back soon. If I find out anymore people turn up dead on your doorstep, or that little girl isn't taken care of, I'll be back and I'll throw you out and see how well you do without the church to protect you."

Gaston's eyes lit up angrily with defiance. "You Hunters, always shoving your way around. You're no different than that last Hunter who came here, or the Raven who chased her out of town!"

"Angela was here?" the man asked but then shook his head. "Never mind. Do your duty for now on, *priest*. You're supposed to be a man of Yohnah, now protect the people and give them sanctuary. I'll be back to check on you when things slow down." And with that, the man turned on his heel and after opening the doors back up, he started to go.

"Sir, wait!" Connie cried out ready to give chase but found that she couldn't cross the threshold to the outside world. "Don't leave me alone… Mummy…"

The man turned and smiled warmly to Connie. He then retraced his steps back to her and crouched down so that they could see eye-to-eye. He then patted her head with a gloved hand, like a parent telling their child that there were no monsters under their bed.

"It'll be okay, sweetie. Father here, he'll keep you safe."

"But the monsters!" Connie argued.

"The church is the safest place for you. No monsters can get in here." The Hunter then glared at Gaston who was watching from the wall, and the priest wilted again. "Trust in your pastor, he'll make sure you're taken care of until morning."

"But… Mummy… Daddy…"

"It'll be okay," the Hunter said with a promising tone. It was like he was begging her to simply have faith in him, and trust that she would be okay. "I promise. Just help Father with everything tonight, and provide sanctuary here. Can you do that?"

Connie wanted to cry, but she reluctantly nodded.

"That's a good girl," the man said wiping a tear away from Connie's cheek. "The sun will come out soon, I promise."

With that, the man stood and started away. Before he passed the iron fence, Gaston was already shutting the doors and telling Connie to back away. He then started to board up the doors with a stray bench.

"Not again..." he whispered to himself. "Not again..."

He looked over to Connie with a pained expression. Was it guilt that he felt, or was he just as afraid as Connie was. Connie remembered seeing Father Gaston every Rishon, so happy and full of life. But now, it looked as if the veil had been removed, exposing him as frightened just like anybody else considering the screaming demons still outside their door.

"Are we really safe here?" Connie asked still nervous.

"Yes," Gaston said taking a seat on the bench with his head in his hands. "The Vampires cannot step onto Holy Ground. The Hunter is right. We're safe here, the church will protect us."

"Okay..." Connie looked at the floor sadly. "They killed Mummy..."

Gaston looked up with a look of agony. He then opened his arms up, beckoning for Connie to come to him. She did, and he hugged her close.

"I'm sorry," he said. "I was just so afraid. If I had opened the door..."

Connie hugged the priest back. "It's okay."

"No... it really isn't. This whole thing... I hate it so much."

Connie hated it too. It was like a nightmare; no matter how many times she tried to wake up or flee from the horrors, they were always there again. She was still asleep, and the night was still young.

Gaston cleared his throat and gently held Connie back. He looked at her with sad gray eyes before smiling softly, almost like something was hurting him. "I'm sure you're hungry, aren't you?"

Connie nodded. Food, that was what she needed. Something to calm her stomach, and distract her from... everything.

"Why don't you go to the kitchens?" Gaston suggested, pointing a bony finger towards the sanctuary behind her. "I haven't anything cooked but you're welcome to the bread in the pantry."

"Okay..." And so, Gaston patted her head and sent her to the sanctuary, and little Connie started her walk through the beautiful church.

She remembered coming in on Rishons, and seeing the pews all in rows with many different people. The aristocrats and wealthy families usually sat up front, while the poor or simple sat closer to the back. But every so often, her own mother and father would sit right up front so that she could really get a better view of the alter and the painted glass window of the dove of Yohnah glistening in the sunlight, the beautiful white bird carrying an olive branch in its beak.

She could almost hear the choir who would sing hymns on either side of the alter wearing their creepy black and red robes and hoods that would conceal their faces. Gaston would be at the podium, teaching and speaking in such a loud and proud voice that was nothing like the voice he had tonight. Though, Connie couldn't blame him; he was just a man, and he was scared. They all were.

Above her, the chandeliers hung empty, and only the thousands of candles around her lit her way as she made her way closer to the alter. She smiled at the window of the white dove, and then took a left to the hall where the staff kitchens were. She then crossed down the dark hallway, passing by chairs and many crates that had a strange smell to them.

That was when Connie heard the growling. She stopped in place, frozen as terror clutched her heart yet again. The growling intensified and in the darkness, Connie saw a pair of glowing yellow eyes. At first, Connie thought it was just a dog, and she allowed herself to relax. It was just Father Gaston's dog, nothing more. She crouched and held out a hand, as if to tell the creature that she wasn't a threat.

That was when she realized that Gaston didn't own a dog, and from the darkness the wolf lunged at her with sharp fangs that tore into her throat and spilled her blood.

Connie tried to scream but all that escaped her throat was the gurgling. She struck the stone floor as the massive paws slammed down on either side of her head, that horrible snout mere inches away from her own face. She stared into those moon-like eyes of yellow, which stared back at her with unwavering dominance.

She was being watched, as she slowly died. And as Connie started to feel no more pain, and feeling the need to just sleep, she heard the muffled voice of Gaston, praying somewhere within the church that he promised would save her.

Te

Angela crept up the walls of the castle after avoiding the main courtyard completely and the Watchmen along it.

Thankfully, there was no one watching the main bulk of the keep, which faced the northern side of the city. With the moon on the other side, Angela was enveloped into complete darkness; as if she herself was a shadow, creeping up the walls like a salamander. Every crack or break in the stone, every nook her fingers and toes could creep into, she found it, and she climbed the tall towers to the nearest window. Far below her, she saw more Watchmen shooting down a Vampire who had tried to overcome the trio. One of the men had died, but the Vampire was shot to the point where it couldn't defend itself as the other two beheaded the dreadful creature and set the body aflame.

As they took care of the wretched creature, Angela got to the window and with nimble fingers, stuck one of her smallest knives into the lock frame and moved the bar to open it. She then slipped inside like a stealthy thief, and upon landing onto the floor, she froze; silent as a mouse, listening.

The hallway was vast and stretched far from both her left and right. Many doors lined the innermost walls of the castle, and torches and windows hung on the wall opposite. Now inside and away from the distant gunfire and shrieks that haunted the outside, the Dhampir was able to better hear who and what was in the castle.

Though she didn't know the layout, she could hear many voices shouting, laughing and even singing down the hall to her right, and she figured that the main hall and throne room was somewhere down that corridor. Deciding to move away from the activity, Angela hugged the wall and started to make her way down the corridor to her left, passing by door after door and torch after torch; which illuminated her pale face like a ghost in sunlight. She continued to venture down until she was forced to turn the corner, and she found that she now stood on an overlooking hallway looking down to what appeared to be a training room where two Watchmen resided. From the shadows, she observed the man and the Nephil in training.

One was who Angela recognized immediately as William who had met her at the gate during her first visit in Irondell. The other, the Nephil, was small and no doubt young, was munching on a large apple as he watched William swing his sword about. The giant-to-be wore only his training gear, and sweat stained the collar of his shirt, indicating he already had his turn now that William was hacking at the dummy as if he were trying to swat a fly. It was amazing, really, just how clumsy humans really were with weapons. Not as fast as most creatures, but fast enough at least for one another; one another was all they were really good at fighting against.

Not Jacob. Angela reminded herself, and felt a pain of regret deep in her chest.

Despite what she had said to the young Hunter, she recognized his talent. He would make to be a dangerous Hunter one day, she could see it. But did she have to be so hard on him? She knew she had to be hard, for him to understand the gravity of the situation.

Then why did I tell him that? she wondered.

Never mind that now. She could apologize or something later, when this night was finished.

Stalking silently forward, using the pillars that held up the upper hallway and ceiling for cover, Angela listened in on the conversation between William and the giant; ignoring the stench the two had on them.

"It's gettin' worse, I tell ya," William said swinging his sword and flicking off sweat off his pale and naked torso, the pungent odor strong in Angela's nostrils. His pants were soaked in sweat, and his bare feet were dirtied by the stone floor.

"We are losin' more Watchmen than we are Vampires, and more and more people are gettin' killed out there. How are we supposed to protect them when that damned Raven won't do anythin' to help us?"

"Andrei's orders," the Nephil moaned wiping his massive chin clean with a large sausage-sized finger. Standing up, the giant appeared to be at least twelve feet tall and was probably as strong as a great many oxen. His speech was a deep rumble, low and slow. "We can't disobey the king, mate."

"He ain't a king, he's a *Count*." William corrected the giant soldier. "Different sort of leader. Don't they have some sort of monarchy back in the mountains?"

"We don't call 'em 'kings', we call 'em 'chiefs.' You punies have too many words that mean the same things."

William snorted with a good-natured smile. "Yeah. Yeah, we do."

He swung a few more times, and then halted at a crouched pose. "Anyways, it still ain't right. The only time that Raven comes out is at night to just look around the castle. He doesn't kill any Vampires, or even helps the citizens getting infected. I haven't even seen him actually aid the Watchmen at all! And *now* he's out lookin' for that Dhampir instead of the fuckin' Immortal still out and about. I should have seen that comin'. I never should have told him... I don't know what to do, Hephus."

Angela halted at the last pillar before the end of the upper hall. She had no time to lose, but she wondered if there was more to what William was saying to the Nephil now.

"You were doing your duty, Will," Hephus groaned popping the rest of the apple into his mouth, core and all. "That is all a soldier can do."

"Even leave the people he swore to protect to die?" William shook his head and tossed his sword onto the ground with an angry clang. "What is the Count thinkin'? Trustin' a Raven? You can't ever trust no one from the Empire."

"Not so loud," Hephus said earnestly. "What if that Raven is here right now? Haven't left yet or something. Or worse, a... a... what are those type of men called? Not scouts, but..."

"Spies. They're called spies, but who cares? I doubt he is even around. He never comes to help during the day, and I haven't seen him whenever I'm outside. Have you?"

"You're not supposed to see them. They are Elite Hunters."

"It's still creepy." William crossed the room and took a seat on one of the bales of hay next to the Nephil. "This whole thing… it's just shit-awful… Elan died last night."

Hephus looked at his friend. "Died?"

"She was attacked. The thing that got to her… he raped her and drank her dry. Remember Cole? He found her, and had to put her down."

"Oh my… I'm sorry, Will."

William shook his head. "Don't be. Tomorrow, I'm goin' to kill all those bastards. Ev'ry last one of 'em. To hell with that Raven, and to hell with Andrei I say. If they won't give a shit, then it's up to us. We should just get everyone out of here."

"How are we supposed to do that? You can't tell for some people, whether they are human… or Vampire."

"I don't know," William said with a frustrated tone. "All I know that if we stay here any longer, Irondell will belong to the dead and so will we."

The horrible and sad truth hung in the air like a bad smell, and Angela slipped away from the training room and continued down the hall. She didn't need to be reminded what was at stake here in Irondell.

As she passed more doors Angela unfortunately caught the sounds of laughing and moaning behind some of them, and was quick to rush away. She even had to take cover behind another set of armor and shroud herself in her cloak, blending in with the shadows until some patrolmen passed by so she could continue. Most were Irondell Watchmen, others wore the armor of the Empire.

As she maneuvered like a thief through the castle, her thoughts returned to William. The man was right to be afraid. They were losing time, and if they didn't end this plague soon, there wouldn't be a city left to save. Angela only had one shot into driving Horla out into the open; wherever he was hiding. She had to find the Raven, and the best way to find him was the source: Count Andrei.

Sneaking into the castle was easy, at least for her. Angela only hoped that Jacob was doing alright outside- and that the young Hunter wasn't doing anything stupid.

I'm not your friend.

She had hurt him, both physically and otherwise on the rooftop. She didn't want to, but it was the truth. She had to go alone, and she didn't want his help. She didn't want Jacob to get into any danger, and she certainly didn't want to linger around him for too long. They were strictly business partners, nothing more, nothing less. She didn't know why she allowed him to get to her like that, but that was a mistake that was quickly corrected. As long as he was safe and out of her way, they could finish this job soon. And the sooner this job was done, the sooner they could go back to Shadowfort and part ways as it should be.

She was a Dhampir; a monster. She didn't belong with him, nor the rest of the Hunters. She was to Hunt alone, it was her fate. It had been her fate since she came into this world kicking and screaming.

She didn't belong with the humans, or the Vampires.

She just, didn't... belong.

You're losing focus, Angela said to herself. This wasn't the time to be thinking about such things. She had to remain focused and alert, and as she turned another corner down to a large hallway, she took cover behind a mannequin of armor and surveyed the armory hall leading the Count Andrei's bedroom. She knew that was what it had to be, by the way there were four guards at the large double-doors at the end of the hall. Also, the smell that she recognized was strong in this direction. Like a bloodhound searching for the rabbit, she had found Andrei's quarters.

The men appeared to be bored and Angela could smell whisky on one of them. Along the walls were hanging axes and swords and glass cases containing firearms and bows hugged the wall along the hall. There was no cover, and the distance between Angela and the Watchmen were too great. She was fast, but there was enough distance to the doors to allow a few seconds for the men to raise their guns. A few seconds wasn't good enough. A *couple* however…

Maybe she would die, maybe she wouldn't, but Angela figured the odds didn't matter.

Backing up to hide behind the corner again and making sure they didn't see her, Angela focused her mind on her eyes. She hadn't done this in a long time, at least not consciously and with a purpose. In fact, she would normally try to avoid using her eyes if possible so that she would never have to see any horrible possibilities for the future. But she saw no windows down this hall which meant that this was the only way into the room without having to go back outside. So, with her clairvoyance, she hoped to find an opening for her to gain an advantage on the men before they could react and fire a single shot, or blow the whistles around their necks for aide- or worse, alert Andrei before she got to him.

Maybe this will limit the visions I get too...

And so, she decided in the end to unleash the power her father had given her, and use her Immortal Eyes. She closed them tight, focusing on gathering enough energy into them to focus on the one possibility she needed: success. When she felt ready, she snapped them open and as they glowed bright and purple, she looked into the near-future.

Lunge to the opposite wall, sprint across it and leap to the opposite side where the leftmost Watchman stands. At this moment, the men will have spotted her and by the sight of her movement and will mistake her for a Vampire but their reaction would be slow and uncomprehending for a brief moment. They will cry out and raise their weapons, forgetting their guns. As she sails through the air, and throw three knives into the necks of the men before they could raise their guns too high and upon landing on her first target; she would run his sword through him, silencing him immediately before rushing back and finishing off the three who at this point would be choking on their own blood.

Complete action would take about three or five seconds. The reaction of the men would be too slow and the noise they would make be minimum. Not at the level that Angela would like, but as her vision faded away, Angela saw it as the best course of action. She would have to be quick to avoid them shouting too loud or reacting too soon.

With a deep breath and a sigh, Angela reached over her shoulder and grabbed ahold of her sword in her left hand. In her right, she pulled out three throwing knives between each knuckle, ready to throw them. She then turned around, and focused upon the far wall close to one of the glass cases. When she felt ready, she tensed up her legs and listened to the men's breathing.

Slow... relaxed. It was when one of them yawned when Angela lunged forward, crossing the floor at such incredible speed as she emerged into the lit hallway and upon landing on the wall took off into a sprint towards the men, running across it like a roadrunner across the southern deserts.

The men reacted as precisely as her vision revealed. They gasped and started to raise their weapons as well as their voices. However, Angela leapt off the wall and sailed towards the leftmost Watchman with the speed of a lunging mountain lion. As she did, she hurled her knives towards the other three men, and the blades dove into their jugulars, sending spasms throughout their bodies and making them forget about their weapons as they groped at their bleeding necks.

The one Angela was almost upon just barely got his gun up before Angela kicked it away while at the same time driving her sword right into his chest. His eyes bulged out in horror and fear as she violently ripped the sword out of his chest, the jagged edges ripping his insides up even more as she turned on her heel and sliced right through the remaining Watchmen.

One was cut right through the side of the head, lopping the top off like a cap. The other was cut clean through at the base of the neck, while the other was slammed against the wall with the force of Angela's sword driving into his side and practically cutting him through beneath the armpits. His armor didn't even protect him from the bite of her blade.

All men dropped while gushing blood everywhere; all over the walls, the floor, and even Angela's own body. Sprinkled with the dew of the men who now laid dead at her feet, Angela stood up and breathed in softly, slowly, calmly. The entire attack took about *four* seconds, and the only sound the men made were mere squeaks even mice couldn't hear, as well as the hollow clunks when their armored bodies dropped onto the floor like sacks of laundry

She listened, trying to sense any change in the castle. She heard no one stopping to listen, she felt no change in the atmosphere. As fast as the attack happened, it was over in an instant; and no one in the entire castle knew of it- yet.

Angela looked down at her fist clenching her sword and saw that some of the gore that covered the blade was now dripping over the hilt and onto her pale hand. She could feel it, sticky and cooling fast on her knuckle, and Angela flicked her wrist in order to splash the blood off her sword. The dew on her hand remained however, like a blotch on her skin.

She glared at it hatefully, but at the same time with a look of longing. She could smell it; the sweet copper-like scent masked in sugar and protein. It smelled to her like fresh honey dribbling out of a bee's honeycomb. She could feel the buzzing in the back of her head, as well as feel how wet her mouth had gone as she began to salivate. She felt a pain in her stomach, as she craved for the blood.

She held up her hand, and stuck out her tongue, ready to just have a single taste of that marvelous dew that humans always carried around with them; wanting badly the sensation that many felt after a sip of wine or mead. She could hear her very instincts screaming; begging for a taste before she continued on her mission. It was screaming! Screaming!

You just can't hide your nature, can you, Angela?

Angela retracted her tongue fast and clicked her teeth shut immediately as she turned her head away with a fanged sneer.

No. She couldn't, not now, or ever again. She had made herself a promise; she would never drink the blood of a human ever again.

She promised him... promised...

Wanting nothing more than to get away from all the blood that pooled around her like spilt syrup, Angela went up to the doorway of Count Andrei, and with a steady hand, gently pushed the door open and as silent as a wraith, closed it behind her; closing her within the Count's bedroom, and the horrible man with his secrets inside.

The fat Count was sleeping in a large bed that seemed to stretch nearly thirty feet from the back wall, with embraided curtains folded just above the lush pillows where Andrei rested his head. On either side of the man were crystal lamps and the lightbulbs buzzed with lighting; and to the far right the remains of a fire glowed in a hearth of brick and marble. Mounted heads covered the walls and the furs of the beasts blanketed the Count, all from bears to wolves and many deer from Andrei's obvious hunts.

To Angela's right, she saw a large painted glass window of what looked like a star among many blazing colors of a rainbow; the many glass tiles glistening in the moonlight that shined through it. To the left a large bookshelf with a small opening that contained a desk and lamp stood against the wall; the desk itself littered with books and papers.

But what caught Angela's attention the most however, were the many runes on the floor circling a pentagram with a sacrificial dagger plunged into the body of a crow right in the center with black candles circled around it like sentries; unlit and dead like the poor bird. It's blood had been drizzled over the runes that looked to have been carved into the hardwood floor rather than etched in chalk or paint.

Angela didn't know what the many runes themselves meant; they were an ancient language only known by a very few people. But what she did know, was that no one in Balkeñoir used sacrificial runes except for Witches, the Wildesding, and any foolish mortal who wished to touch the black magic of Kawfka; the lord of darkness and the dimension of Oblivion.

In her fury, Angela crossed the room and with her sword, sliced right through the markings as she passed by. Seeing that the books and papers on the desk were also ancient grimoires and other teachings for black magic, she ran her hand over the beautifully crafted desk and knocked the writings onto the floor; the books thudding loudly while the blasphemous papers wavered in the air like falling leaves.

Andrei was now starting to stir from his slumber, but Angela was already by his side as his eyes adjusted and saw two furious purple beacons staring down at him. A squeak escaped his throat as Angela grabbed ahold of the man by the bicep and with inhuman strength, *hurled* him over her head and tossed him across the room right into the bookshelf with a mighty crash. Books fell upon the fat man's head who was naked and now desperately trying to cover himself up with a book as he opened his mouth to speak. But Angela was already upon him, pushing the tip of her sword right between the man's eyes, slightly puncturing his skin and drawing light dribble of blood down his pudgy nose.

"Y-y-you!" he stuttered with eyes as wide as dinner plates.

"Count Andrei," Angela said trying to keep her voice level despite the venom that trickled along her low and angry tone. She waved at the pentagram and the demonic literature all around them. "What is the meaning of this?"

"I-I-I dunno what you're-"

"Where is the Raven?" Angela demanded furiously. "Why haven't you tried to better protect your citizens? They are out there, dying while you sleep peacefully in this castle of yours. How many men have died in the place of the Raven who was supposed to save you all? As if all of that isn't bad enough, I come in here, to find you messing around with black magic? Do you even realize what kind of forces you are playing with?! Answer me, *Count*: Explain yourself!"

She added a little more pressure to her sword, making Andrei squirm his body and groan in pain as the blade poked his skull. Angela was so livid that she just wanted to run her sword right through the fat Count's skull; ending his pathetic life right then and there.

Still, she restrained herself, as Andrei stared at her defiantly angry.

"Who do you think you are!?" he demanded. "I am the Count of this hold, and you *will* stand down, demon! It's none of your concern-"

Angela kept her sword against his forehead as she stooped down and seized the man by the throat. He gagged and choked as she squeezed his jugular, not too hard but hard enough to make breathing only a little difficult. Her patience was thin, and the line Andrei was trying to keep between them was thinner.

"I don't care if you are a count or a king. Where is the Raven?" she asked again, determined to break the man if she had to. "And why are playing with the runes of Kawfka?"

Jacob crossed the street and took cover behind a pile of burnt bodies. The smell was horrible but the smoke that still seeped from the blackened corpses provided just the protection he needed from the watchful eyes of the riflemen along the courtyard walls as well as the foot soldiers. There were Gatlings in the corner towers built atop of the parapet, but the rest of the castle seemed quiet; asleep almost.

If Angela had already gotten inside, she hardly disturbed anyone. She really was something else.

Jacob considered his options and his eye lingered to the far right of the courtyard gates. There were stacks of boxes and crates that were probably meant to be shipped out before the quarantine was put in place. They weren't stacked high enough to transverse the walls, but they could in the very least give him the boost he needed. And so slipping away from the smoldering pile of ash and bone, Jacob crept back towards the buildings, giving the Watchmen a wide berth as he made his way over to the other side.

As he maneuvered past the shattered buildings and straying Watchmen, Jacob listened to the distant gunfire and screams of both humans and Vampires. It all pierced his ears and made his stomach flip with every step he took. Still, he managed to make it to the wall and after climbing up the crates, he quickly leapt up to the ledge; his fingers clenching the rain-eaten bricks like his life depended on it. He pulled himself up and after getting a leg up, he was soon on the wall. He took some cover behind the closest tower, out of sight of the patrolling Watchmen.

Inside the courtyard itself just before the large doors leading into the castle was a great amount of space with some training dummies as well as targets for shooting. On both sides of the courtyard were stables where beautiful horses nickered and whinnied as they huddled close together for warmth. Moving fast when he saw the chance towards the nearest one, Jacob leapt down onto the wooden roof and grabbing ahold of the edge he leapt and swung right into the stables, landing right into some soft hay where a horse started to sputter in indignation.

The Hunter managed to calm the beast before it caught the attention of any of the Watchmen lurking about nearby. He peeked through the gaps of the fencing and gates in order to get a better look. There were four guys right at the castle doors, and roughly six more just wandering about inside, smoking and talking amongst themselves. Every time the shrill screech of a Vampire echoed from afar, the men shuddered audibly.

"I hate that sound…" said one.

"Why do they do that?" Said another.

"It's like a call for help. They communicate to one another, kinda like a pack."

"They're monsters- animals, how can they do that? They ain't human anymore. That's nonsense."

"I dunno…"

"Do you think that the Vampire is just the one infected back from the dead? Or is it… something else?"

"No way, that can't be. Their bodies are brought back but those things… they aren't the people we knew before. I don't know how or why, but they aren't the boys we knew back then. You did what you had to do."

"But he said my *name*, Ethan. He knew who I was… if it is a demon, then-"

"Look, I don't know ev'ry damn thing about the bloody Vampires. All I know that they are monsters and to make our boys sleep in peace, we need to send them to Hell where they belong. Ev'ry damn one of them."

Though Jacob found the discussion between the two Watchmen interesting, he had to keep moving. So slowly, while keeping crouched and out of sight, he slowly made his way through the stables. He made sure to stay in front of the horses as to not spook them, and when one started to get restless he would stay and calm them down with a gentle hand. He made sure to rub their noses with his gloved hand, so that he could tell them that he was a friend. It was when he reached the end of the stables close to the doors when he looked back up towards the guards at the door-

They were all dead, and Jacob gasped in terror at the sudden sight that beheld him.

The four men at the doors laid on the stone steps and ground with their blood painting the walls of the castle as well as staining the snow around their corpses. When he looked back, he was shocked to see that the other six men around the stables laid dead as well. Along the wall, he saw no one except for a single Watchman who hung over the edge with his blood dripping down the length of the cold stones like a waterfall. There had been no sound, no scream for help, and the horses were perfectly tranquil.

And was it just him, or had the area become foggy all of a sudden?

Nervous but keeping cautious, Jacob vaulted over the fencing, and taking out his bow, he began to survey the carnage. There was no noise on the other side of the walls, and he wondered if the other men outside were okay.

"What the hell..." he whispered to himself coming close to one of the bodies.

Using his foot to roll the man over onto his back, he inspected the wounds along the neck. Something had *cut* the man's throat all the way to the spine; it was so deep that Jacob could see the shiny bone in the back. The man's face was frozen in mid-shock. He didn't even have time to scream before he was killed. He didn't-

Something struck him in the right side; his blind spot. He felt a sharp sting of pain in his abdomen but still Jacob was able to get his feet back under him before he fell over and throwing his arms and bow up with all his might while ducking, he tossed the man who struck him overhead, his vision blackened with what looked like feathers as the man tumbled across the clearing. Jacob groaned, clutching his side which bled profusely- right between the plates of his leather armor. He looked at the black mass now rising back up and Jacob first thought he was looking at a giant crow.

But what he saw instead was a man wearing a black feathered cloak with a beak-shaped mask of tin. He was missing his right hand which was now covered with a metal cusp and a small crossbow was strapped over the forearm with leather. In his gloved hand, a single jagged sword glistened in the moon and firelight, the blade itself speckled in crimson.

"There is no way my luck is this bad..." Jacob muttered pulling his bloodied hand away from the wound and getting into a stance. He would have to reach up and draw an arrow fast in order to get a clear shot on the Raven. From what he had heard from Angela and

Clockwork, this man was good with a blade. The most logical choice would be to drop the bow and go for his own daggers. The only problem, would be that crossbow…

"I should have known the Black Hand would return," the Raven said his voice angrily muffled beneath his mask. "You traitors just couldn't stay out of my business, could you? Instead, you decide to come back and cause trouble for Irondell?"

Jacob flashed a smile, determined to at least buy himself some time. "Oh, I just do it to meet exciting people like yourself. I mean, *technically*, I was hired by a different employer. So, *technically*, I ain't breaking any laws whether by under the Emperor or by Hunters across the world."

"Oh really?" the Raven demanded. "And so you brought that half-breed *bitch* with you." He spat onto the ground and continued, "As if this situation couldn't get any worse. Now I caught you lot murdering the men and women who defend this hold."

"I didn't do this."

"Who else would know? No witnesses other than you and I."

Jacob narrowed his eyes. "Look, we are not your enemies. The plague is getting worse, you need help."

"I need no help!" the Raven snapped. "And I don't need you lot telling me how to Hunt."

"If you can call it that," Jacob retorted. At this point, he had decided to start lowering his hand so that both were close to his belt. "How many people are dying out there because you've yet to come out until you hear my partner and I are here? How many Watchmen, women, and children are now dead because of you and the Count not seeming to take this seriously?"

"My contract isn't to save Irondell," the Raven said indignantly which made Jacob worry what was to happen next.

If he's telling me this...

"My job is to find the Immortal and kill him. When he dies, those who have been infected will die out as well. Without the head of the snake, the body will wither. But then you lot came around, and I have to eliminate you as well. You, and that abomination bastard." The Raven sneered. "How can you work side by side with that monster? That *beast*?"

"Do you not care about the living?" Jacob demanded loudly, ignoring the question and hoping that his voice would carry and somehow reach Angela. "Why don't you do what a Hunter is supposed to do, and kill all the Vampires? Why hide like a frightened rabbit preaching rather than actually hunting?"

"I'm not going to risk getting myself killed just to save a few," the Raven answered coldly. "My job isn't to save them. My job is to find the Immortal and slay him. And the Dhampir? Well, let's just say I got a bone to pick with her. All for the better, one less monstrosity in the world. And you being a criminal Hunter as well, deserves no better treatment."

Jacob didn't have to stall for time anymore. What he felt was real; and he was *livid*. "I've met a lot of bad men in my time. Men who were cowards, selfish, and willing to let people die as long as they got what they wanted. But you, sir, are the worst."

The Raven chuckled beneath his mask. "Is that so? Surely there are far worse men in the world than I am. There always is. But if you are absolutely certain, then let me throw those words back at you. Do you even know *what* you are working for?"

"I work for the Black Hand," Jacob now had his hand on one of his daggers, loosening it in its scabbard.

"No, you work for the devil himself," the Raven spat onto the ground again. "You traitor's to the crown, believe you can run to a cursed child; a Fallen Star who care not for humans? Think you are above the Emperor's law? No, it is time we take matters into our own hands, not rely on minor guilds to fight monsters; especially those who deal with Fallen Stars- or *any* of the Stars for that matter. It is my job to purge this world of *all* who dare defy Emperor Ion- including those who should have never been born. I will slay you and the Dhampir, then the Immortal. Then those who tried to break the law of the Emperor can burn along with the undead."

"No," Jacob said unhooking the buckle over his dagger. "You've wasted enough time." He then quickly reached for an arrow over his back and the Raven lunged.

He was fast. Not fast enough to kill fifteen men in under a minute and without any sound whatsoever, but fast still. Just when he got within a few feet of Jacob, the Hunter had drawn his bow and loosed the arrow, sending it spearing the man in the shoulder. Immediately after shooting, Jacob got his bow up and went for his knife. The Raven slashed at him, but the bow managed to catch the attack, the wood groaning as the sword bit into it. Immediately, Jacob slashed at the man with his own dagger just as the Raven launched a bolt from his crossbow right into Jacob's chest. Both men fell back away from one another as blood sailed between them like rose pedals.

The Raven clutched his arm while Jacob leapt back, grabbing ahold of the bolt and snapping it at the base where the point had punched through his armor. Then dropping his bow, Jacob grabbed his second dagger and lunged for the Raven, who was already waiting for the Hunter and the two clashed blades just as Jacob heard the shrill shriek of a Vampire- and it was close.

Too close, and the fog was growing thicker and thicker by the minute.

But he would not falter. He would put an end to this Raven before the sun came up. He was going to prove to Angela that he was not useless now.

Father Gaston was praying for forgiveness when he heard the distant scream in the far distance. It was a shrill sound, one that only a monster could produce.

Through the walls of the church, he could hear more screams gathering together; like a chorus of demons ready to fly out into the night. The sound gave him the chills, and he bowed his head again in prayer towards the nuns who lifted up the Dove on gentle hands of stone.

"Oh, Yohnah, Morning Star, Light of the world, you know I am a righteous man. Of my virtue… I am justly proud. But tell me, dear Yohnah, why must I suffer? Why do I shed more blood, in order to protect myself, when your loyal subjects suffer at the hands of the devil's spawn? I should be in the fires of Oblivion for all I've done tonight.

"Still, I am proud, and I am unrelenting. I am a man of God, I am perfect in your eyes; purer than the vulgar filth that is outside paying for their sinful ways. This is… This is a cleansing. Yes… that must be it. I shall live on, and carry on your glory through my own. I shall be here, when Irondell is no more; a mere splotch of what happens when kings give up on you, and turn to lesser Stars."

Another scream, and Gaston again felt chills crawl down his spine like a spider; like someone just raked his back with cold claws. He felt the stone eyes of the praying statues glaring down at him from beneath their hoods. They were angry- but they were jealous. Everything he did, was for a righteous cause. What have they themselves done in their lifetime that he had not? His soul was already saved, there was no reason to fear them. He just had to live; he had to strive on. He was Father Gaston, one of the most righteous men in all of Irondell. If only that Raven was dead and the Count along with him... if only, that she-demon, never came back.

The woman... the Dhampir...

Gaston felt another chill as he conjured the image of that beautiful face. That unnatural beauty that came not in the horrendous and filthy Hunting attire, but instead packaged in garments of black which made her perfectly clean a white skin all the more gorgeous. The way she walked, the way she stared with those lavender eyes...

He shuddered again, and realizing the sin that was slowly growing hard in his trousers, bowed his head again in prayer. For the first time in his entire priesthood, he was glad to not be in the company of nuns or disciples or even the deacons. To pray to Yohnah with the lustful image he made in his imagination of the Dhampir and through it gain excitement, was grotesque but at the same time felt so right.

"Tell me, dear Yohnah, why did you allow her to return here?" he asked with clenched hands; his nails digging into his knuckles deep enough to spill blood. "Such beauty of a fallen angel, why must this Siren return to haunt me so? The queen of the damned... is this what you've been trying to tell me in my dreams, dear God? The night has been forever long, all in order for you to show me, your most valued prophet, *what* exactly? I must be the one to rise above the ashes of death and despair. So why test me in this now?"

You killed many people… he could hear the spirits around him practically whisper. The eyes of the statues glared down at him like the Great Judges, scolding him as the spirits that wander the world taunted him. *You left them all behind… you allowed a little girl to die.*

"It's not my fault," Gaston insisted. "I'm not to blame. It is Count Andrei and the Witch who brought upon this plague. The Raven- he is a fool, but they are all in Yohnah's plan. He… he…"

Behind him, Gaston heard something brush against the stone floor. He turned and saw the wolf that he had allowed sanctuary within the church pass him by, those glowing yellow eyes acknowledging him as it continued to walk down the length of the candlelit sanctuary.

Turning his eyes back to the glass dove high above him, Gaston shuddered. The room… it felt so much warmer, now that the wolf had finally left.

"This is all just a part of your test of faith," he continued to pray. "The Raven will be bled out, and the fires of Oblivion will burn this damned city to the ground for their leader has forsaken thee. All the demons that crawl in search for blood shall burn with that Witch. That Dhampir… such beauty, even though I hate her, and know her for what she is… sin-incarnate, but beautiful… so beautiful… this is what sin really is. It is beautiful; what we want most in this entire world. Temptation… oh how hard it is to resist.

"Is this part of your plan as well, Great Yohnah? Very well, then test me. Don't let this Siren continue to haunt me any longer. Destroy the Dhampir as you destroy this blasphemous city that has turned their eyes away from you, and let her taste the fires of Oblivian."

He paused, a jolt passing through him as he realized he did not *quite* want that. So instead, he made another request.

"Or else... let her be mine. Let her come here, I shall give her sanctuary, purify her with the love of the Dove, and I leave this sinful city, and carry on your great and merciful words. To create a good world, the darkness, the evil, must be casted into the lakes of fire. This entire city, the demons both physically and spiritually, must turn to cinders. That Dhampir, I pray that she will be mine; mine to change, to convert, or she will burn with those who have destroyed this city. I pray, dear Yohnah, let your will be done in my favor, and destroy them all. And the Dhampir, let me save her, or let her burn. That is your test, and that is your will for me. God have mercy on her..."

You killed them all... You've abandoned them, false priest...

"God have mercy on me..."

Murderer... fallen priest, faithless hypocrite...

"This city will be turned to ash, and I shall rise within the new start of a new era; all for my glory through you. And all who oppose me, shall burn. May the Raven never fly again after tonight, may the Immortal be damned as it should have been, and may the Dhampir... if is a part of the plan for me, choose me, or the fire. Burn, Dhampir... or follow me..."

Deceiver...

"Choose me, or burn..."

Thief...

"I am the righteous man of Yohnah, who shall smite the world of darkness and plunge them into the fiery pit…"

Murderer…

"And though she is a fallen angel, she will be mine and rise anew, or she will be purged by the fire. This, is all a part of Yohnah's plan, this is my destiny!"

And so Gaston threw his face down upon the ground, the nails in his fingers scraping against stone as he prayed for the best of his behalf. "I will live… I will prosper… I will, become the next hand of God. I will bring Irondell to ashes, and plant the seeds of a new and glorious future. I am… I am…"

He just couldn't finish. The voices in his head and throughout the church brought him further down onto his face, and the screams of the Vampires outside shattered his will, silencing him as the night continued on, and on, and on.

"You *bitch*…" Andrei gasped angrily at Angela who had him on the floor with his arm twisted at an angle to almost dislocate his shoulder. "Why did you come back!?" he demanded in a loud voice.

"Where is the Raven?" Angela asked again taking a step forward right onto Andrei's left hand while still holding his right arm. She then adjusted her foot so that the toe of her boot got right underneath two of his fingers.

"W-wait!" Andrei pleaded waving his other hand just slightly. "I can explain!"

"I'm waiting," Angela said sternly; impatiently.

"The Raven told me he was taking care of it! He told me my job was to make sure no Vampire left the city and nothing else got in- for fear of getting a traveler infected. My soldiers assist in the patrols at night, while he hunts the Immortal responsible for this."

"You're lying," Angela said. "Your city is burning, and your precious Raven is leaving many to die. You're their leader, so why don't you actually *do* something?"

"I am!" Andrei insisted. "I am trying to prove to the Emperor that I trust him and his Thunder of Ravens; they will purge this world of darkness and-"

"Silence." Angela said as she stepped forward and snapped the Count's fingers backwards with a sickening *crunch*. Andrei screamed loudly as Angela stooped down and grabbed ahold of his jugular again, silencing him almost immediately.

"You goddamned monster!" Andrei shrieked with tears in his bulging eyes, the pathetic excuse of a leader. "You... fuckin' cunt!"

"Charming," Angela said pulling her foot back and allowing the Count to pull his now deformed hand away, glaring at it with a horrified expression with his palm facing Angela.

"My hand!" Andrie cried staring at his broken fingers. As he was staring at his injury, Angela caught sight of what was in his palm, and she grabbed his wrist and pulled the hand closer for her to inspect it.

In the man's palm, was a rune carved into his flesh. The symbol, stood for 'glass'. It sat in the center of a pentagram, likewise carved into his palm and scarred over in white. The man had been playing with the runes, and now he had one literally *carved* into his own hand.

Angela jerked the man's hand around, breaking the wrist while forcing him to stare at it. After the man stopped screaming, she gave her command.

"Explain this."

"Get your filthy hand off me you half-breed sow!" Andrei cried out with tears rolling down his fat cheeks. "You broke my damn hand, and you think I–"

"I'll cut the bloody thing off if that will make it easier for you," Angela said bringing her face closer to Andrei's and making him look directly into her glowing eyes. "Do you not realize what you have done? You have cursed yourself, playing with the very language of Oblivion itself! Who taught you this? Was it the Raven?"

Andrei grimaced as if she smacked him. "Yes! He taught me! He said it was expected of all who followed Emperor Ion now. No one is supposed to know about this!"

"Why?" Angela demanded now greatly disturbed as to how much the Emperor might really know about the devil worshippers under his own command. But to also require the holds to deny Yohnah and take on the markings of the Witch and the star of Kafcaw?

"I don't know!" Andrei began sobbing pitifully. "I don't... I don't know..."

Angela narrowed her eyes. The man really was useless. This mark; these runes and the ritual performed here, it was all terrible news. If Ion was expecting his underdogs to follow such forbidden teachings that even some Witches might not even attempt, that could not be good for the realm, or anyone associated with them.

But first things first, Angela had another job to do for now. She could worry about such things later. Right now, she had to find the one responsible for all this bloodshed, and to find out why he had been teaching the Count such horrible practices.

"I'll ask one more time then," she said giving the Count one last chance. "Where is the Raven? Where can I find him?"

Andrei started breathing fast, like he was about to hyperventilate. "I don't know…"

"You're lying to me again," Angela said in a low voice that almost came out as a growl. "I will end your life right now. Do you want that? I will make sure that the last thing you see in this world before the gates of Oblivion swallow you up won't be pretty. I will make you *scream*."

Andrei then started mumbling something. His mumbling formed mixed words, and Angela realized too late that the man was chanting in tongues, and the rune on his hand was starting to glow and bleed like a fresh wound. Then with her holding his hand, he twisted and clapped his hands together, his other palm now stained by the pentagram.

Angela was just about to run the man through with her sword when the glass window behind her suddenly imploded and shattered with shards of glass showered onto her back, forcing her to flee in order to keep from being impaled. When she landed nimbly back on her feet, a few tinkling bits of glass falling from her shredded cloak, she looked up to see Count Andrei struggling up to his feet.

The Count now stood as large as a Nephil, his spell having converged the painted glass shards around his body that took the form of some monstrous figure of glass with a wolf's head and bulging arms, bellowing and tinkling with shards that occasionally fell away like dead skin. Those that fell away proceeded to roll back to the feet of the monster and return to their original position. It dragged it's curved claws of glass across the floor, tearing the boards to shreds as it stood above Angela, who only stared in awe at the phenomenon.

She narrowed her violet eyes. *So, this is what a bonded rune is capable of...*

Count Andrei's voice sounded muffled within the cocoon of glass, "Now you'll pay for your insolence, you miserable wretch!"

The glass-beast that had covered Andrei suddenly raised a massive arm, and slashed down at her with incredible speed, sending down a shower of glass at the same time in order to rip the Dhampir to shreds. Angela spun aside just as the claws dug into the wood. The glass entity then tried to swipe her aside with its other hand, shredding the bed and making it smash against the side of the room with a thunderous crash. The creature then snarled at Angela again; its bellow somewhere between the sound of glass sliding together mixed with the screams of anguish from a man with nothing to lose.

"I see," Angela said disappointed now. "You have abandoned your faith in order to find comfort in the darkness. You thought you could survive the dark of night by allowing yourself to accept the Raven's black teachings. You've abandoned light, in foolish hopes that darkness could destroy darkness."

"Shut up!" the voice of Andrei screamed within the swirling body of glass. "I am Count Andrei, and I shall live on to continue my Lord's work! I am not wrong! I am not accepting anything other than my Emperor's word! I've done nothing wrong if I am told to do what I must now."

"At the cost of the people you swore to protect and lead," Angela said bringing her sword up and placing a hand on her Blunderbuss. "Humans really are weak fools of no faith. You justify your wrongs no matter how much blood is spilt, and you go on to shift the blame to others because of your insolence."

"*My* insolence!?" Andrei snarled as his glass beast raised another tinkling arm. "I'll show you insolence, when your kind is wiped off the face of the earth!" The clawed hand came down and Angela stepped back, bringing up the gun and firing it at the arm and shattering the glass into shards. The whole arm disintegrated and tinkled across the floor only to return to the body where it had been removed.

"Bitch!" Andrei snarled again and swiped at Angela with its other arm. The Dhampir was already on the move however, kicking the bedroom doors open and sprinting down the hall away from the glass entity. There was hardly any room in the bedroom or this hall- she had to get Andrei out into the open.

Some men turned the corner and though they shouted and rose their weapons, Angela sailed over them as if she had wings. Upon landing on the wall behind them, she immediately turned aside and out of the way as Andrei came barreling in, his glass shards tearing the terrified men into meaty ribbons as he collided with the back wall. Sparks flashed as the bloodied glass scraped against the stone, and Andrei turned his monstrous head towards the Dhampir, who was already moving once again.

With a snarl, he ripped a torn and mangled body off his chest and tossed it aside, splashing the nearby wall with a gory smear. At this point, Angela had turned the corner again and vaulted over the railing down into the training pit where William and the Nephil were already starting to move; the sounds of the fight catching their attention. They gasped as she landed into the pit, and William went for his weapon.

"It's you!" he snapped.

Angela looked up at the two men with a stern and cold expression. "Run." she told them just as Andrei came barreling over the railing, smashing a pillar to shreds as the glass beast crashed down into the ground. Some shards had scattered away from the impact, but they all immediately rolled back to their host and rebuilt the massive body that then screamed at the Dhampir and the two men who stared in utter terror.

"Wh-what the hell is that thing!?" Hephus growled.

"Get out of here!" Angela shouted this time. She didn't look back but kept her eyes on Andrei, who was angry within his protection of bloodied glass.

"I am blessed with the power of the Stars, you cunt!" Andrei bellowed. "I will destroy you!" The glass arm came up again and Angela rolled aside as she moved in close to the entity's torso. However, some shards shot out from under the arm and nearly impaled Angela who just barely managed to make it out of harm's way and create some distance between her and the corrupted Count once again.

"Come on, try again!" Andrei taunted the Dhampir. "Don't tell me you're afraid, *Huntress*. Show me what you filthy bloodsuckers are capable of! Come on- come on you *leech*! Attack me!"

Angela raised her sword again, just as she heard gunshots erupt behind her. Andrei staggered back as bullets struck his glass casing and made the beast stagger back. Angela looked back fast to see both William and the Nephil near the gun racks. William was shooting one rifle after the other while Hephus rushed around the room and came at the Count, swinging a massive club.

Angela shouted, warning the giant not to do it, but it was too late. With a swipe of his arm, Andrei sent forth a volley of glass shards that stuck right into Hephus, dropping him in a flash of red as the crashing of his body shook nearly the entire castle.

"Hephus!" William screamed as he took aim and fired at the creature again. Sparks and chunks of glass flew but just as fast they would roll right back. Nothing could break through the many shards; the only way to destroy it, was to create a weak spot so that Angela could get to Andrei himself.

"Keep back!" Angela commanded William and she rushed back into battle, her sword in one hand and her revolver in the other. One way or another, she was going to put an end to this madness. She would get Andrei to talk, or he would die.

She heard another gunshot and the glass-beast staggered back howling again as a chunk of its head went flying, the wolf's head now missing an ear and part of it's skull. Seizing her chance, Angela leapt into her opening and swung her sword, shattering away fragments of painted glass and nearly hitting the Count within. The shards within the body then stuck out, ready to be launched at Angela but she was already prepared for it; her flashing eyes predicted it.

As the shards came flying at her she whipped her cloak around, snagging the glass and creating yet another opening for her to swing her blade at the same spot again, tearing away more glass. She was forced to back away as the glass-beast swung at her but firing her revolver again and again in the same spot she had struck, she punctured away more chunks of glass with the sixth bullet piercing right through and hitting the fat flesh of Andrei within. The glass-beast howled as Andrei screamed, and the embodiment backed away as blood dribbled from the shards that were quickly closing up again.

"Damn you, Dhampir…" Andrei growled. "I won't allow you to get close like that again!"

That was when Angela heard a gasp of surprise behind her, and realized that William had found out the truth. "My Count…"

"Captain!" Andrei screamed out. "Stop fucking shooting your leader! Kill the Dhampir, and whatever your heart wishes for, I shall grant! She is the enemy here, just like all the undead out there destroying our city! Slay her now and prove your worth!"

"Count Andrei…" William turned his eyes upon Angela, whose back was still to him. "What-"

"William," Angela said keeping her eyes on the glass-beast which was slowly starting to recover. "Your Count has abandoned his people to a Raven who has taught him black magic. You have every reason to hate and fear me. But this man who leads you, he has abandoned you and everyone in this city. He is cursed by the black magic of the demon Kawfka, and such connections to Oblivion must never exist. He is willing to learn the powers of the Dark, in exchange for the lives of all in Irondell."

"It is the Dhampir that lies!" Andrei roared. "Such a dirty, filthy creature- you cannot trust them! She shares the blood of those who had slaughtered your family! Shoot her now, and I promise you, you will achieve greatness in my glory!"

"William," Angela said speaking loud enough for him to hear while at the same time keeping a tight grip on her sword just in case. "He has rejected Yohnah, in exchange for power. Look upon him now, and know the Raven who was supposed to save you all has instead taught him the magic of Oblivion."

"Liar!" Andrei shrieked. "I am a servant to Emperor Ion, just as much as you are, William! He commands, I listen. If he commands us to follow a different god, then who are we to object? If that Raven says he will take care of the Vampire Plague by order of the Emperor, then he will!"

"How well has that been going, William?" Angela asked, hoping and praying that the man wouldn't pointing the next gun at her. By then Andrei was up and now circling to the left, ready to attack at any moment. "Has the situation gotten any better? Have you even seen the Raven actually kill a Vampire? Has the body count fallen at all? If they really were intent on killing all the Vampires, why hasn't the situation been resolved yet, and why is your precious Count taking such a precaution as to make a pact with the devil himself?"

"Enough!" Andrei screamed as he grabbed ahold of Hephus' bloody corpse and *hurled* it across the room. Angela dove aside and stepped back as the glass-beast came charging at her and dig its claws into the floor.

"I will do as my Emperor commands and will rise beyond a human; I will become as one of the Stars! And I will annihilate anyone who gets in my way!"

Andrei came at Angela again, sending another volley of glass shards at her as she nimbly danced through the storm unscathed.

So that's what it is... she thought upon landing again.

Andrei came at her again, an arm raised with many glass shards ready to rip her to shreds. Before he could take a swipe at her however, another thundering gunshot made Angela freeze as she felt the bullet fly close past her head and collide with the chest of the glass-beast, mere inches from where Andrei's own reflection was. Glass sprinkled through the air as the impact tore away a major chunk and exposed the Count's shoulder.

Seizing her chance, Angela stabbed forward, unnerved by the shards that prepared to rain down upon her like dragon scales. Her sword lunged fast and true, and she stabbed the Count through the shoulder, making him scream and causing the glass-beast to go rigid. Using her impaled sword as an anchor, Angela lifted her body up and with a mighty kick, shattered the beast's remaining head into many fragments and exposing the hollow inside. She leapt up onto the shoulder while dragging her bloodied sword out in the process. She then reached in to where the naked Count was, and with a mighty tug, ripped the man right out of the glass-beast, his skin becoming shredded along the edges as she tossed him to the opposite wall. The Count tumbled across the dirt and Angela leapt off and started for him, the beast behind her staggering without the support of its master.

Andrei started backing up still on the ground, panicking with wide eyes and a stammering mouth. "Get away!" he screamed holding out his cursed mark towards her as if to ward her off. "I command you! Kill her! Kill her!"

Angela heard the glass-beast start towards her, it's glass feet scratching the floor as it lunged forward. Another gunshot erupted and its entire chest blew apart. It stumbled and more glass shards fell tinkling onto the floor. Angela then swung her sword one last time, and in that single strike, shattered the entire beast in a glistening rainfall of glass. The shards did not attempt to put themselves back together, and laid glistening on the floor in the candlelight like the remains of a fallen chandelier.

Angela, then turned her attention back to the Count, who was staring at her in horror as she regarded him with cold lavender eyes. "Now wait a second!" He squeaked backing up until he struck the wall. "You don't understand, I-"

Angela closed the distance between her and the Count before he could even dare utter another word. Her sword was then driven into his other shoulder, making the man scream as she pinned him against the wall with nowhere to run. The strong scent of the fatty blood struck her nose, but she ignored the tantalizing temptation. With her free hand, she grabbed ahold of the hand that bore the pentagram and twisted, snapping the bone at the wrist and with a sharp tug, ripped the hand off which dangled pathetically on a single shred of flesh. The pathetic Count to scream in agony as he stared wild-eyed at the dangling hand which bled profusely.

"Where is the Raven?" she demanded, grabbing his face with her free hand and forcing him to look at her.

"He left!" Andrei screamed, the will to keep secrets no longer on his mind. "He left to hunt for you and your partner! He hopes that will bring out the Immortal and end this… this nightmare once and for all!"

"Why did he wait for so long?" Angela demanded. "And why isn't he helping with the fight against the rest of the scourge?"

"He said it wasn't in Emperor Ion's interest to save every single soul in Irondell!" Andrei spat the truth out with tears and snot running down his face. "The Emperor only wanted the destruction of the Immortal, Count Horla. Everyone else- except for me if I followed the Raven's teachings -was and is expendable. It said so in the letter the Raven had with him!"

Angela narrowed her eyes. "Why is the Raven teaching you black magic?"

"So I could better serve the Emperor!" Andrei cried. "He said it was my Lord's will!"

"And you *believed* him?" Angela demanded. With a shake of her head, she wrenched her sword from the man's fat arm. Flesh and muscle were ripped by the jagged edge, making the man scream and clutch his bloody arm all the tighter, torn between his destroyed hand and shoulder.

"You are pathetic, you who have so little faith. It takes a *man* to kill monsters such as Immortals. But instead, you decide to hide in the blackness of whatever madness this Raven has told you. Just like when Emperor Ion made his contract with those devil-worshippers, you merely accepted their words without filly understanding the repercussions. It is ignorant men like you that destroy this world."

"Please…" Andrei said holding up the arm that hung the same hand that still bore the bloody rune. "I only did what my leader commands me. Anyone would have done the same. Please… Show mercy…"

With a blinding swipe of her arm, Angela's sword sliced the rest hand off at the wrist, sending it flying into the air and fall with a bloody splat. Andrei screamed out again as he clutched his bleeding stump into his belly with a sad attempt to stop the bleeding.

"It hurts! It hurts!" he screamed.

"William," Angela said turning her angry eyes to the captain. "Your leader has abandoned you. The Raven, has abandoned you. Keep all the Watchmen inside. I'm going to find him."

The soldier stared at the Dhampir with frightened eyes. "What are you going to do?" he stammered, disturbed beyond questions and unable to truly believe what he had witnessed and heard.

"I'm going to kill the man, and bring Count Horla out into the open." Keeping her bloody sword out, Angela brushed past the man and started to go. "I'll put an end to this nightmare. Have faith in me."

"Have faith in *you*!?" Andrei demanded spitting as he shrieked. "A *Dhampir*!? William, I command you, shoot that monster, now! She is part of that horde that has haunted Balkeñoir since the beginning of time! She is a bastard of a human and an Immortal! She is a creature who should be eradicated from this planet by any means necessary! Surely you believe the same thing, yes? Kill her! Kill her! Kill her! That's an order, soldier!"

Shrrik!

Angela stopped at the sound of a knife slicing through flesh. She turned her head and from the corner of her eye, she saw William standing above Count Andrei with a bloody dagger in hand. The fat leader of Irondell choked on the blood that sprayed from the deep gash in his throat and doused the soldier's pants.

Then Andrei, fell over to his side, twitching and choking still, as he bled out like a stuck pig.

"You traitor..." William muttered with controlled rage as he dropped the knife to the floor. "You... you... bastard..."

Angela said nothing, but merely started to go.

"Dhampir," William called out, making her stop again. He didn't look back to her, and she didn't look back at him. Their eyes were set on something else, both present and future. "Be honest with me… Is Irondell doomed?"

Angela fell silent for a moment. For a long while, the only sound was the whistle of the wind somewhere in the castle halls, and the screams of the undead outside. When she did speak, her voice was so low that William almost couldn't hear her.

But she gave him his answer, as she started to go.

"It'll all be over soon. I promise that much."

La

Jacob vaulted over the Raven again, hooking his legs around the man's neck and slamming him onto the ground upon rolling as he proceeded to try and stab at his enemy's chest.

The Raven was quick though; he kicked up and sent Jacob flying back and forced the Hunter to back off with the toss of a throwing knife that stuck right into Jacob's arm. There was little pain but a numbness came over Jacob's arm. The Raven then rushed for him again and the two locked blades and trembled as they pushed against one another; their weapons grinding and quivering against the opposite strengths.

Now that they were close, Jacob could see the eyes behind the beak-shaped mask. They were brown, like hazelnuts in the long-forgotten spring, but cold and hard; they were the eyes of a warrior. Despite getting stabbed and cut by Jacob and even missing a hand, the Raven was still a skilled fighter and deadly opponent. The human being really was a formidable creature, having been able to adapt to change how they function even after crippling blows to their body. This Raven, despite having no hand and having a clear disadvantage, gave Jacob a fight he would always remember. But Jacob could hear the man's labored breathing; he was just as tired as him, if not more so.

It almost made Jacob smile through his clenched teeth. "Guess I shouldn't be surprised, eh?"

"You are good," the Raven said beneath his mask. "I'll give you that. It is a shame, really, that you chose to work with the Black Hand."

"You really don't know anything, do you?" Jacob asked him. "If you did, you and I wouldn't be fighting now."

"What are you talking about?" the Raven asked in a worried tone, though the pressure pushing back against Jacob didn't falter in the slightest.

"If you don't know, then it doesn't matter," Jacob told him. "Besides, you've only been messing around here in Irondell, when you should be doing your goddamn job killing the beasts and finding the Immortal responsible for this."

"That's just a waste of energy," the Raven's eyes narrowed as he spoke. "You are still a young Hunter. You will soon see that fighting the undead horde will just tire you out. The fastest way to end a plague is to find the source of the virus and eliminate it."

"What about the people who were infected?" Jacob demanded pushing back a little harder. "What about the Watchmen and citizens who have died already and could have been saved if there were less Vampires out there?"

"You can't save everyone," the Raven said solemnly. "My job is as simple as any contract: find the Immortal, and eliminate them. If I run into any superior supernatural beings, I should eliminate them as well. My job is not to hunt every lesser Vampire out there, or save the pathetic scum of this city. Why should I? It makes no difference."

"How cowardly," Jacob said clenching his teeth harder as he shifted his weight and kicked out at the man's ankles, throwing him off balance and striking at him again without waiting.

The two collided again and hacked at one another, their blades clashing and sending forth sparks as they rang with intense and deadly intent. The two Hunters danced around one another like acrobats; their movements quick and nimble while at the same time devastating if one were to slip up. The snow and blood on the ground made it difficult to keep his footing but Jacob refused to allow himself to slip. When he hacked at the man again, his dagger collided with the Raven's face, not harming him but knocking the metallic mask right off to reveal a stubble-ridden chin and cheeks covered in scars. The Raven looked to be in his thirties, his eyes cold and full of anger now that his visor was gone.

But such an action gave Jacob an opening, and he retreated back to have enough room. "Time to end this half-assed game of yours." He threw his last expendable dagger at the Raven to force him to dodge, and with his free hand Jacob pulled back his eyepatch, revealing his Immortal Eye. The Raven, who was now charging right at Jacob, expressed incredible shock as well as the terror for what could possibly come. It was still too soon for him to use the eye again, but Jacob was practically laughing now, determined to end this fight and find out the truth behind this game of lives.

"Stop." he commanded. "You will drop your weapon and-"

But the Raven kept coming and before Jacob could finish his command, he was forced to step back and get his only dagger up to avoid getting stabbed again. He flashed his eye again, commanding the man to stop. But the Raven merely smirked as he roundhouse-kicked Jacob back, making him crash right into the fencing containing the now rearing horses.

"What the…" Jacob groaned as he started to pull himself up. He glared at the Raven, who slowly made his way over to the Hunter as if he had all the time in the world. Taking a bolt from his hip, the Raven even loaded his crossbow as he walked over to the surprised Hunter.

"That's very interesting." the Raven said. "I've never seen a human with an eye-transplant like that before. And Immortal to boot… Red… hypnosis… incredible. Tell me, Hunter, where did you get that eye?"

"Wha…" *Why isn't it working?* Jacob thought frustratedly. He groaned in pain as his eye started to burn like fire; a reaction of the use of the eye. When he felt tears come out of his Immortal Eye he reached up to wipe them. When he brought his hand back however, he saw that his fingertips were stained with not tears, but blood.

"Contacts," the Raven said pointing at his face. "Cuts out certain light patterns that Immortal Eyes give out. It's how they work their cursed magic upon the weak-minded. If you had two eyes, you might have had a chance. But, alas," the man took aim with his crossbow, ready to shoot it while at the same time having his jagged sword ready. "It seems that your little trump card has failed. I will enjoy cutting you up to see what other secrets you might have kept hidden. I knew there was something wrong with you when I came down to see you."

"After killing off the boys, eh?" Jacob said, trying to sound ignorantly confident while at the same time terrified. He felt his hand beneath his glove jolt slightly, as if lightning was coursing between his fingers. Would he have to use it? No... he couldn't, but maybe...

"Where is your partner?" the Raven demanded. "Tell me now, and I'll make it quick."

"Let me guess," Jacob said with a smirk. "You'll kill me slow if I don't? Come on, be original."

The Raven shook his head. "You got some cheek, boy. Now tell me, Hunter, where is the Dhampir? I'm not going to ask again."

Jacob grinned. "How do you folks at Goldendell say it? Oh, yeah... Bugger off, you fucking wanker."

The Raven smirked back. "Cute." And he released the bolt, which stuck right into Jacob's arm. The Hunter, ignoring the pain, rushed up and swung at the Raven, who easily ducked and with his stump, punched at the bolt in his arm, sending out a jarring pain through Jacob's arm again. Then grabbing the same arm, the Raven swung Jacob over his shoulder and slammed him back down onto the ground with a thundering *crash*, his head smacking against a rock in the process.

With the wind knocked out of him, Jacob could only freeze as he felt the cold blade of the Raven's sword press against his jugular. "You get one more chance, Black Hand. Tell me where the she-demon is, you piece of filth."

Jacob chuckled, which then turned into laughter.

"What?" the Raven demanded angrily. "Is this something to laugh about?"

"I'm just amazed is all. You really don't know anything about what is happening with the Raven's and the Black Hand, do you?"

Confusion gleamed across the Raven's eyes. "What?"

"No matter." Jacob smiled. "I guess I understand why they sent you of all people here. They wanted to see if you had a chance, but it is clear that you didn't. You are a coward who hides until the you can find the Immortal- if that day ever comes. You really expect a Vampire to just *come* to you? A *real* Hunter acts like a predator, not prey. You put all Hunters in the world to shame, *Raven*. You don't even deserve to be called such a thing. I'm honestly amazed that Ion signed the Contract of Blood with you lot in the first place. I'm amazed that Angela gave up so easily before, but I guess it makes sense. You were never worth her time to begin with."

The Raven's face twisted red with anger. The man was clenching his teeth so tightly that Jacob thought they might crack under the intense pressure. "You fuckin'…" the Raven growled in his throat. "The Black Hand will *never* best the Ravens! We are the future! Now," and he raised his sword. "Die."

Jacob smiled as he started to slip off the glove from his hand. There was no choice now. "I'm gonna enjoy this…"

The Raven started to stab downward, but he suddenly froze. Jacob would have used this pause to use his last trump card, but found that he couldn't. He couldn't move, and he couldn't breathe. It was as if rusty chains had coiled around his very lungs, taking the breath right out of him and squeezing all the tighter. The air suddenly felt colder, and looking up at the Raven, he saw that the man was suddenly relaxing, his head looking all around them.

Darkness, enveloped them both like a cloud.

Black fog was rising from the ground, circling the two men and condensing more and more over the walls. As the black mass passed over a body, Jacob was shocked to see that the blood spilling from any corpse suddenly rose as if gravity had forsaken it, and mixed in with the darkness until there wasn't a single drop let around or even in the body. It was like the fog itself was sucking the blood right out of the body. The horses in the stall started to panic and cower close to one another in the back of their stalls; frightened beyond words.

What is this? Jacob thought to himself as he felt his spine tingle, causing his entire body to shake with the desire to flee and escape the sea of darkness. *Is this... what terror feels like?*

Yes, he supposed that was what it was; complete and utter terror. He wanted to get away from the fog, which was now condensing into one spot, all swirling in shadow and crimson flow of blood.

The mass continued to grow and accumulate until it took the shape of a large man of pure darkness. From the head, two cat-like eyes of yellow flashed open; a smile with many sharp teeth appeared beneath the eyes, and as the shadow condensed even more, it soon solidified and revealed a tall pale man wearing a black suit and cloak around his broad shoulders. His fingers were long and bony like a skeleton's, and his lips as red as blood. Upon his breast was a brooch of sapphire, and on his left hand, a ruby ring similar to that of Angela's that Jacob recognized.

The man stared at the two Hunters before him, and his lip curled back to reveal two fangs curled over his bottom lip; sharpened to points that even Jacob could not see completely. The Raven immediately got off of him, allowing him to sit up and back away from the towering man, his presence crushing the very air around him like miles of ocean water.

That's an... Jacob thought scrambling to his feet and backing up further away, passing by the Raven who appeared planted right where he was.

"Good evening," the Immortal said with a thick accent and raising an arm and with it the cloak that made him appear as if he had wings of shadow that swirled and churned. "I pray that you'll pardon the intrusion, you two looked like you were having fun. It was quite entertaining, two dogs fighting for dominance. Unfortunately, I did not come to play your silly games."

Then with the same arm that he rose, the Immortal turned and pointed a bony finger at the Raven. "You. Vicar Virgil, I presume?"

"You know me," the Raven chirped audibly. "Sir...?"

At this point, Jacob had backed clear enough away so that he was halfway near the castle doors where his bow still laid in the snow. The pain in his belly was forgotten, and the cuts he had received while fighting the Raven were nothing more than a distant memory. All he felt, were cold hands trying to hold him in place; the presence of the Vampire suffocating him with utter terror.

Is this magic? he wondered, feeling that his mouth had become as arid as the southern reservation.

"Oh, I know," the Vampire replied with a knowing smile both beautiful and frightening; like the look a hangman would give beneath his hood before pulling the lever. "In fact, I've been looking all over for you. You never come out to play at night, and my disciples were starting to worry when they couldn't find you anywhere. The dead always fear their new master; their new god. Thankfully they were finally able to find you here, just where Count Andrei slept."

Jacob crouched down to retrieve his bow, not once ever taking his eyes off the Vampire who seemed completely fixated on the Raven before him. It occurred to him that the Immortal didn't care that Jacob was there.

"And now I have found you." the Raven said getting into a stance with his sword ready to do battle. "You have finally come out of hiding, monster."

"I believe that is *my* line," the Immortal said wagging a finger as if scolding a misbehaving child. "For it is *you*, who was hiding from *me*. Unfortunately, not even the living of Irondell could protect you forever. I'm honestly surprised you haven't run away from here."

"A true Raven never backs down!" challenged the Raven with whatever courage he could muster. Even he was unable to resist the fear the monster was pouring into him like a vase of cold water.

"No, they do not. Not from their demonic religion, nor their stubborn arrogance. You lot really have no place in the world of man, trying to become gods yourself. You really are a disgrace to all humanity. That foolish Emperor of yours must really be losing it now, to be anointing such *filth* to defend his cities; or was that the point all along? I mean after all, Balkeñoir is just a giant chessboard for the kings and lords of the living.”

"You have no say here, Vampire.” the Raven said seeming unnerved by the superior being before him. “It is none of your concern of what happens in the land of the living; all you have to know is that you will not survive this night!”

"Oh?” The Immortal chuckled, amused and Jacob gaped at the Raven as he slowly started to back away a little further; anything to get a little further away from that thing. Virgil either had to be incredibly brave, or downright stupid to say such things.

Horla then gestured with a lazy hand at Virgil. “Then please, indulge me. I would like to see what the man who killed my protégé has in him.”

Protégé...? Jacob stopped moving at the foot of the stairs leading up to the castle. He wanted to just turn and flee into the building where it was safe, but he just couldn’t move. He could only stare into those horrible yellow eyes that glowed like the fires of the very sun.

The Raven said to the Vampire, “I was only performing my duties in making sure no more of your scourge infected the living.”

"And what a marvelous job you have done.” The Vampire smiled, now slowly clapping in lazy mock-applause. “That Huntress slayed my little brother, and I had planned to bring her into my coven as my eternal servant. Unfortunately, you killed her before my brother's kiss could convert her, and I cannot forgive such an act."

"So, all this carnage, for a single bitch?"

The Vampire chuckled with deep and yet somehow begrudging amusement. "Yes, I suppose that is what she should be called for killing my little brother, though I suppose it is justifiable. He was such a simple man, not even grown into his own eyes when we chose to walk the path of true darkness. You Ravens think you are so special, with your black magic when you merely *adopted* the darkness. *We*, had been reborn in it. Unfortunately Takeshi was still not strong enough in the end, and as a result, he was killed by a lesser Huntress. That Huntress, was to serve a fate worse than death. She would have become one of my most powerful servants, in redemption for the blood she had spilt, and you took her away from me. And now, this entire city will suffer because of your sin. Now, I shall give *you* a fate worse than death."

Horla then raised his arms, and hissed with laughter. With his hands raised it also brought a chill that removed all warmth, muddled all sound, extinguished all hope. The very shadows themselves darkened and rippled like restless wraiths emerging to haunt their prey.

"Prepare yourself, Vicar Virgil, to suffer my wrath. You talk a big game, Raven, so come on, attack me! Show me just what the Thunder of Ravens are truly capable of! You've hidden from my undead because you fear them, I can smell it; you *reek* from it! I'll show you how a *true* Vampire does battle! Come on, Raven, attack me!"

The Raven undid his feathered cloak and allowed it to flutter away in the light breeze, exposing his armored torso and tossing his hat into the air as well. "In the name of my lord, and Emperor Ion, Lord of the Eastern World and bringer of justice to the unworthy, I hereby condemn you back to Oblivion where you belong, Josef Horla of the Night!"

Jacob reached for an arrow as he winced. *You fool.*

"Excellent," the Immortal hissed and suddenly the entire world felt like it had dropped another twenty degrees; the snow froze into ice and the breath in Jacob's mouth turned to thick vapor. A shadow seemed to emit from Horla's cloak and began to slowly engulf him. From the abyss of darkness, Jacob could have sworn he heard howling; the hounds of Hell itself, ready to pounce on their next victim.

"Come on, attack me!"

The Raven bellowed and charged towards the mass of darkness. The eyes of Horla suddenly flashed brightly, blinding the world like a beacon on the seaside shores, and Jacob cried out as he felt *both* of his eyes burn from the effect. The Immortal's magic was powerful enough to make him falter, but he did not receive the direct assault as that of Vicar Virgil.

The Raven suddenly stopped charging, and with a shrill shriek he fell back right onto the ground and started to back away from the Vampire. He had completely forgotten about his crossbow and sword and started to quickly crabwalk away from the Vampire, who cackled in amused laughter. Whatever he was seeing now, was not what Jacob was seeing. Whatever the Vampire did, it had turned Vlad into a babbling fool; terrified for his very life. He backed away fast, while the mass of darkness only seemed to remain where it was, taking its sweet time to kill him.

"What's the matter?" the Immortal's voice echoed from everywhere and not just from where he stood. "Come on, attack me! You've been hiding for so long, and talking a big game. Come at me!"

As he spoke, Jacob could have sworn he could see something in the mass of shadow; a snarling beast with a large snout and maw full of teeth, and the eyes glowed brighter and brighter. Those horrible yellow eyes flashed towards Jacob, and he froze in place. He could suddenly see someone... something terrible...

M-mother...

"Come on, attack me!" Count Horla snarled. "Hurry, hurry!"

The Raven only remained seated, cried out and shielded his eyes.

Jacob tried to will his legs and arms to move, but they refused to obey his commands. He was *planted*; stuck in place as his hag of a mother cackled at him. Her eyes burned bright and yellow with terrible delight, and her chiseled teeth flashed brightly with hunger. He could feel the burning on his own flesh, the many knives cutting into him and the many liquids burning his throat as they were forced into his mouth. Every horrible, inhumane thing she had ever done to him, at that moment, Jacob felt all of it; the worst of it being his Immortal Eye, that burned like molten fire and when he felt tears spilling from it again, he saw blood drip down his cheek and fall onto his boots.

What kind of... horrible magic is this? It feels like... all my strength has been sapped away... I can't move...

Jacob's eyes lingered towards the walls, and he saw more Vampires perched along the walls like grinning demons, waiting for the poor souls caught by their master to be dragged down into Oblivion. They all chittered and hissed in both anguish and delight as they laughed at the two Hunters, who despite their best efforts, could not escape the terrible gaze of Count Horla.

"No! Get away!" Vicar screamed. "You are not real! You're not! I would assure my Emperor I was-"

"Silence!" the Shadow snarled. Momentarily, the vision of Jacob's mother slipped, revealing an angry Vampire for a brief second. "Your whining and sniveling *insults* me! Face it: You are not worthy to be called a Raven- or a Hunter for that matter! You are a disgrace to your own kind; you have *failed*."

From the shadow, a clawed hand stretched out and grabbed ahold of Vicar by the neck. He then forced the man to his feet, and the head of Horla emerged from the darkness, smiling terribly at the man who whimpered and shook where he stood. "Now then, shall I give *you* the kiss of death?"

"Kill me!" the Raven begged the Vampire, hot tears rolling down his cheeks. "Please, just end it! Don't... don't show me his face again! Just kill me, please!"

"Kill you? Oh, come now, death is too good for a man such as yourself. I intend to make you *suffer* for not only taking away my Akira, but also for your cowardice."

The Vampire reached out with another hand, and with a swipe of a finger, his claw cut a thin slice into the side of his own neck. Blood ran out of the small wound, seeming darker than normal like aged wine.

"Where is your demon lord now, Raven?" Horla chuckled, and then pulling the man's face into his own neck, he held the screaming Raven there who tried to fight it. His screams were muffled and despite his efforts, Horla did not let up on him. Eventually however, his screaming's slowed down, and then his body seemed to quit fighting altogether.

It was then when Jacob realized that the Raven had tasted the blood of the Immortal; he was now *drinking* it.

A fate worse than death…

Horla smiled brightly and then tossed the Raven aside like a rag doll. Vicar crashed into the nearest wall and curled up into a ball, shaking horribly with his mouth covered in crimson dew. His eyes were wide and he started muttering nonsense, as if he was still seeing whatever nightmare the Immortal has revealed to him.

Jacob finally managed to get his legs to move, and he turned, ready to run for the door.

But then, a cold and yet tempting voice, hissed at him and held him in place. *"You."*

"You."

Such a small word, so simple, and yet Jacob felt his entire body grow cold and his legs immediately stopped running as if invisible shackles had suddenly grabbed his ankles; pinning him in place. The one word had come out like a command, and his body had forsaken Jacob's will in obedience to Horla's own.

He turned his head, and saw that the Immortal was back in his original form, walking slowly towards him with a peculiar expression. All the while, those horrible yellow eyes continued to glow brightly, numbing Jacob's own mind and body. Despite his desire to either fight or flee, Jacob felt his knees trembling as they slowly turned to rubber, his mind a blank slate of terror.

"Oh, you are a Hunter, aren't you?" the Immortal stated in a voice that was so silky and deep it sounded terrifyingly beautiful. "It explains why you were able to hold your own against a Raven. That eye however... it is... most intriguing. You are only the second being in the world I have ever met to have two different eyes like that... But tell me, why have you come here, to Irondell?"

Jacob tried to keep his mouth shut, but he felt like someone was prying his jaw open, and ripping the words right out of his throat. "We have come to Hunt the Immortal responsible for all of this. You, my lord."

"We?" the Immortal asked, and the many Vampires still along the wall started cackling and hooting at the man with burning blue and black eyes.

Horla tilted his head as if he were not hearing the sounds of the damned but instead whispers that were close and yet far. "Yes, that's right. They all mentioned someone else with you. But where-" He stopped, his pointed ears seeming to turn towards another sound.

A flush of black suddenly consumed Jacob's entire vision, breaking him from the Immortal's gaze and making him feel his body again. With a gasp, he fell to his knees as if the chains that had bound him were suddenly lifted. His Immortal Eye didn't feel like it was on fire anymore, and he pulled his eyepatch back over it in order to hide it.

"You fool," the voice of Angela said behind the cloak that hide Jacob from the Immortal. Her sword was drawn, and she was in a fighting stance, ready to thwart the Immortal before her. That similar ruby ring on her finger seemed to glow like blood in the pale moon and firelight.

Jacob smiled despite the pain slowly alleviating from the back of his head. He pulled himself to his feet and stood beside Angela. "Nice to see you too. I've found your Raven, as well as..."

"Count Horla," Angela said, finishing Jacob's words but also acknowledging the Immortal before her. Jacob peeked around the Dhampir's body in order to see Count Horla, who was staring at the Dhampir with a look of both hatred and yet curiosity.

"Well, well," said Horla. "A Dhampir."

Angela said to her partner, "Jacob, run."

"No way." He reached over his shoulder and tightened his fingers around one of his arrows. "I'm not leaving you alone."

"You don't understand," Angela said keeping her eyes on Horla. "He isn't like any other monster you've come across."

"So I've noticed."

Horla breathed deeply, as if taking in the smells of everything around them. The horses continued to cower in the back of their stalls, and the Vampires even seemed to shift at the sudden change in the air.

"So, it is true," the Immortal whispered almost dejectedly. "You're a Dhampir. And I must say... a beautiful one at that. I haven't seen such a face such as yours in over five-hundred years. And you really are beautiful..."

Despite those yellow eyes no longer being focused on him, Jacob could feel his own eyes burning at the sight as the Vampire stared at Angela almost as if those hellish eyes were *absorbing* her. He could almost see the outline of whatever hellish beast he was inside the mass of shadow that he saw lingering around the Count's feet like black snakes.

Angela shifted her purple eyes slightly, and then addressed the Immortal. "I see you've found the Raven."

"Thanks to your human pet there," Horla nodded. "If he hadn't gotten the man to finally come out of hiding, I was afraid my disciples were never going to find him, and I would have to crush this city one brick at a time until he was *forced* to flee. And then I would have to hunt him down to the ends of the planet."

"So, all of this, was because of him?" Angela gathered. "Because he killed your prey?"

"Well, 'prey' is a bit of a stronger word than I would like to use. It *was* my intention, until I saw that my brother had given her the Immortal Kiss. I had planned to have her join *my* coven. It is not very often that humans receive such a Kiss and live. She would have become a very powerful Vampire.

"But then this *man*," he gestured to the Raven who was now struggling to his feet with a hateful glare. "Killed her, before I could return the next evening to retrieve her. And now this man will serve his purpose, now and forever."

"So, what now?" Angela asked. "Will you take the souls you have captured, and leave Irondell?"

Horla smiled. "Hardly. Tell me, Dhampir, you've come out of the castle just now. Does that mean Andrei is alive?"

"No."

"Then it is only fair that this city needs a new ruler," Horla spread his hands out like an actor about to introduce a major character. "Who better to lead the city of the dead, than myself?"

"I can't allow that, Lord Horla," Angela said. "The time of the Immortal Nobility has come to an end. The undead rulers have been slain or scattered. To allow such a thing to happen again would be dishonoring those who have risked their lives to push back the darkness."

"Spoken like a true Huntress," Horla said lowering his hands. "I can respect that. And I see your ring and it's inheritance; I... *acknowledge* it. However, I have no intention of leaving. It has been a long while since I've had this much fun. Besides, having a city of my own, it is *very* exciting. How I would love to bring back the ways of old, in order to bring back the royal families. We have waited so long for a chance such as this; who am I to pass on such an opportunity? This has to be the beginning. This has to be the will of our Ancient Lord."

Angela held out an arm to Jacob, who had just nocked an arrow onto his bowstring, ready to shoot upon her command. "You will do nothing," she told him. "Stay back, and get away from here."

"I'm not leaving you behind," Jacob gritted his teeth.

"You are wounded. You would only get in the way."

"Then protect me then."

"Dammit, Jacob," Angela sounded desperate now.

"Listen to the Dhampir, Human," Horla said to him. "Though it is pointless. The second you ran off, you would be run down like a sheep fleeing wolves. But if you are to stay here, you shall die. I am not like the Vampires you have slain thus far. There is no point in fighting unless you enjoy wasting your energy and struggling. So, what will it be? Will you flee like the desperate Dhampir commands? Or will you stay and fight?"

"There doesn't have to be a fight," Angela said. "My Lord, think about what you are doing here. The people, they do not deserve such a horrible fate. You have shed enough blood in order to search for the Raven. You have him now, isn't that enough?"

"Hardly," said Horla with an air of impatience. "The Watchmen who dared fight against my disciples must be punished. And when the force of Irondell's strength is eliminated, the city will belong to the dead. And as we grow, I shall make Emperor Ion pay for his insolence by destroying the very Empire he worked so hard to create.

The others will see, and they will come. It is what all Vampires everywhere would want; that is what Our Lord would want for his loyal subjects, those who survived and lie in wait."

"The Dark Master is dead, my lord. The Immortal Nobility cannot rise again."

"I expected you to say nothing less, my dear. Dead he is, yes, but I will make sure his glory will not be forgotten; I will ensure our kind is not cast aside again, and all will fear us once more. It is our destiny."

"I see there is no dissuading you," Angela said. "Then you leave me no choice: you have to die, My Lord."

Horla chuckled, amused by such a threat. "Oh, please, 'my lord' indeed. You are no servant of mine, Daystalker. Isn't it told in the human's book of Yohnah, 'those who cry out 'lord, lord,' without cause shall not enter the gates of Kawn?' As such, you won't get much out of me by expressing formalities. I wouldn't expect you to understand what the Undead God would want. We have conquered Kawfka when he tried to create us, to use us. We have conquered death. We were made to conquer the weak human race and inherit this world as our own, as it is written. I don't see why you bother trying to help the human race. They won the battle, but not the war, and it matters not that you help them. Such a poor and naïve Dhampir, cursed to walk the world with no place of belonging. No place among humans, and no place among our kind. Yet you chose to walk the path in helping the humans, who want nothing more than your own annihilation. Tell me, Dhampir, why would you take the side of the humans who hate you so?"

"The time of the Vampire has passed, and their reign of terror must come to an end," Angela answered. "Your kind's time has come, it is time for you all to disappear from the world of Man; back to Oblivion where you belong."

"I suppose it *is* easy for you to say such a thing," Horla sighed. "Considering you are neither human nor Vampire. If you took down the blinders from your eyes, you would see that if you actually *do* carry out your threat you will still never be accepted among the humans. They may hire you, they may rely on you to do their dirty work like a Hunter should; but they do this all only because they need you right now. And if such a day comes when the Immortal is nothing more than legend, when *they* no longer need you, they will cast you out like a diseased whore. They will make sure that the Vampire never comes back out into the light again, including *any* blood relations to them. You will *never* be accepted, Dhampir. No matter how much you wish to be, you are a cursed bastard of an Immortal who dared mate with a human. You have no place in this world; your cause is useless. You-"

An arrow suddenly stuck into the Immortal's eye, sticking right through the socket. The Immortal, having no reaction to being shot, merely grabbed the shaft and pulled both it and his own eyeball right out. But just as quickly, the eye was roped back by its tendon and popped back into its socket completely healed.

Horla's disciples hissed at Jacob, who went to reach for another arrow.

"You be quiet," said Jacob in a low voice. "Angela is a member of the Black Hand, she belongs with me and all the other Hunters. Vampire, Human, or in-between, she belongs with us. And no one, especially not a monster with a bounty on his big head is going to say otherwise."

Dead silence followed this statement, even Angela didn't say something to the Hunter despite Jacob expecting her to.

With a sigh, Horla tossed the arrow aside, the shaft clattering across stone and snow. "Very well. Unfortunately, we are out of time. Look to the east, the sun is now rising over the mountains beyond. I must go, but by this time tomorrow evening, this city will belong to the dead. If you value your lives, Hunters, you will be gone."

Horla then raised his arms up and the shadows encircled his body, lifting him up into the air. The hellish shapes and shadows swirled in the darkness, including the faces of snarling wolves that snapped their jaws at the two Hunters. "Though, I *do* hope you stay. I hope I get the chance to see you both again. I'd love to see what sort of taste your blood has.

"FINISH THEM!"

Then in one united scream, the Vampires leapt off the walls and converged on the two Hunters like demons attacking a broken man. The many naked, snarling and hungry undead, cornered the two who got their weapons up and ready to fight as Count Horla floated over the walls and into the night like a swarm of locust.

"May the Stars you serve have mercy on you!" his voice carried to Jacob's ears just as the horde lunged towards them.

"Stay behind me," Angela told him as she slashed her weapon and sliced one of the undead in half. At the same moment, Jacob nocked three arrows and shot them all into the hearts of three women who tried to circle around the two from the left.

The two were surrounded, and there was just too many of the undead who bared their fangs and claws, their eyes burning with icy hunger and delight. Even with Angela up front and taking down many of the undead horde, she was soon overwhelmed by the masse who completely engulfed her with snarling fangs and slashing claws. Jacob tried to rush to her side but already some of the Vampires started for him instead, making it impossible to save the Dhampir from the monsters who bit and clawed at her, spilling blood and drinking their fill in sick, erotic pleasure.

"Aaargh!" one cried out in twisted glee. "So sweet!"

"Mana from heaven!" cried another.

"More!" snarled another with a bloody mouth. "I want more!"

"Get off her!" Jacob screamed out breaking one Vampires neck and throwing another knife into the chest of another. "Get off her, you fucks!"

He was then tackled from the front, the Vampire grabbing his shoulder and trying to hold him still as she bared her fangs. She stretched out her neck and lashed down like a hungry snake, her lower jaw splitting into something like mandibles and a long forked tongue wriggled out and with a swipe across his left cheek, slit the skin open to reveal some blood which she managed to taste.

With a yelp, Jacob managed to get his hands underneath her jaw to push her back, but he could feel more hands grab at his legs and feet. His vision was completely devoured by the sight of gnashing teeth and blood.

I guess this is it then… he thought as another Vampire came into view and bared his fangs to bite down at his face.

But then the Vampire on top of him suddenly staggered as her face erupted in a flash of bone, blood, and brain. It splattered all over the Jacob and the Vampires nearby, who all screamed as they too were suddenly shot in the head and sprawled out.

More gunshots erupted and Jacob saw many of the Vampires getting blown back or scattering away from the front steps. One even tried to crawl away while missing one of his forearms. Another took a deep breath, ready to scream to the heavens but a bolt suddenly stuck in his throat, rendering him silent until another one put him out of his misery.

Jacob turned around fast to see Watchmen coming out of the castle doors wielding guns and swords. One man who appeared doused in blood pointed towards the monstrous horde, commanding the whole lot to kill all the Vampires. Gunfire erupted like thunder and here and there, the heads and chests of Vampires blew open, destroying them and leaving them crumpling on the frozen ground which was quickly becoming doused in blood.

With his enemies lost in the confusion, Jacob rushed back towards Angela, who still had a few Vampires holding her down and biting her. He shot one of them and immediately they all turned their attention to him and hissed; giving Angela just the opening she needed to lunge up and slice all of their heads off in one swing. Her cloak had been shredded to ruins and she had a horrible gash across her chest and belly. Her shoulders and parts of her neck had been bitten and were bleeding profusely, and she had four deep scratches across her face which covered her in crimson warpaint.

And she looked absolutely enraged as she opened her fanged maw and roared her challenge at every nearby Vampire who had approached her to avenge their fallen brethren.

She then turned and grabbed ahold of the neck of one of these survivors before smashing his head into the ground, spraying out chunks of skull every direction. After disposing of the corpse, she raised her sword and lunged right into the undead horde who were still getting shot up by the soldiers who clashed with the Vampires like a great battle; all the while Jacob stuck close to Angela's, killing every Vampire he came across in order to stay by her side and keep her safe.

As he fought, Jacob saw the head of one man getting ripped off by a Vampire, his blood spilling into its mouth before the creature was stabbed in the heart by another soldier. He saw another man get punched right through the gut and the Vampire ripping his very entrails out as it bit into his neck. He saw another Vampire getting hacked into pieces by three men, their swords covered in gore and spraying blood all over the walls and stables.

It was complete and utter carnage, with the smell of blood clogging the very air they breathed. Even Jacob who hacked at the Vampires with his knife and shot many with his bow, was overwhelmed by the crimson fray. He had been tackled and had to use the arrow he planned to shoot at another to stab into the creature's face, staggering the monster before taking the arrow and shooting it into the heart. All the while, the sun continued to slowly peek above the mountains miles away from Irondell as if hesitant to expose its whole face to the horror being left behind by the two groups.

Some more soldiers were coming in through the front, drawn to the screams and the sounds of anguish bloodshed. Everywhere he looked, Jacob saw looks of pure terror and fear spread through both Vampires and humans; the instinct, the fight-or-flee terror that drove them into one single mindset: survive. It didn't matter if they were Vampire or human, they were all merely animals, fighting just to make it out alive. The Vampires, were told to stay and eliminate him and Angela, but instead, ended up becoming the Hunted by the mass of Watchmen finally coming out of the castle, or coming to the cries for help that seemed to echo through the city and spread like the smoke of fires.

Though she was obviously wounded, slathered in both her own blood and many other's, Angela moved fast and deadly through the Vampires. All who stood in her way were cut down or smashed into pieces. She would hack through an entire group and use her bare hands to tear apart more. Jacob even watched her spin around, smashing her elbow right into the face of another Vampire, it's face shattering like a clay pot and spraying blood all over the nearby horses. In that same movement

Angela swung her sword and sliced the legs clean off another Vampire to knock him down onto the ground before *punching* her fist right through his very chest in order to smash the heart within.

Her eyes flashed dangerously, and she bared her fangs as she leapt up and drove her sword down into another enemy where the shoulder met the neck, and upon wrenching the sword out she grabbed a fallen soldier's sword and hurled it like a throwing knife, spearing yet another Vampire right through the heart. Even as blood speckled the Dhampir's face, Jacob could still see that beastly look about her; that fierce and determined look to slaughter her enemies without thought or feeling. She didn't even bat an eye at the dead at her feet, and merely kept on killing until there would be no Vampires left.

A frightened Watchman even tried to stab her in the back in his panic, and she had spun around and dug her fingers right beneath the man's chin, the tips coming out of his choking mouth and with a mighty tug, ripped his lower jaw right off before kicking him back into a horde of Vampires who accepted the screaming man like an offering. Angela didn't seem to care anymore; all who opposed her were the enemy, and would be reduced to a bloody pulp.

Now Jacob understood everyone's fear for her as a half-breed; why even the Vampires seemed to fear her. She was a killing machine, a creature born not from light or darkness, but somewhere in the twilight where no one dared to venture. She was a beautiful and deadly adversary whose strength and power far surpassed anyone Jacob had ever met.

Angela was just an angel of death and destruction.

Before he even realized it, a mighty cry erupted from within the carnage that was slowly starting to die down a bit. Jacob turned to the front walls and saw Virgil, trying to stand with a hand on the stone bricks. Smoke seemed to be seeping from his pores and he was breathing heavily. When he slowly raised his head, Jacob felt his heart stop in his chest. Those brown eyes were no longer there in the man's head. Instead, they were silver like the glare of the moon that was slowly fading away with the rising sun. Unlike the other Vampires or even the Dearg the Hunters had found, the eyes of Virgil were sharp, cunning, and very much aware.

Virgil bared his teeth and started to open and close his mouth like he was about to puke. He then violently reared his head back and unleashed a hellish scream that dropped everyone to their knees, even the remaining Vampires were affected by this window-shattering screech. One man even stumbled back into the fire, his naked body soon alit with flames that began to consume his body. Even then, no one dared to move as they were paralyzed by Virgil's terrible screams.

As the man did so, his very teeth fell out of his gums, having been pushed out by two large fangs that seemed sharpened into pinpoints. His fingertips slid grotesquely off his fingers as claws shot out of them, shining black like polished marble and dropping crimson dew; and from the many wounds the man had received from Jacob, smoke belched from them, and they slowly began to close up as if his flesh was made of clay. Indeed, even the missing hand of Vicar Virgil had sprouted back like a grotesque flower, it's fingers ending in claws of obsidian.

"Shoot that thing!" someone shouted, and another fired his pistol at the Raven. Blood sprayed as bullet tore through flesh, but black smoke belched from the wound just like the others and then closed up just as quickly.

The Raven then turned his silver eyes upon the shooter and with a sneer, he lunged. Faster than a man is capable, Virgil closed the distance between him and the Watchman and with a single swipe of his hand, he cut the man down as easily as a sword would. The two halves of the man fell away, and the Raven knocked the head of a nearby Vampire clear off her shoulders, sending it flying into the wall and splattering like a juicy fruit.

A few more Watchmen began to converge on the transforming man, who then proceeded to cut them all down with bloody hands. Then standing among the dead, Virgil raised those hands up to his mouth, and with a tongue that was purple and slithery like a snake, he lapped the blood off his fingertips. Immediately, those silver eyes seemed to glow brighter, and he released a heavy sigh.

"No..." he whispered as his tongue continued to slither. He shuddered like an addict suffering withdrawal. "I've..."

His eyes shifted and Jacob watched as Angela lunged for him, swinging her sword and slicing him across the chest. Blood sprayed as Virgil leapt back and onto the roofing of the stables, hissing angrily at the Dhampir.

"No! This cannot be!" And with that, he spun about and leapt high onto the walls and sprinted across them, proceeding to flee and disappear on the other side.

Without even waiting for anything or anyone, Angela took off after him, leaping onto the wall and giving chase along the nearby rooftops; her blood left behind on the stone walls.

"Wait!" Jacob shouted scooping up his bow again and sprinting towards the stables. He wrenched the gates open and grabbed ahold of the nearest horse.

The beast resisted but it eventually Jacob was able pull it out into the open despite the battle that continued to rage. With the sun now shining dimly across the horizon, any Vampire caught in its terrible glare screamed as they clawed at their very skin which began to smolder and burn like blisters. It made it all the more easier for the Watchmen to cut them all down without hesitation. Meanwhile, Jacob mounted the beast and spurred it to run for the open gates. He heard men shouting at him, telling him to stop or they would shoot.

"Let him go!" he heard someone say just as he tore through the gates and took off down the streets of Irondell. He had to catch up with the two Vampiric beings before they got too far away. He had to help Angela. He had to make sure that she stopped Virgil, before he too became consumed with the darkness, and become the very thing he had come to Hunt.

"Sir!" one of the Watchmen cried out to William who had just watched the last Vampire get staked through the heart and lifted up towards the sunlight. The creature snarled and screamed as it thrashed about, its skin boiling over and burning away as the light destroyed all the darkness within it. It was just after when the Dhampir took off after that Raven, and her partner stole a horse in pursuit. Now that the carnage was over, it seemed that-

"Sir!" the same soldier called out to him again. This time, William gave his attention. "Why did you give the command to let them go? We should pursue them!"

"No, we won't catch up to them," William said. "That Dhampir is going after that Raven, and you saw what was happening to him. He ain't our problem anymore, he's one of *them*."

After killing Andrei, some men came into the training room to investigate the commotion within their safe haven. Having seen all the glass and their Count naked and dead on the floor, the men demanded answers. William had some blood on his hands, but he had ditched the knife, saying that the Dhampir was the cause of the Count's death. That was all the motivation the men needed in order to rally all within the castle to go after her, and as a result, clashed with the Vampire Horde waiting for them outside. William didn't believe that the Dhampir was the enemy, not after what he had witnessed in his own leader.

He didn't know *what* to believe in anymore. All he knew was that the Count had abandoned them, and cut them off from the world on the Raven's orders; who was now being chased like a beast by the Hunters of the Black Hand.

They were on their own, and they had to focus on the present situation at hand. There were still some

Watchmen out in Irondell, and he had to rally them all up. He didn't know what this meant for the hold, but if the Dhampir was true to her word, that meant that it would all be over soon. It could get dangerous, and he had to do whatever he could to protect the men Irondell had left, and save the citizens. Andrei had abandoned them, and the Raven was soon to be disposed of.

It was up to *them* now, as Watchmen of Irondell and the Realm, to save the city.

"Sir," another Watchman said standing above the melting corpse of another Vampire. "Your orders?"

William was not the highest-ranking officer in Irondell, but he was still the highest present. He would have to talk to his peers when they all return to the castle, but for now, he was in charge.

"Send out a broadcast. Have all Watchmen report here in the courtyard. The situation has become dire, and all Officers must be present. We have very little time, and we must prepare for tonight."

"What about the Dhampir, sir?"

"We'll deal with her later. Right now, I want all Watchmen present here- immediately!"

"Yes sir!" one man saluted before rushing back into the castle.

"Rally any other able-bodied citizens as well," William added. "Our Count is dead, and the Raven has abandoned us. It is up to us to save Irondell. Once we have control over the situation, we will move on to the Dhampir. Someone- I need someone to ride out to the nearest village and send out a broadcast. We have to do the same here; we need to get ahold of the Empire."

"But sir," another soldier argued. "Count Andrei said-"

"To hell with what the Count said!" William snapped startling everyone present. "People are dying, and we need to get help. All of you, go! Return here within an hour and let us protect this city to the last man!"

"Yes sir!" everyone shouted and they all dispersed to perform their various duties.

As they all left William looked past the main gate, towards the city that belched black smoke still from the horrors everyone had experienced this fateful night. He truly hoped the Dhampir meant what she said, and this would all be over soon.

Hopefully, if she proves to have been right, she will have fled back to the Black Hand, away from here. Because William, had made her a public enemy of the Empire and all of Irondell.

"Yohnah," he whispered. He wasn't that much of a religious man before the plague. But he had no one else to turn to, and he needed something, some*one*, to believe in. "Hear my prayers... watch over them both."

# 51

Vicar Virgil bounded from building to building, desperate to get away from the carnage. His body which hurt everywhere, seemed to act on its own; almost on instinct as he fled.

Before he knew it, he had killed a bunch of men, including a few of the Vampires the Count had left behind. But he had no control over himself, even when he licked the blood

(*their blood!*)

off of his hands. He couldn't help himself back there, he just *did* it.

And the blood...

Never had he ever tasted anything so sweet, so luscious. But... it was *blood*! He had partaken in *human* blood! Every bone and muscle fiber in his body hurt, and every smell around him, from the rotting corpses, to the burning wood, to even the smallest creatures rummaging through the streets, it all struck his nose like a powerful tidal wave.

Not only that, but through his eyes, Virgil could see everything.

Though the sun was barely up, and the city was still slightly shrouded in darkness because of all the smoke from burning buildings and crosses, Virgil was able to see all living things like a hawk. Small silver flames of the souls of men flickered everywhere he turned like a thousand beacons; beckoning him to go, and hunt.

As he passed over another building, his eyes caught five of the souls huddled together away from the windows and doors where another flame of blue hovered by the window, demanding to be let in. He could hear so many voices, cries, and whimpers of agony as if he himself was the cause of such a plague, and now he was hearing the voices of those who suffered from it.

Virgil continued to run, until he came to a stop right on top of the largest clock tower, overlooking the entire city. The gargoyle he was perched on groaned slightly beneath his weight as he caught his breath. The sun... the sun was now peeking over the horizon, and as its rays touched his skin, Virgil felt naked and exposed. He didn't burn, but he felt as if the sun... the damned sun was laughing at him; exposing him for all his sins and for what he was now. Immediately he felt a need to go somewhere dark, to turn out the lights and hide from the sun as to not become exposed to the world. Looking at his own two hands, watching the smoke seep from his pores and the blood that still speckled his clothing, Virgil let out a cry of anguish.

A fate worse than death...

He cried out to the heavens as if calling to Yohnah Himself, who would no doubt ignore him. This wasn't how it was supposed to be. Virgil had become a Raven in order to rid the world of the Vampire scourge of the world. He had given up everything, his childhood, even his faith and god. He gave up his wife, left his family behind, even his unborn child.

But even then, he failed, unable to save anyone because of his fear of the undead. No one, not even the demon lord Kawfka, could save him.

A fate worse than death…

So, desperately, he looked towards the heavens, to the god he had abandoned in order to become who he was. The god who the Ravens were now waging war against in order to prove to the world that He didn't care about anyone. Was He laughing now? Was He silently telling the Raven, that he had failed?

Was he… was he…

"Why?" he asked out to no one in particular. "Why does this have to happen? This cannot be!"

There had to be a way out of this… yes, there has to be!

He had to journey back to Goldendell, where the Thunder of Ravens nested. There he could speak to the Head Raven, maybe find a cure. There were vaccines for minor vampire bites if treated quickly and there was enough of it. Would it work if he had not been bitten at all though? It would take a long time, for it was a long journey, but he had to try. He would hide from the sun, try to resist the temptation of blood that he felt back in the courtyard, and then someday, return to find Horla and make him pay for this.

That's right, this wasn't over yet! It *can't* be over yet! He was a Raven, a Hunter of the Empire! He wouldn't stop now, he would destroy them all- he would kill all of the-

Virgil once again caught another scent in his nose, and he whirled around to see something seeming to fly

right towards him with a torn and shredded cloak that made her appear like a giant bat, her sword swinging towards him as her eyes glowed purple and dangerous. He leapt off the gargoyle just as the Dhampir sliced through the stone and collided into the clock tower.

Unfortunately, he had forgotten where he was, and he plummeted right back down to the buildings below. He crashed right down onto a rooftop and he felt all the ribs in his body snap and shatter. But he felt them moving around inside of him almost immediately, clicking back together and mending as if the fall was nothing. To him it felt like a scratchy throat but in his chest. Once again, he was able to breathe and he was just pushing himself back up when he heard the Dhampir land on the rooftop as well. She had landed softer on her feet, and as she stood up doused in blood that seemed to glow in the sunlight, she pointed her sword right at him. The Dhampir, unobstructed by the sun who sought to expose all sin that had once lurked in the darkness.

"Vicar Virgil," she said. "You have become one with the darkness. I am sorry, but I cannot allow you to escape."

Virgil hissed and stood up upon his feet. He felt his own ears pull back like a cat's and his legs were tense, ready to fight or fly.

The Dhampir... this was all her fault! If she hadn't wounded him, if she just stayed away...

She planned this.

Yes, that had to be it! She *planned* this! She wanted him to become a monster! *It's all her fault!*

With a hiss, acting primarily on instinct rather than rational thought, Virgil lunged forward, his body becoming both an apparition and a familiar as he struck out at her with black claws, forcing her to retreat and move back in with a flash of her silver weapon.

He could smell the blood on her... oh, the sweet stench, she *reeked* of it.

It's enough to make a man sick...

Virgil retreated as Angela hacked at him and he rushed off the building and started to climb the clock tower once again, trying to gain higher ground on the half-breed. Still, the Dhampir followed, climbing just as easily as he did if not better, and seeing that there was no way to outclimb her, Virgil leapt off the tower with the intent on landing right on top of her.

Angela was ready however, and she sliced right at him, slicing a deep cut into his side and Virgil dug his claws into the black bricks of the tower, and while hanging there proceeded to retaliate against the Dhampir who crawled away like a spider.

He pursued her, clawing at her and growling at her like a wild beast. Was that just his body *reacting*, or was it all him? All his fear and rage unleashed? Uncaged?

As he followed her around the clock tower, the bells struck the morning hour, echoing across the city and sending rings of terrible pain through his ears. Still, Virgil ignored the pain; he was no longer there and thus didn't need to understand pain anymore.

He was a monster- and he wanted her blood before he disappeared into the world. It was all her fault, and she had to pay before he even thought of leaving.

The Dhampir then took off climbing further, leaving him behind but Virgil leapt up upon one of the statues inside the brick layout. When he saw her come back around again, no doubt confused as to why he was no longer where he had been, he lunged downward with claws ready to tear and fangs ready to impale. A vicious smile had spread across his grotesque face which at this point had become mutated and bat-like.

But the Dhampir stopped right beneath him and brought her sword point up, and as he fell the sword pierced right through him, spraying crimson all over the tower as she turned her body and allowed him to slide off the blade and fall screaming. His own blood dribbled out like raindrops slowly falling back to earth and when he stuck a nearby building, he rolled right off the roof tiles and crashed right down onto the pavement with a sickening *splat*.

He picked himself up however, his smashed face slowly regenerating back to normal, every fragmented bone reforming and flesh restitching. Ribs were mended, and limbs bent back to their normal positions. But the sword wound in his body smoked and festered as if burnt. The smell was putrid like brimstone. The Dhampir had delivered a killing blow if he were a man, but she had missed his heart, and he was still alive. Although the wound was troublesome, he was not scared.

He was back up just as the Dhampir met him down in the alley.

Virgil then turned a hateful eye to the half-breed, his eyes glowing bright and silver as he observed the flickering flame of life emitting from her body.

White… white like clean smoke, like a holy spirit…
Like purity…

"You bitch…" he snarled and hissed at the same time. Darkness soon began to seep from the shadows around him, merging with his body in the form of what he saw were bats. "You did this to me- *you* did!"

He then lunged forward, letting the darkness carry him and deliver a heavy blow that was too fast and too strong for the Dhampir to react fast enough. The force of his attack sent her skyward, making her fall somewhere on the other side of the building. Using the darkness, feeling light as a feather and as swift as a sharp dagger, Virgil chased after her, the lust for her blood stronger than ever now. He would kill her.

He would kill her…

With hooves thundering down the destroyed streets of Irondell with the sound echoing against all the buildings that blurred past them, Jacob rode the horse as fast as he could towards the clock tower. He had seen the two Vampiric beings fighting along the massive spire and they were now somewhere at the base of the great black building.

He kept his bow out just in case, as he willed the horse to ride faster past the many spiked heads that reeked and smelled of garlic and decay. He could feel the horse's fear as they passed by the many heads and burning bodies of Vampires left in the streets, including the corpses of any Watchman or soul unlucky enough to be out tonight. Still, Jacob told the beast to keep going; that he would protect it.

But even he was afraid as he watched the shattering figure of Angela sail through the air and crash somewhere behind a cluster of buildings.

"You idiot..." he groaned.

Of *course* she would go after the Raven without him. Despite her always scolding him for being reckless, *she* was the one acting reckless now. Something was wrong, and he wondered if it had anything to do with the many bites she had received, or if it was something she had realized. Jacob himself didn't know just how severe it was for one to become an Immortal, but he knew what the end result would be: An ancient monster of supreme power that even crippled himself just being in the presence of Count Horla.

Angela was in the right to be afraid for what would happen in the near future, but she was still an idiot for running after him like that; especially in the condition she was in.

When he saw a breakage within the buildings down a dirtied alleyway, Jacob willed the horse to take off down in that direction. He saw a Vampire trying to wrench a grate off the sidewall and turned to hiss at him as he came barreling past it. It did not give chase however; like many of the undead still in Irondell, it was determined to hide from the sun before it glared down upon them. Jacob wasn't terribly worried about Angela, considering how strong she was, but with her wounds not healing as they should be, he still worried about how she would do in the glaring sunlight.

As he willed the hose to move faster towards the sounds of battle, he prayed to Yohnah, in hopes that he was not too late.

Angela laid on the ground somewhere from where she had been struck by the Raven. Every bone in her body crackled upon movement, and she could feel blood streaming down the side of her head. All of her other wounds continued to bleed as well, and would not let up even with her trying to stop it. All the bites she had received during the fight with the horde had weakened her body, leaving her vulnerable to such a barbaric attack. He was not fully converted, yet, but the Raven was still very powerful thanks to being forced to drink the blood of Josef Horla.

Even as Angela tried to push herself off the ground, the force of the attack still resonated throughout her body like a pulse, spilling more blood out onto the asphalt.

You fool… she told herself. *You should have drank one of them… you should have drank some of the blood…*

She then heard the sound of two boots clashing down behind her and Angela turned her head to see the Raven now standing behind her, the darkness of his own familiars blending in with the shadows. The welts on his face from being exposed to the sun slowly disappeared like a blemish, those hellish teeth glistening hungrily at her along with those dangerous silver eyes. The wound she had inflicted upon him which should have been devastating enough to remain, had stopped smoking and would soon begin to heal as well.

"Blood..." Virgil hissed. "Your blood... oh it sings to me... is this what it is like to unravel?"

Angela pushed herself up to her feet, despite the pain that shuddered through her entire being. For some reason, the Raven didn't strike out at her, but she still kept her guard up, ready for anything.

"So, you've given up trying to fight it?"

"No, this won't be the end," the Raven denied it. "As soon as I drain you, I'm gonna- *gah*! What am I saying!?" He grabbed ahold of his head and bowed down in agony. He began muttering to himself, arguing as if he were two beings at once, one who wished to deny what was happening, and the other embracing it like a lover.

"I have to get out of here!" he gasped out loud, his eyes bulging towards her with hatred. "It's all your fault! *Your* fault!"

He's gone, Angela decided turning around to completely face the man who was lowly coming undone. "You have no place among Man, or the Light. You cannot be allowed to be set free into the world, it doesn't need another monster running amok."

"Shut up!" Virgil snapped his head back with veins popping out of it. "You're nothing but food- no, you're not, but you are! You're a Dhampir- a fuckin' half-breed that needs to be destroyed! I'll... I'll...

"REEEAAAAGGHH!"

The Raven lunged forward, flashing his teeth at Angela as he screamed. "Give it to me!"

Angela stepped back away from the claw that tried to grab for her. She then proceeded to leap further back and out of harm's way, forcing Virgil to come after her.

I need to end this fast, otherwise I'll be killed.

Virgil leapt at her, and she sidestepped the monster's attack, grabbing ahold of his arm and twisting about, she broke it at the elbow and kicked him back. As he staggered, she moved in fast and slashed downward across the monster's back. Blood sprayed but Virgil turned suddenly and clawed right through her armor at the belly, creating a bloody gash in her stomach. It caught her off-guard and despite her stabbing into Virgil's shoulder with her sword, she was grabbed by the neck and slammed onto the ground before being tossed aside like a rag doll. Her body struck the nearby wall and her head smacked against the brick, causing whiplash into her neck and sending crimson stars shooting across her vision.

She dropped to her knees as Virgil started for her again, the sword still stuck in his body. He looked at the new blood in his claws and he stuck his tongue out for a taste. Upon contact, his eyes widened, the corners straining as if threatening to tear and make more room for the silver orbs within.

"Oh, good Stars above and below!" Virgil moaned in ecstasy. He had paused in step, shuddering with sick delight. "It's so sweet, yet bitter… I hate it, but… oh, is this what it means? Is this what it is now?"

He turned his eyes towards the Dhampir with a hungry look, as if he was seeing something new in her now. "Oh, a beautiful little piglet you are… I want to taste all of you… I want to fuck you into the ground, and drink you until you're dry."

He started for her again. His fangs had elongated and his silver eyes were burning all the brighter. His skin had turned paler, and he was looking less like the man he had been before, and more like the monster he was becoming. Indeed, as he was actively shedding away ant humanity left in him, he likewise began to remove his shirt as if suffocated by it.

"Yes, that's right. I *do* want it. I want it all. I *do* want this, why was I so afraid before? It makes no sense..." He shifted in step, as if adjusting himself for growing an erection, making Angela feel for the first time in a long time, horrific revulsion.

Angela struggled to get up, feeling all the strength in her arms slowly fade away. In no time at all-

"Hey!"

She heard footsteps and she turned her head to see a Watchman rushing for her with a gun in hand. It was aimed right for her, and he was yelling nonsense that she couldn't understand; it felt like her own head was swimming in water. Angela opened her mouth to scream, to tell the man to run away before he got caught.

But it was pointless. His feet then came mere inches from her face and then suddenly they lifted right off the ground and out of her sight. The gun clattered to the floor, and then the man's head joined as blood rained down on her, a look of surprise frozen on his dead face. The body then dropped to the ground, as Virgil hovered over Angela like a wraith tormenting an old relative.

"What a nuisance," Virgil hissed. Angela could feel his breath seep through her hood, and it chilled her very spine even as he gently pulled it back to reveal her head of white hair dripping in crimson. Those horrible hands came down and cupped her cheeks, forcing her to look up.

She could see his face lingering right above her with a sinister smile that was bloodstained. The look of a deranged and starved beast, the eyes of a hungry man in search for easy prey.

"Now that we're alone…"

He opened his mouth, and his needle-teeth fangs glared at her, ready to bite her. Angela tried to move her arms, but she was still too weak. She had lost too much blood, and she had been smacked around too hard by this soon-to-be Immortal. There was nothing she could do, and for a moment, Angela thought of just lying still.

Well, this is it then, she had decided. *My time has come. I'm sorry, Velinar.*

Alex… I'm coming…

Suddenly, the point of an arrow stuck out the front of Vicar's throat, speckling Angela with crimson. He released her, surprised and coughing as he whirled around and wrenched the arrow free. Angela turned her head and down the alleyway past the Immortal, stood Jacob with his bow drawn. A horse was fleeing behind him, and he had nocked a total of three arrows to shoot at the Raven.

No…

"Get away from her," Jacob said taking aim with the arrows between his four fingers.

Virgil snarled and started rushing towards the Hunter, his neck completely healed. "You little bastard, I'll wring your scrawny little neck!"

Angela cried out to Jacob to run but no words came out of her mouth. She could only watch as Jacob crouched and released the three bolts of silver into the knees of the

Vampire. The third sailed right between them, striking the stone wall behind Angela before clattering to the ground.

Stuck in both knees, Virgil fell forward and cartwheeled into a crash. Just before he could collide into Jacob, the Hunter leapt over the Vampire and as he landed on top of Virgil's back he had nocked another arrow and shot the man again in the back of the head before leaping off and rushing towards Angela.

"Guess you ain't so agile," Jacob shouted over his shoulder with that cocky and confident smile of his.

Angela tried to warn him again, but it was no use. Unfortunately, Virgil grabbed ahold of the nearest thing which happened to be a tin trash can and he hurled it back after Jacob, smacking the man right in the back of the head and sending him crashing down into the asphalt.

He was dazed and now Virgil was rushing towards him with claws of darkness ready to tear the man apart. Desperate, and wanting to save him, Angela stretched her tongue over her lips where some of Virgil's blood had landed.

The blood was bitter; still changing from the effects of the drinking of Horla's blood. The sensation was that of drinking fresh beer, the carbonation popping and stinging her throat. But it gave her just the strength she needed to reach out with her hand towards the corpse of the headless Watchman, and dip them into the blood that pooled around him.

She didn't want to do this.

She swore to herself that she would never drink human blood again. She didn't want to go through such a hellish feeling again; the feeling of blissful joy and ecstasy mixed with the reminder of what she really was.

But Jacob wasn't moving, and Virgil was almost upon him. If she didn't drink, Jacob was a goner and so would she. Despite her need to suppress her own desire and resist the drinking of human blood, she wanted to save him.

She had to.

When she managed to pull herself closer to the pool of blood, she stuck out her tongue and placed it into the blood. She lapped it up quickly like a dehydrated wolf. The taste was just how she remembered it; sweet like fresh honey, and as addicting as wine. She ignored the taste however, and slurped up as much of the crimson dew as she could. Her body needed it, and as she continued to drink, she could feel the sensation the blood gave her spread throughout her body like a buzzing hornet. She felt electricity spark in her head, clearing all blurry thoughts and bringing new life to her senses.

She was made by the blood, and was both cursed and baptized by the blood, and now this blood she drank gave her new life; mending her bones and pulling her own blood back into her own body. She wouldn't be completely healed, not with the amount of blood she had lost, but for the time being, her spirit had been reawakened. The caged beast within rearing it's head ready to fight at last.

She would not allow Jacob to die, not here, not in this place; and consequences be damned if he saw her drink human blood again.

Resisting the urge to drink more, she pushed herself up and snapped her head up at Virgil who was now right on top of Jacob with a raised claw. Her eyes glowed bright and purple and fast like a cat, she lunged forward and with her sword, slashed right at the man's claw, severing the entire arm right at the shoulder.

"Arrgh!" Virgil screamed as the same hand he had lost before went sailing through the air and spilling blood everywhere. "AGAIN!?" he bellowed in disbelief.

He turned to the Dhampir with a venomous look, but his expression immediately faltered when he looked at her, for Angela, was now reawakened; the blood of her ancestors now broiling through her veins, bringing forth the true Vampire within her. Even Jacob, who was still on the ground at her feet, stared up in terrified awe at her.

White luminescence seeped from her body like a clinging mist, making her appear as if she was a wraith bringing light into the darkness around her. Her white hair flared like fire, and her eyes burned bright as she saw the many futures before her as she leapt over Jacob and attacked the Immortal who was quickly trying to regenerate himself with the speed and ferocity of a savage wolverine.

Again and again, she hacked and slashed and clawed at him, giving Virgil hardly any time to react as she attacked him. She roared like a lion, putting all the strength the blood has given her into every swing of her sword or slash of her claws. Her fangs reflected the pale light around her, blinding the Immortal to the point of screaming. Oh, how he screamed. He was screaming now for the pain to stop. It was so brutal the point where he couldn't regenerate as fast as he was getting attacked and so a slit in his belly left his entrails dangling and a deep slice across his face dislocated one jaw, his remaining hand joining it's brother on the ground somewhere behind her.

All the while, blood rained down upon her and immediately evaporated upon contact with her skin, even her damaged armor and destroyed cloak burned away the many bloodspots both her own and everyone else's. When Virgil suddenly stumbled, she struck with a horizontal slash, and stared Virgil right in the eye as his head went sailing into the air with a loud scream. She then brought her free fist back and striking the Immortal in the chest with all her might, she punched right through the Vampire's heart and with the last of her strength, she roared and threw the body high up above her head where it eventually fell onto the rooftop above, left to burn away by the glare of the risen sun.

Fatigue then washed over her like a splash of cold water, causing her to collapsed to her knees. As she fell, she slowly turned her eye back to Virgil's head, which started to scream. Smoke was rising on the rooftop and the head started to broil and bubble as if it had been put into an oven. Virgil *shrieked* with bulging eyes that slowly evaporated into slime, seeping out of his very sockets and mixing with the melting flesh. Eventually the head stopped screaming, and the flesh and blood of Virgil melted right off the skull and pooled beneath it, revealing a fanged jawline that slowly started to char and then break down into dust.

The sun had burned the body up top, revealing to the entire world what the Raven had become, and what he would return to. For from dust he was born, and back to dust in the light of the sun, he returned.

Virgil, the Raven of Irondell was no more.

With a sigh, the energy left Angela's body like a ghost, and she collapsed onto her side. The world tilted and she smacked right onto the pavement, and all she knew was darkness. Darkness, and the fact that Jacob was alive. And so for now, she would sleep.

Sleep... that was what she needed in order to forget the terrible deed she had done.

Why?... she could practically hear *him* asking at her.

I don't know... Alex...

And Angela knew no more, as she heard him calling out to her, in the darkness where she belonged.

Sol

Jacob pushed himself up off the asphalt and spat a glob of blood out onto the ground. He then tucked his bow behind his back and after slowly dragging himself back up, he started for Angela who laid still down a way's past the melting skull of the Raven. The smell that steamed off the ashes in waves struck Jacob's nose and he felt his stomach do a somersault.

At least he would rest in peace, as a human who had not Turned completely into an Immortal. Jacob left behind a silent prayer for the man's soul, wherever he ended up now; whether that be Kawn, or Oblivion, or some other dimension beyond their own. As he walked however, his prayer became incomprehensible as he felt the world tilt dangerously for a brief moment and he had to pause in order to regain his balance. Only then did he continue to make his way towards the prone Angela.

He stopped beside her and dropping to his knees, he checked her for a pulse. She was breathing, but her breaths were short, fast, and ragged. He checked her visible wounds, and though they had closed up slightly, she was still terribly hurt, and the loss of blood was too great, especially around her abdomen. It was a miracle really that she was still alive.

Being careful, Jacob reached out and gently prided the unique sword out of Angela's hand, and after looking at the bloody and jagged edges, he wiped the blade clean and sheathed it just behind her shoulder. Then taking ahold of Angela, he hoisted her up onto his shoulder and with her arm hooked around his neck and her body draped over his back, he stood up and started to walk out of the alleyway.

"Sorry," he mumbled as he carried her on his back. "But this time I *have* to touch you." He had to get back to the clinic, before the people came out- or worse, the Watchmen who would probably be out for blood since they had left. Had she gained weight all of a sudden? It sure felt like it. The world threatened to tilt again and he had to pause multiple times before he made it out of the alleyway to keep from passing out himself. Gods but his head hurt.

He was just about to turn the corner to go down the pathway leading into the streets of Irondell when a presence stopped him. He looked up and saw three men standing in his way.

Having gotten smacked in the head again, his vision was still blurry, and it made it difficult to see them all clearly. But he did manage to see a few characteristics that were far from the term 'normal,' if anything that has happened here in Irondell could be considered such a word.

They were all only garbed in black trousers with feathered cloaks similar to that of the Raven's. Their torsos were bare, and their terribly thin bodies were paler than snow, paler than even Angela's own skin Jacob was willing to bet. Their faces were painted in what looked like chalk and their eyes were covered in thick mascara, making their faces look like skulls with long black hair that hung over their shoulders. Their nails were black like that of Angela's, and their teeth looked to have been replaced with pieces of sharpened metal when they smiled at him.

At their hips were a variety guns and knives, and one of the men in the back had a massive battle-axe resting on his massive shoulders. Another carried around a brown sack and their leader who stood before them, had a tattoo of three long lines that looked like scratch marks on his left cheek. Around the 'claw marks' were moons and stars that seemed to box it in with four corners. It wrinkled as the man smiled at them. Jacob also noticed that the man had tribal beads in one of his bangs, and strung on his wrists were bracelets of leather with more beads of stone and bones of all sorts; all of which had runes of all sorts carved or seared upon them.

With a sigh that was both out of exasperation and exhaustion, Jacob shifted Angela's weight and reached for his revolver. He was still too weak, but he didn't want to just give up Angela and himself to whoever these guys were.

"Relax," the leader said lifting both hands up as if to show that they meant no harm. His accent was thick and raspy; southern as if he grew up in what was left of Nisthgúl. "We are friends, mate."

"Who are you?" Jacob demanded not relaxing in the slightest or taking his hand off his weapon.

"Name's Zoser." the strange man said. "These are Asim and Ammon. We are friends of Angela."

Jacob looked at the men skeptically. *They know who she is? ...Is that a good thing or a bad thing?* "How good of friends?" he demanded.

"We ain't got alotta time, mate," Zoser said. He had been looking over Angela while they exchanged words. "And I wouldn't go out there if I were you. People are starting to come out of their homes, and the Watchmen are starting their rounds again. Rumor 'round the campfire is that they ain't too happy with your friend on your shoulder- considering they believe she killed their Count."

"Shit…" Jacob swore under his breath. They were on the complete opposite side of the city. The clinic was too far away, even if Jacob was in the best of shape which wasn't enough considering the circumstances. There were too many chances to get spotted, and then they would be caught. If the Watchmen went after them, Jacob wondered if he would even be able to protect Angela for too long.

"We got a place," the bigger creep, Ammon said adjusting the axe on his shoulder. "Not far from here."

"We can help you both," said Asim.

"Why should I trust any of you?" Jacob demanded. "You all look like a shady bunch."

"Is it the chalk?" Zoser asked with an innocent expression which immediately broke into a chuckle. "Mate, to put it bluntly: Because if you don't, she will die. I see her dripping more blood than you are; she ain't got alotta time left. You know this, don't you?"

It was true. Though many of her wounds had healed, Angela still had some bite marks that just weren't going away, and blood continued to seep from them as if her very blood was thick with poison. Where had that aura of power been when she had fought against Virgil? Jacob's cloak had been completely soaked through, and his back was now damp with her blood. They didn't have a lot of time, and even if they were back at the clinic, he wouldn't know what to do. Clockwork, maybe, but still...

Could these three men, *really* help them? Or was this a trap?

"We can help," Asim repeated.

"Just trust us," implored Ammon.

"We promise," Zoser said with a hand over his breast. "We won't let any harm come to either of you. Angela is a... friend of mine. We know each other from way back, and I know how to heal her up- fast. Will you come with us?"

Jacob stared at the men, unsure of what to do. He was desperate. But the feeling he got from these guys... he sensed them to be dangerous. It was like when Horla had appeared, though not as suffocating. The three men, there was something wrong, as if they were hiding something; that *they* were dangerous.

Eyes... that were of a pale yellow in color.

"It's your choice whether you wanna come or not, mate," Zoser said. "Though I wouldn't wait too long making a decision. Because if you two's stay out here any longer, you both will be caught, and Angela will die."

Jacob almost winced at the words coming from the man's metal-infused mouth. He couldn't allow Angela to die. Their job wasn't done yet, and he didn't want to be left alone.

Besides, Angela saved him- again. He didn't want to just leave her behind. He felt no falsehood in the man's words, but he was still uneasy by the aura he felt coming from the three.

But he knew he had no choice; Angela *had* to live, and they had to hurry before night fell again. Before Irondell was doomed to belong to the undead.

"Where do we go?" Jacob asked, hoping and praying that neither he nor Angela would regret this.

The place the freaks had was a small apartment complex down the street. The place had been ransacked by Vampires who had been let in by one of the owners, and as a result the building was marked 'condemned'.

Zoser had helped carry Angela while Asim kept an eye out for Watchmen and anyone taking too much interest in the four shady characters. The other one, Ammon, had stayed behind for some reason. When Jacob asked why, Zoser shook his head saying, "Don't worry about it."

He then led the group through the side window of the brick building and after ascending some stairs, Jacob was led into a small apartment that looked to have been once a young couple's home. Expensive china sets laid in shattered heaps all over the floor and in the bedroom a large blood-splattered bed sat in the corner. The smell of blood and rotting wood was strong in Jacob's nose, and the sound of the building groaning with every step made him feel even more uneasy.

Angela was settled down gently upon a ripped-up couch while Zoser inspected her bite marks. Jacob sat close behind the man, ignoring Asim's request to have him looked at as well. Being close to Zoser himself was unnerving for Jacob, and he kept a hand at his hip, ready to attack should the man try anything to harm Angela.

However, the guy simply inspected the still-bleeding wounds, looking very concerned as he supposed a friend should be.

"Ammon should be here soon," he said. He turned to Asim and told the man to start boiling some 'bat blood' and 'bone ash.' Jacob didn't know why, but he watched as the man moved towards the small wood-burning stove where he proceeded to feed wood into it to start a fire. Zoser then removed his cloak, revealing his thin and pale body that practically glowed in the dim candlelight lit earlier. Jacob was disturbed to see many more tattoos covering the man's body; runes, animals, and tribal markings. On his back between his shoulder blades was a tattoo of a crow's skull; the mark of Kawfka. They all blended together, mixing together a quagmire of some strange ritualistic image on the man's back.

Zoser then turned to Jacob, their eyes met and Jacob felt a chill pass through him. Those eyes, they weren't human, and they weren't Vampiric either. He had been in this hellhole of a city long enough to tell by now. Where the eyes of the Disciples were shiny black and blue and were as dead as their owners, these pale yellow ones looked animalistic and predatory. Not cat-like like Angela's, but almost...

Almost...

"Help me strip her."

Jacob stared at the man. "Excuse me?"

"Help, me, strip, her," the man enunciated starting to undo Angela's tattered cloak. "We need to get her naked; no fabric or jewelry of any sort."

"Hey!" Jacob said putting his hands on the man to stop him. Zoser turned to him and for a brief moment, looking into those ugly yellow eyes, Jacob thought he saw the image of a deadly gleam flash through the pupils. He had only seen such a look in a rabid dog he had seen in the wilderness once upon a time.

Still, he held his ground, staring back into those yellow orbs. "Let go of her; We are *not* doing that."

"We ain't, eh?" Zoser said unmoving. He grinned with those metallic teeth which only made his glare all the more hideous. "Don't you start thinking me dirty, *pal*. You want her to live, don't you?"

"Well, yeah, but I don't see how-"

"This is a *Dhampir*, ya twat. Normal treatment ain't gonna work. We gotta *bury* her. Now, are you gonna cooperate and let me work, or are you gonna be a pain in the arse?"

"What does *stripping* her have to do with healing her?"

"Either you shut up and help me, or she dies," Zoser said ignoring the question. "That is all you need to know."

Jacob looked at the man, and then he looked at Angela who was still out cold. The very thought of stripping... was *appalling*. Angela never liked being touched; Jacob could only imagine the consequences of what would happen if they stripped her naked. He didn't understand why it had to be so, and he wanted to defend Angela's honor with his life.

But if it meant saving her…

This is so wrong…

"Please," he said pleading with the man. "Explain why."

"Like I said: burial," Zoser answered with strained patience. "If I touch anything you don't like, you can let me know however you please. But if we don't move now, she will bleed out and die. Now, are you gonna help me or not?"

Burial?

Jacob groaned with immense loathing, but he agreed to help Zoser and the two men got to work. He didn't want to waste anymore time than they had already.

After the cloak they both worked on the armor and then the shirt and trousers that were beneath it. Then her boots were taken, and her ring was slipped off her finger. As much as he tried not to stare, Jacob couldn't help it. Angela looked… incredible. He felt heat rise in his face as if an internal broiler had been turned on in his stomach. He could only imagine how red he looked.

But even once they got to Angela's under garments Zoser said that it wasn't enough, that *everything* had to come off.

Jacob found himself liking the guy less and less. Nevertheless, he complied and while looking away as often as he could help it, helped peel everything away.

It amazed him how pale Angela's skin was. From head to toe she was so white that if her hair wasn't any darker, he would have thought it was a part of her skin as well- if not for all the blood that was staining various parts of her skin, especially around her wounds.

Lean muscles rippled under that pale skin, and now that she laid completely naked before him, Jacob could now see just how bad the bites were, and he momentarily forgot about her nudity. There were many of them, on her neck, her shoulders and even her arms. Blood dribbled out of them still, dripping onto the floor and staining that beautiful pale skin of hers. The scratches had all healed, and the scabs were now peeling away, revealing small light scars that Jacob figured would be gone really soon.

With the atrocious deed complete, he turned to Zoser. "Now what?"

"You look sick, mate," Zoser snorted. "What? Ain't never seen a real woman's tits before?"

"This isn't the time for jokes, you sick fuck." Jacob dreaded just what Angela would say if she ever- no, *when*, she discovered that Jacob had helped stripped her naked and exposed like this for all to see. His eye accidently lingered towards the Dhampir's breasts again, and he turned away fast with heat gathering in his face with a vengeance.

"Right," Asim said bringing forth a pot of something boiling. The scent coming from the pot was sweet, but it also smelled of decay like rotting fruit. At that moment, the door to the apartment opened up and Jacob went for his pistol but Zoser stopped him with a look. Ammon walked in, carrying the sack that was now full of something, as well as a wineskin that looked stained with maroon wine.

All these eyes, Jacob thought sickly. *Stealing glances at her...*

The big man said he had the stuff and Zoser clapped his hands.

"Right," he said turning to Jacob. "Grab her feet Gotta take her to the lavatory."

Zoser grabbed Angela from beneath the armpits while Jacob got a good grip around her ankles. Upon lifting her up, *they* began to bounce. After looking away, Jacob noticed that the Dhampir had no hair anywhere else on her body other than her head, which to Jacob seemed absolutely alien.

Except that wasn't *entirely* true. The way Zoser grabbed her wrists and exposed her palms towards Jacob, he noticed light fuzz on each palm. He remembered one rumor about Vampires being that they had hair on their palms, but the entirety of Angela being hairless except for her head and palms was simply alien to Jacob. He had never seen a woman- a *human*, like this before.

And that's just it, ain't it? he reminded himself. *She isn't human, not entirely.*

At last the two of them lifted the Dhampir off the couch, all the while Jacob kept his eyes on the floor or at the ceiling out of respect for Angela. Without her armor on, she was even lighter than before; it felt to Jacob like he was helping carry a small child. He wondered how much she actually weighed.

When they entered the once-elegant bathroom, Zoser instructed him to help him tuck her into the large bathtub. The porcelain glistened in the faint light hanging above, and once Angela was placed in the tub, Zoser adjusted her so that she was in fetal position with her head resting on the lip.

"Oh, forgot about this." Zoser dug into his pocket and removed Angela's ruby ring and handed it to Jacob, telling him to keep it safe. Without asking why, Jacob shoved it into his pocket. Having it near him made him feel weighed down, especially after seeing that Horla had the exact same ring on his own finger.

Zoser called over Ammon while backing away from the tub. Jacob did likewise and watched as the giant came over to Angela and after whipping the large sack off his shoulder, he began to empty it into the tub. Black dirt spilled into the tub, covering Angela's entire body and hiding her naked figure completely. Two more sacks were brought in by Asim, and Ammon emptied them. The dirt filled it all the way up to the rim, with only Angela's head sticking out of it.

"Asim," Zoser called, and the man stumbled up and emptied the rolling liquid slowly into the tub, allowing it to soak into the dirt along with Angela.

For a moment, Jacob was concerned that Angela would burn (or worse, wake up), but the Dhampir didn't even react. She didn't even seem to notice the horrible but pleasant scent coming from the batch. After a certain period, Asim stopped and Ammon, who had stepped outside for a bit, came back in with a bowl of crimson liquid. He sat it by the tub, within arms-reach of Angela when she awakens. Jacob noticed the man had cut a gash across his left wrist.

Zoser sighed and cracked his neck. "She should be okay within an hour or so. If she doesn't wake up by then, just waver the bowl under her nose. If she wants it, she'll have it."

"What is it even?" Jacob asked.

"You really need to ask?"

"It's blood," Ammon answered appearing to not care whether Jacob needed to ask or not.

Jacob looked at Angela, who continued to sleep almost peacefully- apart from the fact that she was sleeping in dirt and Yohnah-knows what else.

"Why the dirt?" he asked.

"It's a Vampire thing," said Zoser with a shrug. "To regain it's strength, a Vampire must sleep in a coffin or even in dirt. It's something about resting in the place of the dead that helps them rest and regain strength." Zoser shook his head with a chuckle. "It's funny. To a point, biologically, we can understand how a Vampire works. But there is just so much about them that we still don't understand supernaturally. But then again, where's the fun in understanding everything? Anywho, Angela, is just lucky enough to live in both worlds; a Vampire and human together, otherwise this wouldn't work and we'd be absolute fools."

If not dead, Jacob thought morbidly. And was it just him, or was there an almost hungry if not *greedy* look in the Zoser's eye,

"You still didn't explain who you were." Jacob pointed out.

"So I didn't." Zoser turned to his buddies. "Go pack everything. We leave Irondell before sundown."

"You aren't staying?" Jacob asked as the men walked silently out of the bathroom leaving him alone with Zoser and Angela.

"Hell no. The plague is getting worse, and we ain't sticking around for it. Hopefully you and Angie here will be able to stop them, but better safe than sorry."

'Angie'? Just who did this guy think he was?

"Fair enough," Jacob said instead. "But who are you, really?"

Zoser smiled again, revealing those metallic teeth of his and ground them together, creating a terribly high screech with them. Jacob refused to react however, refused to break eye-contact.

"Ain't it obvious? Mate, we are Wildesding."

Jacob felt his heart stop dead and cold.

Now it all made sense. The tribal markings and beads, the runes tattooed within the animals on the man, the strange sensation Jacob felt around them...

"What?" asked Zoser smiling. "Something the matter?"

"You're the cult that Angela mentioned. The followers of Kawfka like the old Witches."

Zoser tilted his head almost curiously. "Oh, Angela mentioned us? How sweet. Although, we don't really have any connection with any particular coven. We's our own."

"What are you doing in Irondell?" Jacob demanded no longer relaxed. If this man happened to be an enemy, he would have to fight. He kept his hand on his thigh, mere inches away from where his revolver hung. He didn't know what kind of powers the man had, but if something were to happen, he couldn't give the guy even a second to try anything.

"Just observing," Zoser said simply. "Me boys and I were heading for Copperdell when we heard about the outbreak here in Irondell. So, we stuck around. We hunted a few Vampires, drank some delicious mead, fucked some pretty beautiful women, you know, traveler's stuff. We managed to find out quite a lot when we stuck around. We got a lot of Vampire blood in our chest now, perfect for our experiments. Not only that, but finding out the Raven was a follower of Kawfka, and was teaching our ancient ways to the Count? Crikey, mate, that's *gold*! We heard

the rumors about the Thunder of Ravens, but I never
believed it until I saw it with my own eyes!"

"You think this is *amusing*?" Jacob demanded angry
to hear every word coming out of the man's mouth. "Like
this is all some kind of game?"

"Ain't life a game anyway?" Zoser asked. When
Jacob didn't respond, the man leaned back in his seat
against the wall and started picking at one of his black
nails. "The world the Stars created is just a big chessboard,
and we're all the pieces. There are kings, queens, and
pawns the lot of us. But unlike chess, it ain't one on one.
It's a battle against many teams of every shape size, and
ability. Not only here on Lunokean, but above."

He pointed up towards the ceiling as if to prove his
point. "Wildesding is a group of traditions. The art of
magic, unrevealed if you play by the rules. I'm sure you've
been in the game long enough to realize that there are no
rules in this world. There is only chaos, and me boys and I
are always sure to stick around to see if there is anything
worth... learning."

"Angela told me about you lot," Jacob said
unimpressed with the man's word game. "You're a buncha
devil-worshippers, trading your souls to learn the black
magic of the witches of old. You deal with Kawfka, the
rebel of the stars."

"Well, 'devil-worshiper' is a bit of a stronger term.
I'd like to think of us as *free men*. Like I said, the world is a
giant chess game. If you play by the rules, you *might*
succeed. Follow Yohnah and the Stars who serve him,
follow the rules, and you have a chance of winning. Sure
helped the Noyiian's when they invaded our homeland.

But, lemme ask you something else, Hunter. If Yohnah *really* cared, why does he allow such horrible things to come about in this world? Vampires, Werewolves, all the monsters that crawl across the planet, all the plagues and diseases that weaken the human race, all the pain and suffering we endure. I cannot speak for my whole pack, but my boys and I, we just decided we were done following rules. And as for magic? Who doesn't want a little more in life? And besides, it makes life more interesting. In all honesty, it's a good thing too. If we weren't in Irondell collecting Vampire blood and teeth, learning the secrets of the Count- may he rest in peace - then we wouldn't have been able to run into you guys. Now thanks to your cooperation, Angela will be good as new in no time. If anything, you're damned lucky you know us now."

"I thank you for that," Jacob said. "It doesn't mean I trust you still."

"As you shouldn't." Zoser agreed. "Doesn't really matter to be honest with ya."

"How do you know Angela though?"

"Angela and I, we got history. Though, Wildesding, the lot of them, they would be pretty pissed if they found out I was speaking to you lot. The Black Hand and they... they don't get along that well for obvious reasons. You could say that some of the big boys have been having bounties placed on them."

"For good reason, I'm sure."

Zoser laughed. "I like you, kid. I really do,"

"Look, I appreciate you saving Angela." Jacob said trying to change the subject. "In fact, I am truly and eternally grateful. But the last thing I want is to get caught up in any more shit than we are in right now."

He looked at Angela, and his expression softened. "She will be okay though, when she wakes up, right?"

"She will, mate," Zoser assured him. "I promise you. Dhampirs, they are very tough creatures. I wouldn't be surprised if she lived for a thousand years, maybe more. That's just another trait she got from her Immortal daddy."

Sickened at the mention of that, Jacob turned to look at the man. "Thank you, again. Now are we done here?"

"Hold up now," said Zoser raising a hand. "What about payment…?"

Jacob's eyes narrowed. "Payment?"

"You can't catch on for *nothing*, can you?"

"Do I look like I have anything on me in value?"

"Aside from your weapons, no. I don't want your weapons. We don't need 'em."

"Then what *do* you want?" Jacob asked the man, eager to get this all over and done with. The sooner these freaks were away from him and Angela, the better. He didn't care if the two had history, he didn't want to be in the presence of Wildesding any longer.

Zoser smiled, flashing those metallic teeth of his again. "Just tell Angela when she wakes up that she owes me a vial. One vial. She'll understand."

The man then stood and stretched his long body. "Well then, me and the boy's best be going. Don't wanna be caught up in all of Horla's madness."

"If you know so much about him, you should help us," Jacob said and immediately regretted it, thinking about how much longer he would have to put up with this creep.

However, Zoser had his own priorities. "'Nup. Like I said, Hunter, we ain't on the same team. This is just a favor for an old friend."

"A favor that costs something. A vial, or whatever."

"Good, you remember. You'll do just fine." Zoser went to retrieve his cloak, and Jacob stood up abruptly. "Relax, I ain't gonna curse you." He gave Jacob a smirk of amusement.

"Makes no difference to me," Jacob said. "I don't trust you."

"Heh, why? You the jealous type? She and I ain't close, kid."

"No. It's a matter of who you are. Or *what* you are."

Zoser smiled again. "Makes no difference to me either way. But if I were you and Angela, I would get out of here. No, if you're *smart*, you'll get out of here. Irondell is done for, and I don't want the loss of my vials on my conscious."

"I cannot afford to be discouraged now." Jacob told the man. "Angela and I, we've come too far to just tuck tail and run. If she chooses to stay, then I stay with her. I trust her, and I trust that Yohnah will help us stop this scourge."

Zoser snorted and bared his teeth. "Take a look outside that window, Hunter. See all the dead being loaded into the carts? See all that smoke? Tell me, where is your god in *their* time of need?"

Jacob looked Zoser in the eye. "There is no promise of safety or good life. There is only promise of a chance."

Zoser snorted again. "Heh, some chance for the people who are dead and dying. Tell me, these people, what did they do when the plague came upon them? They don't turn to a god, they turn to *people*. They turn to what only themselves can do. Think of that church you took that little girl to."

Jacob felt his heart stop at the mention of the church and that bastard, Father Gaston. "How do you know about that?"

"That's not important. Think about that. That false priest, faithful until he is put to the test. So, he locks himself up in the church, and doesn't allow anyone else in. Tell me, what kind of god should be served by such weaklings such as this, if not weak himself?"

"You're wrong," Jacob said bitterly.

"Lemme guess," said Zoser. "Yohnah's the 'morning star.' The 'light of the world.' Please. Light is just a pathetic sense of self-protection, believing that your soul will be saved by following a set of rules. In the real world, there are no rules. In the real world, sometimes, there is no light. It is best to accept the darkness exists, and take care of yourself. Men are weak, and proud servants of Yohnah are great examples. You are told to be submissive, and you agree to it. Then turn a blind eye when others need help no god is willing to provide."

"Am I turning a blind eye, then?" asked Jacob. "Staying here in Irondell? Is Angela?"

Zoser considered him a moment. "No, I suppose not. But that is you. That ain't Yohnah. And look at you, you are merely a man."

"You're right, and yet men are weak," said Jacob with hardly any hesitation at all. This surprised the Wild One, who narrowed his eyes in curiosity. "Men are weak, and when their faith is put to the test, most of the time, they fall short. I don't know why this world is the way it is any more than you do. I don't know why we have sickness, death, and monsters of the night... or why horrible things happen to us all. But there is another world we are not aware of, that much we know for certain. There is a constant battle against Yohnah and the forces of darkness."

He looked down at Angela, the sleeping beauty hidden beneath the dirt. "Yes, this world is dark, and cruel. But if we allow ourselves to just give in and give up; to just accept everything and not look for a brighter light, then we are no better than the dead. And our immortal souls, that is all they will ever know when it is time to leave this world: darkness. I would rather live in light for the rest of my days, putting my trust that Yohnah is guiding me and Angela, so that we can make the world a better place without the monsters of night to terrorize Balkeñoir and all of Lunokean. I'd rather live hopeful, than accept hopelessness."

Zoser raised an eyebrow. "You say you live in light, but do you really? All the time?" He then shook his head. "Oh, whatever. You have your beliefs, and I have mine."

"Is that why you joined Wildesding? Because you couldn't stand just being a man? You had to gain magic as well- black magic to boot?"

"Yes. Because I value my *own* strength, and the desire to get stronger. Besides, I wouldn't be talking, *boy*." He gave Jacob a knowing look and Jacob thought he felt a tingling in his gloved hand.

He only stared back, not saying anything.

Zoser then wrapped his cloak around his shoulders, and turned to Jacob. "It is late, and we must go. Tell Angela that she owes Zoser *two* vials."

"Two vials?"

"She'll understand." Zoser started for the door and opened it. He paused, and then looked back at Jacob with those dark and hollow eyes. "For what it is worth, Hunter, I *do* hope you are right- for your sake."

Jacob nodded a thanks. "All I know is that if I am wrong, then I have nothing to worry about, because we simply won't exist. But if I'm right…"

Zoser nodded, understanding what the Hunter meant. "Tell Angela not to keep me waiting for too long." He started to go.

"Wait," Jacob said looking at the man. The overwhelming aura the man gave off bothered Jacob to no end, and he had but one more question for Zoser. A question, that would hopefully fit all the pieces together.

"You… you're not quite human … are you?"

Zoser snorted, and without looking back said, "You should talk." And with that, he slipped out of sight, the door closing right behind him. There were some muffled whispers on the other side followed by footsteps and another door closing.

Silence then fell upon the apartment, leaving Jacob completely alone with Angela, who still slept in the tub full of dirt. Jacob finally released his shudder, for the cold hand on his back had finally been lifted. The energy those three had... it was not normal. There was something about them... something that reminded Jacob of himself.

Whoever the Wild Ones were, they were not human at all.

Two vials...

Wanting to forget the whole encounter, Jacob turned to look at Angela. He was glad she was going to be okay, and he hoped that Zoser wasn't lying. He also hoped that he would never see the cultist again. What the man said made sense, this world really was unfair. But was that really reason enough to surrender your soul to the devil himself in order to gain power?

That power... there was nothing great about it. It was black magic that caused his own mother to become a Witch, and kill his father. It was black magic, that both twisted her mind and turned Jacob into what he was.

He felt his one hand burn beneath his glove, and he went to scratch the top of it through the leather.

"Feels like someone just walked on my grave..." Jacob whispered to Angela who wasn't hearing him.

He looked at her again, studied her peaceful expression. "Angela... what sort of people do you *really* know? Why do you know that guy? Why..."

There were so many questions, but Jacob had no right to ask them.

Angela had her secrets for a reason. She was so closed up, and everything she did was strictly business. But she was a good person at heart, Jacob knew that for certain. She was a good woman, a great Huntress, and… and a good friend. Jacob would protect her with his life, and he would trust Yohnah and the Stars to protect them both.

And so, Jacob sat against the wall far enough away from the sleeping Dhampir to keep watch. After checking the time in his silver pocket watch, he replaced it with the ring which he bounced in his hand. The ruby glistened like frozen blood, and he continued to watch Angela sleep, waiting for any sign of life. As he bounced the ring in his palm and watched, he prayed. He prayed for the three men of Wildesding, he prayed for all of Irondell and the poor souls that were lost because of Horla and the greed and stupidity of Virgil and Andrei.

But more importantly, he prayed for Angela to be okay, and that the two of them would live to see tomorrow. He felt guilty, for going so far, because of what he would have to do later down the road. But he truly wished for the best for Angela, and hoped that someday, past tomorrow, she would find the peace that she never seemed to have. It was unfair, but like Zoser said, the world was a big board game.

And they were all on different teams.

"Yohnah, hear my prayers…" Jacob sighed closing his one eye. "Have mercy on me, but mostly on her. Please, watch over Angela…"

His eye opened again when he felt a warm sensation in his side. He placed a hand over it, feeling the slight sting as he pulled it away covered in blood.

"Oh yeah…" he groaned in remembrance.

He tapped his side softly, feeling around and finding that he had three cracked ribs and the wound he had received from Virgil was deep in his side. Other than a few other minor scratches, there wasn't anything else to worry about. But the wound was deep, and blood was still slowly seeping out. The ribs would be a problem as well.

With a sigh, Jacob decided that he had no choice, and he sat Angela's ring onto the floor before lifting up his gloved hand and grabbing one of the fingertips. He then pulled his glove off with his palm facing him, and he looked at his hand that was as gray as stone with cracked skin and fingernails that were black and blue with veins that pushed against his skin like plant roots.

In the center of his palm, was a rune, burned into his skin by both fire and iron; the wound at the time of its creation then spell-weaved and leaving him the rune of the beast. The rune was marked as what looked like a closed eyeball. Around the eye itself, was an hourglass-shaped sealing, with the moon and three stars on each ending point.

As if sensing Jacob's presence, the eye then slowly opened, its black and silver iris glowing slightly in Jacob's palm. It shifted and blinked slightly as if waking up from a nap, looking at its owner with a cold and disgusted look about him.

"Yep, it's me," Jacob said uneasily.

It was never easy to use this; in fact, if Jacob had a choice he would never use his hand or his magic if he could help it. His horrible hag of a mother had burned the mark onto his hand before chanting the words of Kawfka and casting her spell into his smoldering wound. He could still feel the branding rod burning into his hand; the smell of burning flesh still fresh in his mind. She had created the hand, which broke the barrier between this world and Oblivion in order to use black magic whenever Jacob should deem necessary. Unlike most magical artifacts like wands and scepters, Jacob's hand was the focal point of magic energy whenever he would cast a spell like a witch.

He remembered how his mother used to force him to memorize spells and practice them on animals and humans she would capture. The memories were... simply unpleasant. And like most magic artifacts, using his hand usually came with a terrible price. He would feel a burning in his skin, and his hand would slowly start to age faster than his own body.

The state where it was in now, reminded Jacob of leprosy almost. He didn't want to use it. He didn't know how many spells the hand had left in it, but he wondered just what would happen, should the hand die before the rest of him did. Maybe it would be a blessing, but the unknown was simply a question that Jacob could not help but dwell on.

But that didn't matter right now. If he didn't get himself fixed up, he would indeed be useless to Angela and for the rest of the evening.

So, placing his palm over his side, he took a deep breath and closed his eyes. He imagined the cracks in his ribs closing up again like mortar slipping into the cracks of stone bricks, and the torn muscles in the hole in his side weaving back together and knitting themselves to the point where the wound itself would close.

He gasped as he felt magic leave his body and pass through his hand. Immediately, he felt so much better in his side, and when he removed his hand to take a look, he saw that the wound had been completely healed over inside the hole in his armor. Though he was happy he was alright, Jacob watched as his hand seemed to shrivel and shrink slightly in size. It would only be a matter of time before his skin went taunt around his bones, and then tear away to reveal what was beneath. Until that day came, he would have to hide it under the glove he was now putting back on his hand; hiding the eye within it who showed its displeasure by burning his hand again.

"I'm sorry," he told it like he had many times before. "But I can't stand looking at you. You remind me too much of her."

He got up while at the same time scooping up Angela's ring. He then crossed the bathroom and stopped right above her. He found himself staring at her, seeing just her all quiet and peaceful like this... made her seem even more beautiful than before- breathtaking, actually. She was too beautiful to be human anyway, but still, her angle-like beauty mesmerized Jacob, and he his mind wondered around impossible possibilities.

Because the Immortal, Josef Horla was still out there, and Angela had to get up soon if they were going to go after him again anytime soon. Until then however,

Jacob would wait until she's awakened. He would wait, and think.

I wonder… do Dhampirs dream?

Angela did not know how long she had been in her trance. When her body had gone to sleep, she had just accepted the darkness, and allowed it to embrace her in its comfort. It was a stage that all Vampires endured in order to recuperate and regain some of their power; whether they were Immortals or an average Vampire infected by a Dearg.

She dreamt. She heard voices. Some were comforting, welcoming. Others, not so much. One consciousness in particular that brushed against her own, she had heard from him before. It had been so long that she had forgotten about him until this very moment. He gave no words of wisdom, no guidance as before.

All he said before she felt herself returning to her body was, *You're losing your touch.*

She was returning to consciousness. Her mind returning from the different planes of existence and once again back in the reality she had been born in. What she did *not* expect, was the strange sensation she felt on her body upon awakening. Grittiness, warmth, and a sick odor which to her smelled absolutely enlightening.

She opened her eyes to find that she was staring at a cracked ceiling above her. She could hear slow breathing and turning her head she saw Jacob sitting against the wall scribbling in a little notebook. He was completely engrossed in whatever he was working on and hadn't noticed her waking.

She looked forward to see the reason why her skin felt so strange; she had been *buried*. Upon feeling about and finding that the dirt was the *only* thing now covering her body, the realization of what had happened while she was unconscious surfaced like a great beast from the sea, and she gasped in horror and disgust.

"Oh!" Jacob gasped at the sound of her breath. "You're finally awake! Thank Yohnah, I was starting to-"

"*You*," Angela growled covering herself best she could and turning her eyes to Jacob who suddenly clamped his mouth shut at the sight of her furious glare. "You manky son of a bitch. What did you *do* to me!?"

"Wait, wait, wait!" Jacob said raising his hands up and dropping everything in the process, his notebook slapping the floor and his pen clacking tip over end. He had not attempted to get up, which was good for him. If he got even an inch closer to her, she felt ready to rip his throat out.

"I can explain!" he was saying.

"Explain then!" Angela hissed. She wanted nothing more than to lunge out of the tub and rip Jacob apart from throat to groin, but then that would mean having to leap out naked and exposed. As she kept herself covered beneath the soil, she realized that she had no pain in her body, and trailing her fingers around her arms and shoulders, she felt no bite marks from the Vampires.

They had... disappeared. She knew that it had to be because of her burial, but how did Jacob know? More importantly, why did he think it was *okay* to do such a thing?

And so, Jacob went on to explain what had happened and Angela listened silently and intently. As the story unfolded, she felt herself relaxing only a little, but not enough to express that what Jacob had done was necessarily okay. Some things made her eyebrows raise but she still kept quiet as Jacob went on to tell how Zoser had helped him with her, and that was how she was nursed back to health.

"And that's all that happened," Jacob finished breathless and red in the face. "I did not touch you- well, I *did*, but not *after* we buried you in that tub. I swear on my life and the life afterwards that I didn't... *do* anything. I didn't even look at you if I could help it- cross my heart!"

Angela was still angry with Jacob, but she leaned her head back in utter exhaustion. She raised an arm from the dirt and draped it over her eyes. She remained that way for some time, and could sense Jacob growing restless as he watched and waited for her response.

"Zoser, huh?" she eventually said.

"That's right," Jacob said squirming up to his knees timidly. "And... he says you owe him two vials."

"Two, huh? Heh, I suppose I shouldn't be surprised."

"How do you know him? If it's okay me asking."

"It is. He tracked me down one day, doing research I was young and back then was Hunting alone for a living. But that's a story for another day." She removed her arm and looked over at Jacob. "How long have I been out?"

Jacob looked at his pocket watch and winced. "It's nearly noon."

Noon. There wasn't much time then. "Then we have to move. We have to find Count Horla *today*, before the sun sets."

"What about your-"

"My wounds have healed," Angela said. "The burial has ridden me of the bites and their ailments. All my other wounds feel alright as well. I'm fine. What I need *you* to do now, is *quickly*, go grab my clothes and then get out of here."

"R-right," Jacob said standing up fast and rushing out of the bathroom. As he rummaged in the other room, Angela looked back to the stuff he had left behind. Her ring, and his notebook, even his revolver.

Angela frowned, wondering *what* exactly Zoser had said to Jacob. When he returned, she told him to leave again, and he did so quickly without another word. When she was sure he was gone again, Angela emerged from the tub, the dirt falling in clusters all around her until she stood up dirty and naked. She winced at the thought of him having to see her in such a pitiful and helpless state. She then proceeded over to the cabinet and started rummaging for a towel to wipe of the dirty residue off her body. She stopped when she heard something scrape against the floorboard just outside the door.

"What is it?" she demanded of Jacob while grabbing the towel.

"I just wanted to talk while you... changed," Jacob said. He didn't make any more movement, at least none that Angela could hear. She figured he had to have been just standing by the door if not sitting on a chair.

"Is that okay?" he asked. "I'll leave you alone, if you want."

"What is it?" Angela asked wiping down her arms first.

"Are you *really* healed?"

She rolled her eyes. "Yes, I promise I am."

"I'm glad."

"Are *you* hurt at all?" Angela asked. Jacob had taken too many nasty falls, and she wondered how he was doing.

"Nothing serious. Just a few scrapes now." Jacob paused for a moment and when he spoke again, his voice sounded hollow; the voice of a man asking for some shred of hope when there appeared to be none in a dire situation. "Angela, is it true? Was Count Andrei performing rituals to Kawfka?"

Angela frowned. "Yes."

"Did you kill him?"

"No. One of his men did."

"Alright."

"What's worrying you?"

"Nothing anymore. It just makes me angry, when people like that allow horrible things happen to others. They have the power to do something, and yet... they do nothing. In fact, they instead turn to something so despicable that they should never had been allowed to lead or... or..."

"I understand," Angela said. "You don't have to say anymore."

"Okay. Just... this whole mess... it's awful."

Angela swallowed and heard an audible 'click' in her throat. "Is that all?"

"Angela, I uh…" He sighed, and then, "I saw you drink the blood of that Watchman in order to save me. So, thanks."

Angela felt a cold fist close around her heart. *So he had seen after all…* "I'm sorry…" she said now working on her legs and feet.

"Why are you sorry?" Jacob asked.

"Because you saw that."

"Don't give me that, you did it because you had to. If you hadn't come at Virgil like that, I would have been dead meat."

"You shouldn't have come after me in the first place," Angela snapped without meaning to.

Jacob was quiet for a minute and then said, "You really think I'm gonna let you go off on your own like that? We're partners. I ain't gonna leave you behind for any reason. I don't care that I saw you drink blood, you had no choice."

"I *did* have a choice, Jacob," Angela said. "You just don't understand. I was simply going off of instinct. It was either do or die. The Vampire in me got me to drink it, and to survive, I had to. I'm no different than Horla or Virgil. I have Vampire blood in me, and it caused me to drink the blood. I saved you, because I didn't want you to get killed, but it was also because *I* had to survive. It was all instinct, selfish survival and instinct, and you shouldn't have seen that happen."

"Well, I did. And not to be crass, but it wasn't like that Watchman was going to need his blood anymore. I'm not upset, Angela. I'm not afraid of you."

Why? Why, oh why did he have to make this more difficult than it needed to be?

"Everyone is right to be afraid of me, including you. So I don't understand why it doesn't bother you at all."

"Don't give me that shit," Jacob said suddenly. Angela looked toward the door as if it were open and he were on the other side of it, facing her now. She was startled by both his response and her own reaction.

"I saw you lying there- you were practically waiting for Virgil to kill you. You were just going to let yourself die, until I jumped in. When I was in danger, that was when you drank the blood to save me. So don't give me that 'Vampiric instincts' bullshit. You did what you had to do not only to survive, but because you were worried about me. You just don't want to admit it. And secondly, I don't care that I saw you because you did what you had to do. The man was already dead, it isn't like you killed him. If it weren't for you, we would *both* be dead. So please for the love of Yohnah, stop trying to shut me out. I'm not afraid of you, Angela."

Angela's mouth twitched before she said, "You should be. Everyone should be. It doesn't matter the reasons behind me drinking human blood, the fact remains is that I did, right in front of you. It is just another sign that I am not human like you, and why I can never belong among your kind. It is *never* something acceptable by human beings. It is especially not accepted in the Black Hand. But... it is *hard*, Jacob. That's what you don't understand. It is the way of the Vampires, as well as the blood inside of me. It is the reason why so many fear me: because I *do* drink blood, because I am a part of the Vampire heritage. I am a monster who is feared by all, and it isn't just a matter of 'have to' or 'must.' It is because it is who I am. And who I am, is not human, no matter how much there is humanity in me. I am not like you, so I don't understand why you care so much."

"It isn't a matter of whether or not you are like me. It's because you care for me," Jacob said which stunned Angela even as she started to put on her garments. "It's because you're my partner, and my friend. I don't care that you're a Dhampir, and that seems to be the thing that you can't wrap your head around. You... you're different, alright? I'm not going to lie. You're too beautiful to be a normal girl, and you're terrifying when you fight. You... you get resurrected by being buried in dirt, and you are definitely stronger than any man I've ever faced. The Vampire in you... it scares me, I'll admit. But you care about others, I know you do. You helped out Ava, and you get along great with Clockwork. You saved me, *many* times in this crazy hunt of ours. You are more human than most humans are, to be honest with you. You and I, are not so different. You..."

He paused. And during these three seconds Angela found herself waiting with held breath. By the time she realized this and forced herself to take a breath again, Jacob had continued as if on que.

"You're just as human as me or anyone else in the Black Hand or the rest of the world. Half Vampire or not, you're still a person and a damned good one at that. If no one else can see that, then that's too bad for them. Because you're a great person, Angela, and a partner that I can really trust. I'm not afraid of you, because I care about you just as much as you care for me. Whether you want to admit it or not."

Angela frowned, now zipping up her pants and torso. She then slipped on her armor in silent thought.

"Whatever." she said now putting on her boots. "You just don't understand. I saved you because I would have felt guilty if you died."

Jacob snorted, but she ignored the sound.

"Look, not just me, but if you care too much about someone in a business such as ours, then you are more likely to get hurt. Besides, you are a human, and I'm still a Dhampir. Our kinds, were never meant to coexist. After this contract is over, it will return to that way. You will go on your own bounties, and I'll return to mine. And someday, when the fear is great enough, someone will have a Hunter come after me."

"Velinar wouldn't allow that."

"If things changed and I am no longer welcome in the Black Hand, then it will be allowed. It is as simple as that."

"No, it isn't." Jacob sighed. He paused for thought, and then continued. "You can't just shut everyone out, Angela. You just want to deny it, but whether you believe it or not, I trust in you. I know that together, you and I will make it out of this alive, and save the remainder of Irondell... the people you still care about. Unlike Andrei or that Raven, you actually want to save this city. So... you *do* care. That's how we are going to make it out of this. You can't fool me."

Angela pushed the door open and knocked Jacob onto his butt. She brushed past him, and took a seat on the couch in the strange living room they were in. She waited for Jacob to join her in the chair across from her, and she crossed her legs.

"We don't have time to talk about this," Angela said, eager to just end this conversation all together. "I'm not going to argue with you anymore."

Though she would never admit it, Jacob was sort of right. She *did* care, but that didn't matter if she did or not. She was still a Dhampir, she could never belong among humans. Regardless of what Jacob claimed, he *should* be afraid of her. Everyone should be.

Caring only got you hurt, and the sooner this job was over, the sooner she could go back to being alone and he would be a true Hunter of the Black Hand. He wouldn't need her anymore. She saved him, simply because she didn't want him to die. The fact that he saw her drink human blood has already sealed their fate; they were never meant to be partners. She could never belong with him, or any other member. After this contract was said and done, they would return to the castle and she would never take on a partner ever again.

It was all just… simply too risky.

Jacob crossed his arms, clearly wanting to argue more but he nodded. "Very well."

"Now," Angela said. "First, you cannot say anything about me drinking human blood in front of anyone back at the castle. You need to promise me you won't."

Jacob shrugged. "Fine."

"Promise me you won't."

"I promise."

Angela narrowed her eyes.

"You want me to swear or something?" Jacob asked. He sighed and then raised his right hand. "I promise I won't tell anyone. You happy?"

"Enough. Now," Angela crossed her own arms, straight to business. "We need to find Horla before sundown. There are too many Vampires out there, and I doubt that the city will last another night. So, we need to slay the Immortal- *today*."

"But how?" Jacob asked. "We don't even know where he is. Besides, it's daylight out."

"The sun won't bother me."

"It ain't you I'm worried about. The Immortal won't come out as long as the sun's up. And what about the Watchmen? You aren't particularly popular at the moment, you know. If someone spotted you, we'd be in big trouble. No offence, but that hair is like a beacon."

Angela frowned. "Well, we can't just sit here and wait until nightfall. We need to find Horla before he can wake up again."

"Then we have to do something about your hair."

"Like what?"

"I got an idea."

Jacob stood and walked over to the kitchen. He started rummaging through the cabinets and pulling out various ingredients. Cleaning solution, pepper, other spices. He even scooped up some dirt from a nearby potted plant. He then started rummaging through the drawers and took out some maple candy, which he placed in a pot before placing it on the stove. He started to make a fire, his back turned to Angela the whole time. All of this Angela watched, curious as to what he was doing but at the same time couldn't help but think about what he said. About her being his partner and friend... it still amazed her just how stubborn the man was.

She then realized he had said something and shook the thought from her head. "I'm sorry, what was that?"

Jacob grunted as he started boiling the maple candy. "I said 'do you have any idea where to look'?"

Angela frowned. "No, I don't. We covered a lot of ground and still haven't covered *all* of Irondell. What are you doing by the way?"

"I'm making black soup," Jacob said pouring the dirt and pepper into the mixture while adding a little bit of the rotten milk.

"And just what do you plan to do with it?"

"I plan to put it into your hair."

Angela glared at him, and Jacob must have felt a change in the air, because he turned around to see her staring at him.

"It'll turn your hair darker. Don't worry, it'll wash out. I used to do this-"

"That isn't what concerns me."

"Oh?"

"*I*, will put it in. I'm not letting you touch me again."

Jacob frowned. "Look, I already told you, I didn't have a choice in that matter. You were *dying*, Angela. You should have seen what was happening to you."

Angela looked away and sighed. "You probably should have let me."

"Why's that?"

"Just forget it. But... still, thank you, for saving me."

Jacob smiled and returned to stirring. "Don't thank me, thank Zoser. He's the one who convinced me to let him help you."

"Right..." Angela leaned back on the couch with her head hanging on the backrest. "Zoser's payment..."

"What did he mean by the way? By, 'two vials'?"

"Don't worry about it," Angela said. "We're getting off topic again."

With a sigh, Jacob brought the pot of black liquid over to Angela. He warned her that it was hot and she at it on the ground by her feet to cool for a bit. When it was, she would apply it to her hair- as Jacob explained.

"So where do you think we should start?" Jacob said removing his cloak and throwing it away. "Do you have *any* ideas at all?"

"It would be in a dark place away from Watchmen and other people. Nowhere near the castle, and probably not in the sewers. Immortals are very picky about their resting places, and prefer to sleep in homes or beautiful gardens rather than in slums. I've never met a single Immortal who slept in dirt other than that of their homeland. They would want a safe place to have their coffin."

"Do they just carry their coffins around?"

"Sometimes."

"Hmm. They kinda remind me of rich people," Jacob sighed checking the string on his bow. "Sounds like a real pain then. Half the city is burned up *except* the castle."

"That's what I'm wondering about as well..." Angela sighed. She tested the liquid and found it to be cool enough to touch. She then dug her hand in and scooped some of the syrupy liquid up into her hair where she proceeded to run it through like shampoo. She kept her head over the pot, as to not drip any of it on her boots or armor. Worse still, if she got her hood dirty, she would never be able to relax.

What am I missing here? she asked herself. *Where can we look? What am I not seeing here?*

"It can't be a church either..." Jacob muttered. "Vampires don't like churches."

Angela's eyes snapped open and she looked up at Jacob. "You're a genius."

Jacob raised an eyebrow. "Thanks? Uh, what-"

"Isn't the religion around here mostly for Yohnah?"

"That's what everyone says, yes. Well... maybe not for Andrei. But for the most part, yes, it is strictly Yohnah. I don't know of any other temples for the other Stars except maybe the Flutemaster. She's always been one of Yohnah's-"

"That's because there *is* only one major temple for Yohnah. There's no other church in Irondell except for a very few idols dedicated to the other Stars."

Angela started fitting the pieces together and she began to mess with her hair a little more, adding the smelly liquid and turning her hair from white to a nasty spotted-gray color.

"I know where we can start," she told Jacob at last. "We need to get to the Temple of Yohnah."

"That large church with the dome?" Jacob asked in a restrained voice. "Why there?"

"It's just a hunch, but I'm wondering, if that is where Horla is hiding."

"Why would he be hiding there?" Jacob asked. Was it just Angela, or was there a slimmer of fear in his voice? "He's a Vampire, I thought they avoided religious places- holy ground and all that?"

"It won't work if the Vampire never believed in religion when he was a human."

"What?"

Angela explained while squeezing the remaining residue out of her bangs. Her hands were stained black like she stuck them into a vat of oil.

"If say the human believed in Yohnah before rejecting the One True God and succumbing to the darkness, then anything considered holy under The Dove's wings would be harmful against the Vampire. If they believed in Kawfka, any of the cult artifacts or cursed ground would send the beast fleeing. If they believed in any of the pagan gods of old or any of Yohnah's fellow Stars, then anything connected to them would shun the Vampire because of them abandoning their faith in order to seek immortality. But, what if the Vampire in it's original life never believed in any god or immortal being? What if that man or woman, used to be an atheist?"

Jacob started to fit the pieces together, and his bow slapped hard on his thigh as he sat it down. "Then they would be immune to *any* holy ground..."

Angela nodded, now waving her head to and fro in order to dry her smelly hair. "Holy water won't work, crucifixes won't work, though maybe white roses... Since he openly attacked the Raven, it can be possible that Blackthorn doesn't affect him either."

"Who cares about that!?" Jacob suddenly shouted standing up fast. He didn't even bother to ask what any of those things had to do with Vampires, which was unusual for him. "Do you really think Horla is hiding at the church right now?"

Angela looked at him with a peculiar glance. "It's a possibility... but why-"

"I need to go." Jacob started to go but Angela stood up fast and stepped in front of him, stopping him dead in his tracks.

"What are you doing?" she demanded. "You're not going anywhere alone. What's going on?"

"I had a little girl sent there last night," Jacob said in a panicked tone. "I got the priest to let her in. If you're saying Horla is there, then she might be..."

Angela got the message, but she still refused to budge. "Then I'll go look."

Jacob started to try and go around her. "I'm going as well, I-" He stopped when Angela raised a hand and planted it on his chest. She could feel his heartbeat slamming fast and hard inside, and he turned to her angrily. She didn't apply any pressure, which he noticed, but it didn't make the situation any better.

"You're not going," she decided. "You're staying here."

"Like hell I am!" Jacob said slapping her hand away. She didn't bother to resist as he stared at her frustrated and scared. "I have to go make sure that Connie is okay! And if Horla is there, you're gonna need my help!"

"You are *not* going to the church, Jacob," Angela scowled trying her best to keep her emotions in check. She didn't want to appear angry, not when Jacob being completely upset (though rightfully so). The vision she saw yesterday flashed through her mind again, threatening to break through the veil she had placed up.

"If you go there, you will die."

"If you go alone, you might as well," Jacob retorted. "No one goes alone then. We both go together!"

"Not this time," Angela said. She took a step forward, startling Jacob and forcing him to look into her eyes appearing flustered and ready to argue.

"Look at me, Jacob. These eyes contain the Immortal power of Clairvoyance. It allows me to look into the short future and see different possibilities. But is also shows me things that haven't happened yet, sometimes in the form of dreams or sometimes in flashes. I had one not long ago. I saw you in that church lying in a pool of blood. If you go there, then you will die."

Jacob smirked at her and still, brushed past her, stopping right by her side. "Sounds like you're actually worried about me for a change," he said. "I'm going, whether you want me to or not. Are you coming?"

Angela's gaze never broke nor did it falter. He kept his eyes forward, not looking at her. "I can still break your legs and leave you here."

"Then I'll crawl," Jacob said turning to look at her. "I left Connie there. I have to make sure she is alright. Maybe your prediction is wrong, or maybe Horla isn't even there. But one way or another, I'm going there to see for myself. You can't stop me, even if you break every bone in my body. Now, are you going to come with me, or am I going on my own?"

"You aren't going, Jacob," she said, a growl threatening to escape her throat. "I won't let you."

Jacob snorted, as he slowly began to take off his glove. Angela stare at it, shocked to see that his skin was gray and molted, like the hand of a dying man. It looked diseased, unnatural.

"Sorry, 'partner.'" he said placing the hand on her shoulder. "But I'm not wasting anymore time."

Angela was about to tell him to get his hand off her when she suddenly hissed in terrible pain. She stepped back far away from Jacob, seeing that in the palm of his strange hand was a rune in the shape of an eye, that blinked heavily as if it was in terrible pain. She looked down at her shoulder, seeing that her armor had been burned through with a handprint that revealed her dirtied skin which was now turning green.

She looked at Jacob as the sensation of fire burned her and dropped her to knees like a cripple. She sat hunched there, feeling the sensation spread across her back and into her legs.

"What the hell… Jacob! What did you do!?"

"It won't last for long," Jacob assured her, putting back on his glove and hiding his malformed hand. "But I'm not allowing that little girl to die."

"Jacob, you can't! If he is there, you'll be killed!" Angela hissed now falling onto her stomach. Her mind felt warped, and her brain buzzed as if something was trying to shake it out of her skull. *What's happening...*

"I'll take my chances," Jacob said scooping up his cloak and then starting for the exit and stopping just as he touched the doorknob. "I meant when I said, when I said I was your partner and friend. But if you can't trust me to take care of myself, how can I trust you? I'm not like Virgil, who has to wait until things eventually get better. I am a Hunter of the Black Hand, and it is my job to put my life on the line for others against the world of darkness. If you can't understand that, then maybe you were right: maybe we weren't meant to be partners. I'm sorry, Angela, but you ain't stopping me this time."

And with that, Jacob left Angela alone, paralyzed face down in a strange apartment with the door locked behind the Hunter who left her. No matter how many times Angela called his name, he did not return.

"You... damned idiot..." Angela hissed as she laid in agony, feeling the effects of Jacob's spell spread through her very skin, holding her hostage. But the pain was nothing next to the shame of defeat. Jacob had gotten away, and the fool was heading towards his ultimate death if Horla happened to be at the church. Until then, Angela was trapped, until the paralyzing spell wore off.

If Jacob was still alive by the time she got to him, she would make him *wish* he was dead. When she got his hands on him...

This is what happens, when you let someone get too close...

Fa

"Dammit..." Jacob hissed while massaging his cursed hand. "Twice in one day, and it *still* burns. Guess we dyed her hair for nothing..."

He felt absolutely terrible for leaving Angela like he had. Though he mostly reacted out of frustration rather than common sense, he was willing to go alone if it meant going to see if Connie was alright. If Horla was indeed there, then hopefully the Immortal was still asleep, and he could end this nightmare right then and there. Then maybe, just maybe, Angela would forgive him and regret trying to stop him from going out with her.

If she didn't rip his throat out before that happened.

"What a mess..." he groaned as he passed by a burnt chariot, now being pulled apart by Watchmen trying to clear the roads. The men looked worn out and one even had a bandage around his arm. Jacob made sure to keep his head turned away from them, should they be any of the men who saw him and Angela back at the castle.

The burnt chariot wasn't the only mess in Irondell however. There were a great many homes that had been broken into, and many bloody stains were seen all over the streets as well as the fences and statues that still stood guard. A man and a woman cried over the body of a little girl with a stake in her heart just before a Watchman cut off her head right in front of them. More bodies were being burned on crosses, and many more heads were stuffed with garlic and staked into the ground. All the while, many people were leaving their homes carrying small bags. They all seemed to be going in the same direction- being escorted by some Watchmen who kept watch on horseback.

Jacob fell in line alongside an old gentleman with a cane, and asked what was going on.

"All citizens are to go to the castle," the old codger replied while readjusting the glasses on his large nose. "An order from Count Andrei. Apparently, it is the safest place in the city right now. There are so few of us left, that it makes sense though I have no idea what good it will do. Eventually, they'll just break in and slaughter the lot of us."

"Not without an invitation, surely," said Jacob.

The old man snorted. "Hard not to let alone think straight when the ones asking to be let in are your loved ones.:

"Why are they sending everyone to the castle? Why don't they leave the city?"

"Didn't you hear? A few Watchmen went AWOL and tried to leave the city. They didn't get more than fifty feet from the walls before they were shot by snipers. Ever shot with an Oxbow?"

Jacob said that he hadn't.

"Kicks like a mule. Removes everything inside the person it hits."

"Damn..."

That meant the quarantine was still being carried out. The Empire was no doubt outside the city making sure no one left, Vampire or otherwise.

"Incidentally…" Now the old man was looking at Jacob with a piercing look of curiosity. "What's with all the arsenal? You ain't planning on staying out here, are you?"

"No. Not here anyway." Jacob answered pulling his cloak tighter around his body.

"You can't fool me, son. You're a Hunter, ain't ya?"

Jacob was silent for a few steps but then nodded. "Yes, I am."

"Vampire Hunter?"

"Not particularly. I used to be a Witcher though."

"What good is a Witcher when we have a *Vampire* plague?"

"You'd be surprised," Jacob said with a smile. He patted the old man's shoulder, and then broke away. "Don't worry, this will all be over tonight."

"How are you so sure?" the old man called after him.

"I have a feeling," Jacob said without looking back.

He slipped away and out of sight of the Watchmen, deciding to rely on the alleys for now on. He continued to make his way to the church. Up above, some more clouds were rolling in overhead. It could get dark sooner tonight than before, so he didn't have much time. He had to hurry to the church, and fast.

He prayed that Connie would be alright.

"Don't worry, love," he muttered to himself. "I'm coming…" He reached for his booklet and let out another sigh of realization. "That's right… it's still in that dirty bathroom. Dammit…"

When he eventually arrived on the street that the church watched over, Jacob kept back to watch some

Watchmen clearing a nearby bakery. A large pile of bodies was burning with massive flames lighting up the entire area and melting all nearby snow. The smoke hung overhead like a dark cloud, and the smell was horrendous. There were five men in total, with one keeping watch while the other four worked on adding more 'kindle' to the fire. Jacob turned his attention back to the church, thinking of how he was going to approach this.

If Horla was in there, then the possibility of him being awake was slim. But if Connie or even that priest was Converted, that would pose a major problem for him. Jacob thought for a second, and then he looked at the Watchmen with a smile. He then stepped out into the street waving both arms and calling out to them.

"Oi! Friends! May I have a moment?"

As expected, the men were startled and immediately reached for their weapons. When they saw that Jacob was just a normal guy, they relaxed- only a little bit.

"What are you doing here, citizen?" one demanded. "This area is closed off, everyone is to evacuate to the castle."

"I understand," Jacob said. "I just need to take care of something."

"Carrying an awful lot of gear to just 'take care of something'..." another guy said, now all five of them were moving in, looking at him strangely.

"These are dangerous times." Jacob reasoned.

"Wait a second!" a third one exclaimed reaching for his revolver and taking aim at Jacob. "He's a Hunter! He was with that Dhampir last night!"

At the mention of this, everyone drew their weapons and Jacob found himself looking down rifles and pistols as well as the crossbow.

"Relax, guys," Jacob said raising his hands. "I'm not the enemy... huh. Guess that makes me sound *more* suspicious, doesn't it?" He flashed a smile for good measure.

"Where is your friend?" Someone stepped up with a crossbow. "Tell us!"

"I was actually hoping you could tell me," Jacob said reaching up to rub his eye beneath his eyepatch. "See, I'm a little lost..." He removed his hand along with his eyepatch, revealing his Immortal Eye. "I was hoping you lot could help me with a little something..."

The men went rigid but then Jacob watched as their shoulders slowly relaxed. Little by little, their weapons were lowered towards the ground and away from. Their eyes appeared glassy as they were transfixed on his face, never taking those eyes off of his.

"What do you need?" one of the soldiers asked dreamily. His eyes reflected crimson light, as Jacob's spell took hold.

Smiling still, Jacob ignored the blood slowly tearing out of his eye. The pain was excruciating, but he persisted.

"I need you all to check something."

And so, he told them, and leading his new partners towards the church, Jacob smiled still. If only Angela could watch this, maybe she would be proud. But now, there was work to be done, and now Jacob wasn't going in alone.

Hold on, Connie, he thought as the men took the lead and marched up the cracked steps of the temple. *I'm coming.*

The Watchman with the crossbow banged his fist on the front doors. "Open, in the name of Count Andrei!"

Something shattered inside the church, and echoed through the doors. Looking up towards the higher windows to see them cracked but otherwise impenetrated. Jacob's eyes also rested on a gargoyle who seemed to be looking right at him like a bad omen. That monstrous grin looked ominous to him, and he began to grow nervous.

"The Watchmen?" a familiar voice answered from within. "What business does the Count have now? I have heard your warning, I will be leaving soon!"

The hypnotized Watchman was having none of it. "Father Gaston, open the door."

There was a pause, and then slowly, the door groaned open to reveal the bald priest. He was about to say something when he was suddenly shoved aside by the five men. He started babbling and demanding them of what was going on and his tongue stopped dead in his mouth when Jacob stepped inside and looked down at him, his Immortal Eye glowing bright and spilling more blood down his cheek.

"Hello, 'Father,'" Jacob said watching the men enter the sanctuary and begin their search. They checked under the stacks of pews, behind the statues, and two went down one of the hallways together, taking a torch along to light their way.

"Place seems a little empty," Jacob turned his eye back to Gaston. "You didn't have any more visitors, did you?"

Gaston whipped out a crucifix, a small figurine of a dove with wing's outstretched glaring back at Jacob, and immediately his eye felt like it was on fire, something that hadn't happened since his departure from the Bell-Ringers. He quickly reapplied the eyepatch and the burning sensation ceased.

"Do not use your devil tricks on me, *Hunter*," Gaston snapped at the last word as he dragged himself back up. "What are you doing here!?"

"I told you I would come check on you guys." Jacob said wiping the blood off his cheek while glaring at the priest. "Just decided to bring along a few friends. Where is Connie?"

"She's here," Gaston growled. "I promise you, she is. She is asleep though, those ruffians will wake her up!"

"I'm sure she'll be glad to see me," said Jacob. That was when a shattering shriek pierced the church followed by a gunshot.

Another cry of terror sounded from within the sanctuary and Jacob took off running into it without waiting for Father Gaston who remained planted. The three remaining men started to rush in towards the hallway to the left and when Jacob made it about halfway within the sanctuary, a wet crunching sound reached him, followed by another cry of fear. Jacob then watched in shock as a Watchman suddenly *sailed* through the air and stuck right into one of the statue's spears like an ornament. He choked and coughed up blood as he hung there, staring at Jacob helplessly as another Watchmen tumbled across the floor, this one missing his head.

Jacob whipped out his bow and nocked an arrow. He took aim just as another figure stepped out into the now blood-covered sanctuary and he froze just before he could grab an arrow, for standing there, covered in blood and holding a head by the hair, was Connie.

"Hello, Mister Hunter," Connie said with a devilish grin that was stained with blood. Her throat looked like it had been literally chewed out, revealing bone in the back of the neck. Her clothes were covered in blood, and her eyes glowed bright blue and black. She lifted up the severed head of one of the Watchmen, and dropped it at her feet which were bare and sticky with gore. She then proceeded to walk towards Jacob, who was still frozen in utter terror and guilt.

"Connie..." his voice was a mere squeak just above a whisper. "What..."

"You came, just like you promised," Connie smiled as her tongue slithered out and licked her lips. It was forked, like a viper's. "No one ever keeps their promise, not even Mummy or Daddy."

"Connie," Jacob said finally seizing control over his legs and getting himself to take a step back. He had a clear shot, but he felt like he just couldn't pull it all the way back; his hesitation made him feel pathetic. "Connie, who did this to you?"

"It's all right, Mister Hunter," Connie said extending her fingers where black claws began to grow from the tips. "I don't feel pain anymore. You don't have to either. I know you feel guilty, I know you feel responsible. But you don't have to feel that way. I'm all right now, honest. I, don't, feel anything anymore." She opened her mouth and bared her fangs, which dripped in blood-mixed saliva.

They were needle-teeth.

Jacob pulled back on the bowstring even more. "Stay back," he said nearly choking on his own words. "Please…"

"It's too late, Hunter," Connie hissed. "It's too late for either of us!" And with that she lunged with a mighty screech.

Swearing in his panic, Jacob sidestepped and shot the Vampire in the side. Connie still came at him and swiped at him with her claws. Swinging his own bow like a bat, Jacob struck Connie upside the head, giving him time to pull his knife and chuck it at her. The knife stuck into her little chest but it didn't go all the way through to pierce her heart. With another roar, Connie lunged and tackled Jacob to the ground with inhuman strength. Before she could bite down on his neck, he managed to get his bow up and into her mouth, holding her back as she clawed at him like a savage wolf. She managed to scratch him across the cheek and Jacob threw all his weight to the side in order to swing her off.

Connie then scrambled back, hissing in anger as she leapt onto one of the statues overlooking the sanctuary. She shrieked out as she lifted her hands and feet off the stone as if it was hot, and she forced herself to leap off and back away from the glaring monks of stone. Seizing his chance, Jacob nocked another arrow and shot Connie in the back of the head while she was distracted.

The Vampire then turned her attention back to the Hunter with an arrow in her head, the silver-tip ticking right out the front of her face.

"It burns!" Connie wailed clawing at her face and chest where steam started to seep from her wounds. Jacob then closed the distance between her and him and with a mighty kick, plunged his dagger deeper into Connie's little chest and sending her flying back into the alter. She fell, writhing and hissing on the ground as her heart was stabbed through with the silver blade, and with one last mighty shriek, Connie fell silent; her eyes looking up at the window depicting the dove of Yohnah, who would at last allow her to rest in peace as her undead body thrashed in it's death throws and became still.

Panting heavily, Jacob fell to his knees in both relief and despair. He turned his eyes upon the image of Yohnah, as if asking the Lord of Light himself why this had to happen.

"Connie... I'm so sorry..." he whispered. He heard footsteps behind him, and Jacob lowered his head, looking down at the bow in his hands as he soon felt a hand upon his shoulder.

"I'm sorry, my son," Father Gaston said behind him. "I tried to protect her, but one of those beasts managed to get to her. I've been able to keep her here, for you to see. I hope that you can forgive me. I–"

"Cut the shit," Jacob said whirling around fast and punching the man in the gut as he stood up. Gaston gasped out in pain as Jacob proceeded to seize the man by the throat and spinning around again, he slammed the priest right into the alter with a thundering *crash*. Gaston proceeded to gasp for breath as he held onto Jacob's arm and kicked out with his hanging feet. The Hunter then reached for another dagger and pointed it right at Gaston mere inches from his frail face.

"You son of a bitch," he hissed.

"Release me!" Gaston demanded with half of the sound of his voice caught in his throat where Jacob held him firmly.

"You *let* it happen," Jacob said in a low and dangerous voice. "Why else would you still be alive? Now tell me: where is he? Where is Count Horla!" he shouted.

Gaston's eyes stared defiantly at the Hunter. "In here, with us," he choked and he brought his hand up as fast as a striking viper. Before Jacob realized what it was, the priest plunged the syringe into his arm. Jacob fell back as he felt a loud buzz go through his head, and his limbs turn to jelly. He collapsed just like Gaston who was now gasping for breath.

"What the hell?" he groaned with more effort than it should have called for.

"You and that Dhampir are more trouble than you are worth," Gaston said his voice muffled and lost in Jacob's head as he collapsed down to his side. The priest suddenly kicked him in the ribs but Jacob hardly felt it. He was slowly… drifting away.

"Yohnah has given me his answer," said the false priest. "The Dhampir shall burn. You'll be a present to the Ancient One, the new leader of Irondell, both literal, and spiritual. Oh God, have mercy on this soul. Have mercy on me…"

And as the world faded to black, Jacob had only one thought on his mind; a thought that brought light through the darkness and pierced through with a sense of hope.

Angela.

That damned idiot...

Angela thought this again and again almost ritually as she continued to slowly move her fingers little by little. For the last couple of hours, she had remained still, just barely moving her fingers little by little and eventually her wrists and hands. She kept track of time by the length of the shadows being casted by the buildings outside the apartments. She had been lying on the floor in terrible pain, the paralysis spell keeping her limbs from moving should the pain cripple her again.

So, she just laid there, biding her time, moving little by little by the sheer anger she felt.

"That damned idiot, running off like that..." she hissed at the pain in her face from the movement of her mouth. *A gateway in the form of a rune... how interesting...*

When she got ahold of Jacob, Angela was going to make the man wish he was never born.

It had been a long while now, he had to have made it to the church in time. For his sake, Angela truly hoped that she was wrong and that Horla wasn't there. But if he was...

Well, if Jacob wasn't dead already, Angela was going to make sure that he wished he was.

Since his one Immortal Eye wasn't powerful enough to work on her, he instead resorted to his rune to keep her from making him stay put. Now he was in danger; the vision she had even more plausible to become true.

That hand... Angela still could not let go of the memory of such a horrible act of magic. Witchcraft of the worst kind, all concentrated into a human limb and now a burden for Jacob to carry; and he had used it to keep her where she was now.

Just who are you, Jacob Tepes?

That didn't matter right now. Angela just had to get her hands and arms to move slightly, and then the spell would be broken. However, she had to push herself in order to make it in time. The sun was getting lower with the cursed time of winter, and the sun would be setting soon- too soon.

"Alright," she groaned ignoring the pain shooting up her arms as she willed them to move closer together in order to bring her hands closer. She was now able to wriggle all her fingers without the sensation of fire burning her very muscles, and when she was finally able to clap her hands together, completing a circle of energy around her and allowing the power of her ancestors to flow like a river.

Her eyes glowed bright and purple, casting violet shadows upon the walls and sending forth a powerful aura that the nearest dog, cat and even a rat could sense from afar. She slowly brought her hands further apart with only the fingertips touching. She then took a deep breath and released it just as she clapped her hands back together, this time intertwining her fingers at the same time. At this point, a flush of energy surged through her body, breaking the spell that held her steady and Angela finally found herself able to breathe normally without the strain of pain in her lungs.

She stretched her shoulders and her legs, feeling her joints pop and crackle with relief. Then, placing her hands upon the floor, she pushed herself up and raised up to her knees. With eyes burning bright with anger and worry, Angela stood and walked over to the journal and ring Jacob had left behind. She felt disappointed that she had forgotten about her ring.

She placed her family ring upon her finger and tucked the journal into her belt. Then, in one quick and fluid motion, she had spun about and lunged for the nearest window, smashing right through and sending forth a shower of glass as she fell down into the streets four stories below. When she landed nimbly as a cat, the fresh snow sprayed out in a splash, pelting some nearby Watchmen who were finishing up their rounds.

They got over their shock and surprise quickly however, when they saw Angela rising back up to full height with her eyes burning bright and menacing.

"It's the Dhampir!" one soldier shouted raising his gun and firing it haphazardly. The bullet then ricocheted off of her quickly-drawn sword and struck another soldier who cried out in pain as he grabbed ahold of his bleeding leg. The men gasped at Angela's speed.

Another soldier came rushing at her from behind, swinging his sword. "You bitch!"

Clang!

The man gasped in horror as his sword was caught in the teeth of Angela's weapon. She turned her head so that she could look the man in the eye. The smell of piss suddenly struck her nose, and with a sneer, Angela stepped back and forced the man to lose his balance and fall. With the three men now staring at her in horror, she looked at every single one of them with a dangerous and threatening look.

"Don't follow me," she warned them, and with that, she took off running. She leapt up onto a nearby street lamp and then soared up onto the rooftops where she proceeded to sprint across the city towards the church, sailing like the angel of death in search for another soul to take to Oblivion. To anyone who happened to catch a glimpse of her leaping from building to building, she looked like a flash of white mist; a shadow of light that stretched out and soared like a wraith.

She had to hurry. She had to save him.

Jacob... she thought gripping her sword all the tighter. *I'm coming for you.* This was thought both in hatred and anger for what the Hunter had done, but also in concern for what his fate turned to be as of now.

In the far distance, the setting sun disappeared behind a cloud. Sunset was still an hour away. She had to hurry.

Karma... yes. That's what this is.

Jacob had decided this as he slowly slipped out of his state of unconsciousness and opened his eyes.

He was lying down and upon looking about he saw that he was lying upon the alter of Yohnah with the many statues looking down upon him. His hands were tied with rope behind his back and when he looked up, he saw the colorful halo of light pierce through the painted glass window upon him like some ancient artifact from a children's tale. His feet were also bound by the ankles, and he was in fetal position. He heard wet cutting sounds and he turned to his left to see Father Gaston spilling the blood of the Watchmen into five large bowls around a massive coffin, their throats slit like pigs for slaughter.

The metallic casket looked to be made of black metal with silver etchings and sapphire jewels decorating the lid and sides. Upon the lid was the silver carving of a skeleton holding a scythe- the original mortal depiction of the Fallen Star of death, Velinar himself.

This guy's your biggest fan, Master, he thought bemusedly to himself.

The candles all around the room were lit, casting strange and eerie shadows upon the wall as if the spirits within the church were stirring; both angelic and demonic. The priest who had finished placing the bowls of blood around the casket by the four corners including the head, then dragged the now-drained bodies to the side, where he discarded them in a pile. He was mumbling to himself, and his hood was up, hiding his face.

Jacob strained to move his arms, but his movement caught the attention of the priest, and Gaston rose and walking over to the far wall, he grabbed a silver sword with a jeweled pommel and cross guard that seemed to stretch out to look like a crucifix. The sight of the weapon only made Jacob struggle more, trying to wriggle right off the alter that seemed to enclose him like an invisible fence; almost like a crib he could never escape. Father Gaston then raised his sword up to his head, making the gesture look like an upside crucifix of silver as he approached the Hunter. When he stood above Jacob, his eyes seemed to droop down, making him appear older than before.

"The moon has risen, and the light of the world has vanished," the old priest said as if he was praying rather than speaking to Jacob. "The she-demon, the beautiful she-demon, has not arrived. The time has come; the Master Awakens."

"Certainly taking his sweet time, eh?" Jacob said keeping his eye on the sword. "You bastard."

Gaston's mouth twitched. "I am sorry, my son." He brought the blade towards Jacob's neck, touched it, and then raised it like an executioner at a chopping block. "The new Lord of this city shall reign, and I shall no longer fear death when I receive his gift of true salvation!"

And the sword came down but stopped short as Jacob got his legs up and knocked the sword aside. Sparks flew where the blade struck the floor and in the same motion, Jacob lashed out with both feet and kicked the priest in the face. A satisfactory *crack* sounded as the old man's nose was broken. He cried out and moaned while covering his face.

Jacob got his feet beneath him and he leapt back and off the alter. While in the air he looped his arms around his crouched legs to bring them forward just before he landed his limbs still tied together. Gaston recovered quickly and glared at him with a hateful sneer splattered with his bloody nose.

"You should have just tied me down," Jacob said trying to keep his balance with his feet still tied.

With a mighty cry, Gaston rushed for him but he dove aside and scrambled up like a worm trying to stand

and he quickly began to hop away from the mad priest, ducking and thanking the statue that received the blow for protecting him. For an old man, Gaston was fast-and dangerous; flailing that sword around with terrifying skill like a soldier. If Jacob hadn't trained himself to move quickly and fluidly, he would have been dead by now.

As he fled from the priest, he kept his eye peeled for his weapons. He saw his cloak in the far corner and on top of it was his bow and other weapons. He rushed for them and grabbed one of his larger daggers. He then managed to cut the binds on his ankles and get into a stable stance before raising the weapon up to receive the blow from Gaston. Their metals clashed together, ringing throughout the church as Jacob held the man back with a struggle.

Hellfire! He's strong!

Jacob managed to shift his body weight aside and he slashed at Gaston's face as he stepped passed the priest. The man glared at him with a bleeding cheek and lunged. This time, Jacob caught the blade and twisted, managing to slip the sword past him and get his bound hands around the priest's neck. Then bringing one knee up, he kneed Father Gaston in the face, breaking his nose again and using the force of the strike to snatp the bonds off and free his hands. He backed up as Gaston sliced at him savagely in an attempt to repay the broken nose.

The two stood squared then, feet spread and knees bent, both ready to lunge and strike as well as parry and defend. The ropes fell loosely from Jacob's wrists at last and they struck the ground with a muffled thud. Both pairs of eyes watched each other, neither about to back down just yet.

"I used to be a soldier, before I became a priest," Gaston said, grinning with a bloody mask. He began to move his feet slowly moving to the side, forcing Jacob to turn with him. "I was a feared man in my platoon back in Goldendell. Crossing blades with me, especially that little toothpick of yours, is not going to end well for you, *Hunter*."

Jacob flashed a smile despite his fear. "I always liked a challenge."

Growing up, after his escape from his horrible mother, Jacob never trained himself in the way of the sword. Instead, he focused on developing his skill with the bow. The man who trained him, worked him for hours, day in and day out to the point where Jacob actually hated the weapon. But now he was able to pull the string back all the way to his shoulder, something that some trained archers in the Empire were incapable of. He was also super accurate and was always confident in his shots.

But as a result, he never trained himself as a swordsman. And with a mere dagger against that monstrosity in Gaston's hands, he was greatly outmatched.

Still, he is old and mad. I might have a chance.

"Come on, 'Hunter,'" Gaston goaded him. "You're running out of time. Come to me, or run to Horla. Either way, you will die. What will it be, boy?"

"I always hated being called that," Jacob said while adding, "False priest."

Gaston bellowed loudly and came at Jacob with all his might. He swung his sword again and again, nearly slicing through Jacob who just barely managed to keep up with the man with his dagger receiving most of the blows, apart from one major cut in his arm.

I need to end this, fast. Jacob thought as he managed to maneuver around the old soldier with difficulty. *Otherwise I will be dead- or worse, having to deal with* two *monsters.*

"I am a man of Yohnah!" Gaston screamed out as he struck out at Jacob again and again. "I am a righteous man, and so much purer than the vulgar *filth* out there. They deserve their fate; I shall live in the name of Yohnah- I am his chosen servant! And if that means to sacrifice the unworthy who are unfit to live in this city, so be it!"

The foolish Hunter leapt back and slashed at him with the dagger. That pitiful weapon had no reach on it, forcing him to get close enough to Gaston so that he could attack the Hunter without too much effort. He kicked out at the man and swung his sword, but the lucky bastard managed to duck beneath the singing blade.

"There are two men I can never stand," the Hunter roared leaping back and throwing a handful of candles at Gaston and blinding him with a shower of sparks and melting wax.

"Men who use Black Magic, and those who are hypocritical scum who believe themselves to be better than others. Those kind of people, are worse than the monsters who crawl from the depths of this world."

"Shut up!" Gaston bellowed hacking downward with his sword and shattering a stack of pews into splinters. Unfortunately, the bastard managed to leap aside and lunge in close to stab Gaston right in the side. The priest seized the Hunter by the throat with the intent to throw him aside, but the nimble man hooked his arm around Gaston's own and spin his body around.

A sharp snap sounded in the air and Gaston screamed out as his elbow was bent the wrong way. He wrenched the sword free and swung at the Hunter who ducked and plunged the dagger deeper into his side. So, he brought his knee up and got the man right under the chin, knocking him back and Gaston retreated back as the Hunter spat out blood as more of it spilled from his nose. The priest then grabbed ahold of the dagger and with a howl, wrenched it from his side. Blood spilled out as if he was a burst wineskin. He tossed the weapon aside and grabbed ahold of his sword with bloody hands, ignoring the pain in his elbow which burned like fire.

"You bastard..." Gaston seethed as the Hunter stepped back now without a weapon in hand. "You say you hate hypocrites when you yourself are one. That eye, that eye of the devil, you use it on the poor souls you led to their demise. Like a shepherd leading lambs to slaughter, you brought them here, just like that pathetic little child now mere dust at our feet."

The Hunter glowered with bloody teeth. He wanted to just lunge in and kill Gaston, the priest could see it in the man's eyes. Even years after leaving the Empire, Gaston knew that look in his eye.

But then, the man suddenly smiled and then he reached up and removed his eyepatch from that damned Immortal eye of his. "Thank you for reminding me," he said as it suddenly flashed bright red.

"No!" Gaston hissed reaching beside the pews where the vat of holy water rested, and he flung the bowl at the man, spilling it all over his face. The Hunter then cried out as he clutched his eye as if acid had been thrown into it.

Seizing his chance, Gaston lunged and swung his sword with all his might. But the Hunter still had his other eye and saw the attack coming. He ducked beneath the swing and rolled past the priest while scooping up his dagger in the process. Gaston spun back around and attacked the man with all his might, not giving him the chance to look at him with that demonic eye.

He pushed back with all his might, bringing the both of them closer back to the alter behind the Hunter. For good measure, Gaston slashed at the man's head, and as expected, he ducked but not before the tip of his sword sliced through his forehead. Blood spilled into the man's eyes, making him even more blind, but still he managed to get his dagger up every single time Gaston tried to deliver a killing blow. But then the man bumped right into one of the statues behind him and lost his balance. Gaston seized his chance and lunged forward, ready to run the Hunter through.

"Die!" he snarled to the Hunter with a smile on his face.

The man rolled away, and Gaston just managed to stop himself just as the Hunter came at him again, trying to stab him in the back. The dagger was then stuck in the nook of the statue's elbow, and the man couldn't move it out of the way in time. With a laugh, Gaston raised his sword to end this squabble once and for all.

But then, it felt as if Kawn itself had shattered like a pane of glass, breaking the barrier between this world and the unseen world around them. However, it wasn't heaven breaking, but it was the painted glass above the alter, and Gaston's eyes shifted towards the shattering rainfall to see someone sailing right through it in a flash of white mist.

It was the Dhampir, Angela Dragos.

She sailed into the church with the white mist trailing behind her, making it appear as though she had wings. Her hair was darker, and she had a savage and angry look on her face, but she was still as beautiful as the day she first came to Irondell.

The Lord... he had answered Gaston's prayers- she has come to him. It was fate. The fallen angel had come to him at last, and Gaston was mesmerized by the sight as she sailed over him and landed right behind him.

Unfortunately, Gaston allowed him to be distracted by the devilish beauty of the Dhampir, and the Hunter had freed his dagger and plunged it right into the priest's back. The old man gasped as the air was punched out of his lungs and he stared in awe at the Dhampir still even through the pain.

Before Gaston could even process what was happening, his sword was then wrenched out of his hands as the Hunter passed by him and his head was quickly removed from his shoulders with a single slash.

The world spun around him, flashing from the Dhampir to the statues- the Guardians of the dove of Yohnah. In his last moments, Gaston thought he saw the statues turn their stone heads towards him, and their faces were exposed to him in the misty light the Dhampir left behind. But for those last moments, through Gaston's eyes, the faces turned to snarling beasts that seemed to be laughing in victory as the lights went out, and he left the world of man.

Me

Jacob watched as the headless body of Gaston collapsed to the ground and spilled blood all over the floor. The man's head then smacked upon the ground and rolled away like a fallen apple.

He didn't know what kind of man Gaston was before all of this, nor did he understand why a supposed man of Yohnah would commit such heinous crimes against his own people, but it still saddened him that he had to kill a man in such a dishonorable manner.

If he was from the Empire, he should have died a heroic death on the battlefield, defending the realm, or better yet, in his own bed as an old man with his wife by his side. But instead, he died for some pagan ideal like a desperate lunatic demanding answers to questions he can never understand.

Still, Jacob breathed in, glad that the fight was finally over.

"I guess I got to work on my swordsmanship." He chuckled, trying to lighten the mood as he turned to Angela who was now standing up. He was glad to see her here and now, but he knew what would be coming next. Still, he was grateful she had made it, and decided it was best to suffer whatever consequences she saw fit for his action towards her.

"Thanks for that."

Angela said nothing, and kept her back to him.

Jacob started for her. "So, am I in trouble now?"

But his question hung in the air unacknowledged by either as he saw that Angela wasn't looking at him. Instead, her focus was on the casket still sitting in the middle of the sanctuary.

The coffin lid was open.

Black fog flowed over the sides and reached out like hands towards the bowls of blood. The two Hunters watched as the blood seemed to be sucked up into the smokey mist and down into the casket as a body rose straight and stiff as a board with his arms across his chest. His pale skin glowed in the candlelight, and the flowing blood seemed to soak into his suit and cloak that wrapped around his body like a shawl.

When he was finally standing tall and towering, the blood had stopped flowing and all the candlelight immediately went out as if a chilled wind had passed through the sanctuary. The eyes of Count Horla then snapped open, bright and yellow like a cat's. They dilated into thin slits. He smiled, his needle-like fangs barely visible from where Jacob now stood.

The Hunter got close to Angela, who had remained still this entire time.

"Jacob, get out of here," the Dhampir told him without looking.

"Not a chance," Jacob said. "I ain't leaving you behind, not again."

Angela growled in her throat warningly, but Jacob ignored her.

"You can thank me or hate me later," he said, his eyes lingering back to the corner of the sanctuary to his left.

At this point, Horla had splayed his arms out, as if welcoming guests into his home.

"Ahh," the Immortal sighed, his mouth as red and as black as the darkest pit in Oblivion. "The Dhampir Huntress, and her human *dog*. Where is Father Gaston, and that scrumptious little girl... Oh, I see. That's a terrible shame. Terrible, indeed. Such tragedy..."

Jacob wanted to charge right in, to cut that smug look off the Immortal's face. But he knew it would be suicide. Instead, he let Angela take control of the situation, and the Dhampir took a single step forward, bowing her head in respect but not letting her sword dip any lower than chest-level. Meanwhile, he would skirt around, and hopefully grab ahold of his own weapons and not this bulky sword that was made out of regular steel.

"Lord Horla," Angela said, her voice low but otherwise kind and respectful to what Jacob supposed could be her ancestor. She rose back up, her steely eyes fixed on the Immortal. "We have come to bargain."

"You have come to *bargain*?" Horla sniffed, lowering his arms and making them seem to disappear inside his cloak. "You would dare to try to bargain with me? For this city?"

"My job as a Huntress is to end the plague you have inflicted," Angela said. "However that is accomplished depends on what I have to do. You already took the Raven you were after-"

The Immortal cut in with, "And you have slain him for me. Not exactly what I had in mind, but to be hunted down like an animal like no doubt a very *few* of his victims, seems fitting enough. I *do* have to thank you for that. I was hoping that he would have suffered a little longer, having being hunted like the beasts he himself had sought after. But nevertheless, you have my thanks."

"Then why take Irondell for your own?" Angela asked. "What good does it do you, an Immortal?"

"Because I want to show my brethren that the time of the Immortal Nobility is not dead yet," Horla said stepping out of the casket. As soon as his shoe touched the ground, it felt like a draft of cold air had suddenly swept along the floor towards Jacob, who shivered slightly.

"The foolish Emperor who controls the lands of Balkeñoir has seen fit to hire the Ravens in order to hunt us all down, but also spread his pagan religion. Personally, I do not care for the souls of those he rules. But our race has nearly been driven to extinction because of him. The Hunters who hunt all beasts of the world serve their purpose to all living things, but Emperor Ion... that man has a hatred for my kind, as well as yours, Dhampir. Worse than that of even Kawfka himself. He has sent his Ravens to hunt the last of our kind who survived the Vampire War, and yet he seeks the same if not more dangerous power we inherited. Seeking our true Immortal Enemy. You have seen what he has done to the Count of this dying city. Surly, you can see worse things happening to Balkeñoir in the near future?"

"I do," Angela said. "I hate the Emperor as much as you do. In fact, I'd venture that I actually despise him more than most among the living. However, I'm afraid he is right about one thing: The time of the Vampire must come to an end. In the end, it is not just a mere grudge the Dark Lord has for the Immortals. It is also a human matter, and *your* kind has no part in it."

Horla's eyes narrowed at this, and Jacob looked at Angela with newfound interest. What did the Dhampir mean by this; isn't she a member of the Vampire family, the daughter of an Immortal and a human?

"How can you say that?" Horla then demanded. "Are you saying that you actually *side* with the humans in their war against us? You would hunt your ancestors in order to *appease* them? What? Is it to gain their love, something you've never had? All because you were cast out as a bastard? A shitblood?"

"The Immortal families never gave me such a thing," Angela said. "And neither will the humans. In fact, I believe that when the last Immortal is destroyed, a Hunter will be sent after me as well. That is the fate of our bloodline- that, is the fate of the Sacred Bloodline."

Horla hissed. "Do not speak of the Sacred Bloodline like you have any idea of it, *child*. The only reason a *logical* Immortal would never accept you is because of your blood, Dhampir. Either that, or he is foolish you're your Sava Croglin, the blood traitor."

"At the very least he keeps to himself," said Angela. "He understands that the Sacred Bloodline would not persevere. Even your master thought so near the end of his existence."

"How *dare* you!?" Horla thundered. His voice was low and calm but the very air around him became more shadowed and frostier that even Jacob could feel it as he moved. "Your blood is as thin as a human's, you are tainted by the blood of our *food*! Whoever your father was, he was a stupid fool to fall for a mortal woman, and conceive such an *abomination* such as you. *You* are the one with no place in this world, but like hawks must hunt fish, a Vampire *must* hunt humans. Every animal has a predator, and we are the top of the food chain. No matter how many are killed, Immortals will remain superior. I, myself, will never die. I am eternal!"

As the two talked, Jacob continued to slip back and away from Angela. He kept his body facing the Immortal she stood before, carefully inching his way to the back of the sanctuary to retrieve his bow. His only hope was that Angela could keep Horla talking for the time being, and distract him long enough.

"Have you no tongue, Dhampir?" Horla clicked his fangs together. "Do you really despise the fact that you are impure in the eyes of Purebloods that you wish to hunt us all down in your little spat of self-satisfying revenge? You are hated by the humans, feared by them, and the Immortals are the ones to pay? I, myself, am to pay for your parent's mistake of even allowing you to exist? To exist with no place at all?"

"No," said Angela. "The time of the Vampire has come to an end. You tried to intervene in mortal affairs, and in the end, Man still rose and you lost most of your nobility. That is the way of nature- that, is the way the world was meant to be. Full of light, which the humans possess, something that Immortals have turned their backs on long ago."

"Don't patronize me nor my cause, Dhampir. Humans are weak, pathetic, feeble-minded creatures!" Horla hissed. "Immortals are the way of the future, we are the supreme race that should have complete control of this country, and the entire world as well! *We* were meant to be the superior beings, not Man.”

“Immortals are mere shells of what Man could never be,” Angela said with narrowed eyes that were full of both hatred but also pity, Jacob noticed this as he neared his gear. “You yourself, are no different, Lord Horla. The fact that you *chose* the path of darkness; to become a monster, just proves that you were too weak to be human to begin with.”

“Weak,” Horla purred venomously.

“Yes, weak,” said Angela. “You are not a full-blooded ancestor. You are not a true member of the Sacred Bloodline. You’re nothing but a visitor of the past; an ancient relic that is nevertheless *manmade*. But it matters not whether you were born in darkness or molded by it. You all your kind are to go back where you belong; back into the depths of Oblivion where The Vampire Precursor should have gone long ago.”

“How *dare* you?” Horla snarled while raising crooked hands of white. “How dare you speak to me that way? How dare you insult His Highness? Ever since the fall of man, it is our birthright as Immortals to retake what is rightfully ours and plunge the sun into the water and all things Light must eventually burn out into darkness. I chose this ‘path,’ not because I was too weak to be human, but because I knew I could become greater; the evolution of superior beings just like The Precursor and the Great Covenants of Old! You have no right to speak to me that way; you’re just a half-breed bastard from a tramping

Immortal and a human scrubber. You don't even deserve to wear that ring on your hand!"

Jacob's eyes lashed to Angela's hand, and sure enough he could see the blood-red gem glistening as her body shifted like a shadow.

"Neither do you," Angela said raising her sword while adding, "The way you and your brother are, The Precursor would be ashamed. You do not deserve that ring any more than I, Horla, because you are a weakling. And a coward I say."

"Weakling..." Horla seethed, and a black shadow seemed to spread throughout the entire sanctuary, plunging the very air into thick and cold darkness. There was no longer a wisp of frigid air, the whole church had gone cold as if Yohnah Himself had abandoned it to the mercy of this demonic being.

"Weakling, and a *coward*, am I? When I am through with you, you will *beg* me to end your miserable life. I don't know how many Vampires you've killed with that obnoxious sword, but still being a Dhampir means you are related by blood. I will make sure that your fate ends just as all the rest at the end of that blade. You speak blasphemies against The Precursor and all his loyal followers, and you shall pay!"

And so, Horla's eyes flashed bright and yellow, the flash seeming to cut through the icy shadows briefly like a camera flash. Angela staggered, and buckled to her knees.

"Angela!" Jacob said concerned, his gear momentarily forgotten.

Horla then flashed his eyes upon Jacob and Jacob found himself looking into the eyes of a massive black wolf. Jacob watched in horror as the wolf lunged and tore into Angela with bloody teeth. Then before Angela could even fall back upon the ground with her head just hanging by bone, the wolf lunged at Jacob who brought his arms up to protect himself. But still, he couldn't take his eyes off of Angela, who laid in a pool of her own blood, dead and gaping blindly at the ceiling. He didn't take his eyes off the Dhampir, even as the teeth came for his own throat. He gasped out as the wolf suddenly vanished, in a *poof* of shadow.

Bewildered, Jacob then saw that Angela was alive and unscathed, standing before Horla who had covered his head with his cloak. Jacob then noticed the blood on Angela's sword. There for a moment, and then burning away to ash and smoke as the silver burned it away.

"It's an illusion, Jacob." she told him backing away from the Immortal whose cloak was now moving as loosely as smoky water. "It isn't real."

"An illusion..." Jacob breathed, and he looked back to his bow, which was just a few feet away from where he stood. The whole thing... it felt so real that he was still shaken by that bloody image of Angela dying right in front of him. What kind of man; what sort of *creature* could make that appear so real?

Horla then started to chuckle, bringing his head out from under his cloak. A deep gash from his chin to his temple slowly closed and sealed as if he were made of clay.

"Remarkable, I haven't met anyone who could see through such a spell." He was now looking at Angela no longer out of hatred, but mild curiosity. A *hungry* look in those glowing eyes of his- a dangerous and seething look about them

"Dhampir, what did you say your name was?".

"Angela," Angela answered. "Angela Dragos."

"Dragos…" Horla hissed with a vicious grin. "I was going to have some fun with you two, but I see simple spells won't be enough on the likes of you two. I suppose I will have to push myself a little further; this might be a little more fun than I thought, not so boring. I will enjoy watching you both *squirm*. What secrets do you hold? I have to know."

His eyes then flashed again, and this time, Angela crippled down for real.

She started to breathe heavily as she looked up at Horla with an expression Jacob had never seen on the Dhampir before. Gone was her cold and indifferent persona, her cool demeanor. Now having been replaced with the image of a frightened little girl. Jacob didn't know what Angela was seeing, but whatever it was, it scared her.

She was *terrified*.

At this point, not giving the Immortal a chance to turn his way, Jacob managed to grab his bow and in one quick motion, he nocked an arrow straight out of it's quiver and took aim at the Immortal. He loosed the projectile which sailed straight and true, right into one of Horla's glaring eyes. The Vampire screamed out as blood and black smoke hissed from the wound, and he suddenly turned towards Jacob, his attention off of Angela and the Dhampir now suddenly relaxed as the spell was broken.

"Angela!" he bellowed and having heard her partner, the Dhampir lunged forward and slashed at the Immortal with her sword at blinding speeds that Jacob would've missed if he had blinked.

Blood sailed like rose pedals as Horla backed away to evade any more attacks. He wrenched the arrow out of his socket, the eye being pulled with it only to slip back into his head as if the tendon was being pulled by unseen hands. He then vanished in a flash of shadow and the darkness seemed to pass underneath Angela and reappear right behind her. With a swipe of his hand that seemed to grow talons, he struck Angela with such ferocious anger. He stumbled after striking the Dhampir however as another arrow stuck into the back of his head. Then spinning about, Angela removed her shredded cloak and struck out at Horla again, forcing the Immortal back and towards Jacob who started to run along the sides of the sanctuary and losing arrow after arrow into the beast of shadow. Meanwhile every blow of Angela's sword was met with either Horla's talons or tasted his flesh whenever he was not shadow.

With a snarl, Horla flashed his now-healed eyes at Angela again once he was at a safe distance, and the Dhampir let out another harrowing cry of terror. She backed away, holding a hand out as if to ward off an evil entity. Just what was she seeing that was terrifying her so?

Before Horla could get at her again, Jacob shot another arrow, this one at the Immortal's knee and calling out to him as he buckled to the ground. "Hey! Leech!"

The Vampire turned and *roared* at Jacob, and for a brief moment, Jacob thought that the shadow around the

Immortal made him appear like a savage wolf; those glowing yellow eyes hungry and full of rage, the maw splitting into thousands with millions of jagged and bloodthirsty teeth. The very sound of his roar shook the building and threatened to destroy Jacob's eardrums it was so loud.

"You obnoxious swine!" the Vampire bellowed.

"Oh, I'm *really* scared," Jacob attempted to mock while nocking another arrow and keeping the Immortal's attention on him. "Why don't you come face me for a change? Those needle-teeth look about as harmful as a kittens; it looks so *stupid!*"

Horla hissed again. "Let's see if you still think that, when I drain you until you are nothing more than a bag of skin and bones!"

And with that, Horla's eyes flashed bright, consuming all things in Jacob's sight into brilliant light, and faded like an oil painting in sweltering heat. The world around him shifted and faded into a place that the Hunter wished he could forget.

A small cabin, old and decrepit, fenced in with a fence of bones of all sorts. Arm and leg bones held up pieces of ribs and were tied with vines. Perched on the two posts that cut off the fence to a pathway to the cabin, were a pair of children's skulls, their heads containing candles that burned and made the eyes glare back at him. The cabin itself was quiet, but out front, Jacob found himself lying upon a sacrificial table looking up at a blood-red moon.

And leering above him with a broken and toothy smile, was Mother.

Her hair was stringy and a terrible mess, and her face was molted with many wrinkles and blemishes. Her back was hunched like a crow, and her bony body was covered in thin rags as she hovered over Jacob who was naked and now as young as he had been when this had occurred. A young child, exposed and frightened as she trailed a black dagger along his torso from groin to sternum. Her eyes, which were supposed to be hollow and black like a bird's, were now glowing yellow like a cat's once it has finally caught the mouse.

"Such a naughty boy," Mother said in a cold and silky voice like an icicle running across Jacob's temple. She then raised the knife and stabbed it right through Jacob's hand. Though this was a mere memory, the pain felt all too real, and Jacob cried out as he felt the dagger pierce through and into the table beneath it.

"But don't worry," Mother continued with arms splayed out towards the dark skies above. "I shall make you, *perfect.*"

She then began chanting, and just like before, Jacob could feel cold hands reaching out and grabbing him, choking him and holding his limbs in a chilling embrace. Jacob cried out; he *screamed*, begging for Mother to stop but the Witch just brayed with laughter, and continued her unholy chant of power as she circled her hands around the dagger itself. Tears rolled down Jacob's cheeks from both eyes, which were how they had been back then. Both blue, perfect and beautiful, and yet so full of terror and pain.

"Jacob!" a muffled voice managed to seep through the sounds of Jacob's harrowing screams. "Jacob!"

But Jacob could not answer. All he wanted was the memory to end; he didn't want to feel this sensation or hear these horrible words of black magic anymore. He was finally free, having ridden himself of his mother's hellish experiments and spells. To see it all, and experience it all again, and again, and again... he just... wanted it all to end.

A sharp pain buzzed through Jacob's head, and he gasped as the image suddenly vanished from view, having been replaced again by Count Horla, who stumbled above him and with a yelp, Jacob rolled away from where he was lying down and out of the way as the Immortal crashed down on his hands and knees. On the Vampire's back, was Angela's sword, the owner, holding Horla down with a terrifying snarl on her face. Twisting her body and thrusting her hip into the Vampire's side, she forced him closer to the ground whilst grabbing one of his arms and twisting it behind his back. The Immortal roared and lashed out with a taloned hand, barely missing her face by a hair's width.

"Run!" she commanded, and she was suddenly backhanded by Horla who was much stronger than she. The force of the strike sent her flying across the sanctuary and crashing into the wall on the other side.

Horla stood, seething angrily at the Dhampir but he turned his eyes upon Jacob instead, who was up once again with another arrow nocked and aimed right for the heart. He loosed it, but quick as a flash the Immortal caught the projectile between two bony talons.

"Such an interesting Hunter, you are," Horla hissed as he snapped the arrow in two. "Son of a witch, filled with black magic that runs like blood in your veins. Such power… I wonder what would happen when an Immortal drinks your blood."

He bared his fangs again, his needle-teeth still barely visible but the rest of his teeth seemed to stretch and sharpen as if they were made of clay rather than bone.

"I *really* wish to find out."

Jacob sneered, all fear evaporating as he took off running to the side, trying to put as much distance between himself and the Immortal who had dissipated into shadow and appearing right where Jacob had been.

"You want me, you piece of undead gutter-shit? Come and get me."

Horla roared and as he lunged towards Jacob, his entire being shifted to that of a wolf of shadow, which cleared the distance between the two in just a few bounds. When the great beast tackled Jacob to the ground it raised it's head and bit down with its massive maw of teeth. Jacob just barely managed to get his bow up and like fighting a real wolf, he held the beast back with all his strength despite it feeling like he would be forced right into the stone floor beneath him. The wolf's hot breath blasted in his face, smelly and wet with drool, the stink of decay and death accompanying it. But still Jacob held the creature back and just for a brief moment as the wolf backed off and raised a paw, he could see Horla in his original image standing above him with a talon-stretched hand ready to claw him to shreds.

Jacob managed to kick out and strike the Immortal in the leg and he scrambled up to his feet to get away during Horla's surprise. He felt a hand grab his shoulder and reaching for the sword he had dropped upon going for his bow, he swung with all his might and cleaved the Vampire's arm right at the wrist. Horla screamed out as blood and smoke sprayed out, but in the mixture of blood and darkness, the hand grew immediately back, the one sailing through the air vanishing into ash.

Jacob then seized his chance and swung with all his might. The sword dug deep into Horla's collar where the shoulder met the neck, but the sword was stuck just about halfway through. When he tried to pull the sword out, Jacob found himself staring into Horla's eyes again, and he faltered as he found himself looking into the face of his horrible mother.

"You're such a naughty boy," Mother said with the witch's voice overlapping Horla's like something out of a nightmare. "We have to fix that."

Jacob cried out and he gasped out as Horla dug his claws right into his torso. With a mighty throw, the Immortal chucked Jacob clear across the room and he cried out again as he felt himself crash through the alter and shattered it into splinters. He had dropped his bow in the vicious attack, and it was just out of reach of his outstretched hand; and on top of it all, he was bleeding out from the wound in his belly. He looked up to see Horla now coming for him again, the sword of the church now in his own hands.

Jacob reached up and pulled his eyepatch back, and his Immortal eye flashed bright and red. Horla stumbled for a moment, surprised at what he was seeing.

"Stop!" he commanded the Immortal. "Don't resist anymore- Don't take another step towards me."

Horla chuckled, amused and he resumed his pace, rubbing his left temple as if he had a migraine.

"You really are an interesting little creature," he purred. "Your mother must have been a remarkable witch in order to obtain a Hypnosis Eye. Unfortunately for you, that eye won't work on me."

Despite himself, Jacob felt his body begin to tremble with fear. He stared up at Horla, disbelieving.

"Those who carry the blood of the Vampire Line in their veins cannot be affected by just a single eye. In fact, those who are defeated in battle for rule often have one if not both of their eyes gouged out, their socket stuffed with an iron sphere coated with silver which they are not to remove. Not enough to cause severe damage mind you, but enough to burn and prevent the eye from healing. Barbaric times, no? If you had two eyes you *might* have had a chance, but alas..."

Jacob grimaced in frustration and tried to stand. But his leg buckled beneath him, and he felt a sharp pain shoot within his calf. His leg was broken, and he couldn't get away as Horla stalked closer like an angel of death. He then started to go for his glove, thinking of a last resort; just one more chance to use it again without pushing himself too far. Having done it twice in the past 24 hours, Jacob even wondered if he would even be able to conjure up a functional spell.

"I'm going to enjoy tearing you apart," Horla said, his face morphing into that of Jacob's mother, then the soldiers he trained with, even Angela to his horror. Many faces, all wanting to kill him, the wolf among them.

The Immortal then froze and then he spun around fast, catching the sword lunging right for his heart and holding Angela back with a terrible glare. His newly-acquired sword snapped against Angela's own, the silver far more stronger than that of steel. Undeterred however, Horla extended his talons and caught Angela's second strike and held it there.

The two vampiric beings held each other steady by pushing back against one another, sparks flying in every direction as silver grinded against those unworldly talons. Both were glaring at each other, lavender locked with gold, eyes slitted and alert. They appeared to be trying to speak to one another without words as Horla's pointed ears curled back like a cat's along with Angela's. How Angela was holding her own against the might of the Immortal, Jacob didn't know.

At the last second, Angela had turned her blade so that Horla's talons would get caught in the teeth of her weapon. Now the Immortal could not back away pull away and as he lashed out with his other hand, Angela twisted and ducked beneath it, twisting Horla's other arm in the process. She disengaged then and struck out, but once again Horla caught the blade, knocking it aside and lunging in to create four deep gashes across Angela's belly. Her blood squirted through her armor as she dashed back and took a dagger and chucked it at the Immortal, distracting him long enough for her to strike out again, this time severing the same hand Jacob had cut off with the church sword.

It did not grow back this time, and Angela was forced to block another blow from Horla's remaining hand, but this time the Immortal intentionally hooked his fingers in-between the teeth of the blade which has proven time and time again useful for Angela's style of combat. Now they were holding each other again, once more at a standstill against one another's strength. In fact, the two struggling against one another had even caused some cracks to form beneath their feet as if they were being crushed from above. Once more, locked in position, the two vampiric beings glared at each other with their glowing cat-like eyes.

But little by little, Angela's arms seemed to quiver beneath the strength of the Immortal, and Horla smiled hideously at the Dhampir with slowly ascending victory now in his hands. At this point, he was now towering over Angela, his missing hand no longer smoking and now slowly healing over as the affects of the silver slowly wore off on him.

"Even with all the strength of a Vampire, all that training that allowed you to do your fancy twists and turns, you are *still* weak," he hissed to Angela. "You should have died like your whore of a mother."

Angela hissed and tried to push back, but found that she couldn't. Her gamble was not going into her favor, and soon she would be overcome by the Immortal. Deciding against healing himself, Jacob wrenched his glove right off his hand and pointed his palm right at the Immortal. Horla's eyes shifted as if he felt something was wrong. Angela kept her eyes on her target, unmoved at Jacob casted his spell, and a brilliant bright light shined from the eye-rune in his hand. A beacon shining through the darkness like a lighthouse through fog.

Immediately, Horla cried out and hissed as if he was being hit by scalding water. Boils and burns appeared on his face, and he screamed out loud as he suddenly lost his balance and started to fall back in hopes of shielding himself from the sunlight being shone through Jacob's palm.

Angela seized her opportunity and wrenched her sword to the side, throwing Horla off balance completely and stabbing for his heart. The weapon stuck right through the Immortal's back, pushing his cape out as blood spilled beneath him. Jacob laughed out loud in victory as his magic finally depleted from his body, and his cursed hand begin to throb again. Three times in a single day had taken a major toll on it; he would have to not use it for a long time now. He returned his attention back up to Angela-

Who stood alone in the middle of the sanctuary. She stepped back, sword raised as if practicing stance rather than fighting a formidable opponent. Dread began to dawn on Jacob as he discovered where Horla now was. Standing right beside him, both hands still intact, the church sword in his right. In fact, he was completely unscathed and did not appear tired in the slightest.

She had not been fighting Horla at all. It was just another illusion while the real one stood above Jacob now, watching the Dhampir battle some invisible enemy and using all her strength and stamina upon it.

"Amusing isn't it?" said Horla who chuckled at Jacob's expression. "I could watch this all day. As for you…" And quick as a flash, he had turned the sword upon Jacob and stabbed downward into his abdomen.

Jacob cried out as the air was suddenly rushed out of his body from the impact. Nothing serious had been hit, he was still able to breathe, but it hurt like hell and he glared at the Immortal who bent down to him and bared his fangs mere inches from Jacob's face. Those horrible yellow eyes burned like coals, and Jacob stared into the face of his mother once again.

"It's okay to scream," purred the old witch's voice. As she spoke, her skin began to turn a shade of black, and some began to peel away like burning paper. Then her hair was singing away, her lips and nose bursting into flame as if someone had splashed her with oil and set her ablaze. Jacob felt a scream attempt to escape his throat, but all that came out was a barely audible squeak. He had been frightened into silence, hypnotized by the illusion of his mother burning before him.

"In fact, *squeal*," demanded the molting face.

A foot then connected with the side of the hag's head, turning immediately into Horla again and the Immortal whose expression was dumbfounded tumbled away and crashed right into the wall beyond the alter and statues. Chunks of brick fell upon him and he came up again, thrashing about and hissing in anger.

The Immortal roared at Angela, who now stood between him and his prey. Gone were her own wounds, her belly still intact as if Horla had not tried to gut her at all.

"*How!?*"

"I saw it happen before you could even cast your spell," Angela said. "I was able to see through your illusion, and wake up as if from a dream. Unfortunately, I was unable to break away free in time."

Horla growled. "You lucky bitch…"

Her eyes shifted to Jacob and quickly turned back to Horla, who was now picking himself up from the rubble.

"Jacob…"

"Don't worry about me…" Jacob said still speared through by the sword. "As long as it stays in, I won't bleed out…"

But even as he said that, some blood began to pool beneath him, not terribly like he said, but just enough to make him feel dizzy.

"Go get that bastard."

Angela looked pained to leave him, but she raised her sword, ready to fight the Immortal once again.

"I'll get you out of this," she told him. "I promise."

Jacob prayed that she wouldn't have to break her promise.

The truth of the matter was, yes, Angela had seen the illusion coming over her and was able to weaken it's grip upon her. However, Horla's power far surpassed hers and she would have grappled with it until Horla had come to finish her off if she had not heard Jacob's cry of agony.

Now he was horribly hurt, the sword still puncturing his body and seeming to pin him to the floor. She had wanted more than anything to take him and flee, to save him from this monster. But now Horla was up and very angry, and so Jacob would have to hold on until she finished this.

As the Immortal began to shift to the side, shift like a figure drawn in pencil is smudged by a thumb and then re-drawn, Angela moved with him, always keeping herself between him and her partner. Outside she could hear the shrieks and calls of the Disciples whom Horla had made, just outside the church and yet unable to come in even if one was to invite them in. Fear brushed her heart, but Angela kept her eyes on Horla, ready to respond to whatever attack the Immortal would attempt.

She had promised Jacob that she would get him out of here, and she'd be damned before she fell. She would finish this, one way or another.

Suddenly, without hardly any indication or provoking, Horla lunged fast as lightning, and Angela sidestepped and slashed him along the arm. The Immortal hardly reacted and clawed at her, coming at her again with long black talons of shadow. The two danced and slashed at each other at speeds no human being could ever comprehend. They were like ghosts and the wind.

In the midst of their fighting, she managed to get Horla to follow further and further away from Jacob, but little by little, the longer she looked into the Immortal's eyes, the harder it got for her to see the near future and hold out against him. It was not just a battle of strength and speed or even skill, but of the mind as well. Their eyes were constantly locked onto one another, forming the bridge between each other's consciousnesses and allowing both to wrestle for control based on the power of their Immortal Eyes.

And in the back of her mind, Angela felt the past creep up like sin waiting at the door. Faces, places she longed to forget, broke through the haze and casted a veil upon her eyes as she and Horla continued their clashing of sword and claws. If she lost her concentration, the Immortal would slip in completely, and she would be lost.

"*Give, in!*" Horla bellowed with enunciation through each swipe of his claws.

Angela ducked beneath the claws and moved in to try and stab for Horla's heart again. The Immortal disappeared in a flash of shadow but Angela saw it coming and swung her sword again as she spun about, striking the Vampire right across the chest.

"Never!" she snarled through the blood and smoke that blurred past.

The Vampire hissed and came at her again, the wound in his chest closing in the process.

"You resist the urge of your bloodline," Horla snarled swiping and snapping at Angela like a rabid wolf which he had materialized into before returning to his original form.

"You help the humans- *converse* with them! Humans are nothing more than prey meant to be slaughtered just like rabbits to wolves! We are the future- the bloodline that you were meant to *serve*! You would die, for a pathetic creature like *him*!" He gestured to Jacob who was still struggling to keep conscious as he watched the immortal beings struggle.

"That's right," Angela ducked and slashed again. "I would die for him, and all of mankind if I can. You are fighting your destiny. The Age of the Vampire is fading away, and you too shall fade into legend like those before you."

"Lies!" Horla argued with another definitive swipe of his claws which obliterated a nearby pew and gouged great gashes across the stone floor. "We *will* rise again! The humans are weak, and the human inside of you is your own weaker side, *Dhampir*. You don't even deserve to be related to any of us- you never should have been conceived! You fight us, and help *them*! They won't even accept you as their own, you shitblood abomination!"

"And I will continue to fight until my purpose is fulfilled," Angela said leaping upon one of the high statues and upon leaping down on top of the beast, prepared to stab downward with her sword. She missed as Horla disappeared in a flash of shadow and reappeared at a safe distance just as she was up and ready for more.

"I walk in neither light nor darkness," she told the Immortal who hissed in indignation. "I walk in the twilight; the lost barrier between Man and Beast, and I will continue to walk it until Man no longer needs to fear their greatest predator. When that day comes, when my own time comes, I shall sever such a connection so that no one will ever slip between the borders of man and beast."

"Such bold words," Horla hissed and backing away from the harm of Angela's followed attack. He was biding his time, recovering his breath for for the first time in centuries, he was being pushed to the limit. "But you realize this will not end with Vampires. It will not even end when the Lycans are put to rest, or any of the ancient ones still loose in the woods or in the vast oceans. It will not end through all Seven Planes of Lunokean. In the end, mankind will just find another monster to fear in the night."

"That's their business," said Angela when Horla disappeared and then reappeared clawing at her, missing her by inches as she struck out at his side and spilt more of his blood. "And when that comes they will hire a Hunter to take care of that monster, just as one will no doubt be hired for me once you all are gone. It's as simple as that."

Her words angered the Immortal further. They resonated with Jacob who overheard it all, remembering what she had said to him back at the apartments. He gritted his teeth in frustration, and could in a way sympathize with Horla simply because nothing is ever that simple. Nothing in the entire world can ever be so simple.

Now Horla had managed to strike at Angela, causing her to fall back but she somersaulted backwards and got to her feet ready to fight again, despite the four horrible gashes that had appeared across the left side of her face and bleeding profusely. The fury in her eyes and the snarl on her face was just as bestial as the Immortal as she hissed and bared her fangs at him in utter defiance.

"I'll be sure to remember that, when your corpse is left for my disciples to violate and tear apart like the piece of filth that you are. And I myself will bleed that insufferable human you care so much for, right in front of you; and you can *mourn* for him as you both die."

The Immortal's eyes flashed again, a psychic blow more powerful than all the others in his last attempt to exercise all within his power to bring the Dhampir down.

And so Angela cried out as she fell before the Vampire again, with Jacob calling her name somewhere behind her. All bravado and steel had been drawn out of her like blood. Her vision had grown hazy, her concentration lost against the pressure of the Vampire's power. Clairvoyance no longer mattered. It would not have helped Angela anyway. No Immortal Eyes nor any miracle from Kawn or even Oblivion could help her now.

Because she wasn't seeing Horla, or the sanctuary anymore. Instead, she saw a horrible and familiar face looming over her. Towering over her like a fleshy monolith. He stood completely naked, and his disgusting grin glaring down at her hungrily, enjoying her fright as he licked his lips wanting to taste her again and again. His cock was fully erect, and his repulsive and loathsome hands reached out to her as if to embrace her.

Angela felt herself wither under the gaze of the man before her. She felt herself shrink inside herself, becoming a tiny shell of a younger version of herself. Tiny, innocent, fragile. No armor, no sword, no hope.

No... not him. Anyone... anyone, but him.

The figure flickered before her, and momentarily, Angela saw Horla in his wolf-familiar lunge at her with such speed and sharpness that the very teeth would have severed her in half if she didn't manage to get her sword up in time. The wolf bit down onto the blade but immediately retreated before pawing her with such force which sent her falling back. She tumbled across the floor and she smacked not into the shattered remains of the alter, but instead right into the side of an elegant bed with satin sheets and an overhead of purple drapes; the scenery changing once again with greater and more disturbing detail.

The naked man smiled, laughing in drunken pleasure as he removed his crown and placed it on the nightstand. His head of stark white hair was loose and damp with sweat, and from the nightstand he removed a pair of silver shackles. He started for Angela again, who was once again just a little girl no more than six when this all happened. Frightened and naked little Angela, backed away from the beastly man before her, unsure of what to do and nowhere to go, wanting to scream and cry and beg him to stop and go away. But he just kept coming for her, like he *always* used to.

"Come here, girl," the man demanded stroking his erect cock. Angela tried to cover herself, to protect what little innocence remained, and yet the man only laughed, relishing at her tears and begging. "Come *here*, I say. We're gonna do something different tonight. You owe me your life, girl. Don't make me change my mind."

It wouldn't have mattered if she somehow *did* change his mind on sparing her life. He would never leave her alone. There was no pity in those black pits for eyes other than lust worthy of the Vampires.

Black pits, that now glowed bright and yellow and cat-like.

He just…

kept…

coming…

Little Angela closed her eyes, prepared for the worst of which she never believed would happen again.

Little Angela gasped, almost crying out as she turned to see that Jacob was laying beside her, propping himself up with one arm with his other draped over her shoulder. As small as she was in this illusion, he was much larger now, but where the naked man projected defiling menace, Jacob projected safety and warmth. His touch was comforting, and she found herself drawing closer to him in order to access his protection.

He pulled her close, allowing her to seek refuge beside him. Angela let him. Anything to get away from this misery. She noticed that his red eye was focused on her, and he was crying a tear of blood as he did so. Slowly, she began to realize that this was not some part of the illusion, not some trick of Horla.

She was then surprised to see him stretching his neck out and exposing his jugular to her. Little Angela from long ago, naked, afraid, and desperate, looked at the man of today with wonder filling her soon-to-be lavender eyes. What did he see in all of this? Did he see her the way she was? Did he see the naked king?

"Angela..." Jacob said, his voice sounding so weak, barely above a whisper. The sword still anchored him in place through his lower torso. "It's all fake; it isn't real..."

Little Angela sniffed, hearing the growl of the naked man now rushing towards her, slowly as if he was swimming through amber. "Come here, girl. Come here *now!*"

"I can't..."

"Angela..." Jacob said, both his eyes looking at her almost pleadingly. His head tilted back, exposing his throat again which bobbed as he swallowed.

He offered himself to her, saying, "Take me. Please."

Angela, the Angela now; the Dhampir, and the Huntress of the Black Hand, looked at him, and understood. She was scared to do so, had sworn an oath she would never do such a thing, but what choice did they have against an opponent such as Count Josef Horla?

So, tenderly, gently as to not hurt him, she took him by the chin, and held him up so that he wouldn't have to bear his own sickly weight. She then bared her fangs, and then as softly as she could without causing more pain, she bit into his neck.

He shuddered as she drank. For the first time in many years, Angela drank from the neck of the living human who offered himself to her. The blood flowed like honeyed wine, quenching her terrible thirst, but also healing the cuts she had received from Horla's last attack. Her face which had been shredded closed off, becoming beautiful once again. She felt newfound strength pour into her muscles and intense pleasure.

For a brief moment, she kept her eyes closed, wanting to just relish the taste on her tongue and keep feeding, keep feeling this sensation of power and life.

But this was Jacob, her partner, who had offered himself to save them both. She had to save him. So when she snapped her eyes open, the veil was broken and the illusion around her shattered like glass.

She saw Horla, not the terrible naked man, rushing towards her, trying to stop her. She released Jacob, and then spinning about as she stood, she got her sword up just in time to catch the Immortal's claws, their faces mere inches from one another. Horla's own bright yellow eyes glared into her own, which burned brighter than ever with newfound power from the human blood she drank; human blood, mixed with the cursed black magic placed upon it by a witch. Horla could not trap her into a terrible illusion again, and he couldn't push back against her like he had before. Angela, was no longer helpless against this Immortal who stared flabbergasted at this sudden surge of strength and defiance.

No, Angela Dragos was no longer inferior to this Immortal Lord.

Twisting her weapon, Angela forced Horla's arm back to create an opening and she leapt up and spinning about the heel of her boot crushed the Immortal's jaw and teeth as she sent him flying back from her mighty kick. As the Immortal tried to get up, she started towards him as a bright light seemed to emit from her very body, and mist began to encircle her and burn away the shadows of Josef Horla like sunlight piercing the night.

"What is this?" the Immortal roared and then charged at the speed of sound at the Dhampir, who just as quickly deflected the talons coming her way.

The two beings danced around each other like demons, moving fast. But Angela was faster now, catching Horla again and again and forcing him deeper into the church and away from Jacob who he dared to hurt. They shredded pews to splinters, dug deep furrows across some of the walls of the church, causing the very structure to quiver at every blow exchanged by them. Horla swung at Angela, who leapt back and slashed at his claws, severing them at the very base and leaving his hand a bloody stump. Horla then stretched his cloak out and leapt back like a bat ready to take flight. Upon landing, Angela lunged forward, her sword aimed right for the heart.

Snarling in victory, Horla brought his other hand up and his eyes flashed bright and yellow for one more chance to distract the Dhampir and remove her head from her shoulders. However, she ducked and slashed at his other hand, just cutting the thumb right off before her blade cut deep across the man's chest, exposing a bloody wound through the destroyed dress shirt.

"Gah!" the Immortal cried out as those purple eyes seemed to engulf the light of his own, outshining like the moon against stars. Her very aura was commanding, overwhelming, a sensation Josef Horla had not felt in thousands of years.

The last Immortal being who emitted such power had been...

"No, it cannot be!"

Stunned, amazed, her glowered at her. He struck out at her, but she had seen the blow coming seconds before. Everything he did she saw before he did so, and she batted him away and whenever she could not get her sword up in time, she would kick and punch and claw, fighting like a ravenous beast and forcing the Immortal to stumble back. The look in his eyes which glared through the mask of blood that covered his face no longer showed sure victory, but now terror.

Angela stood before him, shrouded in light, her lavender eyes burning brighter still, and her expression that of someone he now understood that he had seen before.

"But… how… Who in the *hell* are you?"

Angela started for him, her sword ready, her eyes burning, reading every possible future and outcome based on both her actions and the actions of her supposedly immortal opponent.

He then raised arm, the remaining four talons in his last hand. He lunged fast, using the power of the darkness for one final burst of speed toward her, ready to intercept her.

"Die, you abomination!"

Blam!

But then something plunged into Horla's other eye; a silver bullet, shot by Jacob's revolver which he had managed to shoot just before slumping down to his side, still spilling blood upon the shattered remains of the alter. Horla screamed, blinded in one eye and in the midst of his charge, faltered.

At that moment, Angela slashed at the Immortal's arm, slicing it completely off right at the elbow and causing a spray of crimson all over the church statues. Horla bellowed and raised his other arm whose fingers started to grow back in blurs of pure shadow, ready to claw at her again.

But this time, Angela was ready, with a flash of her eyes, she saw the future, and with it, maneuvered out of harm's way of Horla's shadowy grasp and then lunging forward, she drove her sword right into the heart of the Immortal.

The Vampire *screamed* as Angela plunged her sword deeper, deep enough to pierce through his heart and out his back. Blood and shadows burst from behind, a spray of liquid death that rose into the air only to dissipate like fog in the morning sun.

"Return to Hell!" Angela bellowed as the hilt of her sword struck the monster's chest, the tip piercing out the back and the serrated edge shredding what was left of Count Horla's black heart.

At last, the spell was broken.

The darkness and shadows vanished in the instant, all like a bad dream. The chunks of the ceiling continued to rain down around them, and the blood from Horla now spilled onto the stone floor, spreading out in little tidal waves. His screams shattered the windows as well as all other glass within the vicinity of the church itself. The armless and bleeding Immortal hunched over against Angela. She simply held him there, staring right into the Immortal's eyes, who stared back in utter shock and defeat, not truly seeing her at all. His eyes which had glowed so bright, were now growing dim.

"Who… are you…?" Horla gasped blindly with blood trickling from his lips and down his chins. His skin turned from pale to ashen gray, as he asked the question a second time.

Angela merely stayed silent, watching the Immortal's body slowly begin to peel like burnt skin. Ashy flakes peeled away and began to float aimlessly before eventually crumbling into smaller pieces. A faster process than a Dearg or even that of a common Vampire, the Immortal began to finally die.

"You killed me…" Horla whispered as his body slowly began to crumble away into ash. It was as if time was finally catching up to the immortal body and returning him to dust from which he came before he chose the path of darkness. As the Immortal spoke, his voice came out as a sigh, almost as if out of relief.

"So… this is what it feels like to finally die. At least, I die in the arms of a beautiful lady. I love that cold look in your eye, Dhampir. I haven't seen such eyes, in a long… long time. I don't know who sired you, but… I long for the day, when those eyes are filled with agony and sorrow."

And as his flesh burned away from his skeleton which also fell away into ashes, Jacob heard the Immortal's last words echoing in the wind as he drifted away from this world to the next, leaving Angela standing there, with the blood on her sword slowly burning away like embers of fire.

"Be prepared… it's coming."

Angela said nothing more, but turned her eyes over to Jacob who was now lying still with the sword pinning him down.

Sheathing her own weapon over her shoulder, Angela approached Jacob and ripped off what remained of his cloak. Then with one pull, ripped the sword out of his body next and he gave a gasp as he began to bleed. She shoved the cloak into both entry and exit wounds, making the man hiss in terrible pain. It was not a permanent solution, but once the two of them got back to Clockwork, it would all be alright.

As Angela grabbed Jacob and hoisted him over one shoulder, she grabbed his bow and then carried him like a kingdom firefighter towards the exit of the sanctuary, as a chorus of screams in anguish echoed from the outside. By now, the terrible spell of Count Horla was slowly dying away, and those who were under his control would soon die with him. The head of the snake had been severed, and therefore the body was writhing in agony, waiting to die.

"Easy…" Jacob moaned.

"Sorry," said Angela, adjusting him so that he was a bit more comfortable. "Just hold on."

"This is embarrassing…" Jacob groaned behind Angela. "Being carried around by a woman like this."

"Don't talk too much," Angela told him. It was going to be a long way back to Ava's clinic, and she didn't want him to waste any strength.

"Is this my punishment…" Jacob groaned. "For what I did to you?"

Angela's jaw twitched at the reminder. "Don't worry about that. My only concern right now is getting you to the professor to patch you up."

"Angela… I'm sorry."

"Don't. You're going to be fine."

"I'm sorry…"

"Don't… please…"

"I'm…" Jacob sighed, the loss of blood finally getting to him and causing him to lose consciousness. He was still breathing, Angela could hear. There was still time.

(I'm sorry)

Damn me for a fool…

"I forgive you," she said as she kicked the doors to the sanctuary out, and stepped out into the cold outside where snow had begun to fall in large clumps that looked like feathers falling from the angels of heaven above.

Her eyes lingered up to a group of Watchmen, who raised their weapons as they converged towards the church. Apparently they had heard the ruckus from outside and had gathered.

She stopped, acknowledging them all as they told her to freeze and set the man down. They all looked scared, weathered by the night and it's ungraceful beasts.

But then one of the Watchmen stepped forward, commanding them to lower their weapons. He turned, and Angela saw the face of the Captain looking back at her. His pale eyes spoke his question better than words ever could.

"The Immortal responsible for this plague, Count Horla, is dead," she told them all. "Those who are infected will all return to the grave. When you find them all, behead them and stuff them all with garlic, just in case. Our work is done here."

With that, she started forward, and William stepped aside to allow her to pass. At his motion, they all did the same, staring at the two Hunters in awe and question as to what had happened inside the church.

As she passed by however, William did manage to voice one question.

"Is it truly over, Dhampir?"

Angela, who kept on walking through the Watchmen who continued to disperse as if she was a soldier passing through grunts. Her eyes were bright but also dim, fierce and yet tired. They were what forced them away, like sunlight to Vampires.

"It is." was all she said, and in silence without looking back once, she walked all the way to Ava's clinic as the screams of the undead returning to the depths of Oblivion shook the souls of those who remained alive in Irondell.

Though the plague and the threat of a Vampiric uprising was finally ending, the city had suffered a terrible loss; one that would take years if not decades to recover from. But there was still hope, as long as the people stay strong and did the best they could, they would overcome this horrible tragedy.

Because that's what made humans so special: no matter how much they endure, or what hell they go through in this world, they always got right back up stronger than ever.

And Angela, had complete faith in the human race.

Including the man who had saved both of them.

By morning the body count was recorded by the Watchmen: over two-thousand dead and more than three-thousand still missing, leaving a very small number of survivors.

The Watchmen encountered no Vampires the entire night before, and there were no signs of those who were still missing. However, in various places they *did* find countless bodies lying about with enlarged canines and upon forcing some of their eyes opened, revealed a pale milky color. Those were taken by the Watchmen to be beheaded and their mouths stuffed with garlic before being stuffed into small coffins.

By mid-afternoon the following day after, news from Goldendell came through and the quarantine over the city was lifted in order to allow the Empire to come in and clean up the mess. As the plague was announced over by the new order of Emperor Ion, Goldendell soldiers and a new Raven swept through the city in it's time of need at last. The nightmare was over, and Irondell was slowly reawakening. It would take a long time for the damage to be undone, but like many cities who encounter Vampiric Plagues, Irondell too shall overcome.

"I still don't understand how all the Vampires just *died* after you killed the Immortal," Clockwork wondered aloud as he continued to work on Jacob who was asleep on one of Ava's surgery tables.

The wound the Hunter had received had gone all the way through and thankfully only piercing his intestines. Clockwork had sewn him up to the best of his ability, but Jacob would have to drink fluids for a long while until his guts healed. He laid motionless as Clockwork worked on his stitches wearing only his undergarments, his right leg in a brace. His glove remained on, under Angela's request for Clockwork to not remove them for personal reasons. Clockwork didn't even argue as he continued to work on Jacob's torso which held most of his attention. The man had been incredible, having taking care of Jacob ever since Angela had carried him into Ava's clinic. The wonders of Professor Clockwork seemed endless.

"It's sort of like bees," Angela explained sitting in the chair in the corner. She had been there ever since they took Jacob upstairs and had not left since; watching Jacob as Clockwork worked on him. "Kill the queen, and the rest of the hive dies out. It isn't *exactly* like that, but that is the best comparison we have. In truth, no one knows the extent of an Immortal's power over the undead; it is one of those things mankind just cannot understand and probably never will."

Clockwork was of course not satisfied with this answer, but he allowed it to pass nonetheless and ask instead, "Is it still possible that a few Deargs or common Vampires survived?"

"It's still a possibility, yes."

"That still doesn't make a lot of sense," Clockwork grumbled reproachfully. "They are all individual beings having been infected by different Vampires. How can the strain merely lead right back to Horla, and then affect them when he himself is destroyed?"

"I wish I knew," Angela lied. "But there are just some things we can never fully explain in this world. The way Vampirism works is one of them. Biologically, we can only scratch the surface. Vampires on their own, are different dimensional beings on their own, and one may never truly understand how the Children of Kawfka work."

Clockwork was still unsatisfied, but he didn't press the matter any further. "So, it is done, then?"

"It is," Angela confirmed.

"I do have one, question- concerning Jacob and his injuries."

"What's that?"

Clockwork backed up in his chair and pointed exactly at what Angela dreaded to answer.

There were two puncture wounds, right in the side of the unconscious Jacob's neck, where she had bitten him. "These... these are bite marks. Did... did Horla do this to him?"

Angela swallowed before answering. "No."

Clockwork looked at her, understanding by the sound of her voice. He opened his mouth, closed it. Thought better of it, asked, "You?"

"Yes. He won't turn into anything however. My bite won't infect him. Dhampir's cannot turn humans into Vampires. But... the wounds will never heal either."

Clockwork looked at the bite, and then looked at Angela. "Like, they won't close up?"

"Not entirely. They will scar, but as holes still."

"Did you have to do it?"

Angela nodded. "He gave himself to me. It was because of him that I was able to stand up against Horla.

But… even though my bite is not infectious, the wound will never go away. They will be there, a marking that will remain for the rest of his life. Anyone who sees him, will believe him to be infected, and his life may be in danger.”

What she thought to herself and wouldn't say aloud was, *Worse, he is marked by me. Marked…*

“What will this mean, at least concerning the Black Hand? Surely you won't be able to hide it forever, at least not from them.”

“I plan to speak to Velinar about this,” Angela told the professor. “Whatever he deems necessary, we will do. I'm sure he will figure something out. My only concern, are the others.”

“Yes, I suppose that makes sense,” Clockwork pursed his lips in thought. “Until then… might I suggest then, a scarf or something else besides your usual hoods to cover up the wounds? It would make getting on the train more difficult. Which reminds me, we can all leave tomorrow when the train *finally* stops at the station. We can have them stop near Blackfort Pass and then I'll mail out both of your payments as promised.”

“Sounds good,” was all Angela could say. Grateful as she was, what she and Jacob both endured last night had been a daunting one, one of the most difficult she had dealt with since the slaying of Daimíya the Puppetmaster.

She was just glad that the Hunt was finally over, and both she and Jacob was alright. She wanted nothing more than to return to her room and her books with Sebastian in her lap.

But before any of that could happen, she would have to explain to Velinar just what happened to Jacob.

She had broken her vow, both personally and professionally. Whatever the ancient deity decided, Angela would agree to it. Though she wondered just where the consequences would take her. Maybe she would head south for the Nisthgúlian Reservation, hide among the tribes there while she found work; with the Empire outlawing contracts, it would be difficult for her to Hunt on her own.

One way or another, she would adapt and move as such. She was more than capable to do what is necessary. Her only hope was that Jacob would continue to have a home in the Black Hand. He didn't deserve to be dragged down with her. After all, this would be exactly as she planned anyway; with her and him parting ways and eliminating this partnership. It was better that way.

It was how it had to be.

The door opened and Ava entered the sickroom with a tray of cups containing a steaming liquid. The smell of herbs and spice struck Angela's nose as the sweet shut-in offered a cup.

"Would you like some tea, dear?"

Angela smiled, and took one of the cups gingerly in her thin hand. "Thank you. Not just for this, but for all you've done for my… my apprentice and I."

Ava smiled sweetly as she offered the other cup to Clockwork who sipped it ravenously. The old professor had not eaten or drank since she had brought Jacob in here. He deserved the tea- and more. Just like Ava.

"Think nothing of it, dear," the old woman said crossing the room and taking a seat to enjoy her own cup of tea. She took a sip, and then sighed contently.

"It was nice, having you all to care for. Ever since my husband passed on and my children grew up and moved away, I got so lonely out here with just my patients to attend to. Taking care of you all, made me feel like I was caring for my own son and daughter."

"I'm older than you, Ava," said Clockwork.

Ava rolled her eyes. "And a brother, I suppose. So, thank you. You too, Professor. It really was nice to talk to someone about the past with."

Clockwork smiled warmly and nodded. "You too, Madam."

Angela looked at Clockwork, and then she turned to Ava. "You both have been wonderful to Jacob and I. And to the Black Hand, so thank you both."

"Think nothing of it," Clockwork said sipping his tea again. "It was beneficial to us both. But that doesn't matter because Velinar and I go way back, back when I was a young Hunter- of course when I was able to walk. It was Velinar who offered me hope, not my boss nor my contractors who saved me, but that man."

Angela gave Clockwork a confused look. "Velinar is not a man."

"No, but he's no god either," Clockwork said. "Not anymore. He is just a cursed man, walking the world in a young body. But you already know that."

Angela's mouth twitched. She *did* knew, but it wouldn't go well if others knew about the deity contained in the cursed child. It would destroy his image: the child who was cursed to walk the world forever. Such a fate was terrible, and the news of this getting out would lose the fear that the Black Hand struck into the hearts of men.

Also, there was the child itself to think about.

"It was that little boy," Clockwork said looking up as if seeing the memory right above his head. "Who gave my wife and I the hope we needed to keep going, and serving the world of Man. For that man, I'd do whatever it takes to help him and the realm. So, thank you, Angela, for serving him."

Angela nodded. "Thank *you*, sir."

"Uh…" Jacob groaned while raising his head for the first time in forever. His gaze looked glassy, as if he was coming out of a drug-induced coma. "I helped too, you know…"

"Rest," Clockwork said pushing gently on Jacob's head and forcing him to lie down. "You need to stay still until we depart tomorrow. News of the city being lifted from quarantine will be spreading across the realm really soon. Connections and phones will be back, and you will need to move fast with us if we are to escape the Empire who will no doubt be on their way to investigate the situation."

Jacob grumbled. "Little too late for that, doncha think? Ahh… my side…"

"Stay still," Angela said from where she sat. "You can relax now. Our job is done here."

Jacob sighed, relaxing for what was probably the first time since the two of them came into this hellhole together.

"So, how did I do?" he asked with closed eyes. "Did I do alright?"

"You were satisfactory," Angela answered.

The eye opened, looked at her. "Oh, c'mon, gimme *something* more than that..."

"Don't talk so much," Clockwork said giving the Hunter a shot in the arm which Jacob winced at. "Don't worry, it's something to help you sleep."

But Jacob wasn't having any of it, and he turned his attention to Angela with a pointed finger. "I mean it, Angela. How did I do?"

"Other than what you pulled at the apartments?" Angela asked to which Jacob's finger wilted like a dying branch at the words, his expression withering just as badly.

She smiled then. "You did alright. Don't worry, Jacob. You're alive, and the job is done. That's enough to be proud of."

"But..." Jacob said drowsily as the drugs began to work in him. "Does this mean... you and I are... done?..." he managed to get the last word out before he went limp and was quickly snoring away in the land of dreams.

Angela watched him sleep, unsure of how to answer even now.

Clockwork looked at Angela with a piercing gaze, and he rolled over to retrieve her now empty cup. Upon taking it and following Ava out of the sickroom, the professor said one last thing over his shoulder.

"You are older and wiser than I. But when you find a loyal partner, you can't let them go, no matter how hard you try."

And before Angela could even say anything even if she wanted to, Ava closed the door, leaving her alone with

Jacob. She watched him for a long time, chewing on Clockwork's advice.

You can't let them go, no matter how hard you try.

It wasn't that simple. It wasn't just a matter of what she herself wanted, but what Angela would have to do upon giving the report to Velinar. In the end, it doesn't matter what she wanted or what Jacob wanted. It was all up to the Black Hand of Velinar.

She just... didn't know.

She remained seated by Jacob's side deep in thought, and wondered about it all night, watching her partner without rest. As watchful as a mother with her cubs, still thinking into the early hours of the morning.

What also caught her attention and held it for the longest time, was the Hunter's back. No doubt that Clockwork had noticed as well, though he hadn't mention anything at all. Angela noticed too, as the professor worked on the man.

On Jacob's back was a large tattoo of black wings like an angel, surrounded by many small runes of strange lettering. The wings themselves stretched out to Jacob's shoulders and seemed to curl down to almost his hips. The runes themselves, which were small and meaningless by themselves, sat nearly an inch away from every feather of both wings. No doubt there was magic in the ink of the tattoo, fueled by the runes around it. It only made Angela pity Jacob more, and wonder just who he really was beneath that calm and confident demeanor he always tried to keep up.

But it hardly mattered now... if what Angela thought would happen came to be, it would no longer matter what the two of them knew about each other. Even if it wasn't, she would have to stay away from him. Having bitten him... there was no going back. It was better, just to let it all go. Angela had this last thought when the moon was high, and sleep finally seized her body like a disease, dragging her to the land of dreams.

She slept the rest of the night away, all until morning when Clockwork woke them both up to go. Ava had made a wonderful breakfast of eggs and bacon and freshly brewed coffee to go with it. After some heartbreaking goodbyes, the three left the clinic, with Jacob limping due to his casted leg and having to be supported by Angela who did her best not to make it appear that she was practically *carrying* her partner with Clockwork leading the way in his chair.

Since there was a lot of activity going on with the Watchmen checking up with everybody and with the survivors helping one another to clean up the mess around the streets, the three had to take multiple detours. It would be a matter of time before Irondell was restored to its former glory, though it was a mystery still as to who would lead the city now, but with all the strong people still around, the city would be alright. It was a good thing that they had dyed Angela's hair after all, for no one gave the three a second glance as they moved through the city and out the main gates.

While passing through the gates, Angela noticed just how many people were coming in from the train station just a short walk away; families and friends of those who have lost their lives to the Vampire Plague. The sight was simply heartbreaking, especially for Jacob who said nothing for the entire walk.

They then passed a group of horsemen and Angela recognized one of them to be William, who locked eyes with the Dhampir. He didn't say anything, nor did he make an attempt to approach the group. Instead, with his stern and sober frown, he nodded a thanks to the two Hunters. Angela nodded, while Jacob offered a wave. No words were necessary at all.

The three of them then boarded the Anguis Express, and in a matter of time, the locomotive started to chug away from the city by high-noon. Angela sat by the window as they rumbled through the woods, seeing the smoke rising above the walls of Irondell. She still was unsure of their future, but their job was done; it was up to them now.

She sat back down, resting against the side next to Jacob who sat across from Clockwork. The two men were playing poker to pass the time, passing occasional words or curses between them both. Angela merely kept silent with a hand on the hilt of her concealed sword and her other holding her head up as she watched the world rumble past.

Hours went by, and eventually, Clockwork passed out, using his entire seat to lay down and sleep, leaving Jacob awake with Angela and one of his books he had borrowed from the professor.

"Man, Clockwork isn't a bad author either," Jacob commented. "His theories, his bucket list of experiments and inventions... all this could revolutionize the Empire to new heights, and create a whole new world for us all. This thing here, the motor-bike, imagine riding that instead of the horses."

"If it runs on oil, it would be a problem to refill the tank," Angela said. "Besides, they're noisy and might scare the horses you pass by."

"A wise man once said, 'if I asked people what they wanted, they'd say faster horses.'"

"Who said that?" asked Angela, intrigued.

Jacob shrugged. "Dunno."

Angela shook her head in amusement and returned her attention to the window. "Just enjoy your reading. I'll enjoy the horses."

That reminded her about something she had almost forgotten, and she dug into her belt and pulled out the journal Jacob had been writing in while she was unconscious. She held it out to him.

"I almost forgot to give this to you."

"Oh! Thank you..." Jacob took the journal and brushed it gingerly, like a priceless heirloom. "I thought I had lost it."

"It must be very important to you."

"It is."

"What is in it? If it is okay, me asking."

"Just silly things. Notes, rhymes... pictures. Silly things like that."

Angela decided to give the man a little bit of confidence. "One of the most brilliant painters, started off in a notebook. What is important to you can never be silly."

Jacob smiled at that. "Yeah, until you see one of them." He then looked at her. "Would you like to see one of my drawings?"

Angela looked at him waiting for him to show her. When he flipped upon the page he wanted, he revealed it to her. It was a young girl with fiery white hair, her hood pulled back into the shadow. Her leaden lips were parted slightly, and she was looking off into some unknown space beyond the paper she was in. She looked...

"Is that me?" Angela eventually asked.

Jacob nodded. "Yeah, I... I did it while you were watching the window one night."

"I didn't even notice."

"You were trying not to pay attention to me. I could tell. You were deep in thought though, as if you were really just gone in a different world. You looked... well... peaceful."

Jacob then looked at the picture, before turning back to her. "If you don't appreciate it, I'll take it out and burn it."

Angela thought just that exact thing, for a moment anyway. But after thinking about it for a minute, she shook her head. "No, it's a good drawing. You should be proud of your hand, and your skill."

Jacob smiled, and then closed his journal before tucking it away. "Thank you. Your words gladden me."

"Good." Angela turned her attention back to the window, feeling somewhat honored that the way Jacob saw her was so... beautifully illustrated. Neither out of lust or perversion. Just... watchfulness, with tender care. His own way of seeing her, expressed in paper and lead.

She heard him shift in his seat, and she could practically feel his one good eye staring at her now. She turned and looked at him, thinking the expression on his face was funny.

"Aren't you going to ask?"

"Ask what?"

"My hand? And what I did to you? You've been quiet ever since… you know."

Angela turned and looked at him. "I already told you: don't worry."

"I *do* worry though." the Hunter said. "I gave you a reason not to trust me…"

Angela's mouth twitched. "You never got my trust."

"Yeah right. Don't give me that," Jacob sighed.

"You don't have to tell me," she said. "Not if you don't want to. But I do know a little. It's a portal, isn't it?"

Jacob pursed his lips. "Yes."

"If you're not comfortable-"

"No, no," Jacob shook his head. "It's a long ride anyway…" He was quiet in thought for a moment, and then while raising his gloved hand said, "Besides, I owe you. It was my mother's last experiment. A portal through unlimited energy from Oblivion itself. With it, I can cast spells just like a witch can with a wand or staff. But it comes at a price…"

"It sucks the life out of your hand."

Jacob nodded. "I had to use it a lot when I was still with her. Now, I try not to use it- too much."

"But you did," Angela remembered. "Twice."

Jacob's mouth twitched, as if he was about to say something else. "Yeah. I'm sorry about that... Truly I am. I was just so angry and frustrated... I couldn't think."

"You did what you thought was right," Angela said, feeling the need to sympathize with Jacob now. "I *was* angry with you, but I'm just glad you're all right. You didn't die, and I have no reason to kill you now." She narrowed her eyes at him then and added, "But, if you *ever* cast a spell on me again..."

Jacob shook his head. "I won't. Never again. After all that we've seen there... I don't even want to use it to heal my leg or wound. Not sure if I can even, after using it so many times in one day. But you have my word I won't bewitch you again."

"Good," Angela said looking away. "Then we're square."

"We're not done though, are we?" Jacob asked. "You and I... we're still partners, aren't we?"

Angela frowned at her own reflection in the window; the last bit of proof that she was just as much human as she was a Vampire. "We will have to see what Velinar says, concerning your neck."

"You said I wouldn't turn into-"

"You won't but that isn't the issue and you know it."

Jacob grunted unhappily. "Yeah, I guess. I hope... I hope he understands."

Angela nodded. She looked at him then and said, "Thanks again for that, by the way. It's because of you I was able to defeat Horla. I couldn't... I couldn't have done it without you."

Jacob adjusted the scarf her wore around his neck, hiding the wound. He was smiling smugly. "Who are you and what have you done with Angela?"

"Jacob..."

He chuckled. "Hey, don't mention it. I remembered when you said blood made you stronger, and how a bite from a Dhampir wasn't lethal. It was a risk, and I was willing to take it if it meant... if it meant giving you the edge."

"Still, thanks. That's a terrible burden to carry."

"Doesn't hurt though. Doesn't even itch."

Angela glared at him.

"Sorry. Proceed."

"As I was saying," said Angela patiently. "It is a burden to carry and any who sees it will think that you're infected. And like I said, depending on what Velinar says is how you and I will proceed. But I don't believe... I don't think we *should* work together again if I am still welcome in the guild. I..."

Jacob nodded, as if he understood. In truth he didn't, and he was only trying to respect her opinion and not reveal his disappointment as best he could.

"What if you *have* to take a partner again? Would you at least... consider me? I... I want to work with you again."

Angela paused, and then said, "Maybe."

The Hunter nodded, seeming content with the unsure answer she had given him. "Also..." Jacob shifted in his seat slightly. "Though we won't be partners on a regular basis..."

"Yes?"

Jacob moistened his lips before daring to speak. "Would you at least consider me as your friend?" He looked at her, that one blue eye seeming to sparkle slightly in the train-car lights. "Would you, Angela?"

Angela thought about it for a long while, staring back at him and absorbing what he had said. He just had to make it more difficult, did he?

Everything that had happened between the two of them as well as in Irondell, it had been a lot for the both of them. Angela had never worked with someone before, and she had to admit that this wasn't a complete and total disaster.

But Jacob... he got too close to her. Could she really risk something like that? Could she really trust someone, like, really? She still didn't have an answer, after everything they had gone through.

"I don't know," she eventually answered but then admitted, "But... I would enjoy working with you again."

Jacob stared at her for a moment longer, and then eventually smiled. Like he expected her to answer as such and could be content with it.

"Alright." he said. "That works for me... partner."

Angela shook her head and looked away. But as she looked at her own reflection in the window with Jacob right behind her and going back to his reading, she suppressed a small smile.

Maybe the rookie... wasn't so bad after all.

The train eventually stopped at the station just before Blackfort Pass around midnight that same night. If you took the road to the east and followed the line of mountains, you'd eventually reach the city of Elvendell that was built right in the face of the mountains just beside the legendary Coldponds that dotted the cliffs. If you took the pathway leading up the mountain range however, you'd begin your climb up the Thousand Steps and eventually, reach Shadowfort Castle, where the Black Hand resided.

Both Angela and Jacob got off at the station, as did a few other travelers heading for Elvendell. Clockwork walked with them, but due to his wheelchair, could not step off the train. Nevertheless, it did not stop him from shaking hands with the Hunters and thank them for their duty.

"Irondell owes you both a greater debt than they could even imagine. I thank you, as do they all."

"It was nothing, sir," Jacob said with a smile. "We were just doing our job."

Angela looked at the Hunter, wondering why he was acting so modest now.

"As promised, payment will be sent to you both as soon as I reach Mistendell. I have a few things to take care of there, but I have all the gold stashed away which I will send to Velinar as soon as possible."

"Thank you, Professor Clockwork," Angela said with a bow of her head. "It has been an honor and a privilege to work with you."

Clockwork looked at Angela with a warm expression, and he looked up at the sky which was sparkling with a million diamonds. In the far distance, beyond the huffing and steaming of the train, even the humans could hear the wolves howling and echoing against the mountains in the distance.

"Life really is beautiful, isn't it?" he muttered mostly to himself.

When he brought his attention back down to the world and the two Hunters, he tipped his hat to them. "Tell the old man I said 'hello.' And for you both, I hope and pray for the best. You both are strong Hunters."

The two Hunters left him then, and Clockwork rolled back into the train and not even a few minutes later, the whistle on the engine screamed; warning all passengers to board or get left behind at the isolated station. Not long after, the train huffed and puffed and began to roll away, off to its next destination.

With that being done, Angela went to meet with the owner of the station itself. There were horses for sale there, since the farm was close by the station itself. It was dangerous territory being so close to the Pass to have livestock of any kind to care for, but the owner had been running the station and the farm for over sixty years, and he never once had a problem with wolves, Wendigo, or even bandits. The two Hunters bought two horses, and then started their way up to the mountains along Blackfort Pass and eventually, began their ascent up the Thousand Steps as they had a thousand times before.

After what felt like hours to Jacob but worse on the horses, the two Hunters eventually saw the lights of Shadowfort Castle near the highest peak.

They passed through the veil of wards around the perimeter and then approached the stables. They placed their new steeds into the warmth of the stalls along with the other horses and the hay to feed them. The older horses took kindly to the newcomers, and they sputtered and whinnied in greeting.

Leaving them, the two then entered the castle, and rushed through it to meet Velinar down in his chambers. Having to pass through the main hall again, Angela noticed that only the Hunters Luca and Sabina were present playing cards over a bottle of vodka. They looked up and waved at the two, saying that they were glad the two of them returned but Angela kept on walking. Though she allowed Jacob to wave back before they passed by the bar and the Ghoul butler behind it before descending into the lower chambers.

The closer they got to the bottom of the stairs the colder the presence felt, and the more nervous Angela got. When they eventually entered the hexagonal room, Velinar was waiting for them, meditating on his scythe like a perched crow.

He turned his hooded head to the two, and smiled brightly upon seeing them. "Ahh, you both have returned alive and well. And from what I hear, Irondell is no longer in quarantine and people are able to move about. A job well done indeed. I assume Clockwork has left for home already?"

"He has," Angela said. Jacob kept quiet- upon Angela's orders. She was to do the talking unless Velinar addressed the eye-patched Hunter directly.

"Good, good," Velinar said lowering himself and setting gently upon the cold floor. "Then tell me, what news do you bring?"

"Nothing good, my lord," Angela said. "We have found some... disturbing things while in Irondell."

And so, together, she and Jacob both told Velinar about the discovery of Kawfka Worship in Irondell; primarily from the leaders as well as the Raven put in charge. This disturbed Velinar greatly, and the deity clenched his scythe tightly in his little pale hands.

"That *is* bad news..." he eventually said, his black eyes reflecting deep thought in his mind. "And they wouldn't let anyone in or out, nor would they do anything to help the people there. They were just after the Immortal, not the Vampires as a whole. But why would the Empire..."

"We don't know," Angela said. "No one did... But the Watchmen got news of it, and as soon as Andrei was killed, they took matters into their own hands- against orders. They lifted the quarantine, which Emperor Ion will no doubt be furious about. There were Goldendell soldiers outside the city walls."

"Why would the leader of Irondell sacrifice his own people for the hope of finding just the Immortal?" Velinar mumbled. "Why not defend his people? None of it makes sense."

"No, it doesn't," Jacob said which earned him a stern look from Angela.

"The Ravens are acting strange now…" Velinar continued. He looked up at the two. "Sabina had returned from her job, alone. She had been chased out by a Raven from the village she was called to. The Raven however, did nothing for the people there. The village is gone."

"Which one was this?" Angela asked, now deeply concerned.

"Fairiron," Velinar replied. "North of Dwarvendell. The entire place was overrun by Trolls. The Raven, was reported to just watching the carnage take place. The sole survivor made it to Dwarvendell, and reported all of this. He said the Raven tried to kill him, but he escaped in the woods. He was found with his throat slit in the very inn he was staying at."

"Damn," said Jacob.

"That doesn't make any sense…" Angela said scratching her chin. "Aren't the Ravens supposed to be the 'new' protectors of the Realm under order of the Empire?"

"They are. But their behavior is suspicious." Velinar shook his head. "The fact that they are now teaching others about their ties with Kawfka, makes it even worse. We might be dealing with something beyond Lunokean boundaries."

"What do we do then?" asked Jacob.

"For now, nothing," Velinar said shaking his head. "The Black Hand will continue to serve the Realm, but we must be very careful. We will have to learn more about what the Ravens are up to- and what it will mean for the future of the Black Hand and all of Balkeñoir. Until then, we will do nothing. We will wait until we get more reports, and then we'll figure it out. Until then, you both have done a fine job enough as it is. Return to your chambers to rest. You've had a long Hunt, and you deserve the rest- judging by the looks of you two."

"We appreciate that," Jacob said with a bow. "Thank you, Master."

The deity dismissed the two Hunters, but Angela asked Jacob to wait. She then turned to Velinar, and took a deep breath. "There is one more thing we have to tell you, Master."

She told the deity what happened, concerning Angela breaking her vow and biting Jacob to drink his blood. Velinar listened with intelligent eyes and a silent mouth as the two explained. For once, Angela was glad to have Jacob there. Without him there to explain in greater detail what had happened to them, Angela doubted it would even sound good coming just from her. When they finished telling him what happened, Velinar looked up as if listening to some faraway voice from somewhere the two Hunters could not see or sense. When he brought his eyes back down to the two, he sighed as if exhausted.

He turned to Jacob. "So, you gave her permission to." It was not a question. "Your own free will."

"That's right," Jacob said. "If she hadn't, we'd both be dead. I believed I wouldn't be infected, so it was worth the risk."

"But you understand that the wounds will never close?" Velinar asked. "Did you two talk about that?"

"I knew about that. Angela told me all about it." Jacob developed a sudden interest in his boots. "I know the risks, sir."

"No, you really don't. The other Hunters won't be happy upon seeing it." Velinar said with another sigh. "But should they find out, I *will* explain to them. Until then, just try to keep it to yourself- for now."

"Yes, sir."

"You may go," Velinar told him. "Angela, you stay."

Jacob looked at Angela, who shrugged. After the Hunter had left, she turned to Velinar who looked at her with an indifferent expression.

"You *had* to make it more difficult, did you? But, you did what you had to do," he told her. "You did what you had to, to survive. For *both* of you, is my understanding."

Angela lowered her head, looked down at the stone floor before her feet. "I'm sorry." It was all she could say.

"You broke your contract, in order to save yourself and your partner."

"I know."

"You bite a human and drank human blood, something you swore that you would never again when you first swore an allegiance to me and the Black Hand. Then again, when I gave you your second chance."

Angela nodded once. "That's right."

Velinar sighed. "You realize, that under contract, I should exile you. You shouldn't even be allowed back in my castle."

"I understand," Angela said. "I will take full responsibility for my actions, and will receive any discipline regarding it. I only ask that you continue to keep Jacob here, train him, and help him to strive for greatness. He is a strong man, and can be a stronger Hunter in the future. He'd be safer here, than anywhere else to reach that potential."

A small smile tugged at the corner of Velinar's mouth. "You think highly of him?"

"Based on my observations."

Velinar chuckled as if amused. "Of course we will keep him here. He is the best shooter we got here- which can be useful. I only wish he would get with the times. That bow…"

He shook his head. "Besides, I hope to make a major profit in the Witching business through him."

"I am glad to hear that," Angela said, truly happy that Jacob would still have a home here.

"Of course," the deity said swinging his scythe and resting it upon his shoulder like a miner hauling a pickaxe.

"And so," he added. "This will remain your home as well."

Angela tilted her head in wonder. "My Lord?"

Velinar nodded. "I said, you can stay."

Angela licked her lips to moisten them. "But-"

"What you did was out of necessity," Velinar said stopping her short with a raised hand. "I am not pleased with it, for that could cause trouble not only for yourself here, but for Jacob as well. Any who see that mark on him, will fear him, as will any Vampire he happens to come across. You have marked him for life, and there is no escape from that. I know of the old noble customs your ancestors once followed and most likely still do."

Angela frowned. "Yes, I know."

"But I have faith in Jacob, as I had faith in you when you were brought here. Jacob is a brave man, so I hope that he can overcome the burden now placed on him and become a great Hunter. You as well, Angela. After all, you two share a bond now."

Angela nodded. "Yes, sir. Thank you, sir."

"Now I have a question for *you*," Velinar said with a piercing look. "Do you *want* to stay?"

"I have nowhere else to go."

"That's not what I asked you."

Angela fell silent, unsure how to word what she felt.

Velinar smiled at her. "You don't have to answer me. Just make sure you know the answer for yourself. The Black Hand is your home as long as you desire it to be, and the world needs your skills. But make sure you understand what you yourself wants, before you try to reason anything. It is okay, to speak your heart. Remember that."

Angela's mouth twitched. "I understand."

Velinar waved her on. "Go on, get some food and rest. I will have another contract for you when you are fully recovered. With how strict things are at the moment, that may be a while. Tell Jacob that as well."

"I will. Thank you." Angela bowed, and then started to go.

"And Angela?"

The Dhampir stopped, waiting for the deity's last words.

"I am glad you came back."

Angela nodded, and continued on her way. Unable to say that she too, was glad to be home.

Di

When she reached the top of the stairs and entered the main hall, Angela was surprised to see that Jacob wasn't there. She crossed the room over to Sabina who appeared to be filling out mission reports which were scattered across the dining table she was occupying. Luca was nowhere to be seen.

"Sabina."

"What?" the Huntress asked not looking up from her work. Her pen danced across the sheets of paper almost as if it had a mind of its own.

"Do you know where Jacob went?"

"He stepped out to make a call," Sabina said still not looking at the Dhampir. "Said if you asked he'd be out there."

"Thank you."

Angela started forward, when she heard Sabina call her name. The Huntress had never acknowledged Angela personally by name, and it brought enough curiosity for her to turn to look at Sabina.

This time, she was looking at the Dhampir. "Jacob told me, what happened."

Angela felt a cold fist close around her spine. *Had Jacob told her? Why would he do such a stupid and reckless thing? Why-*

"Oh?" she said instead trying to prepare herself for what was to come.

"Yeah," Sabina nodded. Her expression was strained, disgruntled almost. "He said you threw yourself in front of him to keep him from getting shot. Is... is that true?"

The memory of the Gatling thundered in Angela's mind, striking her like a sledgehammer and she nodded slowly.

"Really?" Sabina asked with eyes widened with pleasant surprise. "That's impressive. And you're still standing... that's pretty amazing."

"I suppose..."

"Well, good for you, I guess," Sabina said returning her attention down to her work. "Like, good job, bringing him back alive I mean. Can't lose anymore Hunters now."

"... Right."

Angela left her alone to work, still feeling the eyes of the Huntress upon her as she left the meeting hall and stepped out into the foyer. The Armor Spirits said something to her, but she wasn't listening. She made her way over to the side, where the phone on the wall hung. Jacob was there, speaking to it but Angela only caught the word 'bye' as he hung the phone on the receiver.

He then sighed, and then turned to look at Angela with that too-damn-confident smile of his. His eye appeared weary however, as if he were talking to someone who gave him a lot of stress in such a short amount of time.

"Hey," he said.

"Who were you speaking to?" Angela asked curiously. For some odd reason, she felt protective of him, wanting to ensure he was well. Whoever it was...

Who had it been?

Jacob shook his head. "No one important. Just a friend, asking how I was doing. Promised to call if I returned."

His smile seemed a little forced, but Angela didn't press on the matter. Whatever business it was, was his own. All the Hunters had some connection to some people outside the Black Hand, even if they didn't have families to return to.

"So what did Velinar have to say?"

"I am allowed to stay," Angela said, feeling a sense of relief upon saying it.

It had become clear to her that she was glad she was staying. She would have a warm bed to sleep in and a place she could be well-fed. Though the company here was something to be desired, this also meant that she was going to be here while Jacob healed and maybe... just maybe...

"Well, that's good news!" Jacob said, genuinely smiling this time. It made the one he had given her earlier look like a poor attempt. He cleared his throat and added, "I'm, uh... glad you get to."

Angela nodded. "I am as well." She meant it too.

Maybe... maybe having him around isn't so bad.

Jacob smiled, that damn confident and alluring smile of his. It both lifted Angela's heart to see it, but also filled her with dread for what it could possibly mean. Though she still knew the two of them working together would be trouble, especially for him, Angela realized she couldn't very well just walk away from this. As Clockwork had said, this was a worthy partner, and she couldn't very well walk away from him.

But still…

From the look in his crystal-blue eye, it would seem that he too wished the same thing she did.

"Well," she said while turning away. "I must rest. I suggest that you do as well. You have to heal, before you can take any contracts again." She started to head for the stairs.

"Wait," Jacob reached for her but then pulled his hand away before he could touch her.

This both relieved Angela as well as confused her. The man really did care after all. The only time he had touched her, and she had not minded, was when he broke through Horla's illusion to speak to her. But now…

She just wasn't ready still for that kind of contact. She found herself wondering then if she ever would be.

"Look, uh…" Jacob shuffled a foot. "I want to thank you, for allowing me to hunt with you. I… I look forward to our next hunt together."

Angela said nothing, but merely stared at him.

"There *will* be another hunt, right?" Jacob asked.

Angela wished she could give him a straight answer. She had never trusted her life to anyone, let alone had hunting partner before. And Jacob, he had proved his worth. He did not care about the blood in her veins, nor what had happened in order to save them. He treated her like any other fellow human- like any other *woman*.

It both pleased her and disturbed her, for she was still wary and wondered if it was ever a good idea for her to try and find belonging with another human. She was a Dhampir, a half-breed of a Vampire. Could she really…

could she really trust a man that much to allow herself to get too close?

She wanted to. Yohnah knew she wanted to.

But I have placed a mark upon him as well...

This was the most major source of her conflict. That was what caused her hesitation.

Still, time was irrelevant to her. Maybe not to him, but to her, everything was only a matter of time and space.

At last she sighed and gave her the best answer she could come up with at this point in time. "When you are ready, perhaps."

Jacob smiled, content with her answer. "Alright. Until then, let's try not to be strangers, okay?"

Although he obviously was telling her not to be a stranger, she smiled softly at the prospect of them *both* being held accountable for this. It was amusing. Angela may even dare to think it charming.

"Of course."

"Tomorrow do you wanna join me for a drink? Maybe play some chess?"

"We'll see. For now, all I see in my immediate future is a long rest."

Jacob laughed. "That honestly sounds good. Next time then."

"Agreed."

"Well, goodnight, Angela. And... thanks for everything."

Angela paused at the foot of the stairs and said over her shoulder, "You too. Goodnight, Jacob."

She didn't look back once as she climbed the stairs and crossed down the hall silently. When she got to her chambers, she unlocked the door and closed it behind her, shutting herself in her place of peaceful solitude.

She was alone once more.

Immediately, as if sensing this thought, Sebastian came rushing through the room, mewing happily that his master had returned. Angela stooped down and stroked the black cat's agile back as he purred.

"Hey, you. I'm home," she told him. Looking about her room and seeing that nothing had changed, Angela was glad to be home; where it would continue to be so.

But even the happiness of making it back was overshadowed by the darkness of doubt that crept into her mind and planted its seeds. What she and Jacob experienced in Irondell, it would happen again, to someone else somewhere else. The Ravens were up to something, something terrible. Dark times were afoot.

Not only that, but her fear for Jacob now that he had been *marked* by her no less, escalated without limit; as well as what it would mean for her, and the Black Hand itself. Strange tides were rushing in, and she feared for once the unknown future that her eyes could not see. That also bothered her. She hated not knowing. She hated this conflict she felt.

But… I'm not alone, not anymore.

That's true. Beyond these walls, she did have something else. In the Black Hand, she had more than just a peaceful room and bed, food and drink, the necessities to live until her next contract. She had companionship. She had Jacob to join by her side once those strange tides reached their shore.

But until then, rest was what she needed. A good book, a long bath, and then a long, long rest.

Would you at least consider me as your friend?, he had asked.

She did not know if she could bring herself to ever call Jacob a friend, and it took a lot to even consider him a companion and partner in their Hunts together. But even then they could share something. That was proved back in Irondell. At the very least, they worked well together. Despite his flaws as well as her own, Angela felt like they could.

But also, when work was not available, there was more to it than that, and despite how much she feared letting that door open even just a crack, Angela was grateful for the person peeking in, honoring her privacy but at the same time letting her know that he was just outside the door. Outside, and waiting for her should she wish to open the door further and would still understand to respect her should she close it.

But for now, that door to herself would remain open. Just a crack, but it would remain, for now.

"I am home," she whispered again, her reflection shimmering in her ring as she continued to pet Sebastian whose purrs expressed his delight in her return.

"I'm home…"

Do

Clockwork had sat in silence for the rest of his train ride home.

After parting ways with the two Hunters, he had returned to his seat without another word or movement the entire way to Mistendell. When he got to the station two days had passed, and he was already dreading the day ahead. He rolled off the station platform, and continued down the cobblestone pathway through the seaside city of Mistendell. Mist had of course accumulated from the sea spray and the smog from the factories, bringing a sense of welcome to Clockwork as he came home.

He rolled passed all men without a word, nor a tip of his hat to any of the ladies. He was in a hurry, and could not dawdle even for a brief moment. Besides, he was crippled, and needed to waste no more time than he already had.

When he had finally reached his destination at one of the manors just by the sea where the waves crashed against the glassy shores, he knocked on the door and an old maid helped him inside. He rolled into the living room, where the two men he was supposed to meet were waiting for him.

One was sitting in a flowered chair by the window, his chalk-covered body glistening like the snow outside. His dark tattoos burned bright on his body including the depiction of the demon Kawfka himself, the crow's head seeming to twitch and the eye moving while on the man's body. When he noticed Clockwork coming in, he flashed a savage grin of metallic teeth.

The other man who was asking one of the maids politely to leave sat on the couch with his body obscured by the shadow that draped over the corner it was in. His shoes were polished, his blue slacks revealing a slim figure, possible malnourished.

"I apologize for being late," he told the two men. "But the deed is done."

"Excellent," the chalk-covered man said running a hand through his black hair and playing with one of the beads in his bangs. His voice was rough, gravely, a smoker's voice. "I assume the menace is taken care of?"

"Yes," Clockwork said. "And I've found plenty of interesting discoveries while working with the Hunters I've hired."

"The ones within the Black Hand," the man leaned forward, his pale and sunken eyes piercing Clockwork where he sat in his wheelchair. "Will they be a problem?"

"Velinar is an old friend of mine, and is a protector of the Realm. He is no issue to us- not yet anyway. The Hunters did their job, there is nothing to fear from them. They could be useful in the future."

"I ain't working with those scum," said the chalk-covered man.

"We'll see about that," said the pale man. "Clockwork, continue. Please."

Clockwork grunted. "The plague has been expelled and Goldendell is taking over. But there is some news that will no doubt be covered up by the soldiers. The Raven put in charge of the Irondell situation, happened to have some very dark... secrets of his own. He is not only a follower of Kawfka, but also, turns out, a teacher. He had been teaching the leader of Irondell, your religion of black magic, Sir Wepwawet."

The second chief of the Wildesding Cult smiled thinly, revealing his metallic teeth again. "So, the news my scouts have reported *were* true. The Emperor is playing with unfamiliar forces in his castle. Unfamiliar, and not offered."

"This is hardly the time to be excited, *wolf*," Clockwork said in a stern voice. "The fact that he is handling this is dangerous enough. How can we expect to keep the charade up, if he is using such dangerous forces to seek out his enemies?"

"We won't have to worry about that," Wepwawet said licking his lips. "It is only a matter of time before Emperor Ion falls, and Balkeñoir will be ours. Then you won't have to worry about neither the Ravens, or us again. Right, Lord Harker?"

The third member of the party shifted in his seat. Clockwork felt a chill run down his paralyzed spine as those two eyes of pale moonlight shined bright like burning suns towards him.

"You are *certain*, that the Black Hand is no issue as of now?" he demanded.

"Yes, I am certain," Clockwork answered, finally finding his voice. "I mean to pay them upon my return to home. And as I said, I think they can be proven useful while we make further preparations."

"Very good, all debts must be paid," Harker said, tucking his black coat around himself to stay the cold trying to come into the manor by the sea. Such a thin man was unfit for this sort of environment.

"Continue with your duties here," said Harker to Clockwork. "Whatever you find be sure to report to Wepwawet. He will make sure that the information gets to their clans in the east, and I will report them to the Emperor. We move forward with the plan, without delay. Wepwawet already has some volunteers ready."

"Do you now?" asked Clockwork to the cultist. "And Lucius agrees with you?"

"Do not worry about that," said Wepwaet spitefully. "You do your job and I'll do mine."

"Clockwork," Harker said to intervene. "When can you go to Arkon?"

"Not yet," said Clockwork. "Soon though. I need to make some calls to Goldendell and see what we can do. It might be something only the Black Hand can do."

"You've thought this through."

"I try."

"Good. Hopefully Ion does his part as we plan."

"Yes, hopefully," Wepwawet said with a bow of his head. The cocky bastard.

The pale Lycan clearly had no idea just how dangerous his job was at this point. Even Clockwork knew that what was to come was going to be risky- *dangerous* actually, beyond measure. If the wrong ears got ahold of such information, they would all be dead and bound for Oblivion in no time. Such high risks, but even higher rewards.

"Clockwork," Harker then said folding his fingers together which were long, bony, and terribly pale with black nails sticking out like claws at the fingertips. "Make sure to contact Carmilla as well. I'm sure she will be very useful in our next experiment for the Emperor."

Clockwork gulped. "That witch? You would trust her to relinquish her notes?"

"Who better to test the effects of blood transfusions? Whatever you need to do to get it to her, do so. But remember, you are to continue your work for the Emperor and his new army as a first priority. We cannot afford any mistakes or suspicions in our rise to power. I need to seek out the Blue Rams too, we will need their assistance if they haven't done anything reckless yet."

Clockwork was still unhappy with this stretch of trust, but nevertheless, he nodded. "Yes, Sir Harker. It will be done."

"Thank you, Professor. I will admit, I am interested to see your new machines in action."

Clockwork said nothing on the compliment from Harker.

"The letters as well," Wepwawet said trailing a dirty nail across the upholstery of his chair. "Have you completed them?"

"Yes," Clockwork answered. From his traveling satchel, he removed what he had been working on in Irondell and waved them at the Lycan. "I can assure you, the Emperor won't even be able to tell that the Huntress Akira is no longer with us. I doubt the Raven has said anything, after he placed the city and myself on lockdown."

"We have to deal with those fuckin' birds," Wepwawet hissed past his teeth. This hatred, Clockwork could relate with the Lycan. "Who knows what trouble they could cause us if we delay any longer?"

"Patience," Harker said softly. "The Black Hand, they know of the Ravens?" the man directed the question to Clockwork.

"They do."

"Good. Then that is all they need to know. We'll simply let nature take its course. Hopefully they can kill a few of them in the process. Until then, Wepwawet, make sure your clans are causing enough anarchy to draw their attention. I must go to Temptestdell to rally up some more anarchists. Between you and the Black Hand, I'm sure things will work out the way you desire."

"They *piss* on the name of Kawfka and our cause," the Lycan snarled. "If they interfere with anything my boys do, they're *carrion*. We'll seek out any Raven we can find and once any of us finds us a Raven, we'll clip their wings."

"Your pagan religion is the cause of all of their troubling's," Clockwork snapped at the arrogant cultist. "Dealing with the devil for your bloody magic, it is tempting fate, which we cannot-"

"Enough," Harker hissed angrily. "Save your defenses of your gods for another day. *Both* of you. When I am the ruler of Balkeñoir, it will be *I*, who will decide the fate of the Empire, just as Emperor Ion has and all before him. By then, we won't have to worry about Wildesding or the Ravens ever again. And Wepwawet, you will at last bring to your people what your cult has been unsuccessful in doing so. It will be a new era, a new country, for both."

The men agreed with Harker, without looking back at one another and bothering with any pleasantries.

"Now then," Harker said standing up from his seat, and a shadow seemed to rise with him, darkening the room with merely his presence that was overwhelming like a tidal flood. "Let us go, gentlemen. Our new Realm is just within our grasp now."

And so, it was. Clockwork agreed. They all agreed, though a terrible price would have to be paid in order to fulfill their roles in the new rise of power in the realm of Balkeñoir, they truly were close to their goal.

The entire country was just within their grasp, and it was only a matter of time before everything became theirs for the taking with the Emperor's new army as well as their own at their disposal. It was only a matter of time now.

Oh, how terribly, yet wonderfully, it was.

He only prayed that Yohnah will watch over them, especially his friends within the Black Hand.

Coda

To be continued in...

The Road